THE DEITY CONSTANT

NEIL DOMIGAN

Dedicated to Ellen, Elizabeth and Charlotte

Thank you to Tina, Gillian and Barbara for editorial guidance.

CHAPTER ONE

NEW YORK, USA, 13TH APRIL 1949

EVERYTHING ANNA DID today she did for her last time.

Anna circled past a nut vendor and stopped at a fish monger's push-cart. She cast her eyes over his fish and thought of the dinner she would cook to celebrate. The Manhattan street monger had his push-cart in the shade; it was chilly in the shade, but less chilly on the other side of the street where a scatter of pedestrians strolled in the sun with three-storeyed red brick buildings behind. Anna pointed to a striped fish with clear eyes and mirror scales.

'Is that striped bass?' She asked. The heavy-faced fish monger nodded and smiled.

'Fresh caught from Newbury Port.'

'I can see your fish is fresh and it smells of the sea.'

'You know fish,' said the monger.

'My father fishes in Israel.'

'How many you feeding?'

'Three,' said Anna, her accent Israeli.

The vendor placed his knife close to the dorsal fin, his heavy face looked at the young woman. Anna nodded. He lay the fish on a cutting board, cleaved then placed the striped bass chunk on the tin dish of a battered trade-scale. The fish monger eyed the weight on the scale's dial then spoke to the young woman. She nodded and gave the monger a one-dollar bill she had received from her Tel Aviv bank three weeks earlier.

'I've not seen you before,' he said. He liked her light voice.

'I'm new here, I now know where to buy fish.' She smiled. The monger smiled.

In the shade, an olive-skinned man glanced at a teenage boy exchange a coin for a bag of nuts then his eyes flicked back to the young woman at the fish cart. His fingers squeezed the knife in his coat pocket—it felt hard. He wanted to hate her to make it easier, but he had no reason to hate. He didn't know her, she looked pretty and seemed happy, and she made the monger smile. He stepped from the pavement and weaved through pedestrians past the nut vendor and onto the fish monger's push-cart. He looked at the fish monger's knife now lying on top of the half-cut bass. It was hand-forged, a knife of good quality; he liked good quality knives. He was close to the young woman, so close if he wished he could touch her shoulder—her black hair fell in curls. He swept his eyes over her heavy blue woollen coat. A coat like that could deflect the knife. He must be sure of the angle. He stepped away. The monger wiped his knotted fingers on a wet towel then grabbed a sheet of newspaper from a bamboo bin, wrapped the bass and handed the fish and change to the young woman.

Anna left the fish cart and crossed the road; she strode with the warmth of the sun on her back. The man followed. He too was warmed and lengthened his stride and closed the distance to the young woman. As he stepped onto the pavement, he clipped his brown leather shoe on the curb *Watch your step,* he told himself. He told himself lots of things. He'd killed a few hours earlier, and prayed his second would feel easy. The scatter of pedestrians in the side street made her blue coat easy to follow, but once along the boulevard, he would need to be close. Ahead were a couple of beat cops. He stopped, then thought he shouldn't have stopped. If he started again what would the beat cops think? He turned his head and looked into a tailor's window and searched among the mannequins for his reflection.

The beat cops watched the street fluidity; and one cop had observed a man stop and turn with a jerk.

The olive man stared into the window and he could see his outline, but not much more. *That's how the cops see me,* he told himself—I'm just an outline. They don't know I killed a man a few hours earlier—and I'm about to kill again. The cops were between him and the blue coat. The cops moved towards him and the blue coat moved further away. *I'm just an outline,* he told himself. *I have the sun at my back and the cops will squint.* He looked again at his reflection by the mannequins and then started to walk. The two cops were close now and as he passed them by, he glanced at the cops and saw they squinted.

The olive skin man heard the words, 'Police, I need you to stop.' He marched on. There were other pedestrians, an innocent man need not stop. One of the squinting cops turned and darted to his side.

'Police, I need you to stop.' The olive man stopped.

'Are you ok?' The cop glanced down at the clenched fingers in the olive man's black glove. The olive man glanced at the distant blue coat.

'I visit from Syria. Sorry my English bad.'

'What's under your coat?' The cop looked at the Syrian and the Syrian looked back at the cop. The Syrian unbuttoned his coat and spread his arms, the coat opened.

'A Syria tourist.' The cop looked down at his waist then locked eyes with the Syrian and the Syrian smiled.

'Enjoy your stay in New York,' said the cop. The Syrian kept his smile and paced slowly away; his heart pounded and now there was no blue coat. He needed to kill her today; kill her before she found out her Rabbi friend had been killed; kill her before she and her other Jew friend became cautious.

He counted his steps, as he distanced himself from the cops, and after twenty quickened his pace, his eyes scanned for blue and he thought of the horizontal blue stripe on the Druze flag, a blue stripe that represented willpower; the flag he held proud in his homeland, Syria. It suited him to see the blue coat as a message from Allah—an action Allah condoned—to knife the blue coat, knife it and knife it again—until the blue coat moved no more. And then Allah gifted, ahead he saw the blue coat stopped at an intersection. Other pedestrians milled. All eyes on the cop directing traffic. One whistle blast to stop the traffic then the pedestrians heard the two blast signal to cross. A white-gloved finger pointed. The human dam burst. The blue coat crossed with a crowd then swung right past a vagrant hunched by a fire in a drum. The bounce in her step made the blue knee-length coat dance—a dance from the previous day's success—Einstein had been tracked down and was coming to New York.

The olive-skinned man trailed Anna to the next intersection; there were less pedestrians at this intersection and no cop. She glanced left and then right, a yellow cab passed, then at the mechanical screech of a tram, the young woman clutched her handbag and skipped her shoes across the steel-shined tram tracks, skipped to the far side of the road and stopped at a photo booth plastered with adverts—*four poses for 25¢*—*take your own photo*—*no fuss and bother*—*private booth*—*ready in two minutes*. She flipped the grey privacy curtain and stepped into the booth. Unseen inside, she sat on a wooden stool bolted to the floor and read the wall-mounted instructions then opened her purse, pinched a quarter between her fingers and pressed the coin into the slot. Flash … blink, one photo done; she smiled again for two more flashes. One photo left, for a bit of fun Anna struck a movie-star pose, with her head flung back and her chest pushed out. She was being sexy as she anticipated the seduction of Einstein. A secret sexy photo. Anna felt nervous, more than a little nervous at the thought of seducing Einstein, an anxiety she wanted to bury—bury the anxiety by feeling sexy, assertive—empowered and in control.

The assassin stared up and down the street and waited for the tram and a group of pedestrians to pass. He held the knife handle tight, crossed the road then stopped at the photo booth, scanned around then ripped aside the grey privacy curtain and barged inside. Anna's head spun in reflex. Spun so fast her eyes took time to catch up, and when her eyes caught up, she saw an olive-skinned man explode towards her. She threw an arm up as his black gloved hand smothered her mouth and he punched his knife into the blue coat—grazed the fourth rib, smashed the fifth and punctured the lower heart chamber. The domino of destiny fell on the thrusting blade.

Anna's heart screamed, screamed for help with the catapulted release of endorphins, endorphins that generated a false sense of euphoria—a false sense that told Anna she was fine. But her heart knew she was not fine. The blade withdrew and a red torrent followed—blood-stained Anna's blue coat, Blood stained the stool and stained the floor. A mortally wounded bird gyrated in Anna's chest, flapped its wings desperate for flight, but the bird flipped and tumbled unable to leave the ground. She needed to help the bird. Just a little breath to calm its flight—just a little breath—just a little, just … Anna's hand reached for the stool but found air. She fell. Her mouth gaped as she hit the hard floor. A brown shoe appeared at her face. The toe was freshly scuffed, feathered brown leather. The scuffed brown leather was her last sight. The spirit bird threw herself at the door of death and then passed through. There was no chance for Anna to say goodbye to the world of sun and light and night and flowers and kittens and smiles and laughter and love—no chance to say goodbye to all that made life a gift.

The assassin dragged deep breaths as he left the booth, dots of sweat on his brow; it was the adrenaline. He hurried then slowed, put his head down, and moved at the pace of the few pedestrians. Behind him the sound of a female's icy scream; the body found. He checked his step then veered away from a worker who hulked a beer barrel to his truck, then turned left into East Houston Street. There were more pedestrians here; the olive man became one of the herd.

For an hour he wove through New York streets, then the olive-skinned man returned to his hotel. He was the only person from Syria staying there. He said hello from under his cap to a couple he passed on the stairs. His room was on the third floor, and the window looked out to a cold stone building across the street. He opened his door, stepped inside; the bottom hinge groaned then the door clicked shut. The Syrian fastened the security chain then leant against the chained door. His nose wrinkled at the smell of stale cigarettes and he looked at the room's green curtains, green candlewick bedspread and green carpet, but he only saw blue. He crossed the green room and closed the curtains on Manhattan. In the bathroom, he stepped into the shower. His hands fumbled with the taps until the water flowed. It was cold. He moved his head from side to side under the cold spray.

The water soaked through his cap and soaked his black hair and his hand brushed the bulge in his pocket. He pulled the knife from its sheath and his fingernails scraped dried blood from the thick-pointed blade then he slid the knife back into the sheath. He reached up and grabbed a flannel draped over the back of the shower nozzle and wiped his face. The soap container recessed in the wall of the shower held a bar of *Ivory* soap in its blue and white wrapper. He ripped off the wrapper, lathered the flannel and wiped his face again. He stepped from the shower box, wrung the drips out of his wet cap, shucked off his drenched coat, stripped off his other wet clothes and towelled himself dry. He glanced at the clump of wet clothes discarded on the floor, stared at the mirror, looked again at the wet clothes, before he again stared into the mirror. The killer's thoughts swirled, she'd been harder to kill than the rabbi—not the physical killing, the knife thrust was easy.

The killer put on a clean white shirt, pressed brown suit and a fedora. Wearing his clean façade, he left the hotel room and headed into the early Manhattan evening.

Sometime later he met with a fine-featured young Syrian woman.

'Where have you been?' he asked in Arabic.

'To eat.' She thought Khalid's eyes looked wide and distant and dead.

'You kept me waiting.'

'I'm sorry,' she said.

'Remember your time is mine. Einstein will be at the Astor Hotel on the 16th, a university meeting.'

'This is great news.' She didn't know how Khalid had found Einstein. She didn't care. All she needed was the thousand shillings they'd promised. In Damascus, Khalid had asked if she had parents. Such a strange question, so she said no, not knowing why Khalid asked, but thinking *yes* was somehow the wrong answer. She knew little of Khalid but knew enough to know he didn't respond well to wrong answers. The thousand shillings would pay for her mother's medical care.

'Allah has blessed us,' said Khalid. 'Move hotels so you're close.'

'I'll move tomorrow.'

'Don't go looking like a cheap whore.'

'You insult yourself,' she said, staring at his face but not his dead eyes. Khalid would never understand, she could have whoever she wanted because of something within her. Something that people couldn't quite describe. People like Khalid, who didn't have it, would never see it, would never understand.

'What?' Khalid took a step towards her.

She took a step back. 'I know how to dress.' Her voice was firm and confident.

'Don't return to Syria without his seed.'

'I'll try everything.'

'If everything is not enough?'

'Trust me.'

'There's no need for us to meet again, I'll see you in Damascus when you're done.'

◯

Later that evening Khalid lay on his bed in the green hotel room. A flashback kicked down the door, grabbed him by the throat, and punched. Wet with sweat, Khalid dragged himself from his bed and checked the chain. He had triple checked the chain already but knew if he didn't check again, he wouldn't sleep. Moments after he checked the chain, he found himself again flat on his back, the white ceiling above the bed a movie loop screen. A movie loop in technicolour with an accompanying sound track. On the ceiling, gold-rimmed glasses fell and revealed dilated pupils, pupils that accessed a last view of the world. An arm thrust down from the ceiling, too late in defence. Behind the thrust arm, the image of the rabbi's torn lung, a torn lung that gushed blood and filled airways. The sound track of a cough, a red cough that spilt a splutter of choking and gasping and suffocation. Red bubbles frothed and burst on the ceiling, then the rabbi's face appeared with a red trickle from his chin to stain the perfect blue of his winged bow tie. Blue. Blue like the bouncing coat. The ceiling scene jumped to a wooden stool. Writhing legs exposed pale skin high above the knees, pale skin with lost dignity and lost self-respect, self-respect a discarded luxury in death. Khalid looked at the pale skin on the ceiling then saw his hand, free of the glove, grab the hem of the brown dress and pull the hem high, high enough to show blue underwear between the pale-skinned thighs. To break the movie, Khalid rubbed his eyes, rubbed them hard until he saw stars, the night sky a welcome relief, until the loop again threw images of stabbing and a blue bow tie and writhing and high pale skin and blue underwear and death.

Khalid thought of the wise words he heard from Samir in Damascus; Samir a *uqqāl*—a Druze elite with knowledge of religious secrets. Wise words of justification, of promise and of faith, but Samir's wise words did nothing to expel the empty feeling in Khalid's stomach. The empty feeling preferred to generate words of its own, words like guilt and contempt, and shame, words generated when the woman with the black curly hair exposed her thighs and he removed his glove. Khalid wasn't prepared for that; the exposed flesh. He felt bad about himself and questioned—was he good or bad? Did he do wrong or right? Yet he knew it was in the hands of Allah. A mixture of every unpleasant emotion combined, and Khalid knew Allah would help rid the empty stomach feeling—the shame and contempt and the guilt.

He knelt on the floor and dropped his head forward into the vice of vacant darkness. *In the name of our Merciful God and prophet Jethro, I beg forgiveness for my sins today. Oh my God, I have transgressed against your teachings and my soul. I see and feel your anger and bow before you. All my actions are for you God to reveal the Druze wisdom to the world in order to begin a golden age for all in Your Name.*

Sleep reprieved Khalid for an hour or two, but the 5 a.m. alarm saw him rise to hunt a third victim. At dawn, opposite the third Jew's apartment, Khalid passed Katz Deli, the neon sign flashing *We Never Close* made his face blue then red then blue again. He heard a police siren nearby and moved close against the dark deli wall where he still flashed red and blue. Police seemed to be everywhere. The Syrian felt a prickling wind reach his cold vacuum core. Beads of sweat appeared on Khalid's brow as fast as his hand had groped the blue fabric between the young woman's legs, and then Khalid realised the police siren sound was on the Katz Deli radio, the siren wailed onto the street through an open diner window along with the aroma of freshly baked bagels and coffee. The breakfast smells reminded him of his empty stomach; he hadn't eaten the previous day; adrenaline killed his appetite. Once the siren stopped, the diner's radio blasted a new song. Khalid smiled his first smile for some days as he heard a song with a *clippity clop clippity clop* lyric. When the song finished, the announcer said it was *Mule Train* by Frankie someone. Khalid's thoughts jumped to Damascus and to images of blankets and sacks thrown over mules to protect the animals from their burdens; of children who smiled and enjoyed a mule ride and an old man who whispered words of encouragement and words of gratitude to his four-legged friend. Khalid leant his shoulder against the diner wall as he stared across the street at the Jew's wooden apartment door hooded with a cherry-coloured entrance canopy and his thoughts left Damascus and framed the image of exposed thighs and his hand pulling up the dress. Khalid blinked hard and shook his head.

It was eight in the morning when a handful of people left the Jew's apartment building, but not the Jew. Khalid plodded a figure-eight circuit to keep warm, and also to appear not to loiter. He weaved from the diner, diagonally across Huston Street then past the Jew's building, before he angled back to the other side of the diner the figure-eight circuit completed. He appeared to make an aimless glance every few steps, but his glance had an animal focus towards the Jew's door. Midway through a figure-eight, a police car stopped. It was Irish green with black guards, a white roof and an NYPD crest on the front door. Two cops got out. One in a suit the other in uniform. Khalid tried not to, but his eyes fixed on the uniformed cop, with his double-buttoned jacket and peaked hat with its silver badge. The cop appeared to march right at him. A pain erupted in Khalid's chest. Khalid stopped and crouched to re-tie a shoe lace that did not need to be tied. The cops' legs passed him by, and then their backs disappeared into the Jew's building.

Inside his apartment, Meir Eidelman flattened the creases in the blanket on his bed. His new cleaner would arrive soon and he had one chance to make a good first impression. Meir straightened up at a bang on the door. He crossed his new apartment and opened the door to two men. One wore a police uniform with the black cap pulled low over his eyes, while the other wore a dark suit, a pressed white shirt and a black tie.

'Are you Meir Eidelman?' asked the uniformed cop.

'Yes,' he said. 'What do you want?'

'We need to speak with you.'

'About?' Meir took a step back.

'I'm Detective Samuels. A man was killed a few hours ago, and your name and address were in a notebook in the victim's jacket.' The detective reached into his pocket and held out a badge. Meir looked at the letters NYPD. He nodded and pulled the door wide. The cops stepped inside and cast their skilled eyes around the room.

'A man killed? Who's this man? Why did he have my name?'

'The victim had no identification; we hope you can help,' said the detective.

'If I can.'

The detective recited from his notebook. 'The victim was mid-forties, receding dark hair, dark beard with thin gold-framed glasses, medium build, a little under six feet, wearing a suit and blue bow tie.'

'Oh no! No. It can't be.'

'Who is it?' asked the detective.

Meir swallowed; aware the police watched his every move. He grasped a chair and lowered himself. He knew Gamliel always wore a bow tie.

'My friend, Gamliel, he's a rabbi, Gamliel Hirsch.'

'When did you last see him?'

'Two days ago. No, yesterday.'

'You must come with us to identify the body.'

'How was this person killed?'

'There was a knife attack.'

'I'll need my coat and hat.' He pushed himself to his feet and trudged into his bedroom. People are killed for a reason and there was only one reason that sprung to mind. The uniformed cop followed and watched.

'I'm fine. You don't need to worry about me,' Meir said.

'A tragedy like this can distress people in different ways,' replied the cop.

Meir picked up his black trilby and woollen coat and came out expecting to see Samuels standing in the living area. Meir heard a noise in the kitchen and flashed a look at the uniformed cop.

'Maybe the detective felt thirsty and grabbed a water. Hope you don't mind.'

'I'm used to a little courtesy.'

'We're ready to go, detective,' the cop called out to Samuels. Then under his breath he spoke to Meir. 'Samuels is like a woman, you're ready to walk out of the room and he finds something else to do.'

Meir forced a smile, pulled the collar of his coat around his neck then uplifted his apartment keys from a hook by the door. Samuels appeared from the kitchen. Meir pulled open the door, they exited, and all three ambled to the cage lift in the hallway. The iron grille clacked open and Meir's new cleaner stepped out. She stopped dead when she saw Meir with the two cops.

'Hello, Mrs Perez. I'm sorry you'll not be able to clean today.' Meir pulled his wallet from his pocket and pressed a five-dollar bill into her hand. She looked from Meir to the cops and back to Meir.

'Is everything alright, Mr Eidelman?'

'Yes. Everything's fine, there's an inquiry that's all.'

Meir held the lift's grille. 'You can come down with us, Mrs Perez.'

Samuels stepped forward. 'I'll come down with you Mr Eidelman, my sergeant will have a word with … Mrs Perez, is it?'

'Yes.' She shot a look at Meir.

Samuels closed the iron grille and pressed ground.

'Why are you speaking to Mrs Perez?' asked Meir.

'It's routine. We talk to as many people as possible early in an investigation.'

'I've never seen a dead body,' Meir said as the lift lurched into motion. In fact, he'd seen many during his recent time in the Israeli Security Service, but the cop didn't need to know.

'It can be tough, but we'll be there with you,' said Samuels. The lift bounced to a stop and they left the lobby, passed under the cherry canopy and got into a '46 Dodge. Two minutes later, the uniformed cop got into the car too, sat behind the wheel and turned into the early morning Manhattan traffic.

'What do you do in New York?' asked Samuels.

'I'm a writer,' Meir replied.

'Writing about—?'

'The diaspora of New York Jews.'

'Meaning what? I'm a simple New York cop.' He banged a cigarette on its packet then struck a match.

'It's a chronology of the two and a half million Jews who arrived in New York between 1880 and 1920 … looking at why so many settled in the Lower East Side,' said Meir, but he could tell Samuels had little interest.

'You been in New York long?'

'Three weeks.'

'Meet your rabbi friend here?' asked Samuels. He looked over his shoulder and he blew smoke towards Meir.

Meir narrowed his eyes. 'No. I knew him in Tel Aviv.'

'The rabbi been in New York a while?' asked Samuels.

'Around the same time as me.'

'You know why someone wanted to kill him?' asked the cop who was driving.

'We don't know if it's Gamliel.'

'Do you have any kids?' Samuels asked.

'No. I'm not married.'

'I've got three kids, three girls, my middle girl just turned eighteen. They grow up so fast you wouldn't believe it, but boy do they keep you poor, I swear they can smell a dollar bill at ten paces; it doesn't stop, dentists, doctors, new shoes, school fees, birthdays, but God, I wouldn't trade one second of my time with them for a million bucks.'

'Lucky man,' said Meir.

'I've got two boys,' said the uniformed cop. 'I'd let you have them both for a dollar. They yell at each other from the time they wake. "You've got my socks on. I'm next in the bathroom. It's my plate of food in the fridge. He changed my radio station. It's my turn to have the front seat. I washed the dishes last night." They go from dawn to dusk, I tell you.' The two cops laughed. Meir knew the game they played. He let the smile slide from his lips.

○

At Bellevue Hospital, the Dodge nosed through a stone archway and pulled to a stop in an area reserved for emergency vehicles. The cops got out, Meir followed and entered a dim corridor. The uniformed cop pressed a button by a black door labelled *Morgue*. A man in a white coat, opened the morgue door and led Meir and the two cops into a room. Meir smelt the pickle-like odour of stringent solvents.

Samuels directed Meir where to stand. 'The attendant will get the body tray. The body will be covered by a white sheet. The attendant will pull the sheet and expose the face,' Samuels said.

The morgue attendant pulled the sheet like a stage curtain raised for the final bow. Meir stepped forward. The bloodied grey face of his friend stared.

'Gamliel,' he said with a tremor.

'Look at another body,' Samuels said.

'Another body? What do you mean another body?'

'A young woman was killed this morning, in circumstances similar to your friend here.' Samuels nodded to the attendant and he withdrew another body tray and raised the sheet in a similar fashion.

'Oh God, no! Not Anna too!' Meir gagged, coughed and retched bile into his cupped hands. The acrid liquid ran through his fingers and dripped to the floor. The attendant passed a clean white towel to Meir.

'Thank you,' croaked Meir as he took the towel. He wiped his mouth and his hands, then bent to wipe the bile on the floor.

'It's alright, mister, I'll mop this up. You take some time to get yourself steady again,' said the attendant.

'Thank you,' said Meir. He folded the towel to bury the bile before passing it to the attendant.

○

Later, in the Manhattan 5th Precinct, Meir fought his memory to shed light on the botched plan he'd conceived with his two dead Israeli friends. Samuels interrupted Meir's memory search.

'We need to understand your relationship with the two victims,' Samuels said. 'This may give us a clue as to how they lived, help identify a motive, so we can catch who killed them.'

'I've already explained; I knew Gamliel in Tel Aviv and met Anna two weeks ago.'

'You seemed pretty cut up seeing the dead woman. Pretty cut up after only knowing her two weeks,' said Samuels.

'I find that offensive.'

Samuels ignored the comment and continued. 'What was she doing in New York?'

'I don't know,' lied Meir.

'How often would you see them?'

'I met Anna and Gamliel for lunch; I would see Gamliel at the synagogue.'

'Anna have a man friend?'

'I'm a private person; I respect the privacy of others.'

'Both your friends are dead, Mr Eidelman. I understand you're in shock, but this is serious.' The door of the interview room opened and the uniformed cop strode in.

'Detective?' The uniformed cop flicked his head in the direction of the door.

'Excuse me, Mr Eidelman, I'll be back. Try to think of the last time you saw your friends and what was said.' The detective stood up from his chair and followed the cop out of the room.

'What've you got?' asked Samuels. A second uniformed cop held a plastic evidence bag containing a knife coated with dull spots.

'We found this under the kitchen sink at Eidelman's apartment.'

'Why would anyone keep a bloody knife at home?' said Samuels, more to himself than to his colleagues. Samuels thought of the details of the various murder cases he'd worked on. In a surprising number the perpetrators had done little to conceal their guilt. 'I'll charge him.'

Meir sat with his head in his hands; he scoured his memory for a sign he'd missed. Was there an odd face in the crowd? A man's face. A lone man's face. No one in New York knew why they were here. It had to be a man from the Middle East. A tanned face in a crowd of pale skins as the pale skins emerged from the New York winter. Something jarred. Two days earlier when he left the synagogue. Samuels and the other cop re-entered and interrupted his thoughts. Meir looked at Samuels then at the other cop. Both held his gaze—their eyes cold and tough.

'Mr Eidelman, I'm charging you with the murders of the two people we believe are named Anna Cohan and Gamliel Hirsch,' Samuels said.

Meir jumped to his feet. 'What! You have no idea what you're doing. You've got this all wrong.'

The uniformed cop slammed a baton against Meir's back. Meir's knees crumpled and he heard the echoing words, 'right … remain … silent.'

CHAPTER TWO

NEW YORK, USA, 16 APRIL 1949

PROFESSOR EINSTEIN LOUNGED in a corner of the Astor Hotel's Hunt Room, caught a waiter's eye and lifted his hand in a silent request for a second glass of celery punch.

At the opposite end of the room, a young woman who wore a drab black dress pierced an olive wrapped in cheese pastry. She fixed the hors d'oeuvre between her front teeth, withdrew the petite silver fork and chased the olive with a gulp of the Astor's champagne. With a deep breath, she thought of her thousand Syrian pound pay-day, then turned her focus on the white pipe plume that shielded the celebrity physicist. Action time for her rehearsed strategy. She sashayed across the full room, passed the fireplace with its embossed copper smoke hood, entered Einstein's haze and extended a languid hand.

'Professor Einstein. It's a pleasure to meet you.'

Einstein shook his head and glanced at a man who stood close by. The man stepped to the young woman and spoke.

'Please, let the professor be.'

'I'm sorry,' she said and stepped back. At that moment, a waiter with a white jacket and black bow tie approached, one hand on a silver tray and the other on a green drink in a tall crystal glass. The young woman had never seen a green drink before. She confronted the waiter.

'I'll take this for the professor.' She grasped the glass and felt the waiter's grip tighten.

'Thank you,' she said, and pulled the glass free. She minced to where Einstein sat and offered the glass. With a nod, Einstein indicated the oak side table. Her eyes invited Einstein, then she smiled her full-lipped smile.

'I've never seen a green drink before,' she said, bending and placing the glass on the oak table. Einstein unbuttoned his grey suit jacket.

'What's in the drink?'

The same man stepped to her side. 'Thank you for bringing the drink. But now—'

'It's celery,' said Einstein in a clipped German accent. Of course he'd speak with a German accent, but it still surprised her.

'The taste?'

'Try it.'

She sat on the arm of his chair, slipped off her shoes and did an unconscious dance with her toes.

'It has a tang,' she said with a smile.

'It's the lemon juice and ginger and the celery is bitter.'

She sipped it again. 'But I'm drinking it all,' she said as she gave the glass to Einstein.

He held it, but she did not let go. Einstein's brown eyes smiled and fixed on hers blue. She released the glass.

'Who are you?' asked Einstein.

'Becca Goldberg.'

'You're here because?'

'I crashed the gathering to exchange a few words with you.'

The same man stepped to Einstein's side. 'It's time for the meeting, professor.'

'Thank you.' Einstein stood up, sipped the celery punch then placed the glass on the side table. He ran the back of his hand across his cropped moustache then looked at the young woman who sat on the arm of the chair—a featureless black dress covered a slim form, and two bare feet with toes that danced in a room full of lipstick and orchestrated style.

Einstein's gaze stopped at her feet. 'Excuse me, I was giving my feet a rest,' she said.

'The meeting doesn't need me,' Einstein said to the man.

The man nodded and moved away.

'What do you wish to talk about?'

'Did you just skip your meeting?'

'I did.'

'I'm honoured.'

'Blame your feet.'

'My feet?'

'I like bare feet.'

'Feet soulmates.'

Einstein laughed and his brown eyes grew large. 'Where do you get such ideas?'

'I'm a theology post doc at Princeton.'

'Science without religion is hollow.'

'Religion without science is blind,' she said, repeating a statement she knew Einstein had made some years earlier.

'You have me at a disadvantage, Miss Goldberg.'

'It's Becca.'

'What has Becca learnt from Princeton?'

'That there's a greater force at work than many care to admit.'

'We should dine together.'

Becca slipped from the arm of the chair, slipped into her shoes and became three inches taller. 'I'm dressed for dinner.'

'Then we can go,' said Einstein. They left the Hunt Room, exited the Astor through the grand marble lobby and sauntered a block under a shared Astor umbrella.

Inside the restaurant, it was warm with dim lighting. Einstein handed the maître d' the Astor umbrella then a waiter led them past empty tables covered with fine white linen cloths, silver cutlery and white peaked serviettes. The chairs were black cherry with upholstered red seats. The waiter pulled a black cherry seat from the table and held the back while the young lady sat.

'Thank you,' said Becca. She sat opposite Einstein at a table set between the restaurant bar and a carved grandfather clock that watched the room from beside a window. Outside, rain fell; it made the window wet and blurred the lights outside. Two other couples also dined.

'Why did you invite me. There must be many who would—'

'I don't wear socks,' said Einstein.

'Never?'

'My feet like freedom.'

'We're very lucky we both like free feet, don't you think?'

'So far.'

'There's no need to be guarded.'

'Am I?'

'We can be carefree.'

'I'm carefree.'

'You don't seem spontaneous.'

'This dinner.'

'You have me there.'

'Maybe I'm not anymore; in my younger days, I had a reputation for insouciance.'

'Let's be carefree, just keep everything simple.'

'We have a deal.'

'A partnership.'

'A partnership.'

'We need a toast.'

'A toast?'

'A cognac.'

'A little cognac.'

'Did I say little?'

'You did not.'

'Then it's a cognac—not little,' said Becca.

'I see what you mean by carefree.'

Becca lifted a finger to the waiter's gaze and ordered two cognacs.

Einstein wondered about this silky young woman, so fresh, so sensual, so lively, so carefree. What was he to this young woman who at her age thought about life, whereas he thought about death?

'Cognac is a region in France,' said Becca.

'What region are you from?'

'Damascus.' She had no reason to lie. 'Have you been to Syria?'

'No,' Einstein said. 'I visited Palestine and Israel in 1923.'

Becca paused. 'Twenty-six years ago; a different country from today.'

'I'm relieved to see the fighting stop.'

'We should toast peace.'

'You think it's peace?'

'No.'

'Neither do I.'

Their cognacs arrived.

'Alcohol?'

'For a toast.'

'I rarely drink.'

'But?'

'But let's have a toast.'

'To?'

'Free feet,' said Einstein. They sipped their cognacs.

'Syria had tigers and bears and deer and wolves and many others,' she said.

'I didn't know.'

'We had forest, but now most of it has been cut.' She looked away from the table to a distant Syria then again faced Einstein. Becca raised her glass.

'To being caring and carefree.' She emptied her glass and Einstein emptied his. She ordered two more.

'I feel you have a love for Syria,' said Einstein aware of his unforgiving view of Germany.

'Our souls are in the desert.'

'War is the bleakest indictment of humanity,' Einstein said, more to himself than to Becca. Their second cognacs arrived.

'How would you describe the soul?' she asked.

Einstein drank his cognac, then ran his fingertip around the rim.

'Am I being boring?'

Einstein shook his head. 'How God knows you to be.'

'Beautiful, clear and beautiful; the cognac warms.'

'I'd forgotten how cognac tastes.'

'Was there alcohol in the green drink?'

'No. How long have you been in America?'

'Two years.'

'Different from Syria?'

'Liberal,' she said giving Einstein a broad smile.

'Carefree.'

'Can we talk about you?'

'I already know everything about me,' said Einstein.

'But I don't.'

'You're more interesting.'

'What makes me interesting?'

'Courage to be yourself.'

'But that takes no courage at all.'

'It takes no courage when you have courage.'

'Have you always had courage?' she asked.

'I follow my way.'

'A way blessed with intelligence.'

'Intelligence is a symphony; we all have different composers.'

Becca smiled; she knew Einstein played the violin.

'Decided what to eat?' she asked.

'I haven't looked at the menu.'

'You've eaten here before?'

'A few times.'

'What's good?'

'It's all good.'

'The Astor's hors d'oeuvres filled me up, but I'll have a chocolate mousse with another cognac,' she said.

Einstein flicked his eyes over the menu and ordered asparagus and porcini mushrooms.

'The asparagus and porcini sound wonderful. I didn't see it,' she said.

'We can share, if it delights you, we'll order another.'

The asparagus and porcini came served on sour dough toast with goat's cheese. They ordered another.

'The asparagus is crisp,' she said after biting into a stalk. 'I don't like it limp.' She drew out the word *limp* and kept her eyes down.

'It's fresh from up state,' said Einstein.

'Do you like to dip your toast in the porcini sauce?'

'I like using my fingers to clean the plate.'

'Can I be boring again?' she asked.

'You're not.'

'Is there a secret to making a great discovery?'

'When you have curiosity it's easy to seek truth, ask the right questions, keep an open mind and challenge existing ideas.'

'An example?'

'Move close to the problem, real close, like alongside a beam of light travelling through space, close enough to hear it.' Einstein rolled and unrolled his serviette as he talked.

'I've never heard the sound light makes.' She reached forward and touched Einstein's hand and knocked his serviette from the table. He bent low under the table to retrieve the serviette and after some time he straightened.

'Where … where was I?' He touched the napkin to his brow and looked at Becca's slim wrists.

'Light and sound.'

'Yes … yes … light and sound,' he repeated. 'Unless in a vacuum everything that moves makes a sound.'

'How did you predict that light has mass?' she asked.

'It's weary to discuss my work.'

'Try my mousse.' She held her fork to Einstein's lips.

'It's very light.'

'It makes the cognac better.'

'The cognac makes the cognac better,' said Einstein.

'I can't remember when I've drunk like this.'

'I can't remember when I've dined with a lady in bare feet.'

'My shoes are off.'

'I know.' His marvellous wide brown eyes held hers. She allowed herself to sink into his smiling eyes then pushed her hair behind an ear. Einstein's forehead creased.

'How do you know my feet are bare?' she asked.

'Before … when I dropped my napkin.'

'I didn't notice,' she said. But, of course, she did notice, for she had *knocked* his napkin onto the floor, and her bare feet parted and revealed for Einstein a flash of white satin.

'It's getting late, I've kept you and a girl must—'

'It's been a joy, thank you.'

'Is the Biltmore close?'

'I'll ask the maître d' to get you a taxi.'

'Thank you, Albert.' She squeezed his arm. 'You're such a gentleman.'

'Let me escort you.'

'Thank you, I'm fine. I've stolen too much of your time.'

'I've had fun being carefree.'

'Me too.'

A few minutes later they were by the kerb. Einstein held the door of the yellow cab, and Becca shimmied onto the rear seat.

'Goodnight,' said Einstein.

'I'm scared of lifts,' she said from the back of the yellow cab.

'Scared of?'

'Scared of lifts.'

'What floor are you on?'

'Sixteen.'

'Too many to climb.'

'Yes.'

'I could—'

'Would you?'

'Of course.'

She beamed, her eyebrows lifted and she shimmied to the far side of the seat. Einstein got in and she shimmied back close to the middle.

'We have a solution,' she said.

'Sometimes the mind does not seem at all to move step by step to a solution, but rather finds a devious route,' said Einstein. Becca laughed. The cab lurched.

'You must come in and let me give you a cognac for being such a gent.'

'You have cognac?'

'By chance.'

With a soft clunk, Einstein placed the empty cognac glass on the hotel room table.

'A shower?' she asked him.

'Should I?'

'I can soap your back, and then you can soap mine.'

'It's been many years since I soaped a young woman's back. Many, many years.'

'We're lucky you have a good memory.'

Before getting into the shower, Becca turned the bathroom dimmer to cast a sepia glow.

'I feel young,' said Einstein.

'How does soaping a young woman's back fit with relativity?'

'You're too sharp and too lovely.'

'Am I?' Becca slipped her fingers into Einstein's left hand and pressed her other to his right shoulder so he turned to face her. She touched her closed lips to his. As she shut her eyes, Becca thought of Jamal, her first love, her only love, and the fire and intensity and eagerness and desire and lust and love wrapped into their kiss. Once the kiss was over, she turned Einstein around, and directed the shower nozzle to splash the bubbles from the wisps of grey hair on his back.

'All done,' she said.

In the bedroom, with her wet hair hanging loose, and her bathrobe open, Becca continued. 'Returning to your theory of relativity... *kiss* ... can you guess my age ... *kiss* ...

'As a postdoc—twenty-eight,' said Einstein.

'As a postdoc—twenty-four... *kiss* ... what are you going to do to a twenty-four-year-old post doc, *kiss* who is all yours for tonight, *kiss* ... and maybe all yours for tomorrow night, *kiss,* and the night after, *kiss,* are you, *kiss* ... *kiss* ... going to let me test, *kiss* ... my theory of relativity ... *kiss* ... my theory that, *kiss* ... alive within you, *kiss* ... is that dark *kiss* ... handsome *kiss* ... young man *kiss* who just loves women ... *kiss* ... *kiss* ... *kiss.*

○

Becca slept with Einstein a number of times, and two weeks later she missed her period, then four weeks later she missed her period again. Convinced she carried Einstein's child, the woman known to him by the name of Becca Goldberg vanished from Einstein's life and flew TWA from New York to Paris, connected at Cairo *en route* to Damascus.

CHAPTER THREE

DAMASCUS, SYRIA, JUNE 1949

LAMINA FELT A shudder and heard machine noises as the landing gear doors opened and the wheels of the four-prop DC-6 lowered. The plane banked into a light breeze then descended to the Damascus runway. It was noon in June, the first month of summer with a temperature over ninety degrees in one of the oldest cities in the world. A city started when nomads stopped being nomads, after they found water in the aquafers that drained from the Damascene mountains and found food and shelter in the wild date palm plantations. It was 1949, donkey carts were on the streets alongside imported cars and Syrian petro-pounds from the new oil industry infused a national optimism. Medieval sands were shaken from Damascene shoulders as those who could afford to, embraced the fashion houses of Paris and the prosperity of Wall Street.

Lamina paused at the top of the DC-6 stairs, and her lungs greeted the heat of Syria with its hint of orange blossom. She looked north to the rounded Qasioun Mountain, a refreshing vista after the shackled outlook in New York. Closer, the minarets of Damascus mosques stretched tall, and closer still passengers outside the airport terminal waited to board their flights; passengers sat on aluminium chairs and drank tea under orange blossom trees. Lamina placed her palm on her lower tummy.

'Welcome home, baby,' she whispered, but her lightened heart cramped when her eyes locked on a man inside the terminal. His white skull cap menaced behind the diagonal cross of a window frame. Then she felt a bag nudge the back of her knee. Lamina glanced over her shoulder. 'I'm sorry,' she said stumbling forward and holding the round handrail and descending the boarding stairs leading to the black tarmac. Hot air from the tarmac fanned her face and the bottom of her feet warmed through the soles of her shoes. Inside the terminal it was cooler; she cleared passport control, then navigated to where the flights luggage was lined up on the terminal floor. A porter appeared at her side. She pointed to her brown leather suitcase with its two straps and two buckles. The porter lifted the suitcase from the baggage line and followed Lamina to arrivals where Khalid waited. He wore the white *taqiyah* on his head that she'd seen behind the window cross.

'Peace be upon you. I see a woman with radiance,' said Khalid.

'Thank you, we're happy to be home,' said Lamina.

'May God make him a worthy offspring,' Khalid stared at Lamina's tummy.

'By God's will, I will bring my baby in December.'

'Come, the arms of Damascus embrace you and we need to do a pregnancy test.'

A short time later, Lamina faced an obstetrician in his rooms. She felt safe with him; he stood up straight and wore a white coat. After missing two periods, Lamina said she felt pregnant. She gave a urine sample which would be injected into a female rabbit and would induce ovulation if she was pregnant. The female rabbit would take two weeks to ovulate. The obstetrician positioned a blood pressure cuff above Lamina's elbow. She felt the cuff tighten and watched the mercury bounce.

As they drove away from the examination, Lamina asked Khalid for her thousand pounds; she didn't tell him her mother needed to see the specialist in Beirut. Khalid said Lamina would be paid when she delivered a boy. Lamina protested and said it wasn't as they agreed, but her protest was swiped aside. Khalid then said Lamina was to live with Issam, a young man with broad manners and a white heart. She was to tell people Issam was her child's father, they'd met in New York and fell in love, and celebrated a traditional Druze reception and honeymoon in America.

'If you tell any of your friends you're carrying Einstein's child, you'll place them in serious danger; a single mistake will ensure a double misfortune.' Lamina's stomach sickened, her lips parted and a flush coloured her cheeks. Khalid slowed and turned his Buick out of the sparse traffic and parked behind another car at the roadside then gave Lamina the keys to her new apartment. He pulled the heavy brown suitcase from the trunk and laboured beside Lamina to the apartment lift.

◯

After returning to his Buick, Khalid drove to the old city, running his fingers through his dark beard as he thought about their plan. He'd killed two of the Jews in New York and the third Jew was in prison to face trial. Now there was a two-week wait to confirm the pregnancy. He checked his watch, parked at the kerb and paced the short distance to the Al-Nofara Café, which sat near the eastern gate of Umayyad Mosque in central Damascus. The two-hundred-year-old Al-Nofara Café, with its ancient carved wooden beams, was one of the oldest cafés in Damascus. Khalid sat at an inside table with a wide view to the street. He scanned pedestrians as he looked for Samir. Opposite, merchants sold furniture, and on the street, pedestrians lugged bags of food from the nearby bazar. A frail man with a brown kaftan sat with his feet splayed astride a grey donkey. A stationary horse, with a lattice of hanging reins, clips and straps, hitched to the wooden staffs of a two-wheeled cart, twitched its raised ears in response to the call of swifts that darted between buildings and circled the three marble Umayyad Mosque minarets. The solid walls of the great mosque reigned over the heart of the old city. A swift dived close to the tallest minaret, the Minaret of Jesus, so named at the onset of time when politics captured religion for power and money.

Khalid poured mint tea from the ceramic pot, added a spoon of sugar then stirred the cup. He sucked the spoon, put the spoon on the table then swallowed a warm sweet mouthful. A few moments later, he spied Samir's steel grey Oldsmobile pull to a stop on the cobblestones up the street. The driver's door opened and Samir's characteristic Druze cylindrical white cap appeared. The temperature sat at ninety-six degrees, but Samir wore a suit; he always wore a suit. Khalid stood and raised his hand when Samir arrived at the café entrance. Like a number of Druze men, Samir was tall with blond hair and blue eyes. According to Druze legend, their colouring came from intermarriage with the soldiers of Alexander the Great. Khalid stretched beside Samir to make himself taller.

'*As-salamu alaikum*,' said Khalid shaking Samir's hand and kissing him on each cheek. Samir bent his head down. '*Wa-alaikum-salaam.* 'It's good to see you, my friend.'

'And you too. I trust God is looking over your family.' Khalid poured mint tea into another cup for Samir.

'They're in fine health.' Samir's chair legs made a squeak on the wooden floor as he pushed the chair back and sat down. 'And your family?' Samir's voice was deep and slow.

'My father finds it difficult to walk.'

'Ask your doctor what could help, do me the honour, let me assist in this way.'

'Thank you. Your generosity lifts my shoulders,' said Khalid.

Samir smiled. 'I see excitement in your eyes, tell me of our progress.'

'Lamina believes she carries a child. The result of the pregnancy test will be confirmed in two weeks.'

'Wonderful news.'

'God willing Allah gifts us a male child.'

'If Allah decides otherwise, we'll begin our endeavour again.'

'May God bless a boy as just reward for the faith and gold you have bestowed.'

'In several months, God willing, we'll have a baby boy in our care. Tell me, how are you faring?'

'It's forty nights since I killed the rabbi and the woman, my conscience is tormenting, but it's a punishment I bear.'

'We had no option but to take blood; repent, and when God deems, he'll lift the weight from you.'

'I repent with daily prayer.' A vision flashed in Khalid's mind, his hand dragged the young woman's dress up, and his hand tugged at the blue fabric between her pale-skinned thighs.

'Lamina has gone to Issam?' asked Samir. There was no answer. 'Khalid?'

'Yes?'

'I asked has Lamina gone to Issam.'

'Yes, Lamina and Issam are together,' said Khalid.

'Talk to Issam every day, he needs to keep Lamina happy.'

'She asked for money.'

'We can give her some.'

'I don't trust her.'

'No?'

'With money in her pocket she may try to escape.'

'Give her this.' Samir counted fifty pounds. 'Tell her we have people who always watch to make sure she is safe.'

'Will Lamina understand the threat?'

'Did you understand?'

'Yes.'

'Then she will.'

'You think of everything.'

'Any other news? asked Samir, his gold filling flashing.

'Lamina tells me the third Jew has been charged with killing the other two. Our tracks are well trodden with others' feet.' Samir left Al-Nofara Café with a lively face. Khalid stayed, and poured another mint tea, sitting alone with his thoughts about what came next, what came next when he tugged the blue underwear, tugged aside the blue underwear. He gulped a sweet mouthful. His eyes darted. He knew what came next.

Two weeks later, Lamina and Khalid sat in the obstetrician's consulting room. The obstetrician eyed them and shook his head. He said the rabbit test was wrong once in a hundred, maybe twice in a hundred. Khalid asked for the test to be repeated. Lamina sat in silence, watching the two men discuss her condition. She had no faith in the rabbit test, but gave another urine sample.

In the Buick Khalid spoke up. 'You've made me look foolish with Samir.'

'Samir?'

'My friend who paid for you to travel to New York.'

'Tall with blue eyes?' asked Lamina.

'Yes.' Khalid started the Buick and turned into the light traffic.

'I never knew his name.'

'Forget you know.'

'I know I'm pregnant.'

'Your feelings mean nothing.'

'I've missed my period again.'

'You're not healthy.'

'Trust me.'

'The doctor knows more than you. He's the best in Damascus.'

'A woman knows.'

〇

The same day at noon, seated with Samir in the Al-Nofara Café, Khalid heard the *muadhan's* noon *adhan* resonating from loudspeakers attached to the minarets of the Great Mosque. The Al-Nofara Café was empty except for the waiter and two men who sat together in a corner. Khalid looked at Samir's hands, the fingers were slender and the nails cut short. He then stared at his own hands—stubby fingers with the little finger missing on his left hand. His four-fingered left hand grasped the ceramic cup filled with mint tea. When he was asked how he lost the little finger, severed neatly at the knuckle, he said it was a childhood accident. No further details were ever given.

Khalid apologised to Samir and explained it would be another two weeks. Samir said to contact him when he knew, then left the café. Khalid finished his mint tea and headed for the street. The waiter chased after him wanting to be paid. Khalid stopped in his stride. Samir always paid the bill.

〇

So Issam spooned the pomegranate seeds and slowly swallowed them. Issam had soft black stubble with a close-cropped goatee. His high forehead was heavy above his eyebrows and his eyes were set in a harmless face that embodied the Druze tenants of truthfulness, loyalty, patience and perseverance. The sun had set and the fan whirled above his head. How good it felt to live with Lamina but she denied him.

'It's been two weeks,' said Issam. Khalid stated they should live like a husband and wife.

'I'll tram to the Al-Hamidiyah Souq tomorrow morning.' Lamina had not seen her mother for three months.

'I'll drive you.'

'There are some woman tasks I need to do.'

'What do you mean?'

'Accord me the privacy Allah has blessed upon me.'

'Khalid instructed to watch over you whenever you go out.'

'A wife desires freedom if her husband wishes to enjoy all she has to offer.'

Issam reached for another pomegranate.

A fortnight later, Khalid and Lamina sat in the courtyard at the obstetrician's house; the spotless floor a tiled mosaic with pot plants, arched doors and stone façades, while a tree grew on one side and arched across the courtyard to weep down the opposite stone wall. A black cat stretched on a branch and looked at the two people below. Lamina sat on a white couch; a grape in her hand. She peeled the grape, ate the purple skin, then popped the green shiny bulb in her mouth. She wore an American-style dress pinched tight at the waist. Khalid sat opposite, close to the weeping leaves. He stood up, selected a fresh fig from a fruit bowl then stepped to a large glass terrarium that sat on a table at the courtyard's end. The terrarium was four paces long, and inside was sand and grit and small rocks with desert plants. At one edge a grey mouse hunched close against a small rock; it seemed to shiver. And at the other end, Khalid saw a curled brown snake. It was a flat-head viper; Khalid knew his snakes. The head was flat and broad and the snake's back was covered with odd-shaped, keeled scales in different shades of brown. The snake twisted and curled and pushed off a rock to stretch out. If it stretched out full it would be over a yard. The snake seemed to know the mouse was trapped; it was often fed live mice. Fixed on the wall above the terrarium was the graphic design of a red snake curled in a circle with its tail in its mouth. Under the circular red snake was the ancient word *ouroboros* meaning wholeness, infinity, fertility.

An arched door facing the courtyard opened.

'I'm sorry to keep you,' said the obstetrician.

'I was looking at your viper,' said Khalid.

'A symbol of fertility.'

'Fertility?'

'I have good news,' said the obstetrician, 'You're pregnant, Lamina.'

'Are you sure?' asked Khalid.

'Yes,' he said. 'Come, let's see how you are.'

Lamina stood up and lifted her chin high with a bold aspect in her eyes, as she followed the obstetrician. Khalid hadn't seen this look before—a look of confidence, a look of defiance, a look of derision, a look to be turned against her.

◯

Several months later, Samir and Khalid sat inside Al-Nofara Café. It was their favourite place to meet. There was talk of snow. The waiter knew them and brought mint tea without needing an order.

'What's going on?' asked Khalid.

'Going on?' asked Samir.

'The army trucks.' Khalid pointed over Samir's shoulder to the street outside the café. Samir turned and looked over his shoulder at the passing green army trucks. Soldiers sat on both sides of the open decks. They were dressed in olive green with round green dish-shaped helmets. They held guns that pointed up. More trucks passed—maybe thirty. All with soldiers. Samir raised his hand to the waiter. He came to their table.

'The army outside, any news on the radio?' asked Samir.

'Let me … the radio.' The waiter tottered behind the counter and turned on a tube radio that sat in a wooden case. It was tuned to Radio Damascus. The waiter listened for a few moments and returned to their table.

'A military exercise. People are not to group on the streets,' said the waiter

'Thank you,' said Samir, he could hear a distorted radio voice.

'A coup,' Samir said to Khalid.

'But we had the new government formed yesterday.'

'The army waited for those who sought power to step forward and expose themselves.'

A few days earlier the government had fallen after popular opposition to Syria joining the Middle East Peace Command. This Peace Command was a combined American, French, Turk and British initiative, but the collective initiative either paid the wrong generals or did not pay enough. It had been a smart American idea to have Syria join the Middle East Peace Command, but Stalin had other ideas. Syrian oil had started to flow, and with the expectation of vast oil reserves Stalin made sure his coterie of influenced Syrian generals held the guns, made new rules and created justifications. Samir had a large grain business and sat with the Druze elite. He knew the cards and the shuffling game of the power brokers. Tangible cards being replaced by non-existent cards. Then the power broker propaganda convincing the populace the non-existent cards were real.

'We need to be careful,' said Samir.

'Careful?'

'They are against us, against the Druze; we all need to be careful.'

'What does it mean for us?'

'Don't talk about politics with anyone.'

'No.'

'Just make sure Lamina is well.'

'She is.'

'It's good news she is expecting any day.'

'I'll send you a message when she goes to hospital.' Samir looked at the street where more army trucks were passing.

'Yes, send me a message, I need to go now,' said Samir. After leaving the Al-Nofara Café, Samir drove through Adan Malaki Square where he could get a view of the American embassy, an elegant three-storey villa sitting behind a close-cropped hedge with young trees in the front yard. Army trucks surrounded the embassy. Samir knew America did not respond well to crude messages. An opportunity he thought.

○

Three days later, Khalid sent word to Samir that Lamina was in labour.

Lamina opened her eyes when Khalid pushed open her hospital room door. She lay in a single bed with white sheets and a white blanket with the name Damascus Maternity University Hospital embroidered in Arabic. Beside the bed was a cane bassinette with a blue blanket and a baby. A band of sunlight poured through a gap in the curtains and brightened the bassinette and brightened the blue blanket wrapping Lamina's baby boy.

'We have our boy,' said Khalid. Through half-closed eyes, Lamina looked at the bassinette with her sleeping baby and the band of light.

'Shhhh, he's sleeping. Can you close the curtains?' she said.

Khalid pulled the white curtain closed and the light band was gone

'How heavy is he?' Khalid knew little about babies but knew enough to know their weight seemed important.

'Six pounds ten.'

'Is that good?'

'It's good for Antanios,' said Lamina.

'Who's Antanios?'

'I've named my baby, Antanios.'

'It's not for you to name him.'

'I need to sleep.' Lamina turned from Khalid and pulled up the sheet. Khalid stepped closer to the bassinette. The little boy was wrapped tightly, a tangle of dark hair against a thin blue towelling pillow, eyes pinched shut. His mouth opened wide and squeaked a plum yawn and then the plum was gone. Lamina turned her head to the bassinette and then to Khalid, her eyes, with her angled down eyebrows, sliced him. Khalid stepped back from the bassinette and without a word left. Lamina smiled at the bassinette. Antanios had come swiftly. The doctor cautioned her that as she had a slight build and it was her first child, it may take some time. But Antanios departed her cosy warm cocoon with the pep and vitality of a Syrian hare. Lamina thought of the thousand Syrian pounds as payment for conceiving Einstein's child, a child to carry until birth, a child to give up after weaning. But now she wanted to keep her baby; she could never give him up. She would choose the time to tell Khalid she wanted to raise her child; love her child, nurture her little boy's mind and heart. Lamina thought of her own childhood and remembered her mother saying the best sound in the world was hearing the words *Mum, Mum, Mum*. She thought about the soft voice of discipline her parents used to guide a course of action; and with the influence of Socrates on Druze philosophy, of being asked questions to think and discover for herself.

It was snowing five days later when Issam carried the cane bassinette from the maternity suite to his car. The lean young man looked down at the bassinette.

Antanios was wrapped snugly in blue, with a blue knitted hat pulled low, and Lamina glowed at Antanios' side. Her breath clouded the air. When they reached Issam's car he placed the cane bassinette on the back seat. Lamina sat beside the bassinette, and gazed transfixed at her baby.

'It's amazing, I can simply leave the hospital with my little boy.'

'Khalid's very happy with you; he asked if there's anything you want.'

'Can we move to Jaramana?' she asked referring to the Druze suburb on the south-east side of Damascus. It was where most of the Druze in Damascus lived.

'We have a great apartment in Al Malky, it's the best area in Damascus and you have Tishreen Park close.'

'I know, but you haven't let me make new friends; you only want me to have Druze friends, but there are no Druze where we live. I need contact with other mothers.'

'I'm doing what Khalid tells me.'

'We need to move to Jaramana.'

'Don't let Khalid hear you talking like this.'

Issam drove straddling the tram track, and the car shook over the cobblestones in Umayyad Square. Lamina felt herself shake and tightened her grip on the bassinette. A Damascus green and yellow tram stopped abruptly in front, and the car skidded in the snow before the tyres gripped. Lamina lurched in the back.

'Careful, the bassinette almost fell.'

'I'm sorry.' Issam drove sedately out of the square, past Tishreen Park to Al Malky.

'All the nurses think Antanios is the perfect little boy,' Lamina said as she broke the silence.

'Khalid gifted a banquet to welcome you and Cyrus home.'

'Cyrus?'

'Khalid said he will be called Cyrus.'

'I feel like a prisoner. Khalid controls everything.'

'He's giving us money, taking care of us.'

'We need to be given space to live.'

'Khalid's excited about Cyrus; we're all proud of you.'

'Why wouldn't he let me name my own baby?'

'Cyrus is a good name, it means sun.'

'It's a Persian name.'

'Maybe Cyrus's destiny is to unite the Arab and Persian world,' said Issam

'Is this why Khalid wanted his father to be Einstein?'

'Please never talk of Einstein. We have to say I'm Cyrus's father.'

○

The snow was heavier. On the windscreen the wipers collected a white line, the tyres slushed and spat and Issam peered through a steamed-up window into the falling flakes, the coldest day of the year in Damascus. Issam parked outside their apartment and turned off the ignition. The wipers stopped. He folded a blanket over the top of the bassinette, and as he left the car, snow-flakes fell on the blue blanket and formed ice crystals. The ice crystals melted when they entered their second-floor apartment.

Lamina breastfeed Cyrus, cupped him to her shoulder and gently rubbed and patted his back, then tucked him into his bassinette beside her bed; a bed Issam had yet to share. She wandered into the kitchen, yawned, and sat with her head in her hands. A muslin cloth covered the food; she lifted her head then lifted the muslin; a vitality of aroma and colour—pitas, cream-coloured labneh, basmati rice, lamb stuffed with a blend of nuts and spices, cherry tomatoes, a dish of sliced cucumbers and a bowl of fresh wild raspberries and pears. She felt full just smelling the food.

'The food looks lovely,' she said. She ate a handful of raspberries and wiped her red lips.

'Khalid said we need to keep you healthy to feed Cyrus the best milk.'

'Thank him.' Her head rested back on her arms.

Issam hugged his arms around himself. 'I have a new life now, to stand by you and Cyrus, please let me into your heart.' Issam saw Lamina's shoulders rise and fall. She was asleep.

○

Cyrus grew and Lamina's love for Cyrus grew and now six months later in Beirut, the door to the St George Hotel meeting room opened and Samir was glad to see the young couple who entered. The young woman radiated a Lebanese perfume with its smoky rich amber fragrance. She had a youthful form; thoughtful eyes and a white head scarf covered her long dark hair. The man had relaxed shoulders and a soft face with wire-framed glasses and dark-cropped beard that portrayed the look of an academic.

'*As-salamu alaykum*,' said Samir as he shook the man's hand.

'*As-salamu alaykum*,' replied the man. Marwan had been introduced to Samir by a trusted family member. Not all family members could be trusted.

'Thank you both for taking time to meet,' said Samir. They were the fourth Lebanese couple Samir had met on his visit to Beirut but on first impressions Samir thought this couple would be perfect.

◯

Marwan explained how he and his wife Safiyiah had met in Paris while both studying at the Sorbonne. They now lived in Aley, the Druze dominated and Lebanon's fourth largest city.

'Would you move to Syria?' asked Samir.

'Syria?' said Marwan.

'People will not know you in Syria, there'll be no questions,' said Samir. Adoption was not permitted within the Druze faith.

I'm in love with my little boy already, thought Safiyiah. 'We could live in Syria,' she said to Marwan. Her voice implored.

'No need to work, you'll have all the money you need,' said Samir.

'Our own little boy,' said Safiyiah.

'I would want to work,' said Marwan. 'I'm a structural engineer.'

'In time work could be organised.'

◯

Marwan drove his car away from the hotel. His eyes left the road to look at Safiyiah.

'It seems strange,' he said.

'What's strange about a little boy needing a mum and dad?'

'Druze families in Syria could help.'

'Please don't cause a fight with Samir. This could be our only chance to have a child.'

Marwan had a lot of questions, but Safiyiah's excitement drove his questions to that place where you stored silent thoughts. The following day, they met with Samir and finalised details of the secret adoption.

○

Cyrus was six months old and Issam walked the two miles to meet Khalid. Issam liked to walk, because he never knew what thoughts would come. It seemed to Issam his thoughts were constructed by unconscious magic and then revealed at the right time and place to forge a role in his world. He smiled at three young women who passed, they carried books; university students, he thought, their western mid-calf length dresses swirled with each step. The young women didn't smile back, in fact, they didn't look at him, but they did look at an army jeep that charged by, and looked behind the jeep at an army truck with a loud exhaust. The army truck and jeep halted right where Issam walked and a soldier with a khaki-green peaked cap jumped from the jeep and barked instructions. A group of soldiers positioned on the street while others barged into a building. Issam ambled close by a metal-hat soldier who crouched with a rifle and then ambled close past another. Neither looked at him. Issam crossed the road, away from the soldiers and headed for the bath-house to meet Khalid. A street vendor who wore a red felt *tarboosh* and red tunic asked Issam if he wanted a cup of liquorice. Issam paid two *qirsh* and the vendor took a cup from the wooden tray at his waist and poured liquorice syrup from a tin container strapped to his back. The tin container looked like an elaborate sports' tournament trophy. At the bath-house, Issam stripped to his underwear and dropped his clothes on a dry patch of carpet. The attendant gave him wooden slippers and a ripped towel-sheet. He clomped to the smoky communal bath, where everyone seemed to know each other.

In the bath mist, Issam stepped from his wooden slippers, then folded his arms across his sunken chest as he skimmed the faces in the mist. When Issam saw Khalid, Khalid nodded, and Issam stepped into the warm water by Khalid's side. The warmth penetrated Issam's skin and he was soon warmed to the core. As he sat in the water, Issam felt his body sway with the ripples. Cool lines tracked on his face behind sweat beads that dropped from his forehead to his cheeks and chin, and his feet were hot.

After fifteen minutes in the warm water Khalid spoke. 'Soap?'

'Okay,' said Issam. He placed the flat of his hands on the tiles and hauled himself out of the water. Khalid used the steps. They both slipped their feet into wooden slippers and scuffed their way to a blue and white tiled bathing room to soap. When their bodies were covered in soap Khalid made a fist and moved his closed fingers back and forth across his chest in a signal to an attendant, they were ready to be scrubbed. The attendant scrubbed with a rough camel hair glove that left red streaks on both their bodies as dead skin cells were sloughed off. Khalid and Issam then retreated to a recessed balcony away from the noise and mist and smoke.

'I need to know his—' Khalid stopped talking and tilted an ear. 'That sounded like a shot.'

'The army are down the street,' said Issam.

'Are you sure?'

'On the way here, I ambled through them.'

'Ambled through them?'

'Like I was invisible. They paid me no attention.'

'They found who they were looking for… or found someone else,' said Khalid.

'They're on the street more.'

'Shishakli must be worried, killing to grab power and now killing to keep it.'

'Why Shishakli? Selu is president.'

'In name only.'

'Shishakli and Selu must know they lose respect,' said Issam.

'They have lost respect for God; how can they ever ask for mercy when they show none? Our leaders need to observe religion and practice morality.'

'How do you think we can deepen our religion?'

'I've told you before.'

'I want to hear your wisdom again.'

'Our prophets are wise,' said Khalid referring to the Abrahamic, and the ancient Greek philosophers, central to the Druze religion. 'But I agree with Samir, we should also include teachings from our recent history.'

'We pray Cyrus will be a new prophet for us.'

'I will be an old man God willing, when Cyrus reaches greatness.'

'We have our religion, no one can take that from us.'

'Lamina's content?' asked Khalid.

'She's fine, and your wife?'

'She makes demands of me at night but it invigorates.'

'You look well.'

'Men lower their gaze out of respect for Lamina, but their eyes still register her beauty. You're blessed not to be kept chaste.' Khalid saw Issam smile, but his smile was strained, his eyes starved of crinkles. 'Do you know a woman is ready to lie with her man four weeks after giving birth?'

'I'll give Lamina the time she needs.'

The time she needs, thought Khalid, convinced Issam had yet to taste her flesh. 'A man needs to be a man; a man is weak if he doesn't bed his wife. Men whisper.'

'Lamina and I are close.'

'A woman shows no respect when she denies her body.'

'There's respect.'

'Where's your self-respect? If you have no self-respect, you become invisible. I fear Samir and I misjudged you.'

Issam thought of his invisible walk to the bath-house. *It's all Lamina's fault that Khalid's mocking me.*

'Lamina has asked again for the thousand shillings,' said Issam.

'We give you money.'

'The money promised to her for carrying Cyrus.'

'Your apartment, your food, Lamina's clothes, it costs many times what she asks.'

'Ah … I told Lamina Samir gives me money and she said I'm not even Cyrus's father.' Issam knew he was telling a lie.

Khalid closed his eyes and took a deep breath. 'Enough talk of Lamina, how's our little boy?'

'Growing every day.'

'Each day is a blessing.'

The waiter brought them a pot of mint tea, a bowl of sugar and two cups.

'Cyrus no longer takes milk from Lamina's breast,' said Issam.

'Oh …'

'He takes milk from the goat.'

'How long?'

'A few days.'

'Samir has decided Cyrus must live with another family after he's weened,' said Khalid.

'Another family … why?'

'To receive the world's teachings.'

'Lamina agrees?'

'She has no say.'

'I don't understand. Lamina is Cyrus's mother.'

'Lamina has no say when she is no longer around.'

'Where's she going?'

'A Druze devotee will render the sacrifice.'

'Sacrifice?'

'We need one who is trusted.'

'To kill a goat?'

'Not a goat, the boy's mother.'

Issam sat silent for a moment. 'Are you asking me to kill Lamina?'

'You would honour Samir and honour our quest to have a new prophet.'

'What has she done to deserve this?'

'We have no trust in her.'

'But to kill.'

'If Lamina says you're not Cyrus's father, she can tell another.'

Issam looked away with his palm on his cheek, and he spoke in a whisper. Khalid saw Issam's mouth move but heard nothing.

'What?' asked Khalid.

'Maybe I didn't hear right.'

'It's the message you took, and the message another may take.'

'I've thought about it. What Lamina was saying is that *I'm not even Cyrus's father … but I do so much.*'

'Her words hide spite. I've also heard Lamina speak venom like this.

'But—'

'Samir and I agree,' interrupted Khalid. 'There's nothing more unbinding than loose ends. Will you honour the Druze destiny?'

'But I've led a pure life.'

'How do you think of me?'

'I respect and honour you.'

'What if I tell you my hands are bloodied.'

'Blood on your hands doesn't change what I know of your heart.'

'A trail of blood follows all prophets; blood clears a path for greatness. As a devoted servant of God, Abraham agreed to take his child to Mount Moriah to slaughter him in God's name, but God later accepted the sacrifice of a sheep. Blood is allowed to spill in our service to God.'

'But Lamina is not a sheep. All our teachings talk of love and respect for life.'

'God willing, Cyrus will become one of the greatest prophets and will be a Druze salvation.'

'I can keep close to Lamina.'

'She could cast Cyrus as a false prophet, he's not Druze.'

'A false prophet?'

'Cyrus was not conceived by two Druze parents, if Lamina repeats this, Cyrus will become a mirage in the desert.'

'Why would Lamina not wish for the best?'

'Only you know the truths Lamina has shared; the intimate secrets revealed between your entwined bodies in the night.'

Issam swallowed, his eyes darted around, then his shoulders slumped forward.

'Safety and loyalty sleep well together,' said Khalid.

Issam remained silent as he understood the warning.

'By the will of God, Lamina's sun must set,' said Khalid. 'Do you wish to enact God's will and attain felicity?'

'It will be done.'

'History will honour your duty.'

'It will be done,' said Issam. 'It will be done.' Issam knew Khalid's words were a knife to his throat. It was his life or Lamina's. They had lied to him from the start. He realised now that killing Lamina was always their plan. Could he tell Lamina and run? Run together north to Aleppo and then to Turkey away from Khalid and away from Samir. But would Lamina believe him? With no intimate trust between them, he could only guess how she'd react, and if Lamina reacted the wrong way, they'd both be dead. He decided he'd first establish intimacy with Lamina and then tell her.

When he returned to their apartment from the bath-house Issam found Lamina curled in her bed napping. Beside her bed, Cyrus sat in the corner of his cot, playing with a stuffed, knitted, striped tiger that Lamina had made. Cyrus's chubby fingers held the tiger against the light brown skin of his chest. Issam lifted Cyrus from the cot, found his nappy dry, ruffled Cyrus's thick black hair, then Issam said 'tiger' as he pointed at the tiger. Cyrus looked into Issam's face then at the tiger then back to Issam. Issam again pointed at the tiger and said 'tiger'. Cyrus's eyes shone and he pointed his finger at Issam. Issam said, 'Dad.' Cyrus smiled a chubby smile then pointed to a soft ball in his cot. 'Ball,' said Issam and Cyrus chuckled, his eyes saucer wide. Cyrus looked at his wall and pointed to a clock. 'Clock,' said Issam. Cyrus smiled wider, chuckled again and pointed at a wall picture of a Syrian hamster. 'Hamster,' said Issam.

Lamina stirred. 'What are you doing?'

'Cyrus knows objects have different names.'

'I don't think so.'

Issam placed Cyrus back in his cot, left the room and showered then returned to Lamina's bedroom wearing a bathrobe. He pulled back the sheet and lay beside her. As he stared at the crimson fabric that covered her feminine form he thought about her continual refusal. When she'd been pregnant, she claimed it could harm the health of her baby and now as a new mother she said she needed time. Issam placed his hand on Lamina's hip and tugged the crimson fabric. Lamina rolled away and pulled down her nightdress.

'*Qahba*!' spat Issam. In his cot, Cyrus's eyes grew large. Issam shoved Lamina's leg with his hand as he rolled out of the bed.

'What's wrong with you?'

'What's wrong with you?' Issam asked.

'We need to talk.'

'We do talk.'

'Since Cyrus was born, I've been tired every waking minute. I struggle to sleep and have no interest in food,' said Lamina.

'You refuse to share your body with me.'

'I'm a new mother.'

'Never you've shared with me.'

'We have a lifetime to grow together.'

'You're lazy. When did you last cook a proper meal?'

'I'm not lazy, every little task takes a mountain of energy; I need you to understand.'

But Issam didn't understand. Issam grumbled and plodded into the room where he slept, closed the door with a bang and opened the Druze holy book. Through his tears the words he read were unclear.

$$\bigcirc$$

Three days later, mid-morning in Tishreen Park, Issam meandered around a set of trees for the third time, talking to himself and repeating Khalid's words. *We have the grave dug, your knife is sharp, slice her throat like you kill a goat.* Issam's life savings no longer sat safe in the bank, his wallet, hidden in his room, was bulging and fat, enough, more than enough, to take Lamina and Cyrus north to Turkey. Issam returned to their apartment.

$$\bigcirc$$

'You need to get up; we need to leave,' said Issam. He wore a short-sleeved white shirt and dark tie.

'Leave … what do you mean?'

'Trust me. Please get up.'

'Trust you, after you pulled up my nightdress and yelled at me?'

'Please, we need to leave.'

Lamina pulled the blankets over her head and spoke from beneath the covers. 'You need to leave, leave me alone.'

Issam clenched his fists and flung the curtains open; the brass loops clattered a warning on the brass curtain rail.

'A surprise for you. I have a surprise for you,' he said, but Lamina murmured *not now* from beneath the covers.

'A special surprise,' Issam said. 'A country house where you and Cyrus can enjoy the best food and clean air. A country house for retreats. Khalid is waiting to meet us, meet us for lunch at the new country house to see if it meets your desire.'

'I'm tired and Cyrus is sleeping. Please go away and keep quiet.'

'Cyrus is your first child, you talk of mother's instincts, what about father's instincts.'

'Father's?'

'You're blind to everything.'

'Why are you wearing a tie?'

'Respect for Khalid,' said Issam. But it was not the real reason. Issam thought if they passed through an army checkpoint going north, it would make them look a more upright family.

Lamina's fine hand and fine wrist came into view as she pulled the covers from her head and asked Issam to fill Cyrus's bottle from the chilled goat's milk can and put the bassinette in the car. He left the room and Lamina closed her bedroom door and put on a brown knee-length dress.

Outside their apartment they sat in the car in silence with Lamina in the rear seat beside Cyrus's bassinette.

'Wait … I forgot,' said Issam. He hurried back to their apartment, packed a travel case a quarter full of his clothes, raced into Lamina's room and filled the case with a selection of her and Cyrus's clothes and headed back to the car. Issam placed the travel case in the boot then got back behind the wheel.

'What's in the boot?'

'Nappies for Cyrus. I forgot.'

Issam drove from their apartment through the Damascus streets and then stopped at a major intersection. North towards Turkey or south towards the Golan Heights?

'The road is clear, why are we stopped?'

'I'm thinking.'

'Don't you know where you're going?'

Issam sat still holding the steering wheel firmly and looking straight-ahead.

After a few moments of silence, Lamina spoke again. 'Drive or take us home.'

Issam revved the engine and turned north, heading for Turkey.

'How far are we going?'

'A few hours so you can sleep.'

'A few hours?'

'Try to sleep.'

'I'm awake now.'

'We're a family and we'll have more children God willing.'

Lamina screwed up her face. 'I can't think of such things.'

'What?'

'Cyrus is my family; I have no space for anything more.'

'I can lead our family.'

'You are not yet a man.'

Not yet a man? thought Issam. Here he risked his life to take Lamina to safety. What more could a man do? His fingers clenched the steering wheel and he braked and pulled to a stop. Lamina rocked forward.

'What are you doing?' She could not see his distant stare or the look on his face, or hear Khalid's voice in Issam's head saying *men whisper, where's your self- respect.*

'I made a wrong turn.' He waited for an on-coming car to pass, turned side-on to the road, reversed, then turned and drove back the way they'd come, heading to Sa'sa near the Golan Heights. The sun was in his face. He pulled the visor down.

The further they drove south from Damascus the more the green bushes surrendered to the brown and rocky desert landscape and the road became dusty.

'How long?' asked Lamina.

'Twenty miles to Sa'sa.'

'Where's Sa'sa?'

'Near the Golan Heights.'

'Lovely,' said Lamina, thinking the journey would be much less than an hour, yet Issam had said several hours.

Near the small southern town of Sa'sa, Issam turned the car from the sealed road covered with desert dust onto a sand-grit track. His pace was unhurried; the car bumped and rocked and threw up dust.

'Wind up your window, there's dust in the car,' said Lamina.

'We need the cool air.'

'It's too dusty for Cyrus.'

Issam wound up his window.

A short time later he slowed down and turned from the sand-grit track and stopped at a crumbling house. Issam knew the Druze obligations to fellow man by heart. The obligations had not changed in over a thousand years. He was a caring loving honest man but he found that place that people can find when they need to justify an action. Lamina had said and done bad things but she didn't deserve to have her throat slit and spend eternity in a hole dug in the brown dessert grit, but she did deserve to be sacrificed like a goat then buried in the dessert. A sacrifice ensuring the best care for the future prophet.

'Why're we stopping?' asked Lamina.

'We've arrived.'

'This house?' The area was isolated.

'It's your resting place.'

'I don't understand.'

'You're so superior with your smart words and closing your body to me,' Issam said with a sneer.

'Issam, please, where're your thoughts coming from, don't darken your soul.'

'You'll find death rides a fast camel.' Issam sprang from his seat, opened the rear door, knotted his fingers in Lamina's dark hair, and dragged her from the back seat onto the dry ground.

'Issam! No! Stop! You're hurting me. Nooo! In the name of God no. No! Please don't do this. I've done everything asked of me,' Lamina cried out. She dropped to her knees.

'You whore yourself to that old Jew but treat me like donkey shit.'

'Your heart is confused.'

'More smart words.'

'Please! I'm sorry if I didn't understand you.'

Issam didn't answer, instead he drew his knife from the sheath at his waist.

Lamina stared at the knife, then looked up at Issam's face.

'I'm sorry. We can go home and make love like a man and his wife.'

From the car, Cyrus cried out. A sixth sense of his mother's danger or a coincidental cry for comfort. Lamina's terrified eyes turned to Cyrus's call.

'Dearest God. Bless my son's soul.' Her face was twisted and grey.

'Peace be on you,' Issam whispered.

○

Issam grabbed the shovel from the boot of his car. The shovel chinked and crunched as he drove the blade into the pile of brown stoney dirt, then came a thud as he tipped the blade load into the yard-deep hole he'd dug with Khalid three days earlier. A dusty film ran down Issam's cheeks as Lamina's body faded. When the grave was filled Issam moved the shovel back and forward to smooth the surface, much as he had done when spreading donkey dung on his father's garden.

○

Issam turned his car from the dusty track on to the seal back to Damascus. The feelings of fear and doubt and dread had all gone now. Issam thoughts were on the embrace he would receive from Khalid and Samir, and he felt an inner warmth that he had proved himself a man.

'Mum mum,' said Cyrus from the bassinet in the back seat.

○

The following day, Khalid met with Samir, who chose not to wear his white *iaffa*, the cylindrical white hat would be a harassment magnet for Syrian security.

'Will you eat?' asked Samir.

'Yes, thank you.'

Samir raised his hand and the waiter appeared.

'Bring us your finest food.'

The waiter returned with a platter of flat bread, hummus *kawarma,* beet-root *tahini,* lamb meatballs, chicken *shawarma* and salad.

'Let me tell you a secret of the *al-uqqāl,*' said Samir, referring to the wise elite Druze. 'We study the past to understand the trajectory of the future.'

'I'm not sure I understand.'

'The Arab defeat to destroy Israel in 1948, showed how corrupt and inept the Syrian government is. You know Yousuf-al-Attras?'

'Of course, our Druze Leader and the greatest living Syrian soldier.'

'He warned the Jews were well prepared and would be more than a match for the miserable Syrian force. If the Druze had not remained neutral, the Israelis might have been defeated.'

'Why do you speak of Yousuf-al-Attras?' asked Khalid.

'The wisdom we offer does not always fall on receptive ears. And when our Druze words and actions have impact, they are often claimed by others. Attras led the 1925 revolt against the French, and the Syrian Arab nationalists claimed the credit. Credit stolen from the Druze, honour stolen from the Druze, respect stolen from the Druze, the Druze relegated to oblivion. We have a deep knowl-edge like no other, humility has seen us influence from the shadows, but I believe we will impact the future so great, the Druze will gain eternal eminence with no risk of history being rewritten.'

'You're talking of Cyrus?' asked Khalid.

CHAPTER FOUR

DAMASCUS, SYRIA, 1954

THE VOLCANIC CONE in the Hauran region in southern Syria was curved and white. On this side lava flows had created rock and there was little shade. The trees were winter skeletons, and on the barren volcanic plateau a herdsman trudged wearing a coat and carried a staff as he minded sheep. Volcanic rock walls, to confine sheep and goats, made a haphazard grid, and a flat-roofed stone house with a high stone wall sat back from the gravel road in the weak winter sun. Against the stone house was an oak table with four chairs waiting for the car from Jordan. The oak table was shielded by the high stone wall. Safiyiah set her four best porcelain cups on the oak table; each cup cast a long shadow.

Safiyiah and Marwan had been in Syria three and a half years nurturing their little prince. Safiyiah wore the innocence of knowing only one lover. Marwan's beard was still close cropped as it had been when they adopted Cyrus. True smiles lived on his and Safiyiah's faces. Marwan held four-year-old Cyrus against his chest as he sat at the table in the winter sun. He thought the car from the Jordan border would arrive any time soon.

'It will cool when the sun goes down,' said Safiyiah.

'We have an hour,' said Marwan as he glanced at the sun.

'I wish they weren't meeting here.'

'It'll be fine.'

'I don't want trouble.'

'It's helping Samir.'

'We don't need politics.'

'Samir gave us Cyrus.'

'Samir doesn't own our lives.'

'You're too sensitive.'

'Am I?' Safiyiah stepped inside the house and pulled closed the window by the oak table. As she locked the window the window latch wobbled in her fingers. Then she stepped outside and stood by the oak table.

'Could you fix the latch?' she said.

'I will … I know I've said I will … but I will.'

'It's alright, but before it gets too loose.'

Marwan stood up, stepped to Safiyiah's side and draped his arm around her shoulders and pulled her close. 'Everything will be fine, you know.'

'Do I know?' She looked up into Marwan's face.

'You know,' he said bending and kissing her forehead. Just then he heard a car engine.

The engine noise came close, idled for a few seconds and then he heard the engine stop outside the stone wall. Their black German Shepherd pricked his ears, pushed up from his front legs and stared at the door in the stone wall

'They're here,' said Marwan. He squeezed Safiyiah's hand, lifted Cyrus into her arms, patted Aswad's head, said 'stay,' then stepped to the door in the stone wall, turned the cast-iron handle and pulled the heavy door towards him. Through the open door he saw an early 1950s two-tone blue Dodge, that smiled a row of chrome teeth. The front doors of the Dodge and one back door opened. A man Marwan knew stepped from the back door. His face was the colour of tanned sheep leather and when he straightened up, he was half a head taller than the other two. At the rear of the car the tall man lugged a black suitcase from the trunk. He held the suitcase handle with both hands and bent as he shuffled.

'*Marhaba!*' said Marwan. The man shuffled past and the other two followed. Marwan closed the gate. The tall man lowered the suitcase to the ground and took a breath.

'*Marhaba,* Marwan,' said the tall man, his chest heaving. 'These are my friends.' He waved his hand but didn't offer names.

'*Ahala usahla,'* said Marwan, using the more formal greeting for guests.

'*Ahala usahla,'* they replied. One of the men lifted the suitcase, looked at the black German Shepherd watching him, shuffled to the oak table, lowered the suitcase to the ground then shoved the suitcase under the table. The aluminium corners of the suitcase rasped against the stone tiles.

From his mother's arms Cyrus watched the men arrive. He hadn't seen them before. When one bent and towed something big and black, it made a noise on the tiles. He looked up at his mum and closed his fingers on her white head scarf. She smiled and patted him on the back. Cyrus smiled too.

Safiyiah also watched the man with the suitcase. 'How long was the drive?' she asked. The tall man looked at his colleague and then at Marwan before smiling at Safiyiah and Cyrus. Cyrus's brown eyes held the tall man's gaze.

'From Amman,' replied the tall man.

'You must be hungry,' said Safiyiah.

'Thank you, but we need to go.'

'I have food for you.' Safiyiah left and returned a few moments later still holding Cyrus, but also holding a brown paper bag.

'To keep you well,' she said, handing the tall man the brown paper bag of food.

'Thank you, I'm sorry we can't stay.' The tall man bent and whispered something to Marwan, then they turned and left.

Cyrus watched the men's backs getting smaller then disappear through the wall door. He stared at the solid black suitcase by the leg of the oak table and his fingers rolled the gold bangle on Safiyiah's wrist.

'What did he whisper?' asked Safiyiah.

'Another car will come,' replied Marwan.

'To take the suitcase.'

'Yes.'

'What's in it?' asked Safiyiah.

Marwan looked at the black suitcase with its reinforced aluminium corners 'It's for Samir.'

'Money?'
'I don't know.'
'For the opposition.'
'Maybe.'
'They would kill us.'
'We'll be fine.'
Safiyiah took a quick step and extended her hand into the air.
'Look.'
'What?'
'I caught a feather.'
'Let me see.' Safiyiah opened her hand and showed a small black feather
'Did you see the bird?'
'Only the feather.'
'Falling?'
'Floating.'
'From a bird.'
'I've never caught a feather before.'
'You're lucky.'
'Even a black feather?'
'An angel watches over you.'
'Maybe I caught it for Cyrus.'
'I hear another car.'
'For the suitcase?'
'It's stopping.'
'I don't want it here.' Safiyiah didn't understand politics; she understood good people but didn't understand bad people.
'A safe drop-off and pick-up, that's all.'
He opened the door in the stone wall and saw a grey American car. Two men left the vehicle and walked with Marwan to the oak table. Safiyiah was inside watching from the window with the loose latch. Two minutes later, the car drove away and the suitcase was gone. Two minutes after that another car arrived. A new man banged on the door in the stone wall and Marwan opened it.
'*Marhaba,* Marwan. Samir sent me.'
'Yes?'

The man stood still as he faced Marwan. 'Your family needs to move to Jaramana.'

'Why? When?'

'I'm sorry, you have two hours to pack.'

'Two hours?'

'Everything you need is in Jaramana, take what's dearest.'

○

Archibald Roosevelt, like his cousin Kermit Roosevelt, was a senior CIA bureaucrat; both were grandsons of ex-President Teddy. Kermit had orchestrated the overthrow of the Iranian government the year before. Archie had tender optimism to bring Syria's government under American influence and if necessary, arrange for a future coup. Archie's concern was Syria's neutrality and their friendship with Russia. And there was recent talk of Syria establishing a unity government, whatever that meant. America certainly did not need Syria having an independent government, independent thought, and independent people. Who the hell did they think they were? As an appetiser, Archie injected one million dollars into Syria to solidify the compliance and reliability of the Syrian military. The Druze were trusted by the CIA and were a conduit for the one-million-dollar injection. As a Druze elite, Samir facilitated the million into Syria. A million was a lot of money and Samir had ideas of his own.

○

The day after the black suitcase was taken away from Marwan's house, Samir stood inside the Damascus Museum where a large stone lion stared down on him. Behind Samir someone moved; he knew it was the colonel.

'Are they friends?' asked the colonel. Samir lowered his eyes to the base of the statue where the lion's monstrous stone paws held a carved horned antelope and the antelope stretched a delicate hoof over the lion's front leg.

'The antelope is hoping,' said Samir.

'In desperation we crave safety,' said the colonel who now stood beside Samir. Samir turned his head to look at the gaunt colonel. The colonel's dark stubble ran to a neat, handlebar moustache. The colonel removed a red and white packet of Winston's from his pocket then flicked a silver lighter and blew a stream of white smoke. He knew Samir was Druze and didn't smoke. The colonel moved the lit cigarette in small circles, inviting Samir to speak. Smoke curled from the lit tip.

'I hear a lot of money has come to Damascus,' said Samir.

'Money?'

'US dollars from Jordan. The Jabal al-Druze,' said Samir, referring to the Druze living on the Hauran Plateau.

'Who are they buying?' asked the colonel, his thin neck accentuating the rise and fall of his Adam's apple above an open white shirt.

'Officers in the army against the communists and Ba'ath Party.'

'A coup?'

'The CIA were successful in Iran,' said Samir.

'Do you have these officer's names?'

'No names, but officers who are not yet your enemies.'

'Not yet?'

'Money sways,' said Samir.

'The *Jabal al-Druze?*'

'Money from Jordan.'

'Do they think they can influence the government?' asked the colonel.

'They must.'

'They don't have the numbers.'

'Enough to seed dissent.'

'US dollars?' The colonel inhaled above his neat moustache.

'More than a million.'

'A million.'

'From Jordan.'

'Buying how many officers?'

'Ten thousand will buy a general,' said Samir. The colonel ran the numbers. 'We don't have a hundred generals.'

'The rest in colonels, majors, captains, or antelopes,' said Samir. The Colonel's mouth struggled to smile.

'Where's the money?' asked the colonel.

'I have the address.' The colonel nodded.

'What do you want?' he asked. Samir knew what he wanted. The Druze influence in the Syrian army was waning, Druze officers were being marginalised, posted away from the influence of Damascus and as with any waning light, the trajectory, unless reversed, was darkness. Samir wanted the Syrian army fractured, and with a fractured army a coup could be facilitated to overthrow Shishakli and his Social Nationalist Party. The Druze would have increased influence in a post-coup government.

'What do I want?' Samir waved his hand and repeated the colonel's question. 'I want political stability; we don't need another coup.' The colonel nodded again. He knew Samir imported large quantities of grain and Syria's current wheat harvest looked poor.

'How do you deal with your enemies?' asked Samir.

'Killing avoids confusion.'

'A language all understand.'

'You support killing your Druze brothers?'

'They'll understand a message of force.'

'The Druze officers?'

'Civilians,' said Samir.

'There's a risk.'

'It's a political calculation. Kill enough to send a message, but not too many to create the wrong message.'

'Artillery?' asked the colonel.

'Shelling sends a strong message.'

'We need a justification.'

'Citizens will be more accepting of an artillery attack if it follows an assassination, but the Druze leadership will understand the real message. Sacrifice one of your generals.'

The colonel tugged his moustache. 'I know one.'

'You need to act fast, before the million is devoured.'

'Political stability you said.'

'I also have challenges with the Druze leadership.'

'How does shelling the Druze help your challenges?'

'It creates problems and with the problems opportunity.'

'Where's the million?' asked the colonel. Samir reached inside his jacket and handed the colonel a piece of paper.

'It was here yesterday.' The colonel looked at the address and pocketed the paper.

'We have a deal.'

That evening, Samir met with the Syrian Druze Council. The council met in a private house. Eleven men sitting on a rug in a circle.

'Your meeting?' asked the council head.

'I think the army will shell Jabal al-Druze,' said Samir.

As they looked into each other's eyes, the council members had sombre faces.

'We need to warn our families to shelter,' said one.

'No.'

'No?'

'We need casualties to cause a revolt.'

'Women and children will be slaughtered.'

'We know that, better a few now than many more later.'

'My sister's family is in Jabal al-Druze,' said another council member.

'Get them to Damascus, but no more,' said the council head.

Samir didn't know how this was going to work out. No one did. A bullet to Archduke Ferdinand precipitated World War I, but there were people in power in powerful countries ravenous to exploit the shooting. A similar greed resided in Damascus, but this hunger could be channelled, isolated, and even satiated as long as America or Russia didn't step in.

Three days later, following breakfast, in their new Jaramana apartment Safiyiah washed a plate and passed it to Marwan to dry; an opportunity to talk while Cyrus slept. Safiyiah liked an ordered world which challenged Marwan because life delivered disorder. He could give no easy answer about the black suitcase or no palatable explanation for the killing two days prior of a Syrian army general; a killing for which the army seemed bent on blaming the Druze. As difficult as the answers and explanations were, the consequence seemed to Marwan more predictable and more ominous. He didn't want to scare Safiyiah, but they were now safe in Damascus and so Marwan shared his feeling that an army attack on the Jabal al-Druze region was possible. The president would fight to stay in power and the calls for revenge against the Druze would need to be fed.

'You must go back to Jabal al-Druze now,' said Safiyiah.

'Why?'

'To bring Selina, where it's safe.'

'Selina?'

'Yes,' Safiyiah said. 'Selina.'

'I thought Selina was in Lebanon.'

'She was.'

'You told Samir you had no family in Syria.'

'When we adopted Cyrus, she was in Lebanon.'

'Why didn't you tell me she was in Syria?'

'Samir was happy we had no family in Syria; I didn't want to risk us losing Cyrus.'

'Safiyiah … Safiyiah.'

'I'm sorry, I should have told you.'

Cyrus and Safiyiah were his domain of protection, not Selina, but he was compelled to protect Safiyiah's sense of responsibility. Marwan left the room and came back wearing a coat. Safiyiah wrote Selina's Busan address; they exchanged a kiss and Marwan left.

○

Marwan had seen few cars in the latter part of his two-hour drive from Damascus, although, ten miles from Busan, he had seen the Syrian army and off in the brown fields were guns covered with brown camouflage netting. He parked outside Selena's house facing where the road slanted down.

○

Marwan had seen few cars in the latter part of his two-hour drive from Damascus, although, ten miles from Busan, he had seen the Syrian army and off in the brown fields were guns covered with brown camouflage netting. He parked outside Selina's house facing where the road slanted down.

Inside, Selina sat on the floor, bent over a domed pillow, her fingers intertwining threads and sticking pins into the very fine stitches of her lace. She straightened when she heard the knock, draped her traditional white Druze head-veil over her head and opened the door.

'Hello, Selina, I'm sorry to arrive like this but it's urgent, you must come to Damascus.'

'What's wrong?' She stepped back from the door. Marwan hurried past her and into the living room where a small domed pillow held pins and lots of white threads. Marwan regarded Selina and was reminded that if he wasn't married, he'd be talking to her in a different way. It wasn't that

Marwan found Selina pretty, he thought her rather plain, but there was a gripping innocence about her with her modest smile and active eyes.

'There may be fighting with the army. We need to leave now.'

'Let me pack a small bag.'

Marwan stood and waited. Then, without warning a shell screamed close by. There was a pressure wave and a loud blast. He hit the floor with his hands over his head. The house shook. He jumped up and ran into Selina's bedroom. She stood with both hands clenched against her mouth.

'We need to get safe quickly,' said Marwan. 'Do you have a bath?'

'Yes.'

'Quickly, show me.'

Selina ran to the bathroom with its tin bath. Marwan followed.

'Into the bath and lie flat,' he said then raced back to Selina's bedroom as another shell screamed. He dived under the bed; the blast was even closer.

He pulled the mattress from the bed and dragged it to the bathroom where he squeezed into the bath beside Selina, before pulling the mattress on top. The ground shook every minute and Marwan felt Selina shudder. Outside, shells hit the houses and they caught fire and burnt freely. Then they heard a noise like a burst steam pipe followed by a blast and a rumbling and shaking as shrapnel flew everywhere and a great cloud of desert stone and plaster dust fell on the mattress. Selina shrieked at the roar and jolt of the explosion; tears ran down her cheeks. That was the last shell and then it became quiet. The salvo from the artillery guns, which hurled the shells from ten miles away, had lasted thirty minutes.

Marwan pushed the mattress away and they scrambled out of the tin bath. There was fine dust in the air that hurt their eyes and made them cough.

'Outside,' said Marwan.

'Look, my house … the walls … no … it's madness. I thought I was going to die.'

'Praise Allah we're not hurt.

Outside Salina's house the banana smell of nitro-glycerine hung in the air and Marwan saw many houses in the village that were burning and broken from the shelling. The street had crater holes and broken bricks and splintered beams and plaster blasted from the smashed houses. A house across the street had the corner ripped open like a yawning mouth with stone teeth at crooked angles. A short distance away Marwan's car sat at an odd slant in a street crater. The windows were broken and the car side dented. Selina stood still as she bit her fist.

'It's horrible we need to try and help.' Her voice was small and her eyes were wide. Marwan took in her distressed face and her weak voice.

'We need to get safe,' he said.

'Is this who we've been living next to? How can we forgive?' She hung her head and there were tears on her cheeks.

'We need to get food and we must leave,' he said.

'Leave?'

'We'll walk over the fields.'

'There's snow in the fields.'

'Wear two pairs of socks and two pairs of long pants,' he replied. 'Hurry. Get some food, warm clothes and walking shoes.'

Selina spun around and ran back inside her damaged house.

Marwan looked down at his black leather dress shoes; he had no others. In the dust at his feet was a narrow tyre track. His eyes followed the track down the street where he saw a T-trolley and the back of a man leaning forward as he pulled it. Two women wrapped in rugs were on the trolley and a young boy was pushing from behind—survival. The trolley was on a lean, one of the tyres looked flat. Marwan heard a noise. Behind him were two large farm trucks. He moved to the side of the road and the first truck stopped beside him.

'You alright?' asked the driver.

'Not hurt, thank you.'

'Are you Druze?'

'Yes.'

'Get a rifle from our men here.'

'I'm from Damascus,' said Marwan.

'You can fight; we need to fight.'

'I need to get to Damascus. Is the road safe?'

'Maybe safer through the fields.'

The man waved his hand and the truck moved forward. The back was packed high with boxes of rifles and ammunition while the truck behind was loaded with sandbags. They'd known beforehand about the attack, thought Marwan, they are ready to fight.

Selina ran from her house wearing a woollen coat and gripping a small bag. She gave the bag to Marwan.

'A truck passed by. They said we should go through the fields.'

'The tracks are rough there.'

'We'll find a way that's safe.' Marwan looked at the rising crest of the hills beyond the village. He led Selina on a track away from the road to a waist-height stone wall. The ground sloped uphill. Marwan handed Selina the carry bag.

'I'll climb over first.' He gripped the top of the stone wall and swung his leg over. On the other side was a score of sheep huddled in a stone-walled corner. Then he looked across the field to a shell crater. Around the crater, sheep lay on their backs with their legs still and straight; other sheep writhed and gasped in crimson mud. They were bleating weakly. He held Selina's hand and helped her over the stone wall then tugged her behind him as he angled away from the bleating mud crater.

'What?' she asked.

'Keep low,' said Marwan as he bent forward. There were small dips, but they were always climbing. The crusted snow became firmer and then they crossed a tractor track which led to the ridge line. They stopped to rest and ate pita then trekked on for an hour. In the distance, they heard shots and Marwan questioned whether he'd made the right decision to leave the Druze village. His gut instinct told him the Syrian infantry would come, but the Druze men had guns too and the man in the truck said to go through the fields. From the ridge, Marwan saw another village.

'We'll go there.' Marwan pointed.

'You're much braver than I am.'

He didn't feel brave. 'Let's eat the rest of the pita, there'll be food in the village.' He opened the bag he carried, ripped the pita in two and held out the larger bit for Selina.

'Thank you, I'll have the smaller piece. Why is the army attacking?'

'Shishakli, a coup maybe. I don't know. How are your feet?'

'I'm okay.'

Marwan's feet were cold and wet and sore, he knew Selina's would be too.

'Another half hour, a hot drink and somewhere warm,' said Marwan.

She wanted to ask if he thought it would be alright, he would say yes, but, of course, he couldn't know. The village looked bigger now they were close; they'd come across a dirt track with patchy snow that headed down then angled uphill and they both breathed deeply. At the top of the hill the track flattened straight to the village. Three people were standing on the track at the edge of the village.

'There are people at the village,' said Marwan.

'Good. I'm ready for a hot drink.' With each step the outline of the people became clearer. Marwan stared. Three men with heavy coats. Syrian army.

'They are army,' said Marwan.

'Oh no!'

'We'll be okay, let me talk.'

The army men watched the approaching couple. Close now, Marwan could see one wore a green peaked cap; an officer. His feet were wide apart and his hands were on his hips. Behind the three army men two bodies lay face down on the dirt track, their pockets turned inside out.

'Oh ... mercy of God!' cried Selina.

'You two,' said the officer, as he stepped forward and tipped back his green peaked cap and lifted the collar of his heavy green coat. The officer looked at the young woman; there was something about her. She hid her face as she half turned away. Her fingers closed and opened and closed and she stood with her feet turned in. She reminded him of a girl he'd liked in his youth; she'd rebuffed him and made him feel like a fool. If it wasn't for the something about her, he may have let them go, but it was too late, he needed to see her eyes open—open and pleading—open and scared, and he needed to see her feet twisted out. The officer spoke to his two soldiers. Marwan saw his lips move but heard a mumble.

'We're lucky to find you,' said Marwan. The officer was silent. 'Our car was hit; we trekked across the fields.' Marwan stamped his feet. 'Cold, the snow.'

'Where are you from?' asked the officer.

'Damascus.'

'A long way from Damascus.'

'Which way to a main road?' The *clunk* of a round being loaded into a rifle breach startled Marwan. Both soldiers glared and raised their rifles.

'Are you spies?' asked the officer.

'We're Syrians, and we want to get to safety. It's a relief to now be safe with you.' Marwan stared past the officer along the road to the village. The road was empty. Marwan pulled his eyes back to the officer who leant back then reached inside his green knee-length coat, withdrew a black pistol and pointed it at him. Marwan took a second to think of the right words to say then opened his mouth. The officer squeezed the trigger, Marwan jumped—jumped when the bullet hit him mid-chest. Some just fell when they were shot, others jumped. It was about nerves and muscles. Marwan jumped. The officer stepped close to Marwan and shot him a second time— at close range—in the head. A wisp of warm haze rose from the open head wound into the cold air. Selina screamed. Her eyes were wide and white; her black pupils stared at the gaping head wound and warm seeping blood. Her legs could take her nowhere. The two soldiers pulled her to the nearby house. Selina cried out as they dragged her and Marwan lay quiet. The officer pushed the black pistol inside his green coat. His eyes darted left and right, then he followed the two soldiers as they dragged the young woman who screamed. Her scream excited him. Sometime later, with the animal in him satisfied, the officer shot her too.

The following day, Khalid banged his fist on the door of Marwan and Safiyiah's new apartment in Jaramana. Safiyiah tensed. There had been no word from Marwan and he should have returned with Selina the evening before. She pulled opened the door

'Hello, Khalid. Marwan's not here.' A man stood beside Khalid. Dressed like Khalid, and he looked like Khalid. He could be his brother, thought Safiyiah.

'I came to talk to you.'

'What's wrong … Marwan?'

'Is Cyrus here?'

'Yes.'

'Bring him, Jasser will take him for an ice-cream.' The man beside Khalid nodded and smiled. A moment later, Safiyiah returned holding Cyrus's hand. Her stomach knotted. Why was Khalid here taking Cyrus? Where was Marwan? He should have returned with Selina hours ago.

'Ice cream, ice cream, yummy yummy ice cream,' said Cyrus. He left with Jasser and Safiyiah sat in their reception room with Khalid.

'I have bad news; Marwan was killed last night.'

'No! … No! My Marwan … how? … why?' cried Safiyiah. She stood up then sat down again. Her eyes blinked non-stop. She lifted a hand to her mouth and stifled a guttural groan.

'He was shot,' said Khalid.

'No! Are you sure it is Marwan? Where is he? When can I see him?' She stood up, turned her back to Khalid, shuffled to the window and stared over the rooftops.

'Why was he in Jabal al-Druze?' Khalid snapped.

'He was … he was getting Selina.'

'Who?'

'My cousin, Selina.'

'What's she doing in Jabal al-Druze.'

'She lives in Busan.'

'Marwan was found dead on a dirt track; there was no woman.'

'Why? … why? …'

'His car was hit by artillery in Busan.'

'Selina lives in Busan.'

'Cyrus needs two parents.'

'What're you saying?' She turned to face Khalid.

'Samir has talked with me. We take Cyrus, or bring another to you.'

'Cyrus can stay with me if I marry another?' asked Safiyiah, knowing it was normal in Druze culture for a stepfather to insist previous children be taken care of by the new wife's family.

'Yes.'

'I'll marry who you wish.' The joy of being told she could keep Cyrus suppressed her despair and the cold hollow in her stomach.

'Marwan's funeral is at Tishreen Cemetery this afternoon, a driver will collect you at two.' Khalid stood up and stared at Safiyiah, then without another word opened the door, stepped out and thudded the door closed. Safiyiah shook as she folded her arms across her chest. She thought about never feeling Marwan's touch again, the need to protect Cyrus, the funeral service, and about a strange man who would enter their lives. Marwan was dead—her husband had been killed. A whimper rose in Safiyiah's throat. Her lips started to quiver. Her eyes filled with tears and she cried as she plodded to the kitchen and slumped at the kitchen table and cried with her head buried in her arms. After some time, she telephoned her close friend, Amira. The line clicked.

'Hello, Amira speaking.'

Safiyiah dragged a deep breath, but no words came. Tears misted her eyes and her slight frame trembled.

'Hello?' repeated Amira.

'Amira! Oh Amira,' sobbed Safiyiah.

'Safiyiah? … what's happened?'

'It's Marwan … oh Amira … Marwan's dead.'

'In the name of Allah, no, my dearest Safiyiah, what can I do?'

'His funeral is at Tishreen Cemetery this afternoon.'

'Are you at home now?'

'Yes.'

'I'll come.'

Just then Safiyiah heard their apartment door open. *Did Khalid have a key?* Cyrus sprang inside.

'Please come, Cyrus is here, I need to go.' Amira called Khalid, but her call was not answered.

'Hi, Mummy,' said Cyrus.

'Come here, baba.' Cyrus looked at his mother's wet eyes.

'What's wrong, Mummy?' They stepped close together and Safiyiah clasped her arms around Cyrus and held him tightly. Cyrus let go of his mother, but Safiyiah did not let go of him.

'Mummy?'

'Sometimes, very sad things happen, but Allah always takes care of us.

'What sad?'

'Papa, Papa has died in an accident.' Cyrus pressed against her tummy, and clamped his arms around her waist. Then his knees folded and the two dropped to the floor and each cried words to the other's soul. Aswad padded up to them and nuzzled their wet cheeks. Cyrus ran his fingers through the black fur.

'My tummy feels cold,' Cyrus said through tears.

'Your heart is telling you how much you loved Papa.'

'I want Papa to come back.'

'Papa is with the angels now.'

'What's an angel?'

'Angels, angels take care of the hearts of those who die, and the hearts of people who loved them.'

'I want an angel.'

'I'm sure Allah will give you one.'

'I need two,' said Cyrus.

◯

A few days later, with his country facing civil war, Shishakli resigned as president and fled the country. Maamun al-Kuzbari was acting head of state for three days and transitioned a return to the presidency for Hashim al-Atassi and his Peoples' Party. The Druze were given the political and military influence for which they fought.

◯

A month after Marwin's death, Rajin Kasem entered Safiyiah and Cyrus's lives. Rajin was the same size as Marwan, but his steps sounded heavy inside their house. Rajin had seen war and killing. His face was long and his neck was thin. The first night Rajin moved into their house, Cyrus heard a banging noise coming from his mother's room. After some time, the banging stopped, but later it started again. The following morning at breakfast, his mother looked pale, avoided Cyrus's eyes, and shuffled around the kitchen. In the following days, Rajin explained to Cyrus the Druze principle of *taqiya*—the changing of appearance and practices to blend with the environment, while protecting their faith. He explained to Cyrus how their secret faith had survived for a thousand years and told stories of how the Druze helped kings come to power and once in power, how the Druze influenced the thinking and actions of kings.

CHAPTER FIVE

DAMASCUS, SYRIA, 1956

CYRUS'S TEACHER STEPPED from her desk to the green blackboard and with white chalk wrote the words *Syrian Presidents*. Cyrus liked her. She was young and smiled and a brown scarf always covered her dark hair. She also kept the classroom clean and tidy. Cyrus could place Homs on a map of Syria. She came from Homs. When the teacher underlined the words *Syrian Presidents* the chalk made a dry screeching sound and a ripple of children let out their own screeches as they cupped their hands to their ears. A moment later, a second wave of children screeched; they recognised the opportunity to break class order and grasp a few seconds of control. The teacher suppressed the minor rebellion with conciliatory words, and order and quiet were restored. Slumped on his wooden school desk, Cyrus had not protested at the dry-chalk screech, instead he found it funny that friends he thought timid and quiet had joined and even led the opportunistic revolt. His chin rested on the wooden desk top; one arm was forward, the other at the side of his head. He roughed his hair. Every morning his mother would comb it neat with a part, but Cyrus liked it rough. He had Lamina's full lips, her fresh complexion and Lamina's fine bones. Safiyiah told Cyrus he had *hello* eyes, but Safiyiah didn't know that Cyrus's *hello* eyebrows angled down at the side just like Lamina's.

'Let's play hunter after school,' Cyrus whispered to Talal, his best friend. Talal was the same height as Cyrus but had very short hair. Hunter was their favourite hide and seek freeze-tag game. Cyrus and Talal were both six.

'My house?' Talal whispered back.

'It's the best.'

'What's important you two?' the teacher asked. Children shifted and twisted to look at Cyrus. Cyrus was always talking but he always knew the answers.

Cyrus sat tall. 'I was telling Talal that *Shukri al-Quwatli* is our president.'

'You know the rule, raise your hand then we all hear.'

'I'm sorry, miss.' Cyrus felt his leg get kicked under the desk. He kicked Talal back.

A short time later, the door of the classroom opened and two men entered; both wore white shirts and dark suits. One of the men spoke to the teacher. She pointed to Cyrus.

Cyrus's alert brown eyes shifted from the pointing finger.

'Cyrus, please come here,' said the teacher. Cyrus lifted back his chair, stood up and plodded beside the blackboard to the teacher's desk.

'These two men are special teachers. They would like to talk to you,' the teacher said.

'Hello,' said Cyrus as he extended his hand. The man closest smiled and shook Cyrus's hand. Cyrus then extended his hand to the other.

'Hello, young man, we'll go to the room next door; it's empty and quieter.'

Alone with the dark-suited men, Cyrus sat at a desk, a piece of paper and pencil in front of him.

'Your name is Cyrus?'

'Yes.'

'How old are you?' asked one of the men.

'Six.' Cyrus lifted his chest.

'Do you like maths?' asked the other man.

'It's like a puzzle and puzzles are fun.'

'We'd like you to do a maths' puzzle for us,' the man said. 'Write the number *one* on the piece of paper, then double it to get *two* and then double the two to get *four*, and so on. See how far you can go.'

Cyrus scribbled the numbers *one, two, four, eight, sixteen* and continued until pausing at 67,136.

'That's fine, my boy, just fine, we can go back to the class.'

◯

That evening, Cyrus and his parents sat around the dining table. The dining room had a high ceiling and to the side an in-laid pearl mirror dignified the wall. Below the mirror stood a sideboard with its polished wooden surface and family photos. Cyrus got up, leant forward and reached to the centre fruit bowl and selected a fresh fig. The fruit bowl was supported by two polished metal stands that rose from a polished metal pheasant with a neck of fine metal feathers. On his plate, Cyrus cut the fresh fig and spooned the red flesh onto chicken thighs covered with a multi-spice sauce on giant white pearl couscous. He ate a mouthful of the spicy couscous then wiped his mouth with a red linen napkin.

'I played a maths' game with two men today,' Cyrus said.

'What two men?' asked Rajin, his bushy black moustache moved as he spoke.

'Special teachers; they were dressed like Papa for work.'

'At school?' asked Rajin.

'They came into the class.'

'What puzzle?' asked Safiyiah.

'I started with *one*, doubled to get *two*, doubled two to *four*, and kept adding until I got to 67,136.'

'That's great, Cyrus. Fantastic!' said Safiyiah.

'But it's a game I play some nights before I sleep. Adding numbers in my head. Did I do wrong not telling the men I've played the game before?'

Safiyiah smiled. 'You did nothing wrong, honey, sometimes Allah prepares us for life in his own special way.'

'What do you mean?'

'Allah watches over us and takes care of us.'

'How can Allah take care of everybody?'

'I don't know the answer, I'm sorry, but I really don't.'

Cyrus looked first to his mother then to his papa, then looked to the light above the table.

'We have a surprise for you,' said Rajin.

'Yay! I love surprises.'

'Tomorrow, we're going to an ancient Roman theatre in Bosra.'

'Can Talal come too?'

'No!' said Rajin.

'Please, Papa, it'll be more fun with Talal.'

'Papa said no,' said Safiyiah.

'I visited Talal's house last weekend.'

'It's a family trip, just us,' said Rajin.

'It's not fair.'

'I'm happy for Talal to visit our house anytime, very happy, but when we travel out of the city it's good to know we only have responsibility for our family.' Rajin threw a look at Safiyiah.

'Papa's right, it's best when we travel to take care of our own family,' she added.

'But Papa, I promised Talal we'd meet tomorrow, when I promised him, I didn't know we would have this surprise, please let it be a surprise for Talal too.'

Safiyiah raised her eyebrows at Rajin and gave him a loving smile.

'How can I ever win against you two?' Rajin shook his head.

'Thank you, Papa, thank you … thank you,' said Cyrus before he jumped up and down, smiled and gave his papa a hug. Rajin ruffled Cyrus's dark hair.

'We'll go to Talal's house now to ask his parents,' said Rajin.

○

Talal's parents said fine, and Cyrus was now in bed.

'What do you make of the men talking to Cyrus about mathematics?' Safiyiah asked Rajin.

'We know Cyrus is clever. I'll ask the school.'

○

The following morning, Rajin and Cyrus drove to Talal's house. Cyrus was out of the car first, he ran ahead, his feet moved at high-speed in circles and kicked up dust. Rajin followed along a passage between two houses to Talal's house at the rear; a two-storey desert brick house with a flat roof, the front was plastered and painted white and second-floor balcony had iron railing. In the passage an olive tree sapling lay on the ground and beside the sapling Talal's father dug a shovel of brown dirt from a hole, then wiped the back of his hand across his brow. When Rajin approached, he speared the shovel into the dirt, rubbed his right hand on his white singlet, and shook Rajin's hand.

'Look!' Talal said and opened his mouth.

'Wow! It came out. Papa, Talal lost his front tooth.'

'You're getting to be a big boy now,' said Rajin.

'Can I have my hair long like Cyrus?'

'We're all different,' said Talal's father.

'Where's your tooth?' asked Cyrus.

'Look.' Talal opened his hand. The tooth was tightly wrapped in white tissue.

'Are you going to throw it?' asked Cyrus.

'I was waiting for you.'

'Throw it! ... throw it!'

Talal pulled back his arm and threw his tooth at the sun. 'Take the buffalo tooth and give me a bride's tooth,' he yelled following Syrian tradition and hoping the sun would return a tooth to make his smile brighter. The tissue-wrapped tooth arced in the air and fell to the dust. The two boys raced to the tissue.

'It's still wrapped. Throw it again! Throw it again!' said Cyrus.

Talal pinched the dusty tissue between his little fingers and again threw his tooth at the sun. The tissue arced—then fluttered. The tooth was released.

'Thanks buffalo!' called Talal.

A short time later they were all in the car.

'Have we started already?' asked Cyrus.

'We're on our way,' replied Rajin.

'Have you been to Bosra?' Cyrus asked Talal.

'No,' you?'

'No. Tell us about the Roman theatre, Papa.'

'Its best you boys wait and see everything for yourself,' said Rajin over his shoulder.

'Do they have food?' asked Cyrus.

'We'll find somewhere to eat when we need to,' said Safiyiah.

The boys chatted non-stop. Safiyiah smiled at Rajin and he nodded. They were driving south into the Syrian desert towards Jordan; a steppe with sand and gravel, a few hawthorns and smaller grasses. To their left, under the eye of nomadic Bedouin, sheep and goats grazed on the smaller grasses that withered under the implacable June sun.

'Can we open the windows?' Cyrus asked.

'Not too far down,' Rajin replied.

Cyrus cranked until the window was over half-open; he used both hands; it was easier to crank it down than up. He put his right hand into the gushing air and opened and closed his fingers. He smiled at Talal who opened his window on the other side and copied Cyrus. The turbulence of the dry air made the car cool.

As he looked ahead at the road, which he had not driven before, Rajin read a sign that indicated a left turn to As Suwayda, the capital of the governorate. He knew As Suwayda was twenty miles from Bosra, so he slowed down and turned left onto the fine gravel road, and as he did so he churned up a squall of dust.

'Will I check the map?' asked Safiyiah.

'It's part of our adventure,' Rajin replied.

'There are no other cars.'

'We've had little traffic since Damascus.'

'What if our car breaks down?'

'We're fine. Boys, wind up the windows there is too much dust,' said Rajin. The dust had dirtied the windscreen.

Ahead was an unmarked intersection. On instinct, Rajin turned right and continued south. In the distance, a cluster of buildings pushed up from the desert. He'd stop in the settlement, find some water to clean the windscreen, and let the boys stretch their legs.

'Are you lost?' asked Safiyiah.

'I'm driving south, we'll find a main road soon.' Rajin slowed a little as they passed a sign with the village name Nahtah. Ahead to the right a group of children played. Rajin glanced at the dust on the windscreen then stared ahead for a place to stop and get water. A ball bounced across the road and a young child rushed after it.

'Rajin!' yelled Safiyiah.

Rajin jammed his foot on the brake. The car skidded a short distance then he felt a thud before the car stopped.

'Stay here,' said Rajin. 'Everyone stay in the car.' He got out and raced around to the passenger side. A young girl lay under the car. Her chest was crushed. Rajin crouched and pulled her gently into the open. He could see she was dead. The other children who had been playing with the ball surrounded Rajin and the dead girl. They screamed. Safiyiah opened her door and got out. She looked at the bloodied girl.

'What have we done?'

'Get back in the car. Now!' Rajin ran around the front of the car and leapt back into the driver's seat. Adults ran from the nearby stone houses. Rajin put the car into gear and accelerated. The car jumped forward, but a man leapt in front of their car and pointed a rifle. Rajin braked and stopped. He grabbed his handgun from the recess in the driver's door, got out of the car and pointed his handgun at the man on the road.

'There was nothing we could do. The child ran onto the road chasing a ball.'

'Stop the motor!' shouted the man. He was older than Rajin, wore a red and white checked turban and had a short white beard.

'We have money and will do what we need to make this right.'

'Stop the motor!'

'We're leaving now. I have my family in the car. I'll come back tomorrow.' Rajin lifted his pistol towards the man. 'Please! Get out of our way. We do not want to make this tragedy any worse.' Rajin stood to the side of the driver's door, his mouth slightly open. Rajin pointed his pistol at the chest of the man with the rifle; another man, holding a stick, ran in front of the car. He was younger. 'Tell the others to get out of the car,' he said to Rajin.

'No! We're leaving. Get out of my way I'll shoot.' A young woman who crouched beside the dead girl screamed. With his pistol pointed at the two men, Rajin side stepped to the open driver's door, twisted his head and yelled to his family inside the car.

'Get down! All of you get down!' Two more men ran to the front of the car. There were now four. Rajin stabbed a look behind, no one blocked the back of the car, he could reverse. He fixed his eyes on the older man with the rifle. Still the young woman screamed. At the same time, he heard children cry.

'You can't shoot us all,' said the man with the rifle. He moved the muzzle and pointed at Safiyiah bent low in the front seat then the muzzle shifted back. Rajin heard a noise behind, he spun and swung the handgun and at that moment a stick crashed onto his forearm. He felt a bone snap and he dropped the weapon. A second blow smashed across his back and he fell to the ground. With his face in the dust Rajin heard Cyrus scream. 'Help me! Papa! ... Papa! ... Help! ... Help!'

As he lifted his head, Rajin saw several men in traditional dress drag Cyrus away from the back seat of the car.

'No! ... No!' yelled Safiyiah. Cyrus kicked and thrashed then felt a hard bang to his nose. Cyrus heard a crack and tasted blood.

Rajin turned to the man standing over him with a stick. Trying to keep his voice low, Rajin spoke.

'Take the other one.' As he locked eyes with his assailant, he repeated his words a little louder. 'Take the other boy.' In silence, for a moment, the man held Rajin's stare, then called to the men who dragged Cyrus away. Hands tugged Cyrus back to the car and shoved him to the ground. Then, they opened the rear door, grasped Talal's wrists and hauled him out.

'Help me!' screamed Talal as strong hands carried him away.

'Get into the back seat with Cyrus and keep him down,' Rajin yelled at Safiyiah.

'Mummy! Papa! ... Help! What are they doing to Talal?' Cyrus howled.

Safiyiah opened the door and pushed Cyrus onto the back seat, climbed in beside him and shut the door. Cyrus threw himself into her arms and she held him tightly. Blood ran from his nose.

The men threw Talal to the ground and formed a circle. He screamed as he lay on the ground in the middle of the circle. One man bent down and picked up a stone and threw it at the boy. It smashed into his shoulder. Talal cried out in pain. He dragged himself towards the edge of the circle, but the circle moved and kept him in the middle. Another man threw a stone that hit Talal on the knee. Talal curled into the foetal position with his arms over his head. He sobbed loudly, begged for someone to help him.

Minutes later and without a word, the men dispersed, and left Talal's bloodied body on the ground. The man standing over Rajin with a gun moved away from where Rajin crouched.

With his good arm, Rajin pushed himself up from the dust and trudged to where Talal lay. Rajin pulled off his shirt, bent down and covered Talal's bloody head. Using his good arm, he picked up Talal. A sickening pain in his injured arm made him stagger and he nearly dropped Talal, but he righted himself and stumbled. Talal was light yet heavy and grey and warm and bloodied and beautiful. He lay the lifeless boy's body in the trunk. Safiyiah watched from inside the car. They made eye contact for a moment before Rajin retrieved his handgun from the dirt, put it back in the door recess, then started the car. He retraced their path to the highway, then drove north to Damascus.

◯

Cradled in Safiyiah's arms, Cyrus sobbed non-stop on the journey back home. His father's whispered instruction replayed over and over in his mind: *Take the other one*. And now Talal was dead. It was his fault for insisting they bring Talal. And it was his fault Talal's life had been exchanged for his. Rajin glanced into the rear-view mirror. Safiyiah stared. There were no words for their shared despair.

◯

In Damascus, Rajin dropped Safiyiah and Cyrus home then drove to Samir's house. Using the grey cast-iron door knocker, he tapped the wood. Inside, Samir flinched, no one came to his door unannounced.

Samir opened the door, and baulked at Rajin's blood-smeared shirt.

'Cyrus?'

'He's safe,' said Rajin. 'I think his nose is broken.'

'Broken?'

'May I come in?' Rajin asked in a weak voice. As he stood in the marbled entrance Rajin spoke. 'We drove to Bosra, on a back road. A child ran in front of the car, she was killed. They stopped us and tried to take Cyrus. I told them to take the other boy, they stoned him ... killed him.'

'Other boy?'

'Cyrus's friend.'

'Dead?'

'His body is in my car.'

'Shit!' Samir slammed his closed fist into a sideboard. 'Shit!' He slammed his fist again. 'Outside?'

'Parked close.' Rajin cradled his right arm.

Samir climbed a set of stairs and as he climbed, he ran his fingers along the wooden banister and returned some moments later with a clean shirt.

'I'll take your shirt. Give me the car keys.'

Rajin undid the buttons with his left hand, then carefully eased the shirt free.

'You hurt?'

'I had my pistol; they hit my arm with a stick.'

Samir stepped forward and looked at the red band of swelling on Rajin's forearm. 'Is the bone cracked?'

'I'm fine,' said Rajin as he handed Samir the bloodied shirt. Rajin reached across his body with his left hand and dug into his right pocket to get the keys then placed them on the sideboard. Samir opened the second drawer in the sideboard and took out a piece of paper, ink and a quill.

'The boy's address and his father's name?' Rajin spoke and Samir wrote the details.

'I need to speak with Talal's father,' said Rajin.

'Why were you in this village?'

'Driving to Bosra to see the amphitheatre.' Rajin had tears on his cheeks.

Samir glared at Rajin and didn't speak. He didn't need to; Rajin knew, his primary responsibility was to keep Cyrus safe and he'd failed. A few minutes later, Rajin was alone on the street outside Samir's house. He wore a shirt that was too big and began the hour-long trek home. Samir offered to drive him but Rajin wanted to walk. With his right arm held against his chest he thought about what Samir had said. *Take Cyrus to the doctor in the morning. After the boy's funeral we'll go to the village of the attack.*

○

Cyrus lay curled on his side in bed; his eyes were puffy and his cheeks wet. He took a few deep breaths; it seemed like a good thing to do and made him feel better. His nose ached but he didn't care. In his head he said I'm sorry Talal, I'm very sorry it is all my fault. I know you can hear me coz I can feel you in my tummy. I didn't say anything; I didn't tell them to get you. I was talking and made it hard for Papa to drive, and I pushed Papa to take us, and we promised to be kings when we grow up and I'll be a king for you too. Thank you for staying in my tummy so I can talk to you, don't go away. I want you to stay in my tummy forever. Cyrus lay for a long time with his face in his pillow. It seemed as though Talal had his head on the pillow beside him and at last Cyrus visited sleep.

'I should have been driving more carefully,' said Rajin.

'Why did they take Talal?' Rajin sat in silence.

'I need to know,' said Safiyiah as she held his gaze.

'I said …' He shook his head and the tears came. 'I said to.'

'Oh, blessed Allah!' Safiyiah was wretched as she thought of Talal's mother. Thought of the abyss Talal's parent's life had been thrown into. She found no home for her own guilt and knew she would be thankful to Rajin until death.

○

In the morning, Cyrus's legs felt cold. He put his hand on his pyjamas, they were damp. He got out of bed and took off his pyjamas and put on dry ones. He didn't want to tell his mum. But he knew he had to. The sheets were damp too. Cyrus plodded into the kitchen.

'Good morning, honey.' Safiyiah wrapped her arms around him, and squeezed tight.

'I had an accident, Mum.'

'An accident, honey?'

'I did a pee in my bed.'

'I had accidents like that when I was a little girl too.'

'It's my first one, I'm sorry. I'll try not to do it again.'

'How is your nose, honey?'

'It's okay.' It was bent and bruised and dried blood clogged his nostrils.

'We'll let the doctor look at your nose later on.'

At breakfast, Cyrus pushed his food around his plate and only ate a little.

○

The doctor told Rajin and Safiyiah that Cyrus's nose was broken and he needed minor surgery. Rajin had his right arm placed in a cast.

Not long after they returned from the doctor Samir arrived. It was the first time Samir had been to where they lived.

'I met with Talal's parents,' Samir said. 'They hold nothing against you. You can attend the boy's funeral.' Samir didn't say he'd given Talal's parents a lot of money and they'd promised not to go to the police.

'I need to go to the funeral,' said Safiyiah.

'Are you sure?' asked Rajin.

'I'll go alone.'

'I'll come,' added Rajin.

○

At Talal's funeral, Safiyiah wrapped her arms around Talal's mother and cried. Talal's father shook Rajin's left hand. He stared blankly into Rajin's eyes and said nothing. After the funeral, Rajin travelled to the village near Bosra with Samir and twenty Druze police and army. Samir paid the girl's family. He threatened that those who had killed Talal would be shot if anything like this happened again. Samir paid the police in the village. There would be no investigation about Rajin's driving being the cause of the girl's death.

Safiyiah returned home and Amira, Safiyiah's friend, who had been taking care of Cyrus, left. When he and his mum were alone Cyrus spoke.

'What happened to Talal?'

'His spirit is with Allah.'

'What's a spirit?'

'It's the energy inside you that tells you who you are.'

'What about the rest of Talal.'

'His body is in a coffin.'

'What's a coffin?'

'A special box that holds your body safe under the ground.'

Cyrus thought about Talal's body being alone forever under the ground in the box coffin —thinking this gave Cyrus coffin eyes.

No matter what route Rajin took driving from the Jaramana suburb in the south to St Louis Hospital, which was over fifty years old, he had to drive around the old city in central Damascus. Rajin parked his car nearby and he, Safiyiah and Cyrus strolled through the main entrance into the hospital grounds, past white statues surrounded by red roses. Cyrus gazed at the large white building and felt his stomach knot. Then he thought of Talal, Talal would give his all to be here rather than lying in his forever coffin box. Cyrus punched at the knot in his stomach then skipped up several wide stone steps and passed through an arched doorway. On the other side was a polished marble floor and polished walls. Light reflected from the walls and clean ceiling.

That night in hospital, Cyrus lay awake for some time. He shared a room with twin girls who were also six, and told Cyrus they were having their tonsils removed.

'I'll let you girls go first,' Cyrus said. The twins agreed which made Cyrus feel a little less scared. He said he was having his broken nose fixed. He lay awake, feeling a little less scared, and listened to the twins' breathing. One breathed softly, but the other tossed and sighed and breathed in and out quickly.

With the morning light, and it had been light for some time, Cyrus lay in the cast-iron hospital bed, his head enveloped in his arms. When he heard footsteps outside, he peered under his arm and saw a young nurse step through the swinging door into their hospital room. She wore a white cap and white uniform and asked Cyrus and the two girls how they were.

Cyrus lifted his head. 'We're good.'

'Wonderful, so who's going to be first?'

'He is,' the girls replied in unison.

'But, but,' said Cyrus. He rolled on his side, curled and lay still; his fingers gripped the bed sheets. The nurse leant close and placed her hands on his clenched fists.

'Show the twins what a big boy you are.'

Cyrus thought he didn't want to be a big boy. He was six years old and had his whole life to be a big boy. But what could he do, so he released his grip on the bed sheets and the nurse lifted him from his bed onto a narrow bed with wheels and Cyrus saw the room swirl as she wheeled the narrow bed out of the room. Then the corridor swirled and he looked around to see where they were going then the nurse opened a door and they were in another room. There were three people dressed in green with green hats. They were moving around and then he felt arms lifting him onto a hard bed and the young nurse who had wheeled him kept talking but her words did not make a lot of sense. Next, Cyrus felt a mask over his nose and mouth. The lights above the hard bed shone brightly. One of the green people selected a bottle from a stainless tray and a white-gloved hand dripped clear liquid onto the mask that covered his face. Then a strange smell made it difficult to breathe.

'No, no,' said Cyrus's muffled voice. He shook his head from side to side. The strange smell burnt his nose and eyes, so he closed them tightly. In his head, Cyrus saw bright white lights spin round and round very fast.

'Five big breaths and blow hard to make it go away,' the young nurse said.

Cyrus took the biggest breath he could and blew out hard, then took four more big breaths and blew out hard again. The nurse counted, but she said the fifth breath was not big enough. Cyrus took an extra big breath and blew the smell away. The bright white lights that spun in his head bounced up and down and wouldn't go away.

'One more big breath,' said the young nurse. 'Five wasn't big enough.'

'It was bigger than four,' Cyrus said through the mask. Then he realised the nurse was working with the green people and he knew the green people had won. In his head the funny smell was everywhere, and there was nothing in his head but the bright white lights, bright white lights that bounced and spun, and the bad smell everywhere.

An hour later, Cyrus squinted through a fog. His eyes wandered from left to right. A nurse was sitting by his bed. Not the young nurse but an older woman like his mum. He peered past her then heard the nurse say it was all over and everything was fine, and that if he needed to be sick there was a bowl. Cyrus knew if he kept very still and only moved his eyes, he would not be sick.

A few hours later, Cyrus moved more than his eyes and beamed when he saw his mum and papa open his door, step to the side of his hospital bed and give him a kiss and a cuddle.

'The nurse said you were very brave,' said Rajin. He looked at the white bandage across Cyrus's nose.

'I wasn't.' Cyrus was thinking of the big breaths and the big blows and how he'd argued with the nurse and shaken his head and tried to get his hands up to rip the mask free.

Ten days later, the bandage on his nose was removed and the doctor held a mirror for Cyrus. He looked in the mirror and smiled.

'Are you happy with your new nose?' asked the doctor.

'Yes.' Cyrus was very happy. He loved his repaired nose and even more, he loved the tiny nose-kink. Every day he looked in the mirror, he'd see the tiny nose-kink and every day he'd be reminded of Talal.

CHAPTER SIX

DAMASCUS, SEPTEMBER 29 1967

I N THE MORNING the sun was up and Cyrus was dressed for his first day at university except for a tie. He pulled open his tie drawer, and selected the blue silk. He'd lain in bed the previous night and decided on the blue. With the collar of his white shirt folded up, and the blue silk tie wrapped around his neck, he pushed the wide end of the tie through the centre loop, tightened and straightened the knot, stepped back and looked at his image in the mirror. He ruffled his dark hair and thought the tie imperfect so retied the knot. Cyrus then faced the mirror side on left, then side on right, and nodded a final approval at his tie. He had yet to shave and his mum said this was a life-long gift of youth. At a glance, his nose looked normal but a close look revealed a slight kink. Cyrus faced the world square on with his sad coffin eyes—sad coffin eyes with fair eyebrows that tapered down. He stood taller than usual when he entered the dining room. How good it felt to walk tall, a fight against his weak nerves. Cyrus breathed deep the dining room air, the air heavy with aromatics from his mother's homemade pita bread. He glanced at the gleam of silver cutlery on the table as the morning sun shone. The sun was low and came through the window onto a wall tapestry.

'You look smart,' said Safiyiah.

'Too smart?' asked Cyrus touching his hand to the blue tie knot.

'Perfect smart.'

'The university motto is *My Lord, increase me in knowledge.*'

'It's a gift wishing to learn, we're proud of you.' He gave a full smile.

Rajin stepped into the dining room and Safiyiah saw him raise an eyebrow when he saw Cyrus dressed in a jacket and tie. He opened his mouth to speak but caught the shake of Safiyiah's head.

'A new chapter, brave man,' said Rajin slapping Cyrus on the back.

'I feel weak.' Cyrus gave a hesitant smile.

'There are more things in heaven and earth, Cyrus, than are dreamt of in your philosophy,' said Rajin stealing a line from Hamlet. Over the years Rajin and Cyrus had read a number of Shakespear's plays together.

'Thank you, papa.' Cyrus's smile was stronger.

'What'll be your first lecture?' asked Rajin.

'Chemistry.'

'Mum's prepared us fine chemistry,' said Rajin as he moved his hand at the full breakfast table. Cyrus had that nervous excitement. He was really too nervous to eat breakfast but he knew he must. Safiyiah stood over the range wearing a purple apron, she tipped slices of *sujuk*, fermented dry sausage into a skillet. When the skillet became hot, the *sujuk* sizzled. Safiyiah leant over the skillet and turned the *sujuk.*

'Fried eggs?' she asked. Both said yes. She cracked eggs into the skillet and tilted it from side to side to baste the eggs with the hot oil. The egg white bubbled and sputtered and the edges turned dark.

'A double yolker,' said Safiyiah.

'Let's see,' said Cyrus. He stepped to the stove and looked down at the skillet.

'Luck for you,' said Safiyiah.

'It's mine?'

'It's your day.'

'A double yolker,' said Cyrus.

Seated at the table, Cyrus dragged his knife through the twin yolks. The bright vibrant orange ran across the egg white onto the plate. He used a piece of pita to mop up the yolk, then chewed the dense bread with its orange egg yolk coating.

'Oh no!'

'What?' asked his mother.

'Egg … look!'

Rajin saw an orange yolk stain on the front of Cyrus's white shirt.

'Do you have another shirt?'

'So much for luck,' Cyrus said and the three laughed.

'Another?' Rajin asked again.

'Yes, Papa. I think there are five.'

'Are you going to stay in the dorm tonight or come home?' asked Rajin. Cyrus's scholarship also funded accommodation.

'I'll stay in the dorm. I want to get into university life.'

○

In his dorm room, early that evening, Cyrus read Linus Pauling's treatise on the nature of chemical bonds; he heard a dorm door close. He jumped up and opened his door and saw another student in the corridor. Unbeknown to Cyrus, the dorm mate was on Khalid's payroll.

'Greetings, my name is Hazrat.' His ears stuck out and he had a black moustache.

'Like Muhammad's *sahabi*?' asked Cyrus, referring to Hazrat Zaid bin Haritha, who was the only named companion of Muhammad in the Quran.

'You know your Quran.'

'I have an interest in all religions.' Cyrus stood to one side of his door.

'You're not a Muslim?'

'I'm Druze. My name is Cyrus.'

Hazrat brightened. 'I'm Druze too.'

'What are you studying?'

'Religious philosophy. And you?'

'I envy you,' said Cyrus, 'chemical and biological science.'

'Have you eaten?'

'No.'

'Let's go out and eat together.'

'I'll meet you by the front door in two minutes.'

○

Away from Damascus University, the two ambled through dusty streets. Cyrus looked at the cloudless sky that offered no prospect of respite from the three-month drought.

'Still no rain,' said Cyrus.

'Better the sun,' said Hazrat. 'What do you want to eat?'

'Simple and spicy,' replied Cyrus. With few cars they, like other pedestrians strolled on the road. A lot of the pedestrians were women. Most married women wore black or brown head scarves. Bedouin scarves were brightly coloured. Cyrus and Hazrat stepped to the edge of the narrow road and allowed a horse and cart to pass, its large red-painted wooden spoke wheels turned slowly. The horse-drawn cart carried boxes piled high and tied down with rope. They crossed the road behind the slow cart, and both changed direction to avoid fresh horse dung and then Cyrus grabbed Hazrat's arm and sidestepped a man bent over with several empty woven cane baskets on his back.

'Let's go there,' said Hazrat. He pointed to a restaurant frontage painted the green, white and black of the new Syrian flag. The restaurant was long, narrow and dim. A man sat close to a woman, who wore a low-cut dress. Her hair was everywhere, and they were laughing and drinking red wine. At the back of the restaurant a woman sat with two girls. Cyrus and Hazrat sat at a table and looked for a menu; there wasn't one. One of the girls from the back of the restaurant stood up and minced to their table. She carried a bottle of red wine and another girl followed with four glasses.

'Hello, boys,' said the first girl as she sat down.

'Hello,' said Hazrat. The girl looked at the boys' fine fingers and clean nails.

'Are you students?' she asked.

'How did you guess?' said Hazrat. The other girl sat down and filled the glasses on the wooden table that bore decades of dining scars.

Cyrus leant towards Hazrat. 'I don't drink,' he whispered and then realised that Hazrat wouldn't drink either. Upon hearing his whisper, the girl raised her glass.

'Chink glasses with me.' The second girl moved her chair close to Cyrus.

'Or with me.'

'I'm sorry, I don't drink wine,' said Cyrus.

'Drink a red rose with a rose.'

'I'm Druze and I don't drink.'

'Taste the wine on my lips.'

Cyrus looked to Hazrat for help. He got none.

'Do you have a menu?' asked Cyrus.

'I'm the menu,' the girl said and laughed.

'I don't understand,' said Cyrus. He looked at the girl—with her wild dark hair, her red lipstick, and her smile.

'Do you like the way I look? You can pay to be with me.'

'We just want some simple food,' said Cyrus.

'I'm a simple girl; simply the best.'

Cyrus stood up. He thought she had eyes like a snake. 'I have to go.'

'You need to pay for the wine; we can't put it back in the bottle.'

'How much for the wine?' asked Cyrus.

'We want you to come back, only ten *qirsh*,' said the girl. Cyrus paid.

'Did you know?' Cyrus asked when they were outside.

'A bit of fun.'

'For who?'

'Let's find something simple and spicy that we can eat,' said Hazrat.

'Very funny.' The boys laughed, two threads twisting fate.

'She called us boys. You should grow a moustache,' said Hazrat.

'Maybe one day.'

☽

'I know little of science,' said Hazrat as the waiter put two plates of food on the table. They both ordered *fahita*—a grilled chicken dish with an eggplant dip, red lentil balls and salads.

'It's great we're studying different subjects; we can educate each other.'

'It'll be fun,' said Cyrus happy to be in a normal restaurant.

'The Jews need to pay a price for the land they have stolen,' Hazrat said

'The Golan?' Cyrus cut a piece of grilled chicken and dunked it in the eggplant dip.

'Not only Golan, all of it.'

'There's an Arab responsibility,' said Cyrus.

'Why?'

Cyrus chewed then swallowed. 'Arab countries need to accept their military collapse was symbolic of deeper cultural and social troubles.'

'The Jews had a better army.'

'Arabs are exploited by their leaders. Exploited by abusing religion.'

'A battle cry that has won hearts,' said Hazrat.

'A battle cry to what end? Science and logic provide the light to lead us from the middle-ages into the modern world.'

'What should the Arab leaders do?' Hazrat adjusted his glasses and ate a red lentil ball.

'Reform economically, socially and politically.'

'You know more about politics than I do. Later this week I'll go to my uncle's for dinner, come with me, you'll enjoy talking with him.'

'It's most generous, but I don't wish to impose.'

◯

A few days later, when the sun departed the sky, Cyrus followed Hazrat through a vaulted wooden door into the courtyard of his uncle's house. Hanging baskets of white jasmine formed a sash around the courtyard, while a dozen columns supported a brick arched veranda under a second storey. The boys circled around an outdoor table with crimson leather chairs then past a fishpond with plate-sized lily pads and purple flowers that exposed their splendour to the insect world.

Inside, Hazrat introduced Cyrus to his uncle, Samir, with his full head of white hair.

Samir looked at the young man before him. Einstein's child. But only a handful of men knew that secret.

'Come, we'll talk in here.'

Cyrus and Hazrat followed Samir into a large room with a tiled mosaic floor, a bookcase on one wall and ornate woodwork that extended to the ten-foot ceiling. The seats were big and made of leather.

'Would you like a *zouhourat* before dinner?' asked Samir. Both said yes.

'What do you study?' asked Samir.

'Science,' replied Cyrus as he sat in a chair beside Samir.

'As a *Shaykh al-Aql*, I provide social advice to our government,' said Samir.

Cyrus understood from Samir's title his senior political and social Druze standing.

'I'm Druze too,' said Cyrus.

'Do you have an interest in social policy?'

Cyrus stared at Samir's gold tooth. He hadn't seen one before. 'I have an interest in how we live in Syria.'

Samir laughed. 'That's the answer of a politician. You're free to share any ideas you have. Ah, here's our tea. This is my niece, Rasha.' A girl in her late teens with a white head scarf drifted into the room and carried a tray with three cups and a pot of *zouhourat*—a tea made from hibiscus flowers.

'Hello,' Cyrus nodded, his eyes sparkled and he smiled wide and said thank you when she filled his cup.

'Your interest in social policy,' continued Samir.

'Is there value in my views?'

'You represent the younger university demographic. I could pay you to contribute your thoughts. Make your parents proud that you're forging your way in the world.'

'Please, I'll need time to consider.'

'When you and I discussed politics and religion you had some bold ideas,' said Hazrat.

'I don't remember, I often speak without thinking.'

'Tell my uncle what you said about science and logic.'

Cyrus thought for a moment. 'A commitment to both is required to bring social and political progress to the Arab world.'

Samir suppressed a grin. The seventeen-year-old Cyrus was already speaking like a leader.

'What would you implement?'

'We need leaders committed to long-term economic progress, technology development, leaders who don't abuse religion. Leaders who govern with intellect, not force,' replied Cyrus.

'Listen. There's ideology and pragmatism. Let me tell you how business works. When you have a serious business opportunity, doors need to be opened and these doors are controlled by the *wasta* or five percenters. It's not possible to start either a private or public sector business without a mediator, we have a vertical patronage network. Do you know what that means?'

'I think so.'

'The *wasta* gives access to the decision maker.' Samir punched one hand against the palm of the other as he said the word *access*. 'The *wasta* system serves as an additional form of control by the state.'

'By what control?' asked Cyrus.

'The requirement for a *wasta,* fragments the middle and upper classes, and prevents a critical mass being formed that could be organised into an opposition. The regime stability is maintained.'

'I can see how it spreads the wealth to certain classes,' said Cyrus.

'Right, and it supplements the income of government officials tied into the five per cent network. This is not corruption; it's how we do business in the Middle East. The door to business success is to find the right *five percenter.'*

Samir continued his discussion with Cyrus over dinner and decided it was time to set up a meeting to introduce Cyrus to a Druze spiritual leader or *al-ajaweed.*

○

A note pinned to the outside door of his chemistry class said, *Apologies, classes cancelled today.* 'What to do, what to do,' thought Cyrus; a gift of time. Cyrus headed away from the university to Tishreen Park. Tishreen Park held a magical attraction and he didn't comprehend why. He may even find a new café for lunch. A mile from the university, Cyrus spied Hazrat across the street. He drew a breath, and raised his hand to call out but stopped. Hazrat kissed a man's cheek in greeting. It was Khalid. Cyrus withdrew into the shadow thrown by a storefront awning. Thoughts flashed through his head of Khalid berating his papa after Talal's killing, and later Khalid coming to their apartment and raising his voice at his parents. Khalid organised his university scholarship. Maybe he also organised a scholarship for Hazrat, how else would Hazrat know Khalid, maybe because both were Druze. But instinct halted his call, and dragged Cyrus deeper into the shadow of the awning.

○

One can see, or say, or do something, that at the time merits little thought of consequence, but it's the minutiae that can be life-changing. Lamina found that out.

At first Cyrus thought he could just go home. It was Friday evening and he stayed at the dorm for the sole reason of going to dinner with Hazrat, Samir and the *al-ajaweed*. Cyrus heard a light knock on his door then Hazrat's muffled voice.

'Okay Cyrus?' Cyrus pulled the door open and he stood before Hazrat.

'Are you ready?' asked Hazrat. They walked together to the building exit.

'I was checking details of my scholarship,' said Cyrus.

'Scholarship?'

'Didn't I tell you? I have a scholarship to pay my university fees.'

'That's great, you deserve it.'

'Would you try to get a scholarship?'

'My family has money, so I never considered.'

Cyrus felt his teeth clench and turned his head away. Perhaps Hazrat knew Khalid for some sincere reason but if he thought that a truth, he would not have retreated to the awning shadow. A distaste for Hazrat's apparent deception crept in and he wondered how Samir fitted. Was Samir really Hazrat's uncle or was Samir related to Khalid or were they all part of something that he didn't understand. Cyrus knew how to how to protect himself, how to erect a strong wall and how to stand outside the wall and stand inside the wall.

○

Samir smiled his gold smile and introduced Cyrus to the *al-ajaweed*. The *al-ajaweed* wore a cylindrical white cap, black robe and his thick white moustache and combed white beard hid most of his face. The *al-ajaweed*'s eyes held a distant question.

After they had eaten Samir stood from the table and they followed him to a nearby lounge. The *al-ajaweed* held both his hands on a carved walking stick and sat across the room from Cyrus.

'What does science create for us?' Samir asked Cyrus.

In an instant, Cyrus's thoughts returned to the meeting between Hazrat and Khalid. Cyrus's thought flashed back further to when he was a boy, of the men in their dark suits and the numbers' game, the walks in the park with his parent's friend Nabil, from the apartment above, their conversations a deep philosophical exchange, with his father discussing cutting-edge mathematics and science yet cautioning it was not necessary to always let on how smart you may be.

'Our future is in Allah's hands,' replied Cyrus.

'I agree, but how does Allah help us in a changing world of science?'

'That is for Allah to decide.'

'What future do you see for Syria?'

'We need rain, our farmers struggle without rain.'

'I was thinking more of what awaits our people.'

'God willing, may Allah bless us with happiness,' said Cyrus.

'Share your ideas on religion and politics,' said Hazrat.

'Allah gives our leaders strength to make the right decisions,' said Cyrus.

The *al-ajaweed* rested his head forward on his arms and his hands still held the walking stick.

◯

Under the clear night sky Cyrus strolled with Hazarat away from Samir's house. Cyrus undid the top button of his shirt and pulled his tie free. Hazrat quizzed Cyrus about why he had been reticent.

'Sometimes I can't find my thoughts,' said Cyrus.

Alone in his dorm room, Cyrus thought about the meeting with the *al-ajaweed*. He'd spoken a lie and that didn't feel right, but somehow it also felt like the right thing to have done. He wondered how something could be both right and wrong at the same time. In two days, it would have been Talal's birthday. Every September since Talal died it had been the same. At the start of the month, Cyrus would count down the days until the 18th—a private vigil.

◯

After the futile meeting with the *al-ajaweed*, Samir invited Cyrus to dinner on a monthly basis but was unable to invigorate the spark seen in their first meeting, and then the invites became less frequent.

Cyrus immersed himself in the solitude of study, and graduated top of his class in calculus, chemistry and biochemistry and received a scholarship to undertake an honours' degree tracking to a doctorate.

His biochemistry honours' class consisted of eleven Syrians and a foreign female student from Iran. A number of professors favoured the Socratic method of teaching.

'What do we know of enzymes?' asked a professor of protein chemistry.

'They speed up chemical reactions,' replied Darijani, the Iranian female student.

'Many enzymes use the same molecular physics,' said Cyrus.

'In what way?' asked the professor.

'Metal ions in the active site of enzymes create micro-environments of high-density water.'

'What do you mean, high-density water?'

'Water has two liquid states. Low density and high density. High-density water is high energy. The energy to drive many catalytic reactions derives from this nascent high-density water energy,' said Cyrus.

'I'm unfamiliar with this,' said the professor. 'Could you write a short paper on your thoughts and we can use it as a catalyst for discussion next week?'

Cyrus agreed, and smiled at the professor's intended pun. As he left class the Iranian girl stepped to his side. She had studied Cyrus from day one. She loved the way his brown eyes shone and the way his brown eyes followed her. She loved the way his full lips smiled and showed even white teeth. She loved the way he answered questions in class; simple statements of fact or opinion. She loved the way he sat up straight and stood tall. She loved the way his long pants showed his shape.

'A molecular physics expert?' she asked.

'Oh hello. Are you Darijani?'

'You know?' Her face lit up.

'The only girl in the class,' said Cyrus. She had dark hair styled short, and dark eyebrows and dark eyes and her lips were curved and painted with red lipstick. He shot glances at her in class and thought she looked pretty, as if she came from another world.

'I know you're Cyrus,' said Darijani.

'Molecular physics. I read, and my papa talked science to me.' Cyrus thought about his papa speaking of Sierpiński numbers and how they were derived, and about bacterial DNA polymerase when it was discovered. Cyrus's problem was not that he couldn't remember, his problem was that he remembered everything. It had started with numbers. Cyrus had learnt his times table up to twenty times twenty when he was four years old. The answers as accessible as one plus one. The twenty times table created a number file of four hundred numbers he could access and retrieve in an instant. *So, this is how the brain can work*, he told himself. And he found his brain loved to be used this way. Cyrus's brain was a hungry beast, the nicest beast of all with none of the usual beast connotations one thinks of when you hear the word beast. A hungry beast with an appetite that never-ended, an appetite that remembered every flavour, every texture, every fine detail of life, big and small. And then his brain told itself, see how clever I am, we can play this game forever.

'Is reading all you do?' asked Darijani.

'I also cook.'

'What do you cook?'

'I'm cooking a dinner for my mother's birthday tonight.'

'I love to cook. Why don't I help you cook the birthday dinner?'

'What?'

'Let me help you cook dinner tonight.'

'I've never had anyone; I mean a girl to my house. What would your family think?'

'They would be happy I'm having dinner with the smartest young gentleman I know.'

'You must know lots of young men. I mean there are lots of people here at university who are really smart.'

'You have food or do we need to shop?'

'There's special food I want to buy.'

'I'll come, we can buy food together.'

'My house is in Jaramana, it takes an hour.'

Darijani looked at her watch. 'An hour to buy food, an hour to get to your house. We'll be there by five.'

'Do you live on campus?'

'Yes … why?'

'I thought you may wish to go to your room first, to drop off your books … and—'

'And?'

'And to get whatever girls need to get when they go out.'
Darijani stepped close to Cyrus and squeezed his arm. Cyrus blushed.
'I have all I need, thank you, a fine day, and a fine young man by my side.'
Cyrus giggled and Darijani joined with soft laughter.
'What flowers does your mother like?' she asked.
'Roses, pink roses.'
'The damask rose?'
'Yes, the pink one.'
'We'll get some, all girls love flowers.'
'Your favourite?'
'Red tulips, the flower of love in Iran.'
'I'll get pink roses for Mum.'

○

They bought a selection of meats and vegetables and Darijani insisted on pomegranate molasses for the goat kebabs, then they boarded one of Damacus's green and yellow trams which carried them close to Cyrus's home. Cyrus turned his key and opened their apartment front door and called out to his mother and heard her call back from one of their living rooms. With Darijani at his side he entered and beamed at his mother who reclined and read a book.

'I have a surprise, Mum. Darijani from my class is going to help me cook.'

Safiyiah stood up from her chaise lounge, smiled, and reached out to hold Darijani's hands.

'Hello, Darijani. What a wonderful surprise, it's lovely to meet you.'

Darijani swayed gently as Safiyiah spoke. Cyrus watched Darijani. He swayed too.

'It's a pleasure to meet you too, Mrs Zaydan.'

Safiyiah kissed Darijani on the cheeks three times. 'Where are you from, my dear?'

'Teheran.'

'You must tell us about your family in Iran; would you like a tea?'

'Darijani is going to help me cook. I'll get a tea in the kitchen. Oh, these flowers are for you.' Cyrus held out the pink roses.

'Thank you, my favourite, let me take them. I'll get a vase.'

'The flowers were Darijani's idea.'

Cyrus stepped to the kitchen and glanced over his shoulder to see if Darijani followed.

Safiyiah and Darijani exchanged a knowing smile before Darijani followed Cyrus.

Safiyiah glowed. It was the first time since Talal that she'd seen Cyrus with his *hello eyes*.

The food the two prepared was a Persian-Syrian experimental fusion befitting the birthday celebration. After they had eaten, Cyrus borrowed his papa's car and drove Darijani back to her university dormitory. When he returned home, Cyrus parked his father's car in the same place it had been. He took the lift to the third floor and inside, his papa sat in his favourite chair and read in the light from a side lamp.

'Thank you for giving your mother a good birthday,' said Rajin.

'Darijani did most.'

Cyrus saw his papa read the Druze Book of Wisdom.

'Darijani seems an intelligent young woman.'

'And she's very nice,' said Cyrus.

'Remember that as Druze we only marry other Druze,' said Rajin.

Cyrus felt cold and hollow inside. 'Darijani is a university friend.'

'I know, and it's good to have friends. No trouble with the car?'

'No,' said Cyrus. 'I need to sleep now, good night.'

○

Over the following days, Cyrus sat beside Darijani in class or if he arrived in class before her, he chose a seat where there were two free. One evening, they had dinner together at a restaurant near the university. After dinner, when they strolled back to Darijani's dorm room Cyrus felt Darijani slip her arm inside his elbow. After a few steps her soft fingers dropped to his hand. Cyrus closed his fingers around Darijani's thumb. He felt giddy and a wild tingling sensation shot up his arm. His wrist felt bent and it was starting to hurt, but he didn't want to let go. Darijani felt Cyrus tense beside her and she flexed her fingers.

'I'm sorry, my fingers are in the wrong spot,' she said.

Cyrus released her thumb then they cupped hands.

'Is it alright for me to hold your hand?' asked Cyrus who had been holding Darijani's hand for a minute or two.

'It's lovely.'

Her hand was so soft Cyrus felt he held a tulip petal. His mind raced and he thought how thin Darijani's fingers where, how thin her arms were and how thin her legs were, and the thought made Cyrus think about what was between her legs. He wanted to touch more of Darijani—wanted to touch all of Darijani—especially between her legs. Where did these spilt words and dirty impious thoughts come from? The Druze Book of Wisdom and his parents taught pure thoughts and pure actions and cleanliness of living in all its aspects. He wondered how long he'd had this dirty thought and then he wondered how long it had been since he'd spoken.

'It's good that it's dark so I can hold your hand,' he said.

○

A week passed, and when Darijani walked from her dormitory to the university for a morning class a mature Syrian man appeared at her side.

'Is your name Darijani Nasri?' The Syrian man thought she looked like Jacqueline Kennedy.

'Yes,' Darijani replied. 'Why do you ask?'

'I have an air ticket for you to fly to Teheran this afternoon.'

'Who are you?'

'You're being given one and only one chance to leave Damascus. Take the flight today or you'll be arrested. You can guess how the guards will interrogate a pretty girl like you. Talk to no one. Leave now. If you talk to anyone their life and yours will be in danger.' Khalid handed the Iranian girl her plane ticket. Darijani noticed the little finger missing from his hand.

○

Cyrus wished he hadn't let Darijani kiss him on the cheek and rob her of her purity. Was that why she had left, because of the shame? His mother asked when he was going to bring Darijani to dinner again. Cyrus turned from his mother and answered with a jumble of words such as *gone* and *Teheran* and *sudden* and *nothing* and *why* and *sad.*

Following Darijani's unexplained disappearance, Cyrus found shelter in his study, and three years later completed his doctoral dissertation on the use of novel algorithms to predict protein folding, and after receiving his doctorate, Cyrus began a full-time research position at Damascus University.

CHAPTER SEVEN

TEL AVIV, ISRAEL, 05 JULY 2018

ELIAS EIDELMAN SANG to the chorus line in his ear buds, *Hallelujah, for the God almighty reigns,* from Sarah Liberman's hit song *Great is the Lord.* The Mediterranean was across the road and as he sang Elias looked out at the dancing scintillation. It was noon and the sun was high and made the buildings look white. The white buildings cast a slim shadow on the congested Tel Aviv traffic crawling below. In a pair of black Klum briefs, Elias was sprawled on a white leather chair; the sun was bleaching the few hairs on his tanned stomach. From Elias's sixteenth-floor balcony he continued to look through a reinforced glass barrier out to the Mediterranean. As he sang along, he swallowed a slug of *Kafrom arak* he had bought the previous week from a boutique distillery in northern Israel. He placed the empty tumbler on the side table beside a hash pipe and a bundle of envelopes. He stopped singing and thumbed through the envelope bundle to a letter embossed with the seal of the Israeli Ministry of Foreign Affairs. Elias tapped the envelope on his fingers, sprang from the chair, picked up the empty tumbler and padded to the kitchen. His black leather Jerusalem sandals created a soft beat on the tile floor. Elias selected a long thin knife from the utensil drawer and sliced open the embossed envelope; placed the envelope on the granite bench and filled the tumbler a third full with cold water. Elias added two ice cubes then a generous splash of the clear *arak* and watched his drink swirl cloudy.

Back in the white leather chair on his balcony, Elias read the Foreign Ministry's letter and learnt that his uncle, Meir Eidelman, had died while serving a long-term sentence at St Louis Correctional Facility in Missouri USA. The Israeli Foreign Ministry held a package of his uncle's personal effects which Elias could collect. He re-read the letter, finished the *arak*, left the other envelopes unopened, took the lift to his apartment garage, and jumped on his Ducati.

Two hours later, Elias was back in his white leather chair, with a refreshed *arak* tumbler and a bubble-wrapped package. He took a mouthful of *arak,* then picked up the package with its blue sticker that showed the parcel had been opened and cleared by Israeli border security. Inside, he found a wristwatch, details of a Mizrahi-Tefahot bank account and a notebook. The notebook contained twenty pages of neatly written script, which reminded Elias of the hieroglyphics he'd seen on the Rosetta Stone at the Museum of Natural History in London. He called the Mizrahi-Tefahot bank, and moments after the call, he heard the front door open. His girl-friend, Esther, was home.

He got up from his white leather seat on the balcony and wandered inside. He carried his glass. Esther's eyes met his then dropped to the empty glass.

'Another drink?' she asked. Her eyes and teeth flashed white and the multi-coloured beads in her ombre braids danced when she moved her head.

'Thanks.'

'Arak?'

'Put the water and ice in first and then add twice as much *arak* as you intended.'

'I always add the *arak* last.'

'I know when you don't, it makes a film.'

'Why haven't you said?'

'I have,' he said as Esther picked up the T-shirt he'd dropped earlier, folded it and put it on a chair. She then mixed two drinks, with the *arak* last.

'Good day?' asked Elias.

'People carry many problems in their brains.' Esther placed her palms either side of her head and shook her head in her hands. She handed Elias his drink, twirled to grab hers from the bench, ombre braids and colour beads swishing.

'Who's giving you grief?'

'The director.'

'About?'

'He wants me to show my character in the first lines. I told him there's time. The director said you can tell his ex-wife's character the moment she enters the room.'

'What his ex-wife wants must be obvious,' Elias said.

'Huh?'

'You don't know someone until you know what they want.'

'That's cold.'

'Truth is ambient.'

'Listen to my lines?'

'Sure.'

'After dinner?'

'Okay,' said Elias.

'Interesting day?

'A surprise or two.'

'Then it was interesting.'

'I received a letter from the Foreign Ministry; uncle died in an American prison.'

'Prison?'

'My father may have known but said nothing; you know how family's hide secrets.'

'We had none.'

'No secrets?'

'We were always so close, and slept in one room. How long was your uncle in prison?'

'Sixty-eight years.'

'What?'

'Sixty-eight years for double murder.'

'Murder!' Her voice rose. 'Who'd he kill?'

'I don't know. The Ministry held some personal effects which I collected.'

'What effects?'

'His watch and a letter.'

'Letter?'

'An account at the Mizrahi-Tefahot Bank.'

'An inheritance?'

'If there's money in the account.'

'If?'

'I'll know tomorrow when I go to the bank.'

'Let's celebrate.'

'Celebrate?'

'Celebrate getting word of your uncle.'

'A life in prison is no celebration.'

'But you have family news from the past.'

'There was also a notebook with hieroglyphics.'

'Let me see.'

'It's outside.' Elias padded to the balcony.

A few moments later, Esther joined him and placed his glass on the table beside the hash pipe. The *arak* looked cloudy in the glare.

Elias crumbled some hash into the pipe bowl, flinted a light and took a hit. He sat cross-legged on the white leather chair.

Esther scanned the notebook. 'Paleo-Hebrew,' she said.

'You can read it?'

'You joking? We'll need an expert to translate this.'

'How do you know Paleo-Hebrew?'

'I wrote a paper on the Scrolls; they're written in Paleo-Hebrew. I wonder why your uncle wrote in such a rare language.'

'The translation should answer that. When you said celebrate—'

'Yes?'

'Were you thinking inheritance?'

'I was thinking lots of things.'

'Including inheritance?'

'No … I said no.' Esther felt her head spin and heart rate jump. She sat on one of the white leather seats and took deep breaths.

'You need to be honest,' said Elias.

'Drink mixes you up, and drink and hash mixes you up more.'

'I'm sorry,' said Elias. 'I love you.' It was a comment he made from habit.

'You know I love you.' Esther wrapped her arms around Elias's neck and pressed her lips to his.

'You told me when you were a child in Ethiopia you had nothing, but you had everything, you had life, we need to remember that,' Elias said. He loved Esther, loved her as much as any of the others, loved her even more, but the early spark had not become an intense fire; was he expecting too much? Expecting a myth, every discovery about her led to a greater truth, but the discoveries were few, the greatest truth not in sight. She didn't see this part of him, was she blind or was he so camouflaged, or was this the hash talking? No, it was him talking, he had to trust his inner voice, if he couldn't trust his voice he could trust nothing. Was it strange that when he fell in love, it was always with a younger woman than the last, maybe the next would be older, older with a child or two. *If Esther could hear my thoughts now, I'd blame the hash, blame the arak, it would be easy for her, she'd just blame me.*

'Help me cook?' she asked.

'Love to,' said Elias.

Esther drifted to their bedroom then came out a few seconds later without her dress. Esther strolled into the kitchen and it was as though Elias had never seen her before.

'I'll try to find a translator. You cook the meat balls.' She took the beef mince from the refrigerator.

Elias downed his *arak* and poured another.

A short time later, the oven timer beeped and Elias removed the tray of sizzling meat balls.

Esther ended a mobile phone call. 'The Archaeology Department at Tel Aviv University can translate it. We can meet tomorrow.'

○

The following day, Esther sat on the back of the Ducati with her hands wrapped round Elias's waist. She liked to feel the Ducati's vibration.

'I have to stop and get gas,' said Elias.

'We're late.'

'We'll be later unless we get gas, it's close to empty.'

'Why let it get below half?'

Elias remained silent and turned the bike into a gas station.

Five minutes after their scheduled meeting time, Elias hooked the stainless-steel loops of the helmet chin straps onto the bike lock. Esther led the way to the archaeologist's office. His door was half-open. Elias tapped on the wood.

'Doctor Mendel?' he asked.

The short bald archaeologist glanced at his watch. 'You called about a translation?' He sniffed and wiped his nose with the back of his hand.

'Thanks for meeting at short notice, doctor,' said Elias.

'How can I help?' The short man sat behind his desk on the far side of the room.

'I'm Esther, I spoke to you … we have a writing we'd like translated.'

'Sit down.' They both sat. Esther leant forward. Elias leant back and stared at a smudged food stain on Mendel's shirt.

Esther passed the notebook. Mendel opened the first page and skimmed over the dialect before glancing at the remaining pages. Elias saw a glimmer in Mendel's eyes then the glimmer died.

'Where'd you get this?' Mendel asked.

'One of my relatives. I was going to throw it away but thought it would be fun to see what's written.'

'Do you know the language?' asked Mendel.

'I think it is old Hebrew,' said Elias.

'Paleo-Hebrew.'

Esther leant back, stretched her arms and made sure her elbow nudged Elias's ribs.

'Can you translate it?' asked Elias.

'It's no small task. I don't have time for something so trivial.' Mendel tapped his knuckles on the table.

'Could you recommend …?' Esther asked.

Mendel rubbed his hand on his forehead and rocked back in his chair. His eyes flitted between them.

'I could try but there'll be a cost.'

'How much?' asked Elias.

The archaeologist thumbed through the notebook and counted the pages. 'There are thirty pages. Two or three hours a page, probably more. The department charges my time at one thousand shekels an hour.'

Elias mentally calculated and shook his head.

'But maybe I can work out something. How much can you afford?'

'Sixty thousand is more fun than I was thinking,' said Elias. 'We'll get someone else.' Elias leant forward and reached for the notebook, but the archaeologist kept hold of it, and once again rocked back in his chair.

'With cash, I can do a lot better.'

'How much?' asked Elias.

'Five thousand.'

'Finished by?' asked Esther.

'It's urgent?'

'We're interested to see what it says,' Elias replied.

'I can work over the weekend, maybe complete it by Monday or Tuesday.'

'Agreed, you have my mobile number.'

'And the payment?' asked Mendel.

'When you've finished … okay?'

'I need half before starting.'

◯

Back at the Ducati Esther spoke. 'Success.'

'I don't trust Mendel,' Elias said.

In his office Mendel turned the pages of the notebook, a phrase had caught his eye and he re-read it. He thought the young couple were lying. What was the real origin of this script?

CHAPTER EIGHT

DAMASCUS, SYRIA, 10 JULY 2018

CYRUS LAY IN that space between sleep and awake, and with his eyes still closed pressed his fingers to his temples. Mid-morning was his monthly meeting at Syria's Arab Army headquarters. The day was hot and dry and the warm west breeze brought an infestation of black beetles from the Anti-Lebanon mountains.

Cyrus watched a black beetle settle on the windscreen when his driver stopped the Chinese made Faw SUV at the rusting security barrier in front of the army headquarters. Behind the barrier dusty grounds provided a harsh life to three Turkish pine and further back were four storeys of solid grey concrete with bullet-proof slit windows, and a mile in the distance, heading towards Lebanon, the brown mountain foothills. An army guard at the security barrier dawdled around the Faw with a cracked mirror on a yard-long stick, while another guard followed and led a greying black dog that seemed as disinterested in his bomb sniffing task as the guards were in theirs. The guard with the dog ordered Cyrus's driver to pop the bonnet and the boot of the Faw and after a casual glance he closed them and then opened Cyrus's door. He opened the passenger glove box, looked inside then slammed it shut, before he directed the Faw to move on. Cyrus looked past the black beetle on the windscreen, past the security barrier as it lifted, past the green Turkish pines, to a black smudge that surrounded a fourth-floor slit window—a smudge caused by recent mortar fire. *I don't want to be here,* he thought. But it was his main role as a university scientist—the lead chemical and biological warfare advisor to the Syrian Arab Army. The Faw stopped at concrete steps where a guard stood with a black moustache, dark-green uniform and an assault rifle slung across his shoulder. The guard escorted Cyrus up the concrete steps and into the lobby. Cyrus stretched his neck to one side then the other, and rolled his shoulders.

Inside the lobby, they all had black moustaches. Cyrus had his ID checked then he queued behind an army person at the metal detector and bag screen. He passed through the metal detector then took the lift to the third floor where he entered the usual meeting room with its larg-er-than-life photograph of the Syrian leader, Bashar al-Assad. It smelt of cigar smoke. Two men dressed in green and brown multi-camouflage uni-forms with blank epaulettes sat with Colonel Saaraf, who dragged on a large cigar under his black moustache. Cyrus sat down. He knew in the smoke that these army men were killers, killers sanctioned by their uniforms. The table was in the middle of the room. The two in multi-camouflage, who Cyrus didn't know, were introduced as Major al-Atassi and Major Daaboul. Al-Atassi had heavy eyelids—dragged down by the evil he inflicted. He had a huge nose and teeth ground down short. Al-Atassi told Cyrus he needed to win, it was a young man's game, but Cyrus was all they had; speed and great weapons assured victory, Cyrus had failed delivery on both. The Syrian army wanted super weapons, biological weapons were the dream of the present; the dream of nuclear distant because Israel had bombed their reactor. The major with the ground-down teeth said if the Mongols could catapult plague-infested bodies over the walls of enemies six hundred years ago, and the Japanese could release cholera and typhus into thousands of Chinese villages during World War II, then their own brilliant biochemist, even if Cyrus was old in a young man's game, must be able to produce the bioweapons the Syrian army needed.

The major with the ground teeth left his seat, marched behind Cyrus, and Cyrus felt him place his hand on his shoulder and grip hard. He then dipped his face close to Cyrus's ear.

'You wouldn't last in the army, you're weak,' said the major. Cyrus tried not to breath; the major's fetid breath smelt like death. He could think of nothing to say in reply to the major so he said nothing.

'We're under pressure to deliver. A team of Iranian scientists will conduct a site visit and review your botulism bioweapon programme,' the major continued.

Cyrus heard the major talking, smelt the major talking, but the major seemed a long way off for someone standing so close.

'A site visit,' Cyrus said, his own voice echoing in his ears, which pounded like his head. A cold sweat broke on Cyrus's skin. He had engineered deliberate delays to the botulism programme, delays the Iranians would spot in an instant. In his mind Cyrus knew this day would come, but he allowed his heart to deceive him as it pumped virtuous and moral optimism.

○

The major then prowled around the table and glared at Cyrus's face. 'Do you think I'm stupid?'

'A visit by the Iranians is a great idea,' said Cyrus. He paused and touched the back of his sleeve to his brow. Cyrus felt himself start to cross his arms, he stopped and spread his arms wide. 'It's always good to share ideas.'

'What's the lethal dose?' asked the colonel, his voice even.

'It's serotype dependent' replied Cyrus. He knew there were seven serotypes of the clostridium botulinum bacterium with three that caused human disease.

'We need human data on E,' said the colonel. Serotype E was the most lethal.

Cyrus looked at the three officers and their faces said we want to test on humans. To buy time, Cyrus tapped the keys on his iPad as he wondered what to say next.

'We could test on mice and then extrapolate,' he said.

'How many human subjects do you need?' asked the colonel.

'But it could kill,' said Cyrus.

'Isn't that the idea?' said the other major who had yet to speak. His skin showed he ate a poor diet.

'Come, we'll start the experiment now,' the colonel said.

Cyrus thought they were either testing his commitment to the regime or they were serious about infecting people—both were possible.

Cyrus, the colonel and the two majors left the military headquarters. Cyrus sat in the rear seat of the Faw beside the major with the ground teeth and foul breath. They drove past the Damascene Sword Monument with its water fountain at the centre of Umayyad Square then headed down Beirut Road past Tishreen Park.

'I played in Tishreen when I was a child,' said Cyrus. The words were out of his mouth before he realised. So that was why Tishreen had always been a lure.

'Born here?' asked the colonel.

'Yes.'

'And you, colonel?'

'Latakia,' he replied referring to the coastal city which was an Assad supporting Alawite stronghold.

'The sea air,' said Cyrus.

'I prefer the dust. It's where our lives begin and end,' said the colonel.

'You studied science?' asked Cyrus.

'A little.'

'You grasp concepts well.'

'Been to Hospital 601?' asked the colonel.

'No.'

'What do you know of 601?' asked the major who sat beside Cyrus. He smiled a foul smile. 'You can be honest.'

'It holds our most dangerous enemies,' replied Cyrus.

'We'll select ten of those enemies to be subjects in your botulism experiment. What do you think?' asked the colonel.

'I'm not a soldier.'

'You're not a politician, so don't give me a politician's answer.'

Cyrus remembered Samir telling him he gave a politician's answer.

'What's the Druze view of our civil war?' asked the colonel.

Cyrus showed no surprise the colonel knew he was Druze. All advisors were given background checks and he'd been advising the army for over ten years.

'War is the worst thing. I'm against harming anyone but support Syria against those who try to destroy us.'

'What age subjects do you want?'

'Healthy males. Thirty to sixty years,' replied Cyrus.

○

They drove past a signpost to the Peoples Palace, President Asad's residence, an oxymoronic palace name as Asad raged civil war against eighty percent of Syria's people, then a short time later entered the main gate of Hospital 601 and stopped behind a khaki army truck. The truck moved forward and an ever-present security barrier dropped and blocked the road. IDs were handed to a security guard who trudged to a booth and after a short time returned. Cyrus assumed all ingoing and outgoing people were logged. The Faw drove forward under the raised barrier and the foul major jabbed a finger at a building to the left.

'Military obstetrics and the new construction is diagnostic laboratory.' The Major's hand then pointed across Cyrus at a three-story building. Cyrus turned his head to the right. 'Ambulatory, radiology, surgery.' The Faw pulled to a stop in front of a two storied building signed trauma department. Beside the trauma department a small building called morgue but the army opted to store bodies in the nearby garage warehouse complex as there were better logistics for large trucks. The two majors got out and headed to an army truck that unloaded prisoners for their trauma experience. The foul-smelling major swung his arms as he strode. As the two majors strode, they talked about the Druze scientist, talked about his dignity and correctness, his air of respectability; character traits the two majors ranked as having no value, in fact, saw as weakness, when aggression and deceit were the traits the two majors ranked for survival in their world of killing and fighting and war.

Cyrus and the colonel headed in the opposite direction to the majors. Cyrus followed the colonel into the trauma building then down stairs to a basement room with cream paint peeling from the walls. The colonel ordered Cyrus to wait alone in the basement. Cyrus's head pounded. He knew all about Hospital 601. It was a torture complex. Cyrus breathed slowly and deeply. He concentrated on the feeling of air going to the deepest parts of his lungs, felt his ribs expand then relax, then felt and heard his breath pass slowly through his nose. *Another deep breath. Concentrate on slow breathing. Concentrate on slow breathing.* A few minutes later, the door opened and Cyrus saw the colonel.

'Come,' said the colonel who had one eye that looked normal and straight-ahead, while the other eye was opaque and looked to the side. The opaque eye seemed stronger, seemed to demand—*look at me.* Cyrus always focused on the opaque eye when he talked to the colonel.

In the corridor the colonel's boots clicked on the floor. They moved past walls with flaking yellow paint; black beetles nestled in paint clefts. The colonel banged on the door at the end of the corridor. Cyrus followed the colonel into a room close to Hell. Twenty bruised and naked men with roughly shaved heads knelt on the concrete floor. Black plastic ties behind their backs bound their badly bruised wrists, and their ankles were deeply chafed from the metal restraining shackles. They were men who either knew too much or whose families didn't have the money to buy their freedom. One man lay prone and straw-coloured liquid leaked from his left ear. On his body were fresh bruises, red and raised, and his ankles bled around the shackles where he'd kicked against himself. The prisoners had no aura, no surrounding breeze of energy, no vibe of life; they were no more than sketches on disintegrating paper. A dozen guards wearing military green stood close to the prisoners in the oblong room.

'Choose your ten subjects,' the colonel said.

Cyrus stared at the colonel's opaque eye and then stared at the men. Bones protruded through thin skin. One lifted his eyes, sunken eyes with black rings, hollow eyes that wondered what a man with a kind face was doing here. On seeing the prisoner move his eyes, a guard cracked a black baton hard against his head. The man grunted, fell forward onto the concrete floor and began convulsing.

'I defer to you colonel,' murmured Cyrus.

'It's not a request. It's an order. Ten!'

'I'm not in the army,' said Cyrus.

The colonel strode to the far corner of the room, where a pot of black paint and a brush sat on a wooden table-top stained blood brown. The colonel waved his hand for Cyrus to join him. Cyrus trod past kneeling prisoners. With both feet square on the floor, the colonel spoke in a low voice. Cyrus took a step closer.

'Listen,' said the colonel. 'Others brought this war to me. I'm fighting for my life and for my family's life. My men follow me because I'm strong. It's easy for me to be strong. I have no choice. If my men see you stand up to me, they will talk, whispers have their own life. You'll take the brush and paint a black spot on ten heads. If you refuse you leave me no option but to have my men strip and beat you. Let me make this easy, choose ten or we'll use them all.' He handed Cyrus the paint brush. It was an artist's brush and had a chipped wooden handle and fine bristles. 'A dot of black paint on ten heads,' the colonel repeated.

Cyrus dragged a deep breath, clamped his teeth together, then grasped the paint pot. The lid was off. Cyrus dawdled to the closest prisoner and dipped the bristles into the black paint. Cyrus then pressed the black bristles against the back of the prisoner's shaved skull. He felt the bristles bend. A drip of black paint ran from the prisoner's skull to his neck. He stepped to the next prisoner. Again, he dipped the brush into the black paint, then stroked the fine bristles against the rim of the pot. He painted a second black dot. No paint runs this time. Cyrus dotted the next and the next and then he stopped. The skin pinched between Cyrus's coffin eyes. He returned to the colonel's side; he stood by the blood brown table.

'I understood the subjects would be males. The next prisoner is a woman,' Cyrus said in a quiet voice.

'Not a woman but an outlier,' said the colonel. 'Let's see how the outlier fares.' He glared at Cyrus and his opaque eye straightened.

Cyrus trudged back to the row of kneeling prisoners. He skipped the woman and painted a dot on the next male and continued until he'd reached ten. He turned around and plodded to the colonel and placed the paint pot and brush on the blood brown table.

'Paint a stripe on her arm, so she doesn't get mixed up,' said the colonel.

Cyrus traipsed to the kneeling woman and stroked the brush on her upper arm. He returned the brush to the table.

'We're done,' said the colonel before he strode to the door and pulled it open. Cyrus followed along the yellow flaking corridor with its black beetles—an organic mosaic.

'I'll write a report and detail how you selected ten males and a female subject for the botulism trial and singled out the female for amputation,' said the colonel.

'Amputation?'

'We don't need a prisoner with black paint on her arm. If you'd painted her forearm we'd amputate at the elbow, but you signalled the shoulder.'

Cyrus felt his stomach contract; he coughed and swallowed bile. His head pounded. He looked up and down and to the side at the paint flakes and black beetles. The two walked in silence and at the end of the corridor the colonel banged on the locked door. A steel flap in the door clanked opened and a moustached face peered. Cyrus heard a key turn and a bolt slide then the door opened. They passed through two more locked doors and left the building.

'You made a good point, Cyrus … can I call you Cyrus?' asked the colonel when they were in the Maw.

'Of course, colonel.' It was the first time the colonel had called him Cyrus.

'Our destinies are linked; we should be friends. If anything goes wrong with the bioweapons programme, it reflects on me, has consequences for me and therefore consequences for you.'

'I understand,' said Cyrus, his voice sounded meek.

'As I was saying … your good point, you said you were not in the army. My oversight, you are now in the army with the rank of captain.'

'Thank you, but I prefer to be a civilian, colonel.'

'Captain, you'll know when I seek your opinion. I'll drop you at the officer's tailors, you'll be fitted for a captain's uniform. Wear your uniform every day.'

○

It was early afternoon. Cyrus sat hunched in his office after the visit to 601, his face tight-lipped, his stare distant, distant like the stare he'd seen others wear at 601. Ten men—and the poor woman—within a day all would be experiencing double vision, difficulty swallowing, speech impairment before descending into paralysis and death—slowly dying, then dying swiftly—the woman with her arm amputated at the shoulder. He prayed they used an anaesthetic.

Cyrus blinked and both eyes dripped a tear. *Tears for the ten men and the woman, tears for himself, tears for humanity.* Through the ages, rivers of tears had been shed, the dark side of humanity oblivious, or maybe not oblivious, maybe emboldened. Cyrus shut his computer, left his Damascus University office and in the heat plodded west on Al-Nasser Street towards his apartment in the Old Damascus district. He passed the Syrian National Museum, where there were few people as the regular bombings kept citizens from high-profile venues. Near his apartment, Cyrus gazed at the damage caused by a car bomb two days earlier. He felt silent discomfort as he stared at the remains of a stranger's apartment, a twisted mantelpiece, broken furniture and shattered glass. The façade of a multi-storey apartment had been blown off to leave a concrete honeycomb of dark holes. Nearby, a group of young boys kicked a soccer ball in the dust, with a curtain rail recovered from the debris fashioned into a goal. A shot at the goal hit the curtain rail and the black and white ball bounced in the dust and rolled towards Cyrus. Cyrus kicked at the ball and it skewed further away. The boy closest chased after the ball and ran past Cyrus. 'Good try, mister; happens to me all the time,' he said. Cyrus felt warm. This was the soul and future of Syria. He reminded himself this was why he enjoyed walking home. The opportunity to interact with strangers—an honest interaction—people who he would never have to talk to again. Cyrus moved on from the football game through the Souq al Hamidiyeh where he heard the rhythmic percussion of wooden mallets pounding the ice cream in a drum. He bought a cup of the chewy tart ice cream rolled in pistachios and salted cashews. He left the souq as the muezzin called the faithful to the *Asr* prayer at 3.00 p.m. *La illah ila allah. Mohammed rassol Allah.* No God except Allah. Mohammed is His Prophet. The omnipresence of Islam, infusing and reinfusing daily life with self-reflection in the face of God.

As he ate his chewy ice cream, Cyrus thought that the Iranian site visit would conclude he had caused deliberate delays, deliberate delays that could see him spending time in 601. The prospect of prolonged physical torture before he joined a pile of bodies in the morgue was not an option. He would steer a path to appease the Iranian review, but if that didn't work, death was a better route than being held in the clutches of 601. He'd need to have a cocktail combination of anaesthetic and opioid on hand. Cyrus felt like a coward. He was smarter than the malevolent colonel. Smarter than the majors. Smarter than any of them, but he had not broken free. In his rancour, the reasons to denounce, revile and condemn the army were many, but Cyrus reviled himself. The army had taken control of his science and he'd resolved to play defence, obstruction and deflection. So much for the childhood promise to be King of Kings; but when he made this promise, he knew nothing of his life's path. Could he look Talal in the eye today and say, *I've lived the greatest life I could have, the greatest life for both of us, lived the greatest life adventure where I've taken risks and been bold with unwavering conviction?* Cyrus knew he couldn't look Talal in the eye and say this, he couldn't look himself in the eye and say it.

CHAPTER NINE

TEL AVIV, ISRAEL, 10 JULY 2018

ELIAS TAPPED THE back of his hand on Mendel's quarter open wooden door, then stretched his head inside and saw Mendel force a grin. Mendel stayed behind his desk where books and papers made a jumble. Elias and Esther sat at the small round meeting table to the side. Mendel's fingers curled around the notebook. It was the most interesting reading he'd done. He bit his lip, scratched his chin, and his eyes flicked left, then he said the translation took longer than he thought and he needed an extra five hundred. Elias said the agreement was for five thousand, and he'd been paid two and a half. Esther said if the translation took longer, it was fair they paid. No one likes to be stiffed, but Elias let it slide. Mendel picked up a pen with his free hand, clicked it, and smiled at Esther.

'Settled,' he said. Mendel then explained how old Hebrew is written from right to left and contains no vowels with no spaces between the words.

Esther shifted forward in her seat. 'It must be difficult with no vowels.'

Mendel felt the frost from Elias but kept talking and raised his eyes very little. He gave the example of the word *big* and asked Esther if the vowel was removed what letters would be left. Esther said *bg* and received a congratulatory smile from Elias, which she returned with a stare. Mendel continued and said that *bg* would be the same for the words such as *bag*, *beg*, *bog* or *bug*.

'You rely on context,' said Esther.

'Precisely, with no spaces between words it's not obvious where a word starts or stops, with no punctuation marks or even spaces … all a challenge.' Mendel stopped talking and handed Esther the notebook and the A4 printed translation.

Elias stood up and counted out three thousand.

'Could you shut the door please?' asked Mendel as Elias followed Esther from the office.

Elias drew the door almost shut, then pulled it hard. Esther spun around.

'He wanted it shut.'

'Who's the adult?'

'It wasn't your decision to make, to give Mendel another five hundred.'

'I'm sorry, I didn't want one of your scenes. He gave us what we wanted.' Elias chuckled. 'One of my what?'

'A fight over money.'

'Your pass?' Elias held out his hand, and Esther gave him her temporary entry pass. Elias handed both to the ground floor reception. The exit door opened automatically.

'I fight over principal,' said Elias.

'Would you fight over love?'

'There's no better reason.'

'Like *Menelaus*?' asked Esther referring to the King of Sparta who raged war after Paris took his wife, Helen.

'You've been reading Greek Mythology?'

'Come look at this.'

Elias followed Esther to the other side of Mendel's building. Standing on a six-wheeled wooden trolley, was a replica of the Trojan horse, made of thousands of computer and mobile phone components. It was named the *Cyber Horse* and was displayed at the entrance to the annual Cyber Week conference.

'Very cool,' said Elias, the sun reflected off the keyboards, screens and circuit boards.

'I'll take a photo for my parents.' They posed and Esther asked Elias to smile.

'Smile?

'You never smile in photos,' said Esther.

When Elias was young, his mother asked him to be normal in photographs, not to pull a face, but he had not tried to pull a face, he had tried to smile with enthusiasm. Everything Elias ever did was with enthusiasm. He smiled for Esther, smiled with controlled enthusiasm.

◯

Esther crossed her legs as she sat and read Mendel's translation. Elias sat on the balcony with an *arak* and stared at the original notebook pages and his photocopy record. He'd listened to his gut and photocopied the notebook before giving it to Mendel. Elias gave a brief laugh and shook his head. A page from the notebook was missing. He examined the binding of the notebook but could see no evidence of a page having been removed. He turned to the back third of the notebook and continued the comparison with the photocopy. Another page was gone. It made sense that a second page was also gone; the pages were leafed through the binding. By removing the full leafed page there was no residual evidence of a single page having been torn out. He paced from the balcony into the living area.

Esther looked up and saw Elias's tight face. 'Something wrong?'

'That bastard removed some pages.' Elias shook the notebook in his hand.

'How do you know?'

'I photocopied it before giving it to him. Two pages are missing.'

'Could they have fallen out?'

'No. Look!' Elias sat on the arm of the chair and showed Esther the photocopies and the two missing pages. He then showed her how a single page passed through the stitched binding to make two separate pages in the notebook.

'Why would he take a page?'

'Remember what you said last week?' Elias got up from the chair arm, crossed to the kitchen and poured himself another *arak*. He lifted his glass to Esther.

'No thanks. What was it I said?'

'We would know why my uncle wrote in the old text after the translation.'

'You think Mendel found something and he removed the pages to hide it?'

'Is there another reason?' Elias raised the glass to his mouth.

'Are you going to confront him?'

'We need to translate the missing pages.' Elias had endless options to deal with Mendel. 'Another translator, someone we can trust.'

'I've let you down once already by recommending Mendel.'

'You're right, how can I punish you?' He strode across the room and pulled Esther from the chair, tangled his hand in her hair and forced her mouth to his. After several moments, they broke their kiss.

'I adore this type of punishment,' she said.

'Make more calls and see who you can find.' He leant in to Esther and kissed her again, and again, and again.

○

The following morning, Elias pressed the doorbell of an architecturally designed house in the coastal town of Netanya, a few kilometres north of Tel Aviv. Moments later, Elias and Esther faced an elderly man who looked like a retired archaeologist. He was. His shoulders drooped and he had wispy grey hair and a wispy grey beard.

Inside, they sat in an expansive room with original art and museum-quality artefacts. Elias handed Isaac Bereksohn the photocopied pages of the missing text.

Esther pointed to the art. 'May I have a closer look?'

'Of course,' said Isaac with a wide smile. He then returned his eyes to the Hebrew text.

Esther looked at a charcoal sketch of a young boy at the top of a slide. The boy's right hand was on the edge of the slide and the three horizontal lines for the young boy's eyes and mouth and the tilt of the young boy's head conveyed caution. There was no sign in the room of a Mrs. Bereksohn. No photographs. Perhaps in his bedroom thought Esther. Issac seemed happy, fulfilled; he must have shared his life. Esther heard Isaac say *two hours* and she asked when he would have time.

'Eager?' asked Isaac, and Esther replied that she felt like a child excited to open a gift at *Hanukkah*.

'Who am I to deprive a young girl of her gift, by midday.'

'We'll bring fresh bread and hummus,' said Esther.

Isaac twinkled. 'A perfect idea, thank you.'

As they left Isaac's front door, Esther asked Elias why he thought people painted. It was a question he'd never considered. He'd never painted so how could he know, and then he remembered he had painted when he was young at school. Big brushes dipped in a jar of water. The bright watercolour palate losing its definition as the painting progressed, a sheet of white paper accepting paint drips and strokes, and him wearing one of his father's old shirts that also became a canvas.

'For fun,' Elias replied, then he thought of artists who just had to paint for their survival, not financial survival, psychological survival, a pathological need like eating or drinking. After the painter had found a journey within, which provided all but food and water, the ecstasy at seeing the world in its finest detail and the raw satisfaction of then finding brush strokes to reflect. 'For the very best painters, psychological survival, the same for writers and musicians,' Elias added.

Esther wasn't sure what Elias meant and wasn't sure she understood his explanation and didn't want him to feel frustrated with her.

'I'd never thought of it like that,' she said.

○

At midday, Elias carried fresh bread and hummus into Issac's kitchen. Elias placed the food on a bench and they sat down. Isaac had a glint in his eye.

'You were right about your uncle; he had a sense of adventure.'

Esther gripped Elias's arm.

'In the translation there's a self-reflection where your uncle claims his absolute innocence in the face of God, but he goes on to write a most fascinating reference to Einstein. I'll read it for you, but understand I've interpreted the spirit of what's written. The spirit makes more sense than a literal translation.'

My dear friends, Rabbi Gamliel Hirsch, Anna Cahan and I came to America with the idea of Anna seducing Einstein to have his child with hopes of this cherished child growing to be an intellectual genius like Einstein and solving some of the biggest challenges to mankind. I—'

'Sounds creepy, like eugenics,' interrupted Esther.

'Let me continue,' said Isaac.

I have combed why Anna and Gamliel were murdered. The only common link between them is what we planned with Einstein. We swore each other to secrecy, but in a moment of weakness when I was trying to impress a Druze woman in Israel I revealed. I fear I am responsible for their deaths and my sentence is justified.

'Can you provide further context?' asked Isaac.

'My uncle died in an American prison serving a long sentence after being convicted of two murders. Gamliel and this woman, Anna, were the two murder victims.' Elias paused then continued. 'I'm unsure what to make of the Einstein reference.'

'You appreciate the impact of Einstein's life?' asked Isaac.

'He was a great mathematician and scientist,' replied Elias.

'Awarded a Nobel Prize in physics. His ideas contributed to the construction of the first atomic bomb. If Einstein were alive today any government would welcome his thoughts on next generation weapons. It would be a billion-dollar endorsement if he sat on the board of any technology company.'

'A valuable eugenics initiative?' asked Esther.

'If an Einstein child inherited the creative genius of his father, his contribution could be immense.'

'A crime needs a motive,' said Elias.

'From what you've said the first motive appears clear, the killer wanted to stop this group carrying out their plan with Einstein,' said Isaac.

'Why do you say first motive?' asked Esther.

'Perhaps the killer was affiliated with a group wanting to have their own Einstein child.'

Elias felt his heart leap. This could be the reason Mendel removed the pages. Had he arrived at the same conclusion? Could there be an Einstein child to discover? The ultimate hunt for an archaeologist.

'Your uncle suggested his friends were murdered because of this Einstein plan. Why wouldn't your uncle have been murdered too?' asked Esther.

'I'm having the same thought,' said Elias. 'There's other information.' He removed the notebook from his bag. 'This is the original notebook from my uncle. Last week an archaeologist, Mendel from Tel Aviv University translated it. But Mendel stole the two pages you've translated. I know this for certain because I photocopied the notebook.'

'I know of Mendel, he has sparse original thought, is narrow, a struggling academic, an exploiter, a cul-de-sac. When did Mendel take these pages?'

'A week ago,' replied Elias.

'A head-start of a week over us, trying to discover if there's an Einstein child,' said Isaac.

Elias did not miss Isaac's use of the word *us*.

'But as Mendel doesn't know we're onto him he may not have urgency … and he said he was going away to a European conference,' said Esther.

'I wouldn't trust anything he says, we could cause him a distraction,' said Elias.

'How?' asked Esther.

'There are many actions I could take to cause him angst,' replied Elias.

Isaac thought of the angst he could also cause Mendel.

'My advice is focus on our own success strategy,' said Isaac.

'Where do we start?' asked Esther.

'Listing the facts,' replied Isaac.

'The killer is likely to be Arab or Israeli,' said Esther.

'Why?' asked Isaac.

'You said the killer wanted to stop them from carrying out their plan with Einstein. If Anna and the rabbi were killed two weeks after arriving in New York, this is a short time for a complete stranger to discover what they were up to and kill them. It looks premeditated. Remember Elias's uncle said he spoke of their plan to a Druze woman in Israel.'

'I agree,' said Isaac.

Elias looked at Esther and raised his eyebrows. 'If the killing was carried out by Arabs or Jews, and there's an Einstein child, it's likely to have been raised either in America or the Middle East,' said Elias.

'Anything else?' asked Isaac.

'My uncle chose not to disclose this until after his death.'

'Did he have a way to contact people he could trust?' asked Isaac.

'Why didn't your uncle simply write a letter?' asked Esther.

'Prisoner's letters are read and censored by prison staff,' replied Elias.

'He could have written in Paleo-Hebrew,' added Esther.

'Do we have confidence in Mendel's translation?' asked Elias.

'Leave the notebook with me, I'll do a full translation.'

'Where in America were they murdered?' asked Esther.

'My instinct is New York,' said Elias.

'Do we know anyone in New York who could play detective?' asked Esther.

'When did Einstein die?' asked Isaac.

'Wait,' said Esther. 'Google.' After a search on her smart phone Esther said 1955.

'If Einstein fathered a child in 1950 the child would be sixty-eight today,' said Elias.

'If it's still alive,' added Isaac.

'Yes,' said Elias.

'Why 1950?' asked Esther.

'My uncle was imprisoned in 1949.'

'If I wanted to educate such a child, I'd give them a life in academia,' said Isaac.

'We have to narrow our target to every sixty-eight-year-old academic in America, and the Middle East,' said Esther.

'I can begin the search using facial recognition software.' Elias explained how every human face has distinguishable landmarks that make their facial features. The software creates data inputs from eighty of these facial landmarks with typical features captured including the distance between the eyes, eye socket depth, and also nose width, cheekbone shape and length of the jawline. This data creates a numerical code faceprint. 'I would first generate a reference database using Einstein's and Einstein's children's photographs.'

'I think I've got it,' said Esther. 'The software makes a comparison between numerical codes of the unknown face and the Einstein reference.'

'You got it,' said Elias.

'Could Mendel do this?' asked Esther.

'It's the obvious first step in a search like this,' replied Elias.

'Where'll you find your candidate photographs to interrogate the Einstein database?' asked Isaac.

'We'll need to hack into university and academic databases,' replied Elias.

'Now we have a strategy,' said Isaac. 'Before you leave, I have a laden mango tree, come.' Isaac opened the sliding door to his garden, then a few moments later his eyes followed his new young friends walk towards their motorbike. As he watched them get onto the bike, he pondered the favours he could call to generate a crater for Mendel, a crater to occupy his time and a crater to chop him off at the knees.

'Is this a vanity exercise?' asked Esther as she was getting onto the bike

'Huh?'

'Trying to find Einstein's child.'

'We can tell him who he is, maybe bring him to Israel.'

'Him?'

'Generic.'

'Why disturb this life?'

'Would you want to know if you were the daughter of an Ethiopian king?

'I'm my own person; I have family and friends.'

'Great people help shape the world,' said Elias.

'Usually independent of their parents, they rise to their own level.'

'Maybe this Einstein child has achieved greatness that's yet to be recognised.'

'Like discovering a Goya in an attic.'

Elias started his bike, turned around then powered for Tel Aviv.

CHAPTER TEN

TEL AVIV, ISRAEL, 10 JULY 2018

ESTHER FLOUNCED FROM the bedroom into the open living area wearing Elias's favourite lingerie. Elias looked up and she continued her flounce.

'Let's celebrate the Einstein intrigue,' she said.

Elias had just keyed *45Chaya45*, the password derived from his mother's name and age at her death. Google informed him there were two thousand six hundred universities in America. Manually searching the university websites for photographs of their staff would burn months, he needed an automated search strategy. Esther wore pink Victoria's Secret and bright yellow lipstick. The automated search strategy would have to wait.

○

Elias called his cousin. Tzvi worked in the Israeli government's extensive security apparatus.

Later the same day, Elias swung open the glass door of Tel Aviv's Juno Wine Bar. Tzvi sat at the front of the bar and behind his table was a wall of wine with bottles lying flat while others were standing. Tzvi gave a quick lift of his eyebrows, stood eye to eye with his cousin then they embraced. Tzvi's olive-skinned face was young with a short dark beard, but his light brown eyes that watched the world through round glasses were old; two years in a front-line army unit gives those with a soft-heart old eyes. They both sat down. Tzvi had come from work and wore dark trousers, a white shirt, and a yarmulke. There was a wine bottle on the wooden table. Tzvi poured Elias a glass of local red, made from a biblical-era grape variety. Elias took a gulp then replaced the tall-stemmed glass on the wooden table.

'You should come to the gym.' Elias tapped Tzvi on the shoulder. Tzvi shook his head and smiled. Elias often teased him about his slim build.

'What's new?'

'I'm trying to trace an academic in America or the Middle East.'

'Why?' asked Tzvi.

'Because the person's father was Albert Einstein.'

'Einstein?' Tzvi's face livened.

'I'm making a guess we're looking for an academic.' Elias explained the background.

'We have software at work to hack into any database accessible via the web, but I'd be risking my job doing something unauthorised.'

'Who can help?'

'I know someone, but he's expensive.'

'Great.' Elias had more than three hundred thousand shekels sitting in the new Mizrahi-Tefahot Bank account and had six million shekels stashed from the equity exit in his IT start-up.

'He lives in Jerusalem. I'll call him.'

'Anytime tomorrow.'

The meeting was set for mid-afternoon the following day.

'With your tenacity you'll find Einstein's child, if his child's out there. Chris will help. I tell you he's great. What'll you do if you're successful?' Tzvi spoke at a hectic pace.

'Not sure yet, two people were killed and my uncle, your uncle too, spent his life in prison … I need closure, whatever closure looks like.'

'My uncle too.' Tzvi lifted this glass of red in a toast.

'Esther and I are going to a movie tonight, want to come?'

'Sure.'

Elias took out his mobile. 'Hi,' he said. 'Where are you?'

'At home, waiting for you.'

'I'm with Tzvi, tell you more later. Tzvi's coming to the movies with us. Grab a cab and come to Juno Wine Bar.'

'Where?'

'Juno Wine Bar.'

'Juno?'

'Yes.'

'See you soon, tell Tzvi I'm looking forward to seeing him.'

Elias turned to Tzvi. 'Esther's coming, I'll get us another drink.' Elias stood at the bar, his mind not on his drinks order but on the hacker Chris, and what the hacker could deliver.

○

The next day—Friday afternoon, was the beginning of Shabbat, the day of rest and spiritual enrichment. Elias rode from Tel Aviv, and parked his Ducati opposite the hacker's apartment which was close to Jerusalem's Zion Square. He crossed the road, pressed the door security buzzer and glanced above at a camera. The door opened with a waft of hashish and Elias thought he was looking at Sadio Mané. It wasn't just the red Liverpool shirt, but the hacker had the regal head of Liverpool's Senegalese superstar.

'Hey, blood, you from Tzvi?' he spoke in a south London accent.

'Hey, you're a Liverpool fan too,' said Elias as they shook hands.

'I sleep on a Liverpool pillowcase, fam.' Chris looked at Elias's leather jacket and then eyed the motorcycle parked across the street.

'Your Ducati, blood?'

'Yes.' Elias stepped inside.

'Nice bike, fam.' He turned and shut the door.

'Hello … yes … Elias.'

'Got a gig for me, blood?'

As he passed through the hacker's apartment, Elias glanced through an open door and saw a large computer screen. The hacker followed his glance.

'You wanna look inside my work room, blood?'

'I didn't mean to …'

'Man, we all blood, you can see, blood.' The hacker took a fresh date from a packet on his desk. 'Want, blood?'

'Thanks,' said Elias. He pushed his fingers into the packet and grasped a sticky date. 'Stone?'

'Here.' The hacker passed Elias a saucer.

Against one wall stood a rack of hardware where LEDs flashed. In the centre of the room was a large desk with four separate computer screens. The wall in front of the desk was dominated by a mega high-resolution screen two metres wide and a metre high.

'Serious hardware,' said Elias.

'Only as spliff as the software man and my spliff software, blood,' said the hacker as he tapped his skull.

Elias explained the challenge and the hacker asked for two thousand shekels and two hours.

Elias left the hacker's apartment and returned to his bike where he wrote a private prayer on a scrap of paper. He strolled through the narrow cobblestone streets. With businesses closed from mid-afternoon, Orthodox men dressed in black also strolled in the narrow streets, on their way to the Western Wall of King Herod's Temple, while families dressed in their best clothes were going to the synagogues. At the Western Wall Elias pushed his prayer note into a crack between limestone blocks then meandered to Abu Shukri restaurant, a small restaurant that had served the best humus since the 1940s. Elias had an *arak*, pita and hummus.

When he returned to the hacker's apartment, the hacker handed Elias an external hard drive that held more than forty thousand head shots from the Ameri-can Association of University Professors' database.

That evening, Elias keyed software across the American photo archive and created a digital signature for each photograph, but interrogation of the American photos failed to generate an Einstein hit. Elias tapped a pen tip on a yellow note pad beside his keyboard. The next step was to create a Middle East photo archive. He sent the hacker a text and arranged another meet.

○

The hacker passed Elias a joint.

Elias took a drag. 'We need photographs of all academics in the Arab world around the age of sixty-eight.' He passed the joint back.

'Which countries, blood?'

'Egypt, Iraq, Syria, Jordan, Iran, Lebanon, and the Gulf States. University websites provide photos of only ten per cent of their academics.'

'Swear down, fam, can access national photo ID databases, can restrict blood and age male dataset.'

'We need to look at both men and women. Can we run the facial recognition search on your system? You have more horsepower than I do.'

'You get me, I'll need a copy, blood, of the comparative algorithm.'

'Do you have a USB?' Elias opened his computer bag and removed his Mac.

'Swear down, we try this now.' He passed Elias a USB stick.

'Will the national ID databases know they've been hacked?'

'No way, blood, so many doors into national ID databases and a wide spec of internal users. I tell you, to be safe I'll leave an Uzbekistan signature, no back trace to Israel, blood.'

'What's the cost?'

'Where's your target likely located, blood?'

'Iran has the greatest number of academic institutes. But maybe Egypt, Lebanon or Syria.'

'This is taking it, blood … taking it … it's loading like a mother.'

In a few key strokes the demographics for Iran appeared on one of the screens.

'Swear down, blood, eighty million in Iran, three per cent between sixty-seven and seventy, is 2.4 million people, similar number in Egypt, blood, a quarter this in Iraq and Syria, less again, blood, in Lebanon.'

'Should we look at Lebanon and Syria first?'

'This putting me in a spliff, blood, not if you ninety per cent sure the person is in Iran.'

'I'm not.'

'Three hours, blood, for Lebanon, and Syria … the cost one thousand, fam.'

'When can you do it?'

'Now, blood.' The hacker sat at his terminal modifying lines of code.

'What are you doing?'

'Spiffing a *sniffer*, blood,'

'*Sniffer?*'

'We need to change things up now, blood … change things up … spliff code detect and capture … three hours, blood, crunching, blood.'

Elias left the hacker to do his crunching and returned three hours later.

◯

The hacker rolled another joint. They both smoked. After dragging a breath, the hacker held the hit deep, tilted his neck back and exhaled a fine smoke haze in front of the screen.

As he looked through the haze, the hacker spoke. 'No joke … it's no joke … something happening, blood … can't believe it.'

'What've you got?'

'What kinda foolishness is this … I can't believe this, fam … my days. Look at the way this running now, blood … top hit in Syria, blood … a thousand times higher, fam … a male, blood.'

'How old is he?'

'Sixty-eight, fam.'

'Get his photograph.'

The hacker tapped the keyboard then the image of a face flashed onto the large screen behind the desk.

'We've found him,' whispered Elias. The colour photograph was of a good-looking man. He had a high forehead, rough dark hair, a fine nose, sad brown eyes, light-coloured eyebrows and large drop earlobes. Elias stood up and squeezed the hacker's shoulders. Elias tried to speak, but the words stuck in his throat. He swallowed, wiped tears from his cheeks and tried to speak again.

'You … you clever man … you clever … clever man.'

The hacker stood up and wrapped his arms around Elias, sharing the moment but not knowing it's importance. 'Who is he, blood?'

Elias hesitated then listened to his gut. 'Einstein's son.'

'My God, blood, I can't believe this … the Einstein … unbelievable … unbelievable … my days, that was faster than I thought, blood … I can't even lie … I can't even lie.'

'Albert Einstein's child ... a son.'

'Must be an old photograph, blood. He looks fifty not sixty-eight. Why is he in Syria, blood?' The hacker shook his head as he talked.

Elias gave the hacker a brief background. 'I'm not sure where this is heading, but our first challenge is to get this Professor Zaydan out of Syria to meet with him.'

'My lord ... my lord ... anything more, blood, let me know ... ... happy to give my time free, blood, now I know where you at.'

◯

With his visor up, as Elias leant the bike through the corners in the hills out of Jerusalem, he appreciated more than usual, the different shades of plant green as the various species ground their survival in the rocky dirt; the gift of a beautiful beautiful day.

Back in his apartment he found Esther curled on the couch reading a book. Her hazel eyes looked up.

'What you reading?'

Esther glanced at the page number, closed her book then dragged her beaded hair free of the black and white checked scarf around her neck.

'Tell me what happened.'

'We've found him.'

'Him?' Esther jumped from the couch and wrapped her arms around Elias's chest. 'Wow! A son, how exciting. Where is he?'

'Syria. He's Cyrus Zaydan, a professor of biochemistry at Damascus University. Zaydan is sixty-eight years old and scores a thousand times higher than anyone else on the facial recognition score.'

'It must be him. We've found him,' shrieked Esther.

'I believe so ... yes... I believe so.'

'We need to tell Tzvi and Isaac.'

'I'll call them now and see when we can meet.' Elias called Isaac while Esther bounced around him listening to every word.

'Is Isaac free?' asked Esther when Elias finished the call.

'You heard me say we're going to meet with him later this evening. So, he must be free.'

Esther stepped close and cuffed Elias on the head.

'I want the hacker and Tzvi to join our meeting with Isaac.'

'I agree. What's the hacker's name?'

'Chris.'

He then called Tzvi and Chris.

○

Elias lowered the Ducati's stand, waited for Esther to get off, then swung his leg from the bike. Chris appeared at their side.

'Esther, this is Chris,' said Elias.

'Yo lush sister, where you rise?'

'Ethiopia.'

Inside Isaac's house, the setting sun sent low light through the sliding door and through a window where paintings hung on either side. After introductions, Issac served drinks, then offered an update on the ancient Hebrew text.

'I've spent more time looking at the notebook,' he said. 'There's a phrase of significant interest. The literal translation of the phrase is *Child confirm God exist*. In your uncle's writings, all of the references to *Child* relate to Einstein's child. This phrase is early in the notebook and at first, I missed its significance. I believe the reason your uncle, the rabbi and Anna wanted an Einstein child, was to have him prove the existence of God.'

'What? How realistic is it? Mankind's been seeking this answer for thousands of years,' said Esther, saying exactly what the others were thinking.

'We're going through a golden age of understanding the most sophisticated elements of our environment,' said Isaac. 'Proving the existence of God is more likely to be achieved today than at any previous time in history.'

'I'm telling you, fam, this is ridiculous … this is ridiculous.' Chris lifted the rim of his bottle to his lips, and swallowed a mouthful of beer.

'Where would you begin trying to prove God exists?' asked Tzvi.

'The very question we need to ask Cyrus,' replied Isaac.

'Outrageous,' said Tzvi. 'This poses as many questions as it does answers.'

'What questions?' asked Esther.

Tzvi spread his hands. 'Do the Syrians know what the Israeli group planned for Einstein's child? Has Cyrus been given a sophisticated enough education to give him the capability of answering such a question? How can we meet with Cyrus? We need to be clear as to what our opportunity is and what we are trying to achieve.' He spoke rapidly then looked at Chris. 'How much is donated to religions in the world annually?' They sat in silence for a few moments while the hacker searched on his smartphone.

'Six hundred billion dollars, blood, church donations, fam.'

'What do Christianity, Islam, Hinduism and Buddhism have in common?' asked Tzvi.

'The concept of a deity,' said Elias.

'Right,' said Tzvi. 'The *concept* of a deity… the *idea* of a deity… the *notion* of a deity… not the *proof* of a deity. Proving the existence of a deity would be a uniting umbrella for all religions.'

'If we have the proof, blood, a chunk of the six hundred billion is ours, fam.' The hacker's face beamed.

'We need focus,' said Esther.

'Agreed,' said Elias. 'But we all need to be on the same page with our strategic options.'

'You're talking like this is a business deal,' said Esther.

'It could be the business deal of the millennium,' said Elias. 'If Cyrus miraculously finds scientific proof that intelligent intervention is behind life, we'll be sitting on a diamond mine, in a position to literally change the world.'

'We need to change our view about Cyrus coming to Israel,' said Isaac.

'Why?' asked Esther.

'If Cyrus is based in Israel any *deity proof* he developed may be seen by other religions as an extension of Judaism,' Isaac replied.

'Others more powerful than us could take control of Cyrus if he comes to Israel,' said Tzvi.

'And we lose any benefit?' asked Esther. 'This should not be about us.'

'If we were in a country other than Israel, we could put a structure in place to protect Cyrus and what we believe is best for him,' said Tzvi.

'And guarding our fam position,' said Chris.

'You're talking as though Cyrus has discovered a deity proof,' said Esther.

'We all appreciate the chance is beyond remote, but if Cyrus is the one in a billion and finds such proof then we need to be prepared,' said Elias.

'We can assume whatever group was responsible for taking Cyrus to Syria will have continued with oversight on his life whether it's the Syrian state, or another Syrian based actor,' said Isaac. 'I think it's more likely he'd be allowed to leave Syria to visit a neighbouring Arab country, an Arab country, rather than a European country.' He looked at the others one by one as he spoke and when he finished, he invited comment.

'We should engage with our Ministry of Aliyah and Integration and go through the process of applying for a temporary entry visa,' said Elias.

'Why?' asked Esther.

'Keeping options open,' replied Elias.

'Does anyone have contacts in the Ministry?' asked Isaac.

'I do,' said Tzvi.

'Which Arab country for the meeting, fam?' asked Chris.

'Egypt,' said Isaac without hesitation. Egypt had a peace treaty with Israel, easy border access, and a population of over seventy million in which to hide if necessary.

'An idea,' said Elias. 'We could invite Cyrus to a scientific meeting in Egypt, where he's awarded a scientific prize.'

Isaac nodded. 'It may work, we could have the scientific meeting in Sharm El-Sheikh, it's a three-hour drive from the Israeli border.'

'An offer of a science prize to Professor Zaydan would be best to come from someone with standing in the Egyptian Academic community,' said Tzvi.

'I know people at Cairo University, but we'll need money,' Issac said.

'I can pay,' said Elias.

'Anything can be achieved in Egypt with money,' said Isaac.

'When you have progress from one of your Cairo contacts, you and I should go to Egypt,' said Elias.

'You'll need visas for Egypt,' said Tzvi.

'I'll get onto it,' said Isaac.

'Are you free to travel?' asked Tzvi.

'Yes, one of the benefits of retirement,' replied Issac.

'I'm free too, blood,' said Chris.

'It's exciting to have found Einstein's son,' said Esther.

'It's fantastic, really fantastic, well-done Elias and Chris,' said Tzvi.

'Does Einstein have any living relatives?' asked Issac.

Chris searched his mobile phone. 'Last grandson died ten years ago.'

After the group finished their meeting, Elias and Esther rode back to Tel Aviv. In his apartment, Elias poured an arak, and smoked a few crumbs of hash. His thoughts played. His uncle's plan to have Einstein father a child had been implemented by another group. The world was unaware of Cyrus's lineage. Possibly, even probably Cyrus knows nothing of his relationship with Einstein. It's probable that the people who orchestrated Cyrus's conception were unaware of the *real* motive of Anna, the rabbi and his uncle. But the equation had changed with Mendel also having this information. Mendel was unpredictable. If it became widely known Cyrus was Einstein's child then he could be killed—a terrorist's scalp. Cyrus needed to get out of Syria fast.

CHAPTER ELEVEN

DAMASCUS, SYRIA 13 JULY 2018

CYRUS PUSHED THE round start button on the fermenter. The fermenter's four legs stood square on the green resin-sealed floor. In the fermentation room there were no windows and the walls were painted white. Light came from low-glare LEDs set into the ceiling. The LEDs beamed light onto the laboratory bench and onto the ultracentrifuge, the PC II biohazard hood and the stainless-steel fermenter. With the test fermentation started, Cyrus stepped from the containment facility into the positive pressure airlock, and stripped off his disposable gloves, hat, goggles and blue coveralls and placed them into the clothing waste bin. The test fermentation would establish conditions for large scale botulism production. The botulism trial at 601 had been a success with a hundred per cent morbidity. The colonel said two of the subjects had been slow to die, but at least they died.

In the dressing room, on the other side of the positive-pressure airlock, Cyrus pushed his arms and legs into his new military-green captain's uniform. Outside the dressing room, four Syrians in desert camouflage stood guard. The guards saluted when he passed. Cyrus did not. He swiped his security card and took the lift to his fifth-floor office. The red light on his desk phone pulsed and showed a missed call. Cyrus pressed voicemail and listened to a message from Cairo.

He punched one to get an external line then punched 0020 for Egypt followed by the mobile number. The dial tone stopped and the call connected to Professor Baz, head of the Life Sciences Department at Cairo University. Cyrus liked the sound of Baz's voice. Tarek invited him to a vaccine conference to be held in the Red Sea resort city of Sharm El-Sheikh, where he would receive an academic prize. Cyrus's first thought was no, and his second thought was no, but then he thought he could find a way to leverage going to the conference. He said thank you and he'd call back in two or three days. The near-term Iranian site visit review of his bioweapons' programme was a huge problem. His time needed to be used to go over his experimental notes. Hide the delays and mask the deception.

Mid-morning, Cyrus met again with the colonel at army headquarters. The colonel wanted to know every fine detail of the botulism production process. Cyrus talked slowly and thought rapidly.

'Could we … ah … delay the Iranian review?'

'Why?'

'There may be an opportunity to collaborate with Egypt on vaccine development,' he said. He didn't need to add that the vaccine component of their bioweapons' programme was essential or add that scientific ties strengthened political ties and it would make the colonel look good to whoever the colonel needed to look good to. The colonel could join the dots.

'Collaboration?'

'I've been invited to a vaccine meeting in Sharm El-Sheikh. The timing clashes with the Iranian visit.'

'Who in Egypt are you talking with.'

'Professor Baz from Cairo University.'

'You must report all such contact to me when it occurs.'

'I apologise. I was embarrassed.'

'Embarrassed?'

'The Egyptian's want to award me a science prize.'

'Write all this down. Send it to me. Focus on getting everything right for the Iranian review. Good to see you in uniform,' added the colonel.

The military green shirt sat squarely on Cyrus's square shoulders The new uniform itched.

Three days later, Cyrus received approval from the colonel to attend the meeting in Egypt. He called El Baz in Cairo, and El Baz called his friend Isaac in Israel.

CHAPTER TWELVE

TEL AVIV, ISRAEL, 22 JULY 2018

MENDEL WAS AS certain about this as he was about anything.

'Einstein's child is somewhere in Israel.'

'Let me think how we can use a machine learning algorithm,' said Boaz. Boaz Weiss was older and leaner than Mendel, and had springy white hair which Mendel envied as he was bald.

Mendel followed Boaz down the stairs from their lunch at Tel Aviv University's Aroma café. Boaz bounced on the balls of his feet and Mendel stepped flat footed and held the hand rail.

○

Back in his office Mendel heard a grinding noise from his printer. The printer display panel flashed a white cross on a red circle and the words *paper jam*. Mendel turned off the printer, opened the side panel and pulled the crumpled page free. He looked at the crumpled page of Albert Einstein's face. At that moment, Mendel's desk phone rang. It was David Halprin, director of the el-Araj geological site inviting him to visit the el-Araj excavation for his view on the stratigraphy. The high profile el-Araj site was thought to be Bethsaida, the home to Jesus's apostles Andrew, Philip and Peter.

○

Two days later, Mendel drove to the el-Araj site, Halprin was not there, which was strange as he'd confirmed the time. A young female intern escorted Mendel to the excavation site where the field crew had left for a break.

'I'm going to get a coffee; you okay to look around?' the intern asked.

'Of course, I've been to many excavations.'

The intern left the site, and moments later, a young man approached Mendel and said he was writing a piece for the *Independent* in London, and asked if he could have a photograph. Mendel looked at the camera slung around the reporter's neck and his long shaggy hair. Mendel thought it was a cultivated look to try and get girls.

'I'm an archaeologist, but I'm visiting,' said Mendel.

'I'm a journalist and I'm visiting too.' Both men laughed. The journalist asked for an *action shot* and Mendel stepped into the excavation, bent down and cupped a half-hand of soil. The journalist passed Mendel a piece of crusted clay with imbedded lumps of teal glass mosaic. Mendel smiled and held the mosaic on his open hands as the journalist clicked his camera.

'I need another lens, wait, I'll be right back.' The journalist moved away from the site and Mendel stepped out of the excavation. A young woman sidled past the journalist as he departed, caught his eye and continued to the excavation site. In her short skirt, she shimmied to Mendel's side.

'Hello, I guess you must be Doctor Halprin, it must be so exciting.' Mendel introduced himself and said he was an archaeologist but not the site director. The young woman said she'd heard Mendel's name in archaeology circles and asked what he was holding. Mendel looked at his hand and the teal glass fragments bound on the clay surface and said they were gilded glass mosaic. The young woman said that sounded important. Mendel explained that gilded glass mosaics signified that a major church had stood at the site and such mosaics relate to the Byzantine period, AD 330 to 1500. The young woman asked for Mendel's photograph, he was delighted and stepped down into the dig.

She stepped sideways to stand above Mendel. She wore brown leather sandals with brown leather spaghetti straps that circled her fine Achilles. She lifted a sandaled foot an inch from the ground, put it down and then her other foot lifted. She looked down at Mendel and clicked her smartphone.

'What does it feel like standing at the site likely to be the home of the Apostles Peter, Andrew and Philip?' she asked.

Mendel said it wasn't certain this was the site of Bethsaida.

'But evidence of the early Roman bath-house where you're standing suggests this was a major urban settlement and is therefore likely to be Bethsaida, correct?'

Mendel looked up at the young woman, and stared. Mendel's stare began at her brown leather sandals with their spaghetti straps and then he stared up and up. She smoothed the front of her skirt. Mendel stepped out of the dig and placed the glass mosaic with the other artefacts. *Click.* He dusted his hands. Mendel said the first-century historian, Josephus recorded Bethsaida as a fishing village, but the site where they were was over a mile from the coast. The young woman asked if coastlines move with earthquakes and Mendel said yes, over the last two thousand years the coastline could easily have changed. The young woman shook Mendel's hand and thanked him. He held her hand for longer than was necessary. Then she left. Mendel waited for the *Independent* journalist, but neither the *Independent* journalist nor the intern came back.

The following day, an article on Mendel appeared in the Israeli Newspaper *Haaretz.* The headline read: *Famous Archaeologist Finds More Evidence of Byzantine Church at el-Araj Excavations.*

The article started with the paragraph:

Dr Mendel (pictured), a famous archaeologist from Tel Aviv University is making a significant contribution to the excavation at el-Araj. In an interview at the site yesterday he explained there had been some controversy as to whether the site was, in fact, Bethsaida, home to Jesus's apostles Andrew, Philip and Peter. The controversy stems from the fact that Bethsaida was known to be a seaside village, yet the excavation is over one mile from the coast. Dr Mendel explained that earthquakes over the last two thousand years have likely caused the coastline to move. It is thought that a Byzantine Church was built on this village site. In the photograph above we see Dr

It was late morning. In his university office, Mendel scanned Google search results for the term *synthetic identity image Einstein*. Just then, there was a knock on his closed door. The door opened and Amos Dayan, head of the Archaeology Department stepped in. Dayan's face was tanned—he'd been sailing in Mauritius. It annoyed Mendel that Dayan wore a tie. No one else in the department wore a tie. Mendel stood then sat back down and glanced at his computer screen with the *synthetic identity image of Einstein*.

'Something important?' asked Dayan. Mendel uttered the word 'research.' then lifted his eyes to Dayan's face. Dayan said he'd fielded a call from David Halprin, director of the el-Araj geological site. Dayan placed a copy of the morning's *Haaretz* on Mendel's desk. The newspaper lay open at a page with a large photograph of Mendel. Mendel glanced at the newspaper, then stared at the newspaper. He snatched it and started reading. The colour drained from Mendel's already pale face. Dayan asked Mendel where he got the *gilded glass mosaic* and Mendel said from the male reporter.

'Christine Kleban wrote the *Haaretz* article and took your photograph. What did you do with the piece of mosaic you're holding in the photograph?'

'It's in a tray with the other artefacts.'

'Halprin confirmed they found the mosaic with the other artefacts, but it's from a different time period and it hasn't come from his site.'

Mendel shook his head.

Dayan gazed out of the window at the distant sky rises then asked Mendel about his earthquake theory moving the el-Araj geological site several kilometres from the sea. Mendel said he just agreed with what the girl said. Dayan outlined the university's lawyers had contacted *Haaretz* and the journalist Christine Kleban stood by every word she'd written; it was routine for her to tape interviews on her smartphone.

'Lawyers! A bit hasty,' said Mendel.

'You weren't around when this broke early this morning. We needed to know where we stand.'

'Where do you stand?' asked Mendel

Dayan advised Mendel to discuss the situation with his lawyer, get independent advice for his own protection. Dayan thought if this was the cut that finished Mendel, he would not complain. He left Mendel's office, and Mendel called his lawyer and arranged an immediate meeting.

◯

In his lawyer's office, Mendel picked up the newspaper and slammed it on the table as he summarised the events at the el-Araj excavation. He had vivid recall of the brown sandals and her slim legs but kept this detail to himself. Mendel's lawyer leant forward and eyed Mendel. He wrote as Mendel talked and placed arrows beside the words *intern*, *Independent* and *Haaretz*. When he wasn't writing, the weighty lawyer rested his chin on clasped pudgy hands. He had the shadow of a moustache.

Mendel stopped speaking and his lawyer spoke.

'Do you have any personal issues with any of your academic colleagues?' Mendel pushed his glasses further up his nose.

'Not from my side, why do you ask?'

'This doesn't sit right; sounds like *entrapment*.' Mendel immediately thought of Elias Eidelman. At their second meeting, he detected an intelligence to Eidelman's character, deeper than he'd first assumed. He'd dug into Eidelman's past, and discovered Eidelman was an ex-officer in the IDF. This discovery made him think taking the notebook pages had not been the smartest move.

'If I wanted to anonymously provide a document to the *Shin Bet* what would be the easiest way?' asked Mendel. He referred to Israel's internal security police.

'Give the document to me. As long as you're not directly or indirectly involved in any criminal action, it's unlikely you'll hear anything further. Tell me what's been going on.'

CHAPTER THIRTEEN
HAIFA, ISRAEL, 24 JULY 2018.

REZNIK GUZZLED FROM his large can of Red Bull Zero then placed the empty can on the table. He sat alone, but he wondered for how long. A man he'd not seen before had followed him the short distance from his Haifa apartment to the Naima Café. Reznik was a Shin Bet agent. He'd killed a number of people for the Israeli government. He didn't look like a stylised killer, he looked thin, almost feeble. Reznik's head was shaved bald and a red birthmark stained his neck.

'May I sit?' Reznik looked up at a non-descript, middle-aged man.

'Sure.' Reznik gestured to the seat opposite. The man had selected Reznik for the mission. Reznik's greatest loyalty was to the State, loyalty to himself a close second. He had the characteristics they needed. Someone with an ego and lack of conscience; a deceitful sociopath.

'I'm in the family too,' the man said as he sat down. He used the colloquial term for the Shin Bet. Reznik licked his lips and tasted the sweet tart of Red Bull Zero. He remained silent, sat back in his chair, and scrutinised the man at his table.

'You impressed in the Gaza operation.' The man's mouth cut a rigid line. *He's read my file,* thought Reznik, and wondered what would come next. He had used a Portuguese passport, posed as a humanitarian worker and crossed the Erez checkpoint to shoot the target with a silenced weapon—a clean hit and a clean getaway, supported by the micro-detail planning of Shin Bet.

'I need someone who will not give up on himself; see it through to the end.' The man touched his fingers to his chest.

'Who are you?'

'You don't need to know, this is a black op. Call Jachin and he'll tell you your application for one month's leave has been approved.' Jachin was Reznik's Shin Bet boss. Reznik made the call, one month's leave that he hadn't applied for had been approved.

'The op being?' asked Reznik

'We need Einstein's son eliminated.'

'His location?'

'Unknown. He's due to meet with Elias Eidelman; an ex-Unit guy.' Reznik heard the warning. Sayeret Matkal, known in argot as the Unit, was the Israeli Army's special ops. The Unit trained men in camouflage techniques, fast tactical shooting, martial arts, unconventional raid tactics, and… the list continued on and on.

'Meet where?'

'We don't know. Suggest you put eyes on Eidelman and find out. Eidelman visited Cairo three weeks ago.'

'Why Cairo?' asked Reznik.

'You tell me.'

'Einstein's son have a name?'

'We don't know, he's illegitimate.' Reznik reflected; a no-name person living in a no-name country, who may be meeting somewhere with this Eidelman ex-special op guy. I know nothing. I need an army.

'Resources?'

'Plan what you need then give me a budget.' He handed Reznik a burner phone.

'Why kill him?'

'Does the bullet need to know?'

'My guess why Eidelman visited Cairo is that Einstein's son is in an Arab country now, maybe government employed, easier to travel to another Arab country, if he's not already living in Egypt.' The man shrugged in such a manner to make it clear to Reznik that his guess had not impressed.

'You've spent time in Egypt.' The man made a statement.

'Two years.'

'If there's any problem you'll be on your own. On your own,' he repeated

Already feeling on his own Reznik's mind raced as he gulped a slug of Red Bull. He'd always had political cover. He pressed a fingernail into the fleshy part of his thumb. *On your own* meant no other agency people. But there were ex-agency people, ex-army people, ex-Mossad people—all private contractors

'Not a word to anyone that your target is Einstein's son, and I mean no one.' The man stood. Reznik eyes followed him as he disappeared around a nearby corner. No name, no Shin Bet rank, but the nondescript man seemed used to giving orders. Reznik crushed the empty Red Bull can. The theory was simple, know when Einstein's son was going to show up at the kill shot location. All he needed to do was identify the location. Say it fast enough and it sounded easy but Reznik knew theory and practice were cards dealt from different decks.

Later that same day, Reznik strolled on Tel Aviv's Tayelet Beach Promenade, with the Mediterranean Sea on his right, and ahead he saw Yaakov Arad with his full dark beard just where he was supposed to be, seated on a bench, opposite the Orchid Tel Aviv Hotel. Arad stood up and was taller than Reznik. Reznik shook Yaakov's hand and was reminded of Yaakov's strength. A strength he'd felt when they'd sparred together in hand-to-hand combat training during their army days. Yaakov had a solid build but could move at speed. He'd topped his IDF Mista'arvim class, a secret security group tasked with intelligence and counter-terrorism. They strolled side by side.

'I need a six-person hunting pack,' said Reznik.

'The rabbit?' asked Yaakov.

'An ex-Unit guy.'

'Six is lean. Where is he?'

'Tel Aviv.'

'Starting?'

'Now.'

'Duration?'

'A week, maybe two.'

'What's the brief?'

'Follow and report.'

'Because he's ex-Unit we should have twelve.'

'Okay—twelve.'

'Sixty thousand shekels a day, seven days in advance.'

'If the surveillance isn't needed for seven days?'

'Then you save yourself a second week.'

'But—'

'One week minimum.' Reznik nodded.

'Deal. I also need help with another project.'

'Uh huh?'

Reznik paused while a pedestrian passed, then leant into Yaakov. 'A targeted killing.'

'Who?'

'A civilian.'

'Location?'

'The surveillance of the ex-Unit guy will determine the location.'

'Twenty-six were involved in Dubai,' said Yaakov referring to the Mossad assassination of a senior Hamas operative eight years earlier.

'There's no budget and time for such planning.'

'Who's running this?'

'It's sanctioned but black.'

'Sanctioned by?'

'That's all you're getting.'

'I can't help you then.'

'Don't go soft on me. I need a couple of guys lined up ready to go.'

'You know the planning involved for your Gaza op. You're alive now because of that planning.'

'A civilian target, not a high-profile target in a war zone.'

'Then do it yourself.'

'I intend to, but want back-up.'

'State protection?'

'Assume not.'

'In Israel?'

'Not sure, maybe Egypt.

'If it's in Egypt, two-fifty US.'

'A quarter of a million.' Reznik mulled the figure.

'Each,' said Yaakov. He guessed Reznik to be a killer not a negotiator.

'Each,' Reznik spat.

'You want it done right?'

'Okay. Here are the details on the rabbit.' Reznik handed Yaakov an envelope.

'Half up front.'

'Throw in a shoe,' said Reznik using spy jargon for a false passport.

'Why?'

'Don't know how this will run, always useful to have a back-up passport no one knows about.'

'I'll need your photographs.'

'In there.' Reznik pointed to the envelope.

'The money?'

'I'll call you when I have it. Can you start the surveillance?'

Yaakov turned his head and gazed at the Mediterranean for a few seconds then said 'Sure.'

CHAPTER FOURTEEN

TEL AVIV, ISRAEL, 25 JULY 2018

ELIAS PUNCHED THE blue display screen to increase the cross-trainer resistance for the last two minutes of his workout. Around him the cadence of running feet on treadmills, sliding rowing machine seats and flywheel hum, while above was the thrum of two large extraction units attached to the wooden trusses of the warehouse. The two extraction units pumped sweat-sour air. Elias drove his arms and pumped his legs and thought only three days until the meeting with Cyrus in Egypt. The following day he would travel to Egypt, rent a vehicle and book a hotel for he and Cyrus; take some time to discuss with Cyrus options for his future. At time zero Elias stepped from the cross trainer, grabbed his towel and headed to the shower. At the end of his shower, Elias turned the temperature to cold and blasted his body for a minute then towelled dry. His high protein and low carb diet kept away the fat and he looked fresh for his thirty-eight years. With the towel slung around his shoulders, Elias padded to his locker. The light on his smartphone flashed. He dressed in black briefs, black jeans, a polo shirt and sneakers then picked up the phone and touched the screen. A missed call from Tzvi. He pressed dial and the call was answered.

'The Shin Bet know about Cyrus,' said Tzvi.

'How do you know?'

'A tip-off from someone who was in IDF with you, he knows you're my cousin.'

'Who?'

'Anon.'

'What's Shin Bet's interest?'

'Track you to get to Cyrus.'

'Get to Cyrus?'

'You know the Shin Bet.'

Elias did know the Shin Bet. And the Shin Bet's sisters, Mossad and AMAN. And the three letter agencies in other countries. The security agencies could justify any action for any reason, a reason that may be real, a reason that could be perceived as real, or a reason known to be fictitious with any threat to the agencies' mandate or to the agencies' control eliminated. And then there were rogue agents and secret cabals who played their own power games.

◯

Elias's default setting—assume the worst-case scenario. If Shin Bet planned to kill Cyrus, then he too could be a target. How much did the Shin Bet know? But how much they knew didn't matter.

His mobile screen displayed 11:06. The Allenby Street branch of the Mizrahi-Tefahot Bank was nearby. There was still time before the midday Friday closing. Elias snatched his helmet and backpack, ran to the Naim Gym exit then strode at an easy pace to his bike. He swung the helmet onto his head and out of habit scanned the street. People moved in all directions. Moved with an unconscious awareness of others, a street fluidity, but fifty meters behind, a stationary motorcyclist angled between two parked cars prompted a passing car to break in caution. *That's one I can see*, thought Elias, *and if I can see one there could be ten*. He pressed the starter button, then revved the engine before dropping the bike into gear, heard the *click* as first gear engaged, eased the clutch and eased the throttle and drove down the narrow one-way street. The watching motorcyclist pulled out to follow fifty meters behind. Elias turned left into Kibbutz Galuyot Road, then headed to the Jaffa flea market two kilometres away. As it was Friday, the busy market would provide the opportunity to drop his tail, but then Elias saw the motorcyclist behind turn left at an intersection and then he was gone. Elias thought the bike was a black Honda. A kilometre later, Elias kicked to a lower gear, nudged the left indicator button and steered through the concrete entrance to an underground car park. He glanced at the graffiti art—purple smiley faces and pink love hearts that decorated the concrete. Inside, Elias parked his bike where *motorcycles* had been painted in orange on the concrete floor. The bike park was surrounded by more graffiti art. He locked his helmet to the side of the bike seat knowing he would be using neither for some time. He then strode to the car-park lift. Behind him he heard the sound of a motorbike. The black Honda appeared, and a second later the lift opened. Elias strode slowly towards the open lift, then did a half skip and took four quick paces to reach the lift before the doors closed. A woman and her young son were in the lift. The young son had reddish brown hair with payot side locks and came to his mother's waist. She wore a dark sheitel wig.

'Can I push the button mum?'

'Push floor one.' The doors closed. He pushed a button and the lift doors opened. Elias glanced down at the key pad. The number one had been worn off its button.

The Honda was now parked by his bike. The rider came through the lift doors. The doors closed. Elias's eyes swept from black Nikes to the tail's close-cut dark hair. He wore a tan and white scarf and his clothes hung on him.

Elias shuffled into a back corner of the lift. The lift accelerated then jolted to a stop. The tail had to move; he was closer to the open door than Elias. The tail stepped a few paces from the lift, then stopped, looked left and right to give the appearance of indecision. Elias sauntered past and felt the tail drop in behind. Without Tzvi's warning it was a normal scene. Elias wondered how many other tails were close by. If they didn't already, it was a short matter of time before they'd also have eyes on him. At an alley entrance to Jaffa Market, Elias paused and glanced up at a lamp post with an Israeli flag that flapped in the wind, lower down at eye level, lamp post stickers advertised mobile numbers of some of the ten thousand Tel Aviv prostitutes. Elias crossed the road to the covered alleys of the oldest section of the Jaffa Market—the Turkish Bazaar. For a moment, when Elias turned into a bazaar alley, he was out of sight for two seconds. He darted between other pedestrians then low dived into a clothing booth. Elias crouched in a rack of garments and watched legs and shoes walk by. A pair of black Nikes paused at the shop entrance then continued along the alley. Elias ripped off his grey summer-weight bike jacket and stuffed it into his backpack. He bought a black T-shirt and a black cap from the vendor, changed, scanned for the tail, then pressed into the alley, where people moved shoulder to shoulder with the din of a hundred voices, and around the sound of drums, a dog barking, a piano accordion and a female voice singing a Yiddish folk son lost in the din of the crowd. Elias angled through the crowd, eyes under the peak of his cap and at the landmark Jaffa clock tower, where palm trees swayed and pigeons beat against the stiff sea breeze, Elias slid into a taxi. He kept low in the back seat and fumbled low with his backpack at his feet, as the cab headed away from the bazaar to the Mizrahi-Tefahot Bank. A short time after entering the bank. he then left the grey stone building with its red and black Mizrahi-Tefahot infinity symbol, and climbed into an Uber. In his wallet a new debit card loaded with US$50,000 and a slug of US dollars. From the bank, the Uber drove to a mall where Elias bought and changed into orthodox attire, then headed to his apartment. He guessed the tail, probably tails, at the bazaar would be rattled. They'd have a watch on his apartment building. He walked straight from the Uber to his building entrance. No obvious tail; he'd find out later. Inside the lift, Elias stared through glasses with thick glass lenses as the distorted floor numbers flashed to 16. He held his apartment key card in his left hand. The lift doors opened. Black Nikes, but different black Nikes, Airmax on the side of the sole. Elias slid his left hand with his apartment key into his pocket.

'*Shalom,*' he said with his head tilted. His wide black brim stopped the man at the lift from seeing his eyes. Even if they are behind glasses, people remember eyes. Elias turned right along the floor-sixteen corridor, away from the lift, away from the black Nikes—away from his apartment, shambled away with sloping shoulders and a strained stride. Elias had not heard the lift door close, and he knew the man with black Nikes had eyes on him. He could feel the man behind look nail-hard at his scuffed black shoes, his creased black trousers, creased black jacket and his wide-brimmed black hat. Elias knocked on the door at the end of the corridor in the hope that his neighbour was home. There was no sound and he tapped on the door again. He heard movement. The door opened and his neighbour stepped back with her mouth open, then she saw Elias's eyes behind the thick glasses. Her face showed she knew who he was.

'Hello, auntie,' said Elias as he stepped inside and closed the door.

Five minutes and an invented explanation later, Elias left his neighbour's apartment. The black Airmax Nikes were gone. Airmax had been in his apartment. His laptop had been moved. Only moved a fraction, but enough for Elias to know. Elias guessed Airmax had tried to clone his hard drive. Good luck with that. He locked his laptop in his safe, pocketed his passport and took the lift to the ground floor, then caught an Uber. A car followed them. Elias asked the driver to drive to the suburb of Bnei Brak, the centre of Haredi Judaism in Tel Aviv. Following a lone black sheep in a paddock of white sheep was easy, but it was a different game when that same black sheep joined a ten thousand black sheep flock. After he lost the tail in Bnei Brak, Elias took another Uber to a mall, changed clothes again then flagged a taxi to the Eliat-Taba crossing, three hundred and fifty kilometres to the south. He promised the driver an extra five hundred shekels to do the trip off-metre. At dusk, the taxi passed the Bislak Airbase, halfway to the Eliat-Taba crossing and the Egyptian border. As he sat in the back of the taxi, Elias gazed at the brown rock and sparse greenery on either side; with the less than ten centimetres of annual rainfall everything was brown. He called Tzvi and asked for a contact person in Cairo, anyone; he didn't want to be in Cairo blind. Thirty minutes later, Tzvi called back, his sister had a friend called Noya with an Auntie Ophelia in Cairo, and Ophelia was Jewish. He asked Tzvi to call Esther.

It would be close to midnight when as a ruse he'd check into the Taba Hilton. Elias knew when being pursued, time and distance are your allies, get as far away as possible from those chasing; buy time. Now was not the time to stop.

'Is it a woman?' asked the taxi driver breaking the silence.

'Huh?' Elias was on his smart phone looking at a map of the Sinai and Gulf of Suez.

'Either we're running to them or running away from them.'

'Is it obvious,' he said to the driver. 'There's a girl who works in a hotel in Taba.'

'An Arab girl?'

'A girl from Jordan.'

'I chased an Arab girl for a while, when I was younger,' said the driver.

'What happened?'

'She thought I was her way out. It was never going anywhere.'

'Maybe she loved you.'

'She never said.'

'A girl may hesitate to say she loves, in case you don't say it back,' said Elias.

'She could never have loved me, why would she? No.' In silence, the taxi driver then focused on the road. Elias focused on the map. After meeting Cyrus at Sharm El-Sheikh Airport, they would need to zig zag to Cairo.

○

Elias handed the taxi driver a bunch of shekels, grabbed his backpack from the rear seat and headed into Taba Airport, the location of the Eliat-Taba border crossing into Egypt. The last flight had gone, and Elias continued to the border post. There were intermittent security guards and no civilians. He passed through a standard security bag scan, filled out a customs form, got his passport stamped and then passed a final checkpoint where he showed his passport again before entering Egypt. He hired an Egyptian taxi, drove the short distance to the Taba Hilton and asked the elderly driver to wait. The high threat of terrorism in the Sinai kept tourist numbers down; no need to pre-book accommodation. Elias paid for his room in cash and gave a cash deposit for expenses. He pulled the bed duvet onto the floor, tossed a white bathrobe onto the bed, headed back to the lobby and jumped into the waiting taxi.

Three hours later the headlights lit up a triangular sign showing a bend and *Sharm El-Sheikh*. Elias used google maps to give the driver directions and then told him to stop.

'Here?'

'Yes.'

'There's no hotel.'

'My friend's house is close,' said Elias. The taxi did a U-turn and Elias flicked his eyes as the rear red lights disappeared. A short time later Elias entered the reception of a small boarding house. A young man slept behind the counter. The young man, with his ruffled shirt, insisted Elias give his passport before he'd hand over a room key but, in the end, instead of his passport, the young man was happy to accept a hundred-dollar bill with its image of Benjamin Franklin.

The next day Elias saw no sign of anyone coming after him. He needed to show his passport as ID, but paid cash for a ferry ticket from Sharm El-Sheik across the Red Sea to Hurghada on the western side. Hurghada had an international airport. Elias walked away from the ticket office, away from the passenger ramp to the ferry and dropped the ticket into a rubbish basket. If those chasing had access to sophisticated electronic surveillance they may find he used his passport as ID.

Elias then hired a car from a one-man outfit. He drove to El Tor on the Sinai side of the Gulf of Suez, arranged with a fisherman to cross the Suez Gulf to mainland Egypt in two days' time, then returned to Sharm El-Sheikh. In two days Cyrus would arrive at Sharm El-Sheikh airport.

CHAPTER FIFTEEN

TEL AVIV, ISRAEL, 26 JULY 2018

REZNIK SNATCHED HIS mobile the moment it buzzed. A minute later he ended the call. Eidelman had crossed into Sinai via the Taba checkpoint nine hours earlier. Reznik took a long slow breath as he recalled his guess about Eidelman going to Egypt. He chewed his fingernails. Eidelman's travel to Egypt was either in accord with a pre-arranged schedule or rushed because Eidelman had discovered a tail. He'd been told Eidelman had disappeared in Jaffa Market—he must have been spooked. Reznik needed to deal with the now. Where was Einstein's son? Was he already in Egypt or flying in! He didn't have resources to watch all fourteen international Egyptian airports. Every operation required calculated risks; airport selection a piece of the risk paradigm. Unless other intel turned up, he'd go with the closest airport, Sharm El-Sheikh, and if Einstein's son was already in Egypt, then he'd need a new plan. Reznik called Yaakov and told him to get his guys to *do their fucking job*; he needed them in Sharm El-Sheikh. Reznik made another call, he wanted an electronic search of hotels and transport businesses to see if Eidelman's passport details were on record.

Two days later, Elias nosed a hired van out of the Jaz Farana Resort car park and drove the fifteen kilometres to Sharm El-Sheikh Airport. He expected Einstein's son to arrive from Syria in three hours' time. Reeds of light fanned the early sky. He rubbed his eyes; only two hours sleep. A night spent organising an escape from the airport in case things turned bad. On the approach to the airport, Elias stopped at the security check where there were the usual dogs, mirrors and guns and beyond the security check the airport was surrounded by a wall topped with barbed wire. A guard wearing a white uniform and black-flak vest waved a finger for Elias to go. A security pole across the road lifted and Elias inched the van into the walled airport and entered a covered car park. At this dawn hour, the car park was near empty. He parked near one of the car-park exit barriers then used a set of binoculars to focus on the car-park entry. The darkened side windows of the van provided cover. After two hours, and a hundred or so cars, Elias turned the centre focusing wheel of the binoculars and sharpened the image of the driver as he entered the car park. He had a shaved head and a birthmark. Sitting beside him was a man with short dark hair and a closely cropped beard. When their car stopped the man with the beard lifted a pair of binoculars and swung them in an arc.

'Anything?' asked Reznik.

'No.'

'Go and see if he's in the terminal.' Hadar placed the binoculars on the dashboard. Reznik had received intel that Eidelman had checked into the Taba Hilton and the following day purchased a ferry ticket from Sharm El-Sheik to Hurghada. Six of Yaakov's men had been sent to watch Hurghada airport.

'So, it's going to be this way,' Elias said to himself. He pulled the van keys from the ignition, and slid out of the front passenger door and kept the van as cover between himself and his two tails. He worked his way through the car park to a distant lift. Inside the terminal, Elias gazed up at the arrival's board, flight SYR046 from Damascus was delayed by an hour. The civil war in Syria delayed every flight out of Damascus. He meandered away from the arrivals board then stopped at the information desk ... yes ... the Damascus flight was delayed by an hour. As he meandered Elias appeared to show no interest in those around but he had a laser interest.

Beside the information desk he intentionally made eye contact with an Egyptian security man.

'You meeting someone?' the security man asked.

'Yes,' said Elias.

'I can give you security escort from the airport,' the security man said and pulled the strap of the automatic weapon slung over his shoulder.

'No, thank you.' Elias nodded with a smile, then angled away past a group of men who held name cards and faced the passenger arrival gate. Hadar sent a text to Reznik. *Eidelman's wearing a Jaz Farana Hotel uniform.* Reznik commanded Yaakov's two men in Sharm El-Sheik to check out Eidelman's connection to the Jaz Farana Hotel. A short time later Reznik received word that Eidelman had booked three days accommodation for himself and a Professor Zaydan.

Elias bought a coffee then sat with his back to the concourse. He stared out to the runway and the distant southern Sinai hills, a brown barren rocky landscape. After ninety minutes, a plane with a white fuselage and the blue tail of Syrian Air, landed and taxied on the concrete apron towards the terminal. Elias strolled to an arrivals' board and saw the Damascus flight was still listed as thirty minutes late. Then a moment later, he heard an announcement that the in-bound Damascus flight had landed.

A man beside Elias spoke.

'Are you waiting for the Damascus flight?'

'Yes,'

'It's landed, the board's wrong,' said the man.

'Thank you,' Elias smiled.

Elias was dressed like a Jaz Farana Resort employee; he wore a dark suit and red tie and carried a card with the teal-green Jaz Farana Resort logo. Witten on the card was the name Professor Zaydan in bold black letters.

The tail with the dark hair and beard watched Elias talk to a man by the arrivals' board. Elias knew the tail watched him; knew he had watched him for over an hour.

○

Cyrus felt the plane bounce on the tarmac. The Syrian army major with ground teeth and foul-smelling breath sat beside him. The major had given instructions on what to do and repeated these instructions as their plane taxied to the terminal.

'Wait on the other side of immigration if you clear before me,' said the major.

The two Syrians left the plane and followed the arrows that said *Hijra* / Immigration Cyrus and the major joined a short queue at the immigration desks. After a few moments, Cyrus stepped forward and handed his deep-blue Syrian passport and travel documents to the immigration officer. The officer looked at documents, but what the officer relied most on was instinct. Is the person nervous; does he look bad? Cyrus had stepped forward with relaxed shoulders, his chin high and he moved his head slowly. The officer glanced at his passport photo then at Cyrus and skimmed through the travel documents. 'Welcome to Egypt, professor.' He stamped Cyrus's passport, handed him his documents, and the double glass swing barrier gate opened. Cyrus stepped through the swing barrier, waited for the Syrian army major, then together they headed for the baggage claim. Cyrus smiled as bags tumbled from the conveyor mouth onto the carousel. It was Cyrus's first time flying.

'Give me your passport,' said the major, his eyes ugly. Cyrus slipped his backpack from his shoulder, pulled open the zip on a pocket and handed his passport to the major. Their two bags tumbled from the mouth and Cyrus hauled his bag onto a trolley and the major used a separate trolly. They exited via the green lane.

Elias searched the first trickle of passengers. He checked the greeting card w*as orientated the* right way, then lifted it to chest height. Then Elias's heart pounded and he felt a smile. He saw Cyrus, tall and erect with his arms relaxed. He looked just like his photograph, a vibrant fine-looking man who looked fifteen years younger than his sixty-eight years. Elias's attention shifted to the man with Cyrus. He moved like a soldier. The unknown man's eyes lifted and locked on Elias, then he spoke to Cyrus and pointed his finger. Elias flashed a smile and raised his palm. Elias knew he could get rid of this unwanted Syrian, but first he had to shake the tail.

Cyrus pushed the trolley towards the man who raised his palm. He held a card with his name written in large black letters.

'Professor Zaydan?' the man asked.

'Yes,' Cyrus replied. The man holding his name card had light skin and spoke Arabic with an accent. Cyrus looked on as this black-suited man put his and the major's bags onto a single trolley; both kept their carry-on backpacks.

'How was your flight?'

'My first time flying,' said Cyrus.

'Welcome to Egypt.'

'Where are you from?' asked the military-looking Syrian.

'The Jaz Farana Hotel.' Elias had a simple smile and pointed to the hotel name on the card.

'You're not Egyptian.'

'Morocco, France, I'm Egyptian now.' Cyrus and the major followed Elias to a lift. Elias steered the baggage trolley as a barrier to prevent anyone else from entering; however, the tail with the short dark hair and beard pushed past the trolley into the lift. Elias nudged the trolley against the tail's leg; the tail stepped to the rear of the lift and Elias backed against him. Elias felt in control. With the airport security the two tails wouldn't risk carrying weapons into the airport complex. The lift stopped at the car park level, Elias strode to the van, quickly loaded the two bags and his two passengers. He started the van, accelerated past a car in front and stopped at the car-park barrier. The tail's car was two vehicles behind the van. Elias slid his parking ticket into the slot and the barrier arm lifted. Before he pulled forward under the raised barrier, Elias pressed his fingers into an open jar of petroleum jelly that sat between the front seats then stretched out and smeared the jelly into the ticket slot. He pushed his right foot down and the van lurched forward. The barrier arm dropped. Elias turned his head and snatched a view of the car park. The tail's car was moving.

'What were you doing at the barrier?' asked the miliary looking Syrian.

'Huh?'

Elias touched the brakes and the van jerked. 'Sorry. I need to concentrate.'

Reznik sneered as he thought of the kilometres of open road to catch the sluggish van. He braked to a halt behind the car at the exit barrier; the car in front did not move forward. Reznik leapt from his car and ran to the stationary driver.

'Go,' yelled Reznik. The middle-aged man driving stared up, opened his drivers side window, and extended his hand with his parking ticket. Reznik snatched the ticket and his fingertips stuck to a jelly; a jelly that blinded the optic scanner. He threw the ticket down, spun and saw cars queued behind.

'The ticket reader's … back up,' shouted Reznik. He ran from car to car and shouted and waved his arms at the immobilised drivers. Horns tooted. Reznik stared at the line of cars then looked across the carpark at a second exit. It would take at least five minutes.

○

Three kilometres from the airport, Elias saw the black Nissan parked on the shoulder; he slowed and stopped behind.

'Why have we stopped?' asked the military Syrian.

'He may need help,' said Elias.

'Keep driving.'

Elias stepped out of the van and pulled open the van's side door beside the Syrian.

'Whaa—' the Syrian's word was cut short as Elias punched his jaw. The Syrian slumped forward in his seat belt.

'Quick, where's your passport?' Elias asked Cyrus.

'What's going on?'

'Later, we have to move fast, trust me, where's your passport?'

Cyrus liked the look of the driver's blue eyes. They looked like eyes he could trust.

'Jaamal's backpack,' said Cyrus.

Two men from the parked black Nissan led Cyrus from the van to the front seat of the parked car.

Elias found Cyrus's passport in the backpack before he stowed it in the Nissan's boot. Then he started the Nissan, turned the car onto the road, and pressed his foot hard on the accelerator.

'Stop! What are you doing?' asked Cyrus.

'Changing cars makes us safe.'

'But—'

'I'll protect you with my life,' said Elias.

'Why do I need protecting?'

'We'll have time to talk, now I need to drive.' The needle pointed above one hundred and sixty. Some minutes later, Elias turned onto highway 523, the road followed the eastern side of the Gulf of Suez north towards El Tor, sixty miles distant. He passed a speed camera, it flashed. It was an hour to El Tor and relative safety. Elias glanced at Cyrus, stunned by his youthful looks. Only a little grey was visible in Cyrus's thick black hair.

'Who's Jamaal?' Elias asked as he broke the silence.

'My guide.'

'Does he work with you?'

'For the government.'

'Military?'

'What's going on?' asked Cyrus.

'We organised the conference in Sharm El-Sheikh as a pretext to meet with you.'

'A pretext, who are you?'

'I am here to tell you who you are.'

'I know who I am.'

'Do you know who your biological father was?' asked Elias.

Elias pressed the digital control for the air conditioning, pressed again and felt a cool blast in his face. Then he returned his focus to the road ahead. In front, was a dark, flat bitumen tape in the copper brown dust, and to the right the Sinai mountains were jagged spearheads. The few cars made for rapid driving.

'I'm sorry, this is all so complex, but do you know who your father was?' Elias asked again.

'Of course, where are we going?'

'Cairo.'

'Cairo?'

'Your father was Albert Einstein.'

'You're crazy.'

'There's an envelope under your seat.'

'What?'

'Reach under your seat.'

Cyrus leant forward against his seat belt, his fingers felt, then grasped an envelope.' For the next few minutes, Cyrus had his head down as he read the facial recognition report written by the hacker.

'Compelling analysis,' said Cyrus.

'Sixty-seven years ago, a rabbi and two of his friends travelled from Israel to America. The woman planned to seduce Einstein and carry his child. And then educate this child in the hope that some of civilisations great questions could be solved. One of those two men who travelled from Israel to America was my uncle. We believe a Syrian-based group learnt of this plan and killed the Israeli woman and the rabbi. My uncle died in prison after being convicted of their murders. A Syrian woman then seduced Einstein and gave birth to a son. That son is you.'

'You're kidnapping me?'

'I'm saving you. Powerful people in Israel want you dead.'

'Dead ... why?'

'Einstein was asked to be prime minister of Israel.'

'I didn't know.'

'You're the son of the world's most famous Jew—a potential threat.'

Cyrus was silent for a moment. 'Why trick me to leave Syria?'

'The people in Israel who want you dead could let the Syrian regime know you're Einstein's son.'

'They would ... they would ...' But Cyrus stopped and thought about Hospital 601.

'Israel has agents in Syria, if the Syrian government didn't kill you then an Israeli agent could.'

'Why ... why've you waited so long ... so long to contact me?'

'I've ... we've just found out.'

'We ... who else?' asked Cyrus.

'What family do you have?' Their checking had found none, but Elias wanted to know.

'None ... now.'

'Before?'

'My mama and papa, I had two papas, my first was killed by the army, but you tell me I have a third.'

'What do your friends do?'

'I have none. I've wanted to be left alone.'

'Why?'

'For them.'

'I'm not sure I understand.'

'Trouble finds me,' said Cyrus.

Both sat in silence for several minutes.

'The only evidence is the photographic comparison?'

'We can do a DNA analysis. We can access Einstein's DNA data.'

'I'm not Jewish. My mother was Druze.'

'I consider you Jewish. I'm a Karaite Jew and we hold Judaism can only be transmitted through the father.'

'Usually the mother.'

'You're right. Mainstream believe either the child of a Jewish mother, or a convert to Judaism to be a Jew.' Elias flicked his eyes to the rear-view mirror. The road behind remained clear. 'In the early days, there could be conjecture as to who a child's father was. Of course there was never an argument about the birth mother. With paternity testing available today, historical social dogma has no relevance.'

'Why hit Jamaal?'

'Is he military?'

'A major.'

'Would he let you travel to Cairo?'

'No.' Cyrus knew the major would kill him to stop him going to Cairo.

'Why Cairo?

'We need to get you to safety; after Cairo we'll go to Europe.'

God works in his own way, thought Cyrus. He'd been concerned with the Iranian site visit, concerned they'd find he'd stalled the bioweapons pro-gramme and now there was talk of new life in Europe; a welcome discon-nect from thoughts of suicide.

Elias stared at the road ahead. 'I can't believe you're in your late sixties; you look fifty, less even,' said Elias.

'We have a saying in Arabic, *al'iinsan hu ma yakul*—man is what he eats.'

'We say the same. You take a youth tonic?'

'Careful diet, two litres of water a day, walking, stretches, palates, yoga and I suppose good genes.'

'Whatever you do works.'

Elias drove in silence. Cyrus looked left at the sea. He'd never seen the sea before.

'The Red Sea?'

'Yes, this is the Gulf of Suez.'

'I've never seen the sea before.'

'We'll cross the Gulf in a fishing boat later today.'

After some time Cyrus asked, 'What did you mean, civilisation's great questions?'

'One question my uncle and his two friends sought to answer had special interest.'

'Yes?'

'To prove the existence of God.'

'*Prove!*' Cyrus shook his head and Elias heard him mutter something to himself.

'Is it a question you've ever considered?'

'Is such proof possible? You have an unrealistic expectation.'

'Your father was a creative genius. He observed what others could not.'

'You know, I agree solutions can be found where others haven't looked, but what a question.'

'Assuming such a proof was found.'

'Yes?'

'The implications?'

'The role of religion in society would increase, even dominate.'

'A reason for powerful people wanting you dead.'

'But I have no proof.'

'People in power don't like uncertainty, and they dislike the idea of a higher power even more.'

CHAPTER SIXTEEN

SHARM EL-SHEIKH, EGYPT, 28 JULY 2018

REZNIK GRABBED A large can of Red Bull Zero, from a chiller bag at his feet, and pulled the tab. The can felt cool and damp in his hand. He guzzled, then belched and guzzled some more, then dropped the can into the dash board drink holder. He overtook a car in front and powered towards Sharm El-Sheikh. Reznik's mobile buzzed; a call from his intelligence contact in Tel Aviv.

'Yes?'

'Zaydan is Syrian, head of Syria's bioweapons programme.'

Reznik thought *what the fuck?* then said 'Thanks for the update.'

'You heard that?' The mobile had been on speaker phone.

'Yeah,' said the tail who Elias had jammed in the lift.

'Even more reason to kill him.'

Moments later, Reznik's mobile buzzed again.

'Eidelman's van arrived.'

'And?'

'Three men are here. One is hurt, staggering about, holding his head.

The other two entered the hotel, neither was Eidelman, and too young to be Zaydan.'

'*Frayer!*' cursed Reznik.

'Description of the man hurt?' asked Reznik.

The voice described the Syrian major.

'Zaydan's colleague,' Hadar said as he listened to the description.

'Keep your eyes on him.'

'Right.'

'We're two minutes,' said Reznik. He stopped the call.

'Eidelman and Zaydan have vanished,' said Reznik. 'They must've switched vehicles after leaving the airport.'

'What now?' asked Hadar.

'My guess, Zaydan's colleague is Syrian military,' said Reznik.

'He looked military.'

'We'll kill him, give an eye-witness description of Eidelman and Zaydan to the Egyptian police; get a man hunt going.'

Hadar wasn't so sure, but he kept his thoughts to himself. Killing the Syrian, a probable Syrian army officer, blaming an ex-Israeli special forces' guy and the head of Syria's bioweapons programme. Too many volatile pieces, too hard to control.

○

Elias braked and turned from the black road into a wadi; a dry dusty stream bed cut through the sand and grit and stone. He stopped by a stunted acacia tree, a wild bonsai with a tenacity for life.

'Why've we stopped?' asked Cyrus.

'Change clothes.'

Elias grabbed two traditional *galabeya* robes and *keffiyeh* head scarfs from the car's boot. One *galabeya* was dark blue, the other light blue. He gave Cyrus the light blue, buried their original clothes under a pile of rocks, dusted his hands, and called Tzvi.

'The people following me in Israel are here in the Sinai; all of you need to hide deep.'

'I'll take care of Esther and tell the others.'

'Get a clean mobile, and text me.'

'Okay.'

'I need to go. Talk soon.'

Cyrus stood in the shade of the bonsai acacia and studied the rough fibrous bark and the parched fern-like leaves. He thought about the leaves' constricted leaf pore stomata, and how they squeezed tightly to stop water loss; the low turgor pressure inside the leaf, membrane protein pumps maintaining ion strength and pH. He visualised the eighteen hundred different proteins in the leaves and thought of their molecular evolution. Cyrus silently recited the Druze *Book of Wisdom; We have removed from you your veil and piercing is thy sight this day.*

Cyrus was under the acacia tree, and Elias watched Cyrus gaze open-eyed and move his head from side to side and take several small steps.

'Cyrus?' Elias placed his hand on Cyrus's shoulder. 'Are you okay?'

Cyrus formed *No* in his throat but his mouth remained silent. For the first time in his life, Cyrus had descended into the pico-world; his face in the crowd of pulsing multi-coloured atoms and electrified molecules. Dulcet-coloured molecules with an ultra-high frequency buzzing that he could feel but couldn't hear. Not the spinning and bouncing white lights that had dragged him towards an ether death, but this time heavenly coloured atoms and molecules inviting him into the secrets of their pico-world. Cyrus turned and Elias saw two brown eyes, wide and open and deep—brown eyes looking past Elias to somewhere silent and distant.

'Time to go,' said Elias.

Cyrus blinked and there was a hint of a smile. He felt Elias's hand on his shoulder as they returned to the car.

Elias steered the car from the wadi back onto the bitumen road.

A short time later, they passed a green road sign—*El Tor 10 km* and Elias spoke. 'Ten minutes and we'll be in El Tor.'

Elias's thoughts shifted to the fisherman and his boat. They were late, but then this was Egypt, at least they were only an hour late and not a day late.

The intermittent date palms on the side of the road cast thin shadows from the high sun and drifts of red-brown sand from a recent sandstorm lay at the base of their trunks.

'Every date palm in Sinai will be owned by someone,' said Cyrus.

'Handed down to family members over maybe two hundred years.'

'The same in Syria?'

'The same.'

Ahead Elias spotted something. He picked up the binoculars from the dashboard and stared at the road. Two men with rifles over their shoulders leant against an oil drum painted with red, white and black stripes. In the middle of the road were red cones and black steel barriers.

'A police checkpoint. Let me do the talking.' Elias braked as they approached, then slowed the Nissan to a stop. A few steps in front of the car, a policeman who wore a dark uniform, black cap and sunglasses raised his palm. Elias lowered the driver's window and handed the policeman both passports.

He studied the passport photos then bent to stare at Elias and Cyrus. He nodded then scanned the passports with a portable scanner.

'Where are you driving to?'

'Port Said,' replied Elias.

'Where are you from?'

'We're engineers. What better place to learn about waterway engineering.'

'Pull over.' The policeman pointed to the side of the road.

'Why?'

'Road's closed.'

'Closed?'

'The army is taking over the checkpoint.' The policeman waved his hand and pointed behind the car. Elias turned and saw a distant dust cloud on a side road. He knew there was strong security collaboration between Israel and Egypt in the Sinai. Was there a chance Israel had asked the Egyptian Army to intercept them? It was not an option to wait and find out.

'Has Allah blessed you with children?' asked Elias.

'Two boys,' replied the policeman.

'Buy them a surprise gift.' Elias stretched out his hand with several hundred Egyptian pounds. The policeman's obsidian eyes blinked then blinked again.

'We need to go to Port Said,' said Elias.

'You need to pull over.'

'We don't have time. Our passports please,' said Elias. The dust cloud was closer.

The policeman took two steps back, and slipped the passports into his tunic breast pocket. 'He has children too,' the policeman said as he waved at his mate.

'Allah has blessed him too,' said Elias.

'You talk of Allah, but you are a Jew. He tapped his tunic breast pocket containing the two passports.

'We all come from Abraham,' said Elias. 'My Syrian friend is not a Jew, but he's my brother.' Cyrus smiled.

Elias stretched out his hand with more Egyptian pounds. The policeman stepped forward, grinned and grasped the wad. He pulled the two passports from his pocket and handed them over. Elias looked behind their car. Sand coloured army jeeps were on the sealed road a quarter mile behind.

'The barrier please,' said Elias.

The two cops talked; one pointed at the jeeps.

Cyrus looked over his shoulder. 'They are coming close.'

Elias leant his head out the window. 'The barrier please.' The cops continued to talk. Elias pulled his head back inside the car, jammed the car into gear and turned the steering wheel. The Nissan's front bumper knocked over a red traffic cone as he curved around the low barrier pole, onto the desert grit and then swung back onto the bitumen. Back on the right side of the road, Elias accelerated and was soon clear of the barrier and the sandy army jeeps. Ahead in the far distance, Elias pointed out El-Tor Mountain, where Moses received God's Ten Commandments. Closer, they could see the El-Tor water tower and the towering twin minarets of a mosque. A few minutes later they entered El Tor and Elias turned away from the coast onto a road that ran to the right, where they drove past a row of derelict buildings. At an intersection his eyes shot around, then he turned right along a deserted paved street, slammed the black Nissan to a stop, ripped open a loose gate then parked out of sight behind a run-down building. To his right, through the rough angles of a derelict building, he could see the entrance of the harbour with glistening white boats moored at a new marina. At the southern end fishing boats lay at anchor.

'We'll stay here for a bit,' said Elias. He looked at his watch. The fisherman could wait.

They stayed out of sight for four hours. Cyrus dozed.

'We'll go now,' said Elias. 'Walk ten paces behind me.'

'Why?' asked Cyrus.

'In case the army is looking for two people.'

They had to leave the old city and walk a few hundred metres on the main road to get to the harbour. A sand-coloured army Ute and a sand-coloured jeep passed by. The rear red brake lights on the jeep flashed. The jeep stopped. Elias continued past the jeep and the driver called out. Cyrus was close to the jeep

'A black car?' said the jeep driver to Cyrus.

'I'm sorry?' said Cyrus.

'A black car … have you seen a black car?'

'I've been at our mosque; Glory to Allah,' replied Cyrus. He turned and moved his arm towards the twin minarets.

'Glory to Allah,' said the jeep driver. The jeep drove away in the direction of the harbour.

'The fishing boats,' said Elias as he led Cyrus to the southern end of the harbour and onto a stretch of beach. The fishing boats were of identical design with high flared bows and flat decks with a single mast that carried a lateen sail—the decks were covered with an array of ropes, nets and coloured buoys. All the hulls were teal with an eye the size of a dinner plate painted either side of the bow. Arabic names on the hulls conferred uniqueness.

The distant sound of a police siren caused Elias to look towards El Tor. Three sets of flashing blue lights dashed from the town to the port.

Elias called out *Sahar* to a man moving on the deck of one of the fishing boats. The man pointed towards a group of three boats anchored together further down the bay. Moving faster than Cyrus, Elias ran along the foreshore to where the three boats lay at anchor. A dog appeared from nowhere and barked and snapped. Elias stopped, picked up a broken buoy on the high-tide line and threw it at the dog and hit its back. The dog yelped, backed up, but then more dogs rushed out at him. Elias threw a stick that hit another dog and the dogs stopped. Elias ran on until he was opposite the three boats with their bows pointing towards the shore and called out the name *Sahar*. There was no reply. He called *Sahar* again. The engine of one fishing boat coughed into life. A man appeared on the deck and waved towards the shore. Cyrus surprised Elias when moments later he arrived at his side. He was breathing heavily.

'He wants us to wade out. Are you safe in the water?' asked Elias.

'I can swim.' They stepped into the sea. Cyrus felt the cool water rise and it was above his waist by the time he reached the boat. Elias gave Cyrus a lift from behind and the fisherman took a firm hold of Cyrus's arms and hauled. On board, Cyrus thanked the smiling fisherman who wore a black beanie, and a well-worn jacket with a high collar to keep out the spray and the wind. The smiling fisherman had a thin grey beard that extended under his chin and a weather-beaten face, beaten into a perpetual smile with the pleasure of living on the sea. Moments later, Elias too stood on deck and looked at police lights that flashed in the port car park. The fisherman followed Elias's gaze.

'I don't want trouble with police.'

'Maybe they've caught a gun smuggler,' said Elias. He pulled off his backpack and held it up. 'Maybe they think I have rifles hidden in here.' All three men chuckled.

'Need help to get underway?' asked Elias. The fisherman waved his hand towards the foredeck.

'Find somewhere to sit and be careful of the nets.' The fisherman engaged a winch and with a grinding sound the bow anchor lifted then the boat reversed into deeper water.

A police car raced along the breakwater to the harbour entrance. 'Quick, inside the cabin,' said Elias. When the two entered the wheelhouse, the fisherman said they'd be fine on deck; the boat wouldn't start to roll for some time.

'Don't want to give the police an excuse to stop your boat,' said Elias as he pointed to the police car with flashing lights. The fisherman scrutinised the two men. Nothing about them suggested trouble and he'd been paid well.

'Sit on the floor,' said the fisherman. He steered the boat towards the harbour entrance, and passed closer to the police than he needed to.

Smart man, thought Elias.

'Across the Gulf to Ras Ghareb?' asked the fisherman.

'Yes, Ras Ghareb.' It was as Elias had organised with the fisherman two days earlier.

The fisherman looked at the blue police lights that flashed and then at the two men who sat on the floor of the wheel-house. 'We may get stopped by the Gulf boat police, we may not.'

'If we're stopped, can you say we are friends of yours from El Tor, Going to a funeral in Ras Ghareb.'

'Why?'

Elias reached into his pocket and held out two hundred US dollar notes.

'Alright. A funeral in Ras Ghareb.'

Free of the harbour, a brisk wind blew from southern Egypt towards the Suez Canal in the north. Outside on the deck, Cyrus watched a number of kite boarders, with multi-coloured crescent sails race across the white chop, then trim their sails before they were lifted into the air where they flipped and spun.

'What's that called?' asked Cyrus.

'Kite boarding,' replied Elias.

'Looks dangerous.'

'They're experts.'

Away from the harbour, larger waves hit the boat on the port side, the boat pitched and rolled and a rinse of salt water sprayed across the deck.

Cyrus sat against a pile of nets away from the spray on the starboard side. Terns beat their wings as they danced and flicked on the surface. The terns snatched bait fish then caught by the wind left the surface in a slant. Above, a brown booby soared. It spotted a fish, folded its wings and led with its conical beak into a Stuka dive. With wings folded close, the booby hit the water like a high-speed torpedo then surfaced with a silver shimmer in its beak. With a shake of the head the shimmer was gone.

○

'There's going to be a moon tonight,' said the fisherman as he looked back towards the shore. Elias looked too and saw light on the clouds above the jagged Sinai mountains. The bow of the boat pitched, rolled to port then shuddered as the bow punched into the bottom of the wave.

'Your friend's going to get wet if he stays outside.'

'Do you have a wet-weather jacket?'

The fisherman took a yellow jacket that hung from a hook and handed it to Elias. Elias steadied himself on the deck with his feet wide apart. Cyrus was vomiting.

'You okay?'

'Action-packed day.'

'Do you want to come into the wheel-house?'

'I'm better here.'

'The spray.' Elias handed Cyrus the yellow jacket before he returned to the wheel-house. With his arms out stretched Elias took short staggered steps.

On the foredeck, Cyrus welcomed being in the fresh air and welcomed the spray, but he also welcomed being alone. *Einstein's son.* He lay sprawled on the deck and gazed at the fishing net feeling a new confidence in the relative light.

'How's your friend?'

'Not so good,' said Elias. 'Do you have tissues?'

'There,' said the fisherman as he pointed to a roll of toilet paper on a wheel-house shelf. The fisherman then glanced at his navigation screen before he renewed his stare into the gloom.

Elias ripped off two arm's lengths of toilet paper and took them to Cyrus.

Once he was back in the wheel-house, Elias asked how long the trip would take.

'Maybe three hours.'

The fisherman picked up a crumpled brown paper bag. 'Do you want a *hawawshi?*'

'Be great, thank you.'

'Your friend should have one, and sweet tea, he'll feel better.' The fisherman passed the brown paper bag to Elias. He took the bag and stepped from the wheelhouse onto the deck.

'The fisherman gave me a *hawawshi.* Do you want one?' asked Elias.

'Yes, thank you, hope I can keep it down.'

Elias unwrapped the pita stuffed with minced beef and spices and handed it to Cyrus.

'You should dink sweet tea.'

'Okay.'

The fisherman lit his gas cooker. The flames glinted on the metal consol dials. Elias tipped a spoon of black tea into a mug, added boiling water then sugar. The boat rolled from side to side, and Elias anticipated the roll movement as he tried to keep Cyrus's tea level. He handed Cyrus a cup two-thirds full. Elias then made tea for himself and the fisherman. They drank the tea as they ate *hawawshi*. As Elias reflected on events, he thought those who chased wouldn't try to follow their tracks; they'd leap-frog ahead, leap-frog to Cairo. The options after they got to El Minya on the Nile were through the desert to Cairo, by road to Cairo or Cairo via the Nile. Each had advantages. Each had disadvantages. Or should they head south, away from Cairo, into the heart of Egypt. If he ran alone the heart of Egypt would be a real option—but Cyrus was sixty-eight years old.

CHAPTER SEVENTEEN

SHARM EL-SHEIKH, EGYPT 28 JULY, 2018

REZNIK SQUEEZED THE trigger. The Syrian slumped; dead before he hit the ground. He could blindside the Shin Bet, let them find out when the shit-storm struck. But it cost him nothing to give the non-descript man a heads up. May even help. He needed to cut into Eidelman's lead then cut into Eidelman. He used the burner.

'Yes?' The non-descript man answered.

'Einstein's son is Cyrus Zaydan, head of Syria's bioweapons programme. Zaydan travelled to Sharm El-Sheikh with a Syrian army major, the major's been shot and killed. Eidelman and Zaydan have been identified as suspects.'

'Location of Eidelman and Zaydan?'

'Don't know, speculate heading to Cairo.'

'Who killed the Syrian?'

'What?'

'Who killed the Syrian?' He ground his teeth hard.

Reznik bent down and hit the burner phone on the concrete. 'Breaking …

breaking up … can't hear …' Reznik ended the call and turned off the burner. He'd given the Shin Bet the heads up they needed.

The ice machine hummed and clunked and cubes dropped into Agmon's empty glass. He poured mineral water into the glass and the bubbles fizzed against the ice. As he took a cold gulp, the director of Isreal's internal security agency stood beside the blue and white Israeli flag and the blue and white Shin Bet flag and gazed from his top floor office over Park Hayarkon in Northern Tel Aviv. Agmon wore an open-necked white shirt and looked to be in his sixties; although Agmon had sparse streaks of grey hair, the heavy bags under his eyes and deep fold lines that ran from the side of his nose to the edge of his rigid mouth revealed his age. Below his mouth was a square dimpled chin. Agmon got where he was because he had outsmarted the others, a self-selection process. If you're smart enough to get the job as head of Shin Bet, you're smart enough to do it, but Agmon wanted more, he wanted to be the next prime minister. To be prime minister, Agmon needed a political environment he could manipulate. Einstein's son could be sand in the gears of his manipulation strategy. Two thousand years had passed since a Jewish prophet had threatened Pilate's Judaea. An Einstein prophet, even a false prophet, could reach pre-eminence in Israel, change the fabric of political conflict and social control, and derail his strategy to rule the Knesset.

The non-descript man called his boss, Agmon.

'Einstein's son, a Professor Cyrus Zaydan, arrived at Sharm El-Shekh from Syria a few hours ago. He heads Syria's bioweapons programme.' *I know his name thought* Agmon. 'Zaydan had a Syrian army major as an escort, the major has been shot, killed. Zaydan and Eidelman are on the run.'

'Who shot the major?'

'My guess Reznik.'

'Fuck.'

'Reznik said Eidelman and Zaydan are the suspects.'

'Killed to recruit the Egyptian police.'

'Exactly.'

'Fuck. Call Reznik off.' Agmon could see this getting further out of hand fast.

At the Mossad's headquarters, five miles to the north in Herzliya, Yossi

Cohen the director of Israel's external security, Mossad, took a call from the director of Egypt's GID, Abbas Kamel.

'Greetings, Ahmad,' said the Mossad director.

'Hello, Yossi,'

'How's Layla, and the rest of your family?' The Mossad director consulted his notes to make sure he had his counter-part's wife's name correct.

'We're all well, thank you, and Aya and your family?'

'They're well. A coincidence you should call, at breakfast this morning my family were discussing a visit to the upper Nile.'

'You must, let me know when and we'll host you.'

'A very generous offer, thank you,' said Cohen.

'We have an issue, the reason for my call.' It was an unwritten rule that neither side would embarrass the other regarding spies or diplomatic *faux pas*.

'Yes?'

'A Syrian army major was shot and killed in Sharm El-Sheikh this afternoon. Two suspects, an Israeli, Elias Eidelman and a Syrian army captain, Cyrus Zaydan. Zaydan is head of Syria's bioweapons programme. Eidelman and Zaydan have disappeared.'

'Appreciate the background. Sounds complicated and serious. I'll brief the PM. Can you send me all the intel you have, I'll see what we have on Eidelman?'

'President El-Sisi has been informed because foreign nationals are involved plus the bioweapons angle.'

'Understand. Have you called Syria?'

'I'll call Syria next.'

'Press?'

'Blackout.'

'Good, suggest we work together. Find out what's going on before any press.'

'Agree.'

'Keep an open line on this for our updates.'

The call ended and Cohen called his colleague at the Shin Bet, Nadav Agmon.

'*Shalom,* Nadav.'

'*Shalom,* Yossi, how are you?' Agmon's fingers were in a fist.

'Abbas Kamel called. One of our citizens, Elias Eidelman is associated with a killing in Sharm-El Sheikh, will send you what we have.'

'Who was killed?'

'A Syrian major.'

'Press?'

'With Egypt, Syria and us involved, a matter of time. Cyrus Zaydan, head of Syria's bioweapons programme is apparently also involved with Eidelman.

'He was shot too?' asked Agmon.

'No, he's also a suspect in the killing.'

'The PM needs briefing,' said Agmon. He expected Cohen to have done so.

'The PM knows there's an issue. We need the details.'

O

Cohen gave his Mossad two hours to find what they could on Eidelman, military service history, work history, address, mobile number, vehicle movements. The Shin Bet would be hunting too; there was no harm in overlap.

Cohen's head of the case file, called the Israeli company TOKA, the IT intelligence company founded by ex-PM, Eduard Barak and funded by Mossad's venture capital. TOKA provided the previous two months GPS history of Elias's Ducati and SUV. An address where the Ducati had been geostationary a number of times was flagged for review.

O

When Isaac's doorbell rang, he strolled to his front door, pulled the door open and saw two middle aged men.

'Isaac Bereksohn?'

'Yes.'

'We're from the Mossad.' The two men showed their IDs. 'We need to talk.'

'Do you know Elias Eidelman?' one of the men asked once they were seated inside.

'Yes.'

'In what capacity?'

Isaac described their circumstance.

'You're convinced Professor Zaydan is Einstein's son?'

'Yes … what's this about … why are Mossad involved?'

'Who else knows you suspect Zaydan to be Einstein's son?'

'More than suspect.'

'Who else?'

'Elias's partner, Esther, his cousin, Tzvi and Chris, an IT guy.'

'You have their contact details?'

'Yes.'

'We'll need them … no one else?'

'No … well yes … Mendel, an academic in the Archaeology Department at Tel Aviv University.'

'How's Mendel involved?'

Isaac gave the backstory … all the backstory, including how he set a trap for Mendel.

◯

Two hours later, Cohen chewed on a protein bar in his office and tried to make sense of the intel summary provided by his agents. Key points stuck. Eidelman was ex-Unit, and Zaydan appeared to be Einstein's son. Mossad intel suggested Zaydan was hampering biowarfare development in Syria. The assassinated Syrian was an army major in military intelligence. And Dr Mendel from Tel Aviv University had alerted Shin Bet.

Cohen called Agmon.

'*Shalom*, Nadav.' Cohen paused.

'*Shalom,* Yossi.'

'My friend, we need to meet; this Syrian major's killing has become complex,' said Cohen.

'I can meet now,' said Agmon. 'I'll come to your office.'

'Suits well. See you soon.' Agmon's driver drove the fifteen minutes to the Mossad headquarters.

◯

Agmon sat in Cohen's office. At forty-five, Cohen was young to be head of Mossad. Cohen had narrow eyes, under a heavy forehead. He was clean shaven and had his hair cut every week so every day he looked the same with his steel aura. His only vulnerability was when sparring with other Aikido black belts, but even that was controlled.

'You should have discussed this with me,' said Cohen.

'Some decisions need individual accountability. I made a call,' said Agmon.

'What do you know of Zaydan?'

'An illegitimate son, we think a Muslim group based in Syria orchestrated the pregnancy, chaperoned his education.'

'Why?'

'Not sure, seems an Israel group, ex-Shin Bet people had the initial plan with Einstein almost seventy years ago; we believe the Syrians killed them, and copied their plan.'

'Einstein plan?'

'The Israelis hoped Einstein's child could prove God's existence.'

Cohen flash-thought endless ramifications. 'And?'

'We need to pre-empt Zaydan getting anywhere near a proof; you appreciate the gravity if Zaydan's successful.'

'You have a strategy?' Cohen asked.

'I'll give you some names, Martin Luther King, Rasputin, Anwar Sadat, Jesus Christ, and likely Mohammed.'

'You tried to kill him?'

'We block any extremist influence on our society.'

'Have you tried to kill him?' asked Cohen as he eyeballed Agmon.

Agmon remained silent.

'You have tried to kill him.' Cohen answered his own question. 'How could you fail against an academic?'

'Eidelman's resourceful,' said Agmon.

'Our fault, we train them too well,' replied Cohen.

Agmon gave a smug smile and Cohen continued.

'Erasing Zaydan will be more difficult now you've tried and failed.'

'Which is why we're talking,' said Agmon.

'Where's Zaydan now?'

'Somewhere between the Sinai and Cairo.'

'Did Eidelman kill the Syrian major?'

'Don't think so.'

'Then who?'

'My guy who's been chasing Zaydan.'

'Right, right—not ideal, is it?'

'Ah … no.'

'Where's your guy?'

'He's gone dark.'

'Want us to find him?'

'Yeah,' said Agmon.

'Find him, bring him back?'

'Find him,' said Agmon.

'The Egyptians want an Interpol arrest warrant.'

'One way to clear this up.'

'I'll sign off a red notice on Eidelman and Zaydan,' said Cohen referring to the Interpol arrest warrant.

'You read the Egyptian report?'

'They passed through an El-Tor checkpoint this afternoon.'

'Driving to Port Said or crossing the Gulf?'

'Or heading deep into the Sinai or doubling back,' said Cohen.

'They'll travel through the night.'

'There are checkpoints on the roads around the Gulf.'

'On the Gulf?' asked Agmon.

'Coastguard and police are checking small craft, unless we're lucky, little we can do to stop Eidelman getting to Cairo. I'll activate a Cairo team,' said Cohen

'The PM?'

'I'll cover for you, but you know the bottom line.'

'Thanks Yossi, can't ask for more.'

O

Hadar punched his mobile and spoke to Cairo's leading newspaper, *Al Ahram* newsroom. Knowing the call would be recorded, Reznik didn't want his voice on tape. Within twelve hours, photos of Eidelman and Zaydan would be all over Egypt as criminals wanted for killing a Syrian army officer.

T HE SWEET TEA and *hawawshi* settled Cyrus; he leant with his back against the wheelhouse and looked behind the stern; the moon was higher and made the wake a moon-stream dance. In the wheelhouse two cigars glowed in the dark.

A couple of hours later, Cyrus heard the pitch of the diesel engine change and felt the deck vibrate as the fishing boat left the open waters of the Gulf and entered the port of Ras Ghareb at five knots. The fisherman steered his boat around the harbour as he searched for a drop-off point then focused on a jetty with poor lighting. Elias stood on the foredeck, dropped a buffer between the boat and the jetty, then stepped across the gap. Cyrus passed Elias their backpacks, and Elias held Cyrus's arm to help him across.

'Lucky we've got a moon,' said Cyrus as he altered his gait to step over a broken jetty plank as they headed for shore. On shore they made their way to the main port entrance gate where their pick-up waited. Elias had called ahead to say they had been delayed. Behind them the fisherman headed out of the port and waited. Elias had paid him to wait another day, to wait for him and Cyrus to return to the port, and then cross the gulf with the fisherman back to El Tor. A journey Elias knew they would not take, but it was another day that the fisherman was unable to talk to anyone.

The next morning, in the early light, Elias stepped from the house onto the veranda. The house was built of brown desert plaster; everything everywhere was desert brown. A twist of charcoal smoke rose a few steps from the veranda. Behind the smoke twist, a grey-veiled Bedouin woman rolled pita dough with a smooth wooden stick then hand tossed the pita into a thin disc. She then slung the thin dough disc onto a convex hotplate. The smile she flashed was broad. Elias raised a palm and returned her smile as he heard footsteps behind him—Cyrus. Their eyes said good morning.

'My favourite smell to start the day,' said Cyrus in Arabic.

'Stays with you for life,' replied the Bedouin woman. She flipped the shrunk pita disc with bare fingers.

'Takes me back to my mother baking,' said Cyrus.

'Where were you?' she asked as she folded the brown charred pita into a cane basket. An iPhone sat on the seat beside her.

'Damascus,' replied Cyrus.

Elias nudged Cyrus and gave him the slightest shake of his head.

'I didn't know you were from Syria,' she said. A few paces behind the Bedouin woman and her flashing jewellery, a buggy guide, a small man, strapped containers with food, water and fuel onto the red buggies. There were three dune buggies under a roof.

'Let's check out our buggies,' said Elias. From where he stood, Elias could see the buggies had large shock absorbers with coiled red springs.

Cyrus and Elias stepped down from the veranda and crossed the desert grit courtyard to where the buggies were parked on a desert-brown cement floor. Timber poles held up the roof.

Cyrus leant close to Elias's ear. 'I'm sorry, I forgot.'

Honest men don't disguise truth with ease.

'Good morning,' the guide said. 'I'm Malik.' He wore a white turban and grey *galabeya*. The desert owned his face.

'Hello,' said Elias.

'We need water, the buggies can overheat. And spare fuel to be safe.' Malik tightened a strap on a water container.

'How many miles to the gallon?' asked Elias.

'Twenty.'

'El Minya is one hundred and twenty miles from here, isn't it?' asked Elias. The guide nodded.

Cyrus counted three khaki five-gallon jerry cans; they wouldn't be running out of fuel. Each buggy had a spare tyre strapped to the open roof cage.

After eating breakfast, with freshly made pita, Cyrus and Elias put on full-face helmets.

'My chin strap,' said Cyrus, his fingers fumbled.

'Sure,' said Elias.

With his strap secure, Cyrus wrapped his blue and white scarf around his neck. The guide wanted Elias as a passenger in one buggy and Cyrus in another, but Elias insisted he drive the buggy that carried himself and Cyrus.

'Have you driven a buggy before?' the guide asked.

'Yes,' said Elias. The correct answer was *no,* but he'd driven a motorcycle for years; two wheels were more of a challenge than four, thought Elias, and as Cyrus's bodyguard, Elias wanted him close.

'Follow to one side, up wind, less dust,' said the guide.

Once they sat in the buggy they clipped on padded seat belts. Elias started the buggy; it barked and sputtered then ran smoothly. He scanned the fuel and temperature gauges and the speed and rev dials, engaged automatic drive then followed the lead buggy off to one side. The ribbed tyres lifted brown dust that hung in the air behind for a quarter of a mile. The desert was the same on both sides. Up to the horizon was brown sand grit. Everything that wasn't brown seemed covered in it; the leafless markh trees with bare brown branches and slender brown twigs and a lone brown acacia.

After an hour of brown dust, the guide's buggy climbed a dune then dropped out of sight. Elias followed to the top of the dune; the left front wheel of his buggy dug into a patch of soft sand and the buggy tilted left sharply on its shocks.

'No!' Cyrus shouted. The buggy levelled and Elias gave a thumbs up. Cyrus smiled and raised a thumb. The buggy ahead veered into a wadi, one of the many valleys seaming from the high mountain ridge. Elias followed. Behind him was the other red buggy with two guides. One would drive Elias's buggy on the return journey. There was more life in the wadi; in heavy rain it would be a riverbed. The front guide stopped his buggy and pointed to two Nubian ibexes. The male with huge curving horns, sat in a rock pit looking down then ran up the near sheer rock face. The female ibex followed.

'See the ibex?' asked Elias.

'Yes,' said Cyrus. 'I think our guide would see a beetle move.'

A mile into the wadi, the lead buggy stopped again. Elias pulled in close and the third buggy stopped too.

'All okay?' asked Elias.

'Yes thanks.' Cyrus unclipped his helmet, pulled off his goggles and sneezed.

Elias opened Cyrus's door. 'Need a hand?'

'I'm okay.' Cyrus's ears were ringing.

'The seats are low,' said Elias.

'It's not easy.' He held Cyrus's hand and pulled him up.

'Thank you.'

After Cyrus lifted his legs out of the buggy, he took a few cautious steps.

'All okay?' asked Elias again.

'I need to walk after getting bounced around.'

'Good for you, you're doing great, pretty much twice my age, going non-stop for two days.'

Two days, thought Cyrus; he had no idea you could cram so much living into two days. He was exhausted, but ten times more exhilarated than the days in Damascus, and he knew the exhilaration had just begun.

'No chance of a police checkpoint,' said Elias with a smile. This was the reason for their traverse through the eastern desert to El Minya, the city a day's river travel upstream from Cairo. At the Nile they would be almost safe, one step from Cairo. The guide unrolled a fabric sheet, tied guy ropes to the buggies and propped up the middle of the sheet with a pole to craft a shade.

Cyrus sat in the shade, his back against a buggy wheel. He felt cooler.

Elias headed behind a rock pile and a few moments later returned to the shade as he bent his head under a guy rope.

The guides boiled water for tea.

'Normal or spicy tea?' asked Malik.

'Spice please,' said Cyrus.

'We call our tea Bedouin whiskey; its strong and very sweet,' said Malik.

Malik added cardamom pods to a litre of water and then a full tea glass of sugar, and when the water boiled, he added dried loose black tea.

Cyrus swivelled his head and looked up and down the dusty track and up at the sky where there was a single white cloud, and then he looked at the shadow the cloud threw against the warm and bright golden brown rocky hills. He thought of the tea glass of sugar added to the water, the sugar would dissolve, diffuse, with equilibrium reached when the sugar molecules were as far away from each other as possible. Life didn't evolve in water, thought Cyrus, in water the life-giving molecules would be too far away from each other—he ran through a mental check list of exactly what was needed for life to evolve.

As he drank the sweet and spicy cardamom-flavoured tea, Cyrus sat heavily in the sand as he continued to lean against a rear buggy wheel with his head tilted forward with his blue and white *keffiyeh* now hanging loose over his head. He picked up a handful of sand and gazed from under the *keffiyeh* at the release of grains in a slow hour-glass stream. He thought there were ten billion times more molecules in a single cell than sand grains in his fist. Molecules, he thought, a lifetime he'd spent with molecules, a feigned interest in molecules as his heart lay in the arts. He knew he was a true romantic with a capital 'R', he needed no one or needed nothing to feel free or was that his second-level conscious talking. He'd spent much time in his second conscious level; he'd observed others interact with his living lie. He now knew it began when he was four. He'd painted on a smile the day after Talal's stoning because he had hidden the secret of Papa telling them to *take the other one.* Cyrus knew it taught him to live two lives, one without and one within, and it was the life within that carried the most intrigue—the most surprise—the most fulfilment. An infinite journey with unlimited signposts, signposts carrying no writing and therefore offering no direction while inviting misdirection. No signpost pointed this way to Utopia or that way to Camelot and there was no danger signpost for dystopia. As a solution to this signpost challenge, Cyrus had found a way to go on multiple simultaneous mental journeys and found it a paradox that he travelled faster when on two journeys and faster still when on ten. As each sand grain fell, Cyrus accelerated towards an unseen light; it was odd, the strongest light he'd ever seen, but it had no light. He knocked on a thousand doors and when one opened there were a thousand more. He knocked on one of the thousand and it opened immediately. He was back in the pico-world and had a stunning idea.

'We're moving again,' Elias said as he touched Cyrus's shoulder.

Cyrus stirred and pushed his *keffiyeh* back from his face. 'I've been asleep.' He rubbed his eyes with the back of his hand; they felt sandy and heavy and he wondered if he really had been asleep. He'd been thinking about molecules and cells; it seemed all too vivid, too clear to have been a dream.

Behind him he heard the rasping sputter of a dune buggy.

'Ready to go?' asked Elias.

'Yes.'

'Riding okay?'

'It's bumpy.'

'Move with the buggy. No need to grip tightly, your seat belt will hold you.

'Too many years of city living,' said Cyrus.

They drove for ninety minutes and stopped for lunch in another wadi. Once again, the guides set the shade cloth.

'Come, we'll get fresh fruit,' Malik said to Elias. Elias followed Malik from the buggies. A narrow passage cut away from the main wadi. They navigated along the cut, the small guide's eyes roving on the rocks with such intimacy it seemed he could hear the rocks breathe life.

'Up there,' said the guide pointing to a hawthorn bush with its red berries. Elias reached up, tugged the rock face and tested the hand-hold. After climbing two steps he was level with the red berries and wedged in tight. The hawthorn berries hung like cherries. Elias pulled maybe fifty berries free and with the red berries in a bag slung over his arm, he inched down. Malik had collected yellow fruit and plant stalks.

Underneath the shade cloth, the guide used his traditional *shibriya* knife, to cut open the plant stalks and scoop out the moist flesh with the knife tip. Next, he cut the sweet yellow caper fruit that he said was called *lassaf*. The other guide sat on the rug, stirring the pot on the portable gas cooker.

'Smells great,' Elias said.

'*Zarb*,' said the guide stirring the food with a wooden spoon.

'*Zarb*?' asked Elias.

'We cooked it first at the house in the *Zarb* earth oven—goat, chicken, vegetables and spices.'

Like *cholent* in Israel, thought Elias, every culture has their own version of stew.

'Halfway?' asked Elias.

'Over half now,' said the guide. 'What do you think of the desert?'

'It's all the same, but it's all different,' replied Elias.

The guide beamed; the desert was his living room. 'Sit down,' he said. 'Want to eat?'

'My friend,' said Elias. He moved towards Cyrus who was once again sitting against a buggy wheel.

'Stew and pita,' said Elias. 'And fresh fruit.'

'Now?'

'Yes.'

They returned to the mat, sat down and made sure their heels and soles did not point to anyone else. The guide spooned the Bedouin stew from the pot on the cooker onto five tin plates and opened the cloth wrapped pita, made by the Bedouin woman with the flashing jewellery. The guide passed the first plate to Cyrus because he was the eldest. Cyrus tore a piece of pita bread and dipped it into the stew. The sauce gave the pita a rich savoury meat flavour.

Elias spooned yellow *lassaf* onto his plate.

'First time?' asked the guide next to him.

'Yes,' said Elias.

'Swallow, don't bite. The capers are bitter.'

Elias swallowed. It tasted sweet.

The guides repacked the buggies after the lunch stop and the dusty journey continued.

Sometime later, the front buggy stopped, Malik jumped out and called to Elias.

'We go up and over a pass now. It's tricky at the top.'

Elias raised his thumb.

They climbed slowly; the track was rough with fist-sized rocks. At the top, Elias stopped and he observed the buggy in front. Malik undid his seat harness, pointed the buggy uphill, and traversed a rocky scree with a side-drift much like a plane crabs through the air in a cross-wind. Elias knew the guide undid his seat harness in case he needed to jump.

'We'll walk across,' said Elias.

'Safer,' replied Cyrus.

'No need to use any luck, either good or bad,' added Elias.

Once the lead buggy was across the scree, Malik stopped and got out

'We'll walk,' Elias called out. 'Take our buggy.' Elias linked his arm with Cyrus and they trod across the shingle scree. Cyrus looked down the mountain; if the buggy slipped it would not be retrieved. With a wide smile, the guide raced Elias's buggy across the scree. The ribbed tyres bit into the grit and sprayed dust as the buggy tilted and crabbed on an angle. The third buggy followed.

Downhill, the track was easy going and they were soon down and driving at speed in the desert. After another short stop for mint tea and snacks they arrived on the outskirts of El Minya. The sun was midway in the afternoon sky as they looked down on the grey-blue Nile with its fringe of irrigated green—rice, corn and sugar cane. The dust covered desert buggies dropped down from the red-brown desert onto a sand-blown road. Litter, mostly paper and plastic, edged the road. Below, absorbing the sun's heat, were thousands of mud domes; each dome covering a tomb. Cyrus looked to his right then his left. The domes were jammed together and stretched for miles into the desert haze; a necropolis of white half-circles—the city of the dead—Zawyet el-Maiyitin, one of the largest cemeteries in the world, a sea of dead bodies without souls, each soul released at death after higher or self-judgement.

The six-hour desert trek had provided Elias time to form a plan. He knew the security arm of Israel had reach to turn over any rock in the Middle East, but with twenty million people in metropolitan Cairo there were lots of rocks under which to hide.

Elias turned the buggy from the sand-blown road onto a track leading into the cemetery, then stopped. 'We'll get an Uber from here.'

'Incredible cemetery; I've seen nothing like this,' said Cyrus.

'Great courage today; I'm sorry it's not been easy,' said Elias.

The other two buggies pulled up alongside. Elias opened the door and grabbed his backpack.

'You stopping here?' asked Malik.

'We'll take a walk through the cemetery then head to Luxor, thank you it was a fun trek.' said Elias.

'Thank you, an exciting time, great food, go in peace,' said Cyrus. He stretched his arms high and arched his back.

'In God's protection, stay safe with your travels,' said Malik.

'Luxor? I thought Cairo,' said Cyrus above the sound of the departing buggies.

'A deception.'

'We go to Cairo?'

'Yes … to Cairo.'

'The Nile?'

'A riverboat.'

'Can we walk for a bit, loosen up?' asked Cyrus.

They walked along the dusty track into the domed cemetery.

'Tell me about your parents,' said Cyrus.

Elias told Cyrus he was an only child, both parents nurtured his heart and brain. His father was an electrician and his mother taught early school.

'I realise now, my father used psychology to motivate me.'

'My father wasn't subtle in his motivation. I'm not complaining; he was motivated to do his best by me,' Cyrus said.

'Company,' said Elias as he glanced down a side path. A group of youths wearing jeans, watches on their wrists and gold chains swaggered close.

'This is our place,' one of them said. They asked for money and the youth talking pulled a knife from under his striped T-shirt. He shifted his weight from one foot to the other and called on his friends to pick up rocks.

Elias focused on the knife, then stepped to put himself between the knife and Cyrus.

'Your watch, old man,' said the youth who wore a low-cut black and white striped T-shirt with rolled-up jeans. All the youths had rolled-up jeans blanched by cemetery dust. Some looked as if they worked with stone, or pressed weights; their muscles bulged.

'You shame yourself, you shame your parents, you shame Allah,' said Cyrus.

'Stone them,' said the youth holding the knife. One youth threw a heavy stone. *Ayreh feek!*' he yelled. Cyrus shuffled against a domed tomb with his arms at his sides. The rock curved towards his face. He lifted his chin and accepted the strike. A glove challenge. The rock tore the skin below his eye. Blood flowed.

'Red face old man.'

With gentle fingers, Cyrus touched below his eye. There was a sticky bump coming up, and his fingertips were red.

'Your watch!'

'Fun's over,' Elias told the youth with the knife. 'You've got five seconds to leave or you'll never walk properly again.' The youths laughed. Elias counted aloud. After five he closed the gap to one pace to the youth with the knife. The youth slashed the air from side to side. Elias didn't move. He stared at the youth's eyes. Their eyes locked and the youth knew. He stepped back.

'We don't need them. We see you again, you'll be sorry,' said the youth. The youths traipsed back along the side path. Elias knew how brave they were from their backs. One turned and from a distance he threw a rock.

'Thank you,' said Cyrus.

'Your face,' said Elias.

'What?'

'It's bleeding.'

'It's owed to me.'

'Owed you?'

'Nothing. I'm fine.'

'You'll have a black eye.'

'The price for my watch. Thank you.' *Only a black eye.*

They caught an Uber, and a short time later, Elias bent down with his face at the window of a Nile ticket office. The ticket seller asked Elias where he was from, where he had stayed, what was the address, how long had he been here, and about his travel companion. Elias dipped his head so he could look into the ticket seller's eyes. He came from upper Egypt; his skin was dark; his eyes were dark. Elias gave incomplete answers and waved a fist of Egyptian pounds as he asked for two cabins on the next cruise to Cairo. The next cruise left immediately and it would be five thousand for two luxury cabins including food and beverage.

Elias and Cyrus crossed a battered, pink gang-plank that led to the first level deck. The gang-plank was dragged back to the dock almost as soon as Cyrus stepped on board. A call came from the bridge to cast off, ropes were dropped into the water and Cyrus felt the propeller engage and power the boat from the wharf into the blue of the slow Nile.

At the brown house in the desert, the grey-veiled Bedouin woman with bright jewellery was chopping zucchini for the evening meal. She put down her knife and answered her mobile; she took the bookings for camel and buggy treks.

'Hello,' she said and the man calling asked if this was *Desert Treks*, and then said he was from the Ras Ghareb Police and he was looking for two men, one about thirty-five, the other seventy. The Bedouin woman asked if the older man was from Syria and the policeman said yes. She said they had crossed the desert today to go to El Minya. The Bedouin woman thought the two men seemed nice, very nice, but knew which side of her pita had hummus.

CHAPTER NINTEEN

THE NILE RIVER, EGYPT, 29 JULY 2018

THE NILE WAS smoothly slow and looked dark in patches where a waft annoyed the surface. Behind their cruise ship were three other cruise ships in a lazy line. The ships all had three stories with a sun and pool deck at the top. Cyrus leant against the safety rail on the pool deck and looked down. Two ropes dragged in the water. A wooden skiff motored alongside and a man on the bow of the wooden skiff leant down and grasped a rope. He pulled the rope through the running guide on the skiff's bow and wrapped it once around a cleat. It was an open wooden boat with no cabin. On board were two middle-aged men, both wore light-coloured *galabiya*. The man at the stern called out to Cyrus, and with outstretched hands he showed him a blue linen shirt. Cyrus liked it and lifted his hand to the man. The man wrapped the shirt around something, tied the shirt with a red string and tossed it in an arc. Cyrus caught the shirt—it was a perfect throw and an easy catch. The shirt was wrapped around a small can with a screw top. Cyrus lifted the blue shirt against his chest, and the size was good. The man spread his fingers and called out five hundred. Cyrus got five hundred from Elias, then dropped the tin to the man at the front of the skiff. He caught the tin, and the other man clapped.

❍

In his room, Cyrus stepped from the shower, dried himself and put on the blue linen shirt. It was good to feel the dust gone.

On the sun deck Cyrus and Elias watched the clouds turn from white to pink, heard shore birds call and then everything was dark. They descended a flight of stairs to the dining room. A buffet was set. Around a hundred other guests were seated or tracked to and from the buffet. The most popular dishes were replenished by chefs dressed in white and wearing tall white hats. At their table beside a window, Cyrus gazed outside. The full moon speared a thin line across the river; the moon line fragmented by ripples on the Nile. He warmed to the moonlight, the light had seen him, and he had seen the light. Inside the dining room, alabaster lights glowed and threw russet rays onto modern paintings of ancient Egypt. Two men with guitars played soft music. One was tall the other was shorter and fat. The last song they played was *Moon River.*

❍

After eating, Cyrus and Elias climbed to the top deck. Elias drank a glass of grape juice and Cyrus drank mint tea. After finishing his tea, Cyrus lay back in his blue linen shirt on a soft recliner. He looked at the stars and silently identified the major stellar constellations. Couples left the top deck and took the seductive melody of *Moon River* with them. Cyrus sat up.

'I thought of an idea when I was looking at the fishing nets crossing the Gulf and then in the desert with the sand.'

'You had the chance to look at the nets closely?' asked Elias with a grin.

'While I wasn't being sick.' Cyrus smiled.

'The idea?'

'To develop a scientific proof. The net looked like replicating cells and the desert grains like molecules. It occurred to me, in fact, *we, we* being the scientific community, now have an extraordinary knowledge to apply to develop this proof. We know a cell must have a certain number of key proteins and other molecules to be capable of self-replication. And this led me to the answer.'

'The answer?'

'How to find the proof.'

'You've found an approach to the problem?' Elias straightened up and leant towards Cyrus.

'I've found the solution to the problem.'

'What! You think you have the proof God's real?'

'I know I have the proof.'

'Tell me!' said Elias, his mind raced and spun… a giddy whirl. What a moment of truth. Elias had a thousand questions, but he told himself to let Cyrus talk.

'I conducted a thought experiment.'

'A thought experiment?'

'Thought experiments give us some of the deepest understandings of science, no physical experimentation is done, from start to finish the thought experiment is based on rational thought and deduction. In all experiments, it's necessary to have positions of certainty.'

'That makes sense.'

'At a specific point in time there was no reproductive life on Earth; an obvious fact.'

'Agreed,' said Elias.

'This is the first position of certainty. We also know that at a later point in time there was the very first form of reproductive life; another obvious fact. These two facts set the boundaries of the thought experiment.'

'Okay.'

'Another important point is there would have been no selective pressure to generate various components to form a living organism. All the complex molecules required to make the first living organism would need to have been made by chance at more or less the same time and place.'

'Okay.'

'We can assume the first form of reproductive life was not a camel but a bacterium-like, micro-organism—maybe like cyanobacteria. This is the simplest life-form we know that is capable of self-replication or *living*. At some point in time such a micro-organism did not exist. Then at a later point in time the very first micro-organism existed.'

'What is a micro-organism such as cyanobacteria made of?'

'A fatty wall or membrane encasing proteins, DNA and a vast assortment of small molecules.'

'Are you saying all of these molecular components needed to come together at the same specific moment in time to form the first living organism.'

'Exactly … and I've calculated the random chance of all these components being formed and coming together.'

'What's the chance?' asked Elias.

'First, I'll tell you the chance of having the correct proteins needed for self- replication.'

'What's a protein?'

'Proteins are made of building blocks called amino acids. There are twenty different amino acids. A protein's function relates to which amino acids are joined together, how many amino acids are joined, and in which order they are joined. For a specific protein to function correctly it needs to have the right amino acids in a specific order or sequence.'

'How many amino acid building blocks are in each protein?'

'It varies; many proteins have around one hundred amino acids.'

'Are you saying for a protein to work properly, it'll need each of the one hundred amino acids to be in the correct order?' asked Elias.

'Yes.'

'And there are twenty different amino acids.'

'Yes.'

'There must be theoretically trillions of possible amino acid combinations.'

'The probability of having a correctly sequenced protein, purely by chance is a phenomenally small number. As a perspective, if you roll a dice, the chance of rolling a six is one in six.'

'The perspective?'

'The random chance of forming one protein with the required structure and function is the same as rolling thirty die with a million-sides and getting a six on every die.'

'That is crazy small—impossible.'

'Yes, impossible.'

'How many proteins are needed in a micro-organism?'

'About three hundred different proteins for a micro-organism to replicate and grow.'

'Do all of these three hundred proteins need to be present when the first micro-organism is formed?'

'No … only about twenty proteins would need to be present. These twenty could then activate the DNA in the first micro-organism to make the remainder of these essential three hundred proteins.'

'What's the random chance that these twenty proteins would be correctly formed.'

'The same as rolling 350,000, trillion trillion die with a million-sides and getting a six on every die.

'Beyond impossible.'

'Beyond impossible'

'What's the relationship between DNA and proteins?'

'DNA encodes the information or template to make proteins. It's essential that DNA is also present in this first micro-organism. DNA is needed so that when the first micro-organism divides, both daughter cells carry the genetic information required to further replicate.'

'You've lost me. I'm confused. I've heard of DNA … but what is it?'

'DNA is made of four building blocks or bases: the four base are guanosine, thymine, cytosine and adenine.'

'How many bases long would the DNA be in this first micro-organism?'

'A great question. Each self-replicating micro-organism would need about one million DNA bases in a very specific sequence. This is the microbial chromosome. The chance is impossibly small for the four DNA bases to randomly assemble into the correct order to code for a self-replicating organism.

'And you said the DNA would need to code for about three hundred proteins.'

'Yes, that's correct.'

'So, if about twenty proteins may have to be present in the first micro-organism the other say three hundred essential proteins could be made inside this micro-organism using the DNA as a template?'

'Yes, but only if all the required amino acid protein building blocks were present.'

'And there would also need to be a supply of amino acids inside the daughter-micro-organism to make the required proteins.'

'Exactly,' said Cyrus. 'And there would also need to be 100,000 DNA bases to make a new microbial chromosome for the daughter cell.'

'Impossible then.'

'Impossible.'

'Returning to what a microbe is made of; you also said fat molecules and a lot of small molecules.'

'The DNA and proteins are encased in a fatty wall, a membrane or skin of organic lipid molecules. There are also many minerals and other small molecules like water.'

'How would this fatty wall, the amino acids and the DNA bases, minerals and all the other small molecules as-semble into a living organism.'

'The accepted scientific theory is that life emerged from a primordial or prebiotic soup of amino acids, DNA bases, lipids and other small molecules. Such a theory is complete nonsense. The chance of this happening is mathematically impossible as you can see from the phenomenally small numbers.'

'So how did the first living microbe happen?'

'Simple logic dictates it's mathematically impossible for the first micro-organisms to have been formed by chance. There are only two choices, by chance or not by chance; we've ruled out chance. By implication, there was intelligent design, the hand of a deity.'

'You're certain about what you are telling me?' Elias *knew* Cyrus was certain.

'I have no doubt. I've simplified my science arguments to you but have not deviated from known scientific facts.' Cyrus wrote the formula on a paper napkin.

$$\Xi = YM(20^{-PX})4^{-L}$$

'We could call this formula the *Deity Constant*.'

'What do the letters mean?'

'Y is the probability of the transfer RNA and ribosomal complex forming DNA; M is the probability factor for all the requisite small molecules, co-factors, and membrane lipid molecules that must be present; P is the average length of the preformed proteins needed to activate and read the DNA; X is the number of preformed proteins required; L is the number of DNA bases in the microbial chromosome.

'What are the transfer RNA and ribosomal complexes? You've not mentioned these.'

'The transfer RNA and ribosomal complex are required for the cell to make its three hundred essential proteins.'

'And this is to make one cell capable of replicating itself?'

'Yes.'

'You have proven God exists.'

'God, a deity.'

'I can understand what you say; it makes sense to me and I know little science.'

'As I said before, a micro-organism has a wall around it. This wall is made of small fat molecules. In an optimal chemical environment, these fat molecules will form a micro-bead trapping other molecules inside. To form a micro-organism exclusively by chance you would need to trap the building blocks for DNA and the building blocks for proteins inside this bead. There is no natural environment in Earth's history where all of these essential building blocks could exist in such close proximity where they could be trapped inside such a randomly formed bead. But assuming these building block molecules were trapped inside the bead they would then need to order themselves in such a way to create the proteins and DNA sequences to generate reproductive life. There are deeper levels of complexity required for these protein and DNA molecules to interact with each other in such a way to generate reproductive life. Also required are an array of smaller molecules such as salts, trace metals and complex molecules that transfer energy to make essential reactions happen. I repeat, there is zero chance, zero chance reproductive life would have, or could have, occurred without intelligent design.'

'How can you convince people when this deity constant theory clashes with their beliefs?'

'Solid science survives the test of time.'

'What if nobody believes you?'

'Truth is not a voting contest. To anyone trained in biological science my proof is elementary; true science is elegant in its simplicity. Major scientific discoveries have always suffered their cynics. Copernicus was not believed with his theory of the Earth not being the centre of the universe; Darwin experienced similar cynicism. I've found science critics fall into two categories, those who have a genuine belief based on their own convictions and those who object out of scientific jealousy.'

'I'm speechless. I'm speaking, but I'm speechless. I've never heard anything like this. I don't know what to say. In my heart, deep in my heart I didn't think a proof was possible, exciting, phenomenal … so exciting. What form is this deity; where is it now?'

'I don't have answers to either of those questions.'

'Is it possible a deity existed to form life a billion years ago, but today this deity no longer exists?'

'Energy forms wax and wane, stars are formed then disappear, we can say that a deity created life, but there is no certainty this deity is with us today. I despair with what I have witnessed in Syria and it has led me to question what Allah is doing; a barbaric brutality equivalent to any of man's actions in history, but then we witness extraordinary acts of love.'

Cyrus sat with his hand on his forehead; a moment of humility Elias would never forget. Science teaching a truth, a truth so simple and obvious some would claim it a truth always known; let them scream this truth, we always knew God was real.

'Our plan in Cairo?'

'I'm not sure yet.' Elias was thinking about the deity constant, and in its shadow with and without the sun, the Jewish community in Cairo, the Israelis chasing them, Noya's Aunt Ophelia, the need to find a safe haven, the risks of hotels, their false Egyptian ID cards, airports, boats and overland routes out of Egypt—how to keep Cyrus safe. They sat in the quiet of the starry moonlight for some time. The ancient city of El Minya behind them and further back, the Aswan Dam, holding water that originated from Lake Victoria in Tanzania. To the left was the Sahara Desert and four thousand kilometres away the Moroccan coast, while to the right was the Eastern Desert, which he and Cyrus now knew well from the buggy ride. And to the north down-stream lay Cairo; breakfast and Interpol arrest warrants waited.

CHAPTER TWENTY

CAIRO, EGYPT, 30 JULY 2018

CYRUS AWOKE EARLY and climbed the stairs to the viewing deck—an ozone sky, a sand-coloured hillock, rocky outcrops and palm trees, a Nile mirror with papyrus reeds and blue lotus lilies reflected at the water's edge. Cyrus felt Elias behind him.

'God's beauty,' said Elias before he placed the palm of his hand between Cyrus's shoulders. 'You're the first major prophet we've seen since Mohammed.'

'No.'

'I see a prophet as someone who speaks on behalf of a divine being or deity, interpreting the signs of the times, your deity constant is the ultimate prophecy.'

'I'd never think of myself as a prophet.'

'We have a joint responsibility to protect you; take your message to the world.'

'But now let's eat,' said Cyrus with a glint in his eyes.

After breakfast, Cyrus and Elias stood on the portside looking at the pyramids; structures predating Abraham by a thousand years. The Egyptians chose the west side of the Nile to bury their kings because they believed the home of the dead was towards the setting sun.

'We need to go to my cabin,' said Elias.

'Why?'

'Our ID cards show men with moustaches; we'll give them moustaches.

Thirty minutes later, the boat's communication speaker announced they would be arriving at Gezira Island in five minutes. On deck, by the stainless rail, Cyrus looked across the Cairo skyline while Elias scanned his smartphone. Close by was the Cairo Tower with its honey-comb veneer and nearer a grassed park with monuments and palm trees.

'The tallest building I've ever seen,' said Cyrus.

'The Cairo Tower,' said Elias before he re-focused on the day's headlines in *Al-Ahram,* the leading Egyptian daily newspaper. *Israeli and Syrian Sought in Sharm El-Sheikh Killing.* Beneath the headline were passport photographs of himself and Cyrus. Elias sat down. After reading the article, he thought, *a lie enlightens the world before the truth has risen at dawn.* He searched Google for a Cairo café and wrote Naguib Mahfouz and the address on a napkin. Then using his burner phone, Elias called Chris in Jerusalem.

'Hi, Chris.'

'Blood?'

'My time's short. Cyrus and I had our passports mobile-scanned in El Tor on Thursday at midday. We need a time stamp of the scan.'

'Egyptian Police?'

'Yes, a checkpoint.'

'Got it, blood.'

At Gezira Island, the propeller churned the water and made the water eddy through the concrete piles as the ferry berthed against the dock. A deck hand threw a rope. Elias stared down at the dock and counted four uniformed police. He decided there was no urgency to tell Cyrus about the major's killing. Better that Cyrus be relaxed if he was stopped for an ID check.

'The police on the dock may check your ID,' said Elias. 'After you pass the police, walk along the dock and wait by the second monument.' Elias pointed.

'If I'm held up get a cab to this café and wait for me.' He handed Cyrus the napkin with the address of the Naguib Mahfouz Café.

Elias, stood at the bottom of the gangway, flexed his toes in his Nikes, and observed the policeman in a black uniform glance at Cyrus's forged ID and point at the bump near Cyrus's eye; in his head Elias ran game theory, fast actions should things go wrong. Cyrus nodded and smiled. Elias was pleased the policeman seemed easy to distract. A police car was stationed close by. Cyrus had his ID back from the policeman. Cyrus glanced at a clipboard the policeman held and saw his and Elias's passport photographs. He headed towards the second monument. *Why would the police in Cairo be looking for them? What was Elias not telling him?*

Two other passengers stood between Elias and the police check. They spoke German and were a couple. He had a wispy beard and blonde hair tied high in a bun. The woman was thick-set with a square jaw. Elias thought she was masculine enough for both of them. The policeman flagged the German couple through. Elias was next.

'*Ahlan*,' Elias said, handing his ID to grimy fingers. Elias slipped his backpack from his shoulders and tugged at a zip slider as though looking for something. The policeman looked at the ID in his grimy fingers, then at Elias

'Eyes up,' said the policeman. His eyes darted from Elias to a clipboard and back again. The policeman's hand twitched at his hip then grabbed the butt of his pistol. Elias spun on his toes, bounced his shoulder off the passenger behind, then he blurred past other passengers and raced for the river. A black-uniformed man tried to head Elias off, and yelled for the police behind to help.

Cyrus heard the yell and turned to see ferry passengers on the dock scramble and within the scramble Elias wore his dark blue *galabeya* and dashed for the river. Cyrus knew what to do. He continued past the second monument. There would be a few moments with the police focus on Elias, then they would realize he too was close. He hurried away from the dock with his head down. Cyrus itched to look back but looked forward for the fastest getaway. A police car raced by and stopped a hundred paces ahead. The doors were flung open and four policemen leapt out. Cyrus swivelled his head. A youth was hunched over his mobile phone beside a motorbike which was jammed in-between two parked cars on the other side of the road. Cyrus crossed over.

'Excuse me,' he said.

The youth held up his hand and thumbed his screen. Cyrus looked up the road where the four police had stopped all pedestrian and vehicle traffic. Another police car raced by.

'Can you take me to the Citadel of Saladin?'

'I'm not an Uber.'

'I'll pay well.'

'A hundred?'

'Agreed.'

The youth flicked his head towards the police. 'They looking for you?'

'No reason to be.'

To the youth this sounded like a *yes*.

'Listen,' said the youth. He shook his finger close to Cyrus's kinked nose, opened his mouth and said nothing. Then after a moment he spoke quickly. 'A thousand, I'll get you there safely, but we got to move now.'

'Okay.'

The youth pointed. 'Go into the textile shop, all the way through to the back. Behind the shop is an alley. Turn right. I'll find you there.'

Cyrus nodded and stepped into the shop past colourful stacks of fabric and dresses. He heard the youth's motorbike start. The shop's owner told Cyrus the back of his shop was private, but then he showed Cyrus to the back alley after he listened to Cyrus's soft words and looked into Cyrus's soft eyes. In the alley, Cyrus got on the back of the bike. They turned left down a one-way road. At the Citadel, Cyrus hired a taxi and stopped a block from the Naguib Mahfouz Café.

○

Elias's feet pounded across the concrete walkway. He slung the backpack, dragged in a deep breath, then dived—arms outstretched. The water looked dirty. His arms hit, then his face. It felt warm and tasted like musk. He kicked down hard as he fought the backpack's buoyancy. He moved his arms in a strong breaststroke. The water was warm at the top, but he stroked into cool, and in the cool he swivelled and swam deep in the direction of the river bank. The water grew dark when he swam under the concrete walkway piles. Hidden from view, he floated to the surface. To his right were concrete piles, and beyond, the open river. To his left was the concrete wall of the river bank. As he trod water, he pulled off his sneakers and pushed them into his backpack and took quick deep breaths. He heard a yell above, and pulled off his *galabeya*, his shirt and long pants and jammed the wet clothes into the backpack too. Wearing only briefs, he put on his backpack and swam freestyle. Three strokes and a breath on one side, three strokes and a breath on the other. He stroked steadily upstream into the slow current. The backpack straps chaffed the skin on his shoulders. Then through the water he heard the high-speed sing of a propeller. Elias lifted his head and looked between the piles down river. A white boat was behind—white bow spray—the Nile River police. He started swimming again as the high-pitched sound grew louder, then the pitch changed low as the police boat slowed and headed to where he'd dived. Elias was two minutes swimming upstream from where he'd dived in. Elias swam on for a hundred meters before he heard another outboard. Ahead, police were coming down river. The police boat turned in close to the walkway. A man dressed in black was crouched at the stern. He held a spotlight, which he shone under the walkway. Elias pulled the backpack from his shoulders, and pushed it deep underwater. It bubbled in the murky water. He gulped, took a deep breath and dived into the cool with one hand against the concrete wall at the river's edge to feel for something to hold onto. His fingers groped the rough concrete as he swung his hand in an arc, back and forth, searching the rough concrete wall as he scissor-kicked forward. Then his fingers felt a small crack and he forced his fingers in tight. He looked up through the watery gloom. A light beam danced on the surface. He hoped no bubbles floated from his backpack. The light beam drifted downstream and then disappeared. The water burnt his eyes and his lungs burnt too.

'I see something,' said the cop with the light. 'Hold the boat.' The driver engaged reverse. Elias heard the prop spin; it sounded close. Underwater, he held his grip in the crack and counted to twenty, then he counted to twenty again. His lungs wouldn't let him count anymore. He released his grip on the wall and kicked to the surface, and gasped for breath as soon as his head broke. Only his head was out of the water. The police boat was close. Maybe ten meters away. The light beam swung. On the police boat a gunner moved the barrel of his semi-automatic rifle with the arc of the searchlight. Elias gasped for breath and pulled himself down against the wall. Ten feet down, at least, Elias shouldered the backpack and breast-stroked and kicked upstream. He stroked with his burning eyes open. There was no swinging light on the surface upstream. He carried on until he felt his chest would explode, then he surfaced. He looked around. The police boat was fifty metres downstream. Upstream, a storm-water drain exited two metres above the river's surface. The drain looked big enough to climb inside. He lifted his eyebrows, widened his eyes, and stared at the concrete wall. The concrete looked rough below the drain exit, chipped out by the stormwater. A few cracks too. There was dark slime on the concrete. He tasted blood. His nose was bleeding. Elias only needed one hand-hold and one toe hold above the waterline then he could reach the drain and haul himself in. He felt exposed as he reached up from the water, and jammed the fingers of his right hand through the slime into a crack. Straight arm. Hip against the wall. He reached up with his left arm, then jammed his fingers into another crack. The concrete was hard and rough against his fingertips. His feet scrambled, and his toes scraped against slime on the concrete wall as he searched for the toe hold he'd seen. Elias talked to himself. *Grid search up and down. I can hang on for another ten seconds.* His left foot moved up and down—higher than he thought the toe-hole was. His left arm shook. He was going to drop. He pressed hard against the concrete and lowered himself back into the water. The police boat moved further away and its light scanned. Elias knew the boat would be back. He breathed deeply. Both arms and his shoulders ached. He tried again but knew right away he needed more rest, and again he slipped back into the Nile and felt the warm water rise up his legs, rise up his body to his neck. He stretched his fingers and rolled his shoulders. The police boat was on the way back. Elias lined up his hand-holds and the toe hold and tried again. One, two, three—he reached up and grabbed the edge of the storm-water drain. He pulled hard on his right arm, straightened his left leg, hauled his right knee into the opening of the drain, then he was in. He threw himself forward low and flat and snaked deep into the drain, out of police sight. His head pounded and felt split, but he gave no life to the pain. Elias gasped several deep breaths. An insect lodged in his throat; he spat the insect and blood. In his ears he heard the high whine of mosquitos. He rolled onto his back and pinched the bridge of his nose. After a minute, the bleeding stopped.

It was dark in the drain, but deep in the distance there was a beam of hope. Elias crawled commando style, elbows forward and dragged his body. There was no other way to move in the tight drain. Close to the beam in front he heard a scurry and screech. *Of course there'd be rats.* At the beam, he took off his backpack and stood in a narrow pipe that led upwards to what looked like a street grate. Elias tried to reach his arms up, but there was no room in the narrow pipe to lift his arms from his sides. He crouched in the drain where there was a little more room. This time, he stood up with his arms already above his head. He grabbed the metal above and pushed the heavy street grate aside, hooked his foot through the backpack straps and dragged himself out of the drain onto the street. Heads turned as Elias emerged from the drain. On the street, he ran to an alley, where he pushed his arms through the wet sleeves of his shirt and his legs through the wet legs of his trousers before, he pulled on his wet sneakers. He bent over, breathed in and out fast and felt his head clear.

Close to where he'd run into the alley, was a men's clothing shop. It was called Concrete and was made of concrete. Elias headed for it. A clean-cut young man wearing a zebra-striped shirt, open to his mid chest, sauntered down the concrete steps as Elias entered. Elias felt zebra's eyes inspect his Nile wet body. Inside, an attendant with a sharp hairstyle turned his head to greet Elias. There were no other customers. Egyptian pop played. Elias bought two *galabeya*, dark and light brown. He fished a wet hundred-dollar bill from his backpack. His fingertips bled, and the hundred-dollar bill was dotted with specs of red. The attendant smelt of cologne, spoke in a high-pitched voice and hung onto his vowels. The attendant screwed up his face at the wet hundred-dollar bill with red blood spots like it was a dead rat.

'Tripped and fell in the Nile,' Elias said.

'Drink the Nile's water and you'll return,' said the attendant with a broad smile. The attendant grabbed a pair of gloves under the counter, picked up the wet bill in a gloved hand then pressed the bill inside a folded cloth. He then opened the cloth, inspected the damp bill and handed Elias a few Egyptian pounds in change.

Outside, Elias flagged a taxi and drove from Gezira Island across a four-lane bridge to downtown Cairo. Flags, with their horizontal red, white and black stripes, flopped limply from every bridge lamp post. The taxi driver's attention jumped between the horn, the accelerator, the brake and the radio volume. The taxi dropped Elias close to where Google maps showed Naguib Mahfouz Café. As Elias entered the café, he wondered how they were going to get out of Cairo, get out of Egypt. Lots of bad ideas but no good ideas yet. The café had three teal blue awnings attached to polished brass poles facing the street and a heavy wooden door decorated with embossed leather. Elias pulled open the heavy door, stepped inside and saw Cyrus at a table in a small recess where there were red woven rugs on the wall.

'I'm very happy now,' said Cyrus as he stood up and embraced Elias.

'Me too. Well done getting here,' said Elias.

Cyrus looked at Elias's red eyes and swollen eyelids. 'What happened?'

Elias lowered his voice. 'The police, so I ran to the river. A swim and a scramble.'

'I saw.'

'You get a taxi?'

'A motorbike. The police were about. I had to pay him a thousand,' Cyrus spoke softly.

'Well done.' Elias patted Cyrus on his back.

'The police had our photographs.'

'The Syrian major was killed,' said Elias.

'What?'

'I saw the news just before we docked. I didn't want to stress you.'

'Killed?'

'Shot. They are blaming me. It's a set-up.'

'What can we do?'

'It changes nothing. It's the same as before. We need to get out of Egypt to Europe.' But Elias knew it changed a lot.

'But if we get caught.'

'That's why I'm here, to make sure we don't.'

Cyrus shook his head and eyeballed Elias with a smile.

'I'm sorry, I need to go and find Ophelia. You okay here?'

'Somewhere to stay?'

'Yes, somewhere to stay.'

'I'm fine here.'

'I'll be back as soon as I can. If anyone asks, say you're from Jordan and change into a new *galabeya*.' Elias passed Cyrus a package.

CHAPTER TWENTY-ONE
CAIRO, EGYPT, 30 JULY 2018

ELIAS PLACED TWO purple scarves on the counter, waved his debit card, but it flashed declined. *No surprise.* He paid cash for the scarves and the new set of clothes he wore.

Elias was now dressed like eighty per cent of the Egyptian men, with dull-coloured pants and shirt, but he had a cap. Elias strolled along Cairo's Kodak Passageway, an upmarket green oasis walkway in Cairo's new art and film district. His eyes took in everything. At the end of the walkway, on the other side of the one-way street called Adler Street, was Cairo's *Sha'ar HaShamayim* Synagogue; it stood like a stone fort. In front of the synagogue, heavy steel hoops rose from the footpath; a preventative barrier to a vehicular terrorist attack. On the near-side of the street, the driver of a parked white tow truck swivelled his head and scanned both pedestrian and slow-moving one-way vehicle traffic. A policeman wearing a black beret, ambled with his right hand resting on his holster, a submachine gun slung over his shoulder. The submachine gun was a Czech Scorpion Evo 3. The policeman with the black beret lifted a finger to the driver in the tow truck, and moments later, the policeman with the black beret inclined his head to a male pedestrian wearing street clothes. *How many plain-clothed police mingled with pedestrians in the synagogue area?* The police knew he was in Cairo and would be looking for him. Elias knew Mossad may not have agents on the street, but they could be giving intel support. There were plenty of Mossad resident in Cairo, maybe fifty. In an instant, reality struck; if he and Cyrus were caught, they'd be killed. The slaying of the Syrian major evidence of the game in play. Should he take a more conservative option? Not only his life. Ophelia may need to run with them too, someone else to watch out for. How could Ophelia help? Somewhere safe to sleep for a night or two until her contacts were chased down, maybe she could help with access to money—a creative exit from Egypt. A fast plan and a faster run. Two people passed by dragging suitcases; the suitcase wheels clattered on the passageway tiles. Elias back-tracked along Kodak Passageway, and avoided other pedestrians' eyes. He stepped into an art gallery which was located on two floors; the second floor overlooked the synagogue. No Mossad agents on the second floor unless octogenarians were recruited. The synagogue's afternoon service or *Mincha* had ended. Elias checked a couple of windows then found one with a clear view of the synagogue steps. Beside the window, Elias glanced at an oil on canvas that depicted a hand-cuffed prisoner smoking a cigarette. *Not today* he thought then stared through the gallery window at a middle-aged woman with dark curly hair and a dark green jersey. She fitted the description given by Tzvi. She pointed a finger as she talked to a group of men on the synagogue's marble steps then she raised her hand to the men, descended the steps, turned, and walked south on Adler Street. Elias darted from the art gallery window, took the stairs two at a time to the ground floor then cut back a block to intercept the lady with the green jersey that he hoped was Ophelia.

As Ophelia wandered, she thought of the rabbi's sermon, *how do we know to trust the past prophets of Israel, or a future one if one comes along. There have been many charlatans claiming a mystical vision and inventing a new religion, recognising that prophecy is by its nature a private experience. A true prophet will be fully righteous and learned, never ruled by evil inclination or passion and with a message to compliment the words of Moses.*

When Ophelia stopped and bought freshly baked pita, she didn't notice the man who followed her. She moved on. The man moved on. Ophelia smiled at two children eating a sweet treat. Both laughed freely, as children laugh. They chased after a ginger cat on a pile of vibrant fabric. The owner of the fabric scolded the children and told them to take themselves away with their sweet pastries and their sticky fingers. Ophelia turned into a one-way street, unsealed and littered with paper. To her right a van door slid open and a man took out a sack of onions to display alongside red, yellow and orange root vegetables spread on a table under a faded brown umbrella; an elaborate stage of fruit that encroached onto the unsealed street. The Cairo vendor's mantra, the more goods in the public eye, the greater the sales—a cluttered order of survival.

Ophelia twitched her nose at a smoke breeze that carried the spice of chillies from meat cooked on hot coals. Ahead, a parked truck created a pedestrian bottleneck, people were jammed close together. At the jam, Ophelia felt her shoulder jostled and a man's voice spoke Hebrew close to her ear.

'Shalom, Ophelia, I'm a friend of Noya's from Tel Aviv. You're being followed, take this. I'll call.' Elias pressed a burner mobile wrapped in a purple scarf into her hand then strode into the crowd ahead. Ophelia stared after the man, curled her fingers in her pocket and buried the mobile.

Elias waited fifteen minutes, then called Ophelia.

'Hello,' she said. Her voice trembled and was soft. 'Who are you?'

'Can you speak up, please?' asked Elias.

'Yes.'

'Thank you, I can hear you now. Are you Ophelia, Noya's auntie?'

'Yes.'

'I'm Elias, from Israel, sorry for all this, but you were being followed.'

'Followed?'

'A plain clothes policeman.'

'Police! Why?'

'My travelling companion has important information; the police are looking for us and are keeping watch on Jewish people in Cairo.'

'What do you want from me?'

'We need a safe place to stay.'

'How do you know Noya?'

'My cousin knows her.'

'Why not go to the Israeli Embassy?'

'Not an option.'

'Where are you staying now?'

'We arrived in Cairo today, no place to stay.'

'I see, let me think, yes. We need to do something. I need to make calls.'

'Please use this mobile, your calls may be bugged.'

'What've you done?'

'Nothing, I promise. I'll explain later.'

'I'll call you when I know.' Ophelia ended the call and put down the mobile with shaking hands. She trusted the Israeli Embassy, people at the embassy were her friends, but the stranger knew Noya.

◯

A walk and ten blocks later, Elias pulled the peak of his cap down and opened the door to Naguib Mahfouz Café. There were more people inside but Cyrus sat alone in the recess; it felt snug.

'All okay?' asked Elias.

Cyrus shifted his gaze. 'The returning warrior.'

'Ophelia's trying to help.'

Thirty minutes later, Elias received a call.

'Hello, Ophelia,' he said.

'My physician friend has a place for you in Alexandria.'

'Can we go tonight?'

'Yes.'

'I'll call you again in around an hour, please wear the purple headscarf.'

'I have it.'

'Do you have a credit card?'

'Yes, why?'

'Please bring your card, and your passport.'

'My passport?'

'Yes, I'll explain later. What's your address?

Ophelia told him. The call ended.

'Back to battle?' asked Cyrus.

'Maybe an hour and a half, I'll be back with Ophelia.'

In that café, now alone, Cyrus studied two people sitting opposite. The man was older with his hair brushed back and the woman was good-look-ing. She ate falafel with her fingers and after each bite she licked her fingers and touched her napkin. The man didn't eat. He held a glass of beer in one hand. At another table, two young women chatted; one had dark long hair and the other short dark. All during their tea, the long-haired girl gazed at her mobile phone, showed her friend then thumbed the screen to show her friend again. The long-haired girl dabbed her eyes and more than once her friend circled her arm around her shoulders.

◯

For an hour, Elias crisscrossed the streets, in the neighbourhood surround-ing Ophelia's apartment—thankful he had an hour to identify opportunities and pitfalls. Three blocks from Ophelia's apartment, Elias stopped at a large intersection; traffic moved at walking pace; cars and trucks double-parked at the road side. Beside where he stood, on the back of a double-parked truck, a dark brown goat with bloodhound-like ears stared at Elias through wide rectangular-shaped pupils. The goat bleated and stomped and didn't smell like a bloodhound. Elias glanced at the goat; it would not be leaving the city. His interest was not the goat but in a group of three Uber motorcyclists across the road. They were on their smartphones and sat side-saddle. He needed a motorcycle; a driver no. The drivers looked to be in their late teens. Elias took several Egyptian bank notes from his backpack and pushed them into his pocket. One driver pressed his mobile into his jeans pocket, started his bike and raced off. A few moments later, a second bike left. Elias crossed the road and scuffed at a patch of sawdust thrown on spilt oil. He spoke to the remain-ing motorcyclist; he was a teenage boy and Elias spied the keys in the ignition.

'Gezira Island,' said Elias. The boy nodded; there were no helmets. Elias reached into his pocket, fumbled and dropped several notes on the ground. The boy leapt from his bike to retrieve the money. Elias slipped his leg over the motorcycle seat, turned the ignition key, saw the green neutral light and pressed the start button. The engine started and the exhaust barked.

'Hey! ... what ... stop!' yelled the boy as he left the last few notes on the ground and tried to grab Elias. Elias kicked the gearshift into first and sped between the walking-pace traffic. He turned left, travelled a few hundred metres then turned right and stopped. He called Ophelia.

On the motorbike, fifteen minutes later, Elias tracked behind Ophelia. The street was one-way until ahead where a red and white striped barrier pole manned by unarmed men in khaki extracted *baksheesh*. On the far side of the striped barrier, the road was wider and two-way. Parked cars and bikes shared the pavement with produce for sale. Many pedestrians were on their mobiles. A man paced with an even stride around the barrier then glanced over his shoulder at Ophelia. The man touched his hand to his ear and seemed to speak. Then he continued along the two-way street away from the barrier and the khaki men. *That's three,* thought Elias, they seemed to be running a classic ABC foot surveillance with two following and one in front. *How can they be so predictable?* But they were Egyptians. Where were Mossad? Elias braked the motorbike to avoid a cyclist who balanced a tray on his head piled high with bread. At the barrier, Elias ignored the khaki men's calls and waving arms. Twenty paces ahead on the faster two-way street, Ophelia's purple scarf bobbed. Elias rode past Ophelia and stopped sharply. Ophelia had been told by Elias what to do. She stepped to the bike, swung her right leg across the seat, but her leg touched the hot exhaust and she stumbled off and stood on the road.

'I'm burnt!' she shrieked.

Elias heard a shout. He glanced behind him. Ten paces away, two men were running and closing fast.

'Get on quickly!' he yelled.

'What's hot?'

'Get on!'

Ophelia stepped back to the bike and swung her leg over the seat.

'Hold on.' Ophelia wrapped her arms around his waist. Just then from the front, a man ran towards them; his right hand held a pistol. Elias angled away and darted the bike behind a boy who pushed a cart stacked high with cardboard boxes, then Elias braked hard. Ophelia jolted into his back. The stacked cardboard boxes created a shield from the man with the gun. Elias bent low and accelerated forward. Ophelia bent low too. Two motorbikes going the other way sped past. In his side-mirror Elias saw the bikes hit red brake lights. Elias turned left through a building arch into a dead-end street, but he knew a narrow alley ran a block from the dead-end and exited to a four-lane road. He raced down the alley, thumb on the bike's horn.

People scattered. Elias glanced in his side mirror. The two motorbike headlights were some distance behind. They left the narrow alley and Elias felt
Ophelia grab closer behind as they raced flat out onto the four-lane road
and passed cars on the way. Elias rode for four hundred metres, braked hard
then turned left off the four-lane road into a one-way street. At the start of
the one-way street a large truck was parked.

An Egyptian policeman gave chase on his motorbike, two hundred
meters behind. The bike with the passenger wearing a purple scarf, turned
left from the four-lane road and disappeared into a one-way street. In the
one-way street, the policeman saw the purple scarf ahead; the bike had been
slowed down by a traffic jam. The policeman drove a quick high-risk inside
line and got ahead of the two on the bike. He slammed to a stop, dropped
his bike and pulled his pistol. The second policeman's bike closed in and
blocked the rear. The rider they were chasing stopped his bike and raised his
hands. The policeman came close and pointed his pistol at the man's chest.

'On the road, face down,' he yelled. Cars stopped. The female passenger
with the purple scarf screamed. The second policeman pulled the screaming
woman from the bike to the ground, a knee on her back, as he hand-cuffed
her wrists. The policeman with the gun had the bike driver on the ground.
He kicked him hard in the ribs. The man grunted and the policeman kicked
him again before he cuffed him too. The second policeman dragged the
woman with the purple scarf to her feet and pulled the scarf from her head.
Her hair was dark and short and straight.

Elias and Ophelia were a kilometre away in the back of an Uber; the
jack-in-the-box had worked. Elias had paid and set up the second bike to
play a trick on a friend, and ride down the one-way street when he appeared
behind the parked truck. Elias had turned into a garage repair shop beside
the parked truck. He had paid the truck driver too. When people see what
they expect to see, or hear what they expect to hear, they are, at least for a
period of time, under your control.

'How's your burn?'

'I'm sorry I was slow.'

'You did great, how's your burn?'

'I've forgotten about it.' Ophelia lifted the green dress from her ankles
and saw an ovoid burn on the inside of her lower leg.

'Go to the bathroom at the café and put cold water on it.'

'That man had a gun.' She spoke quietly.

'We're safe now.' Elias also kept his voice down.

'Why did he have a gun?'

'It's complicated. I'll tell you later, thank you so much for helping us.

'Scary, we raced so fast.'

'I scouted the area first, knew where to ride.'

'Like a rollercoaster.'

'Tell me about Alexandria.'

'My friend has a villa, for as long as you need.'

'You said he's a doctor.'

'Gamal's a cardiac surgeon.'

'There could be police checkpoints between here and Alexandria. Could your doctor friend get an ambulance?'

'To hide in?'

'To get through checkpoints.'

'I'll call him.'

The Uber dropped them near the Naguib Mahfouz Café. Inside, they found Cyrus reading the Druze *Book of Wisdom*. A pot of mint tea sat on the table

'This is Ophelia,' said Elias.

Cyrus stood up and extended his hand. 'Hello, Ophelia.'

'Cold water on your burn.'

'Yes, thank you.' Ophelia headed to the restroom.

Elias borrowed a chair from another table and the three huddled together when Ophelia returned.

'I know you're Cyrus,' she said. Ophelia had a willing and humble smile.

'Please sit, would you like a drink, something to eat?' asked Cyrus.

'A *koshary* tea, please; we had such a fright.'

'A fright?'

'A man with a gun and a motorbike chase.' As Ophelia spoke, she pointed with all fingers extended and angled her hand from side to side.

'Welcome to Elias's life,' said Cyrus.

Ophelia wasn't sure what to make of this. 'Are you from Israel too?' she asked.

'Damascus,' replied Cyrus.

'We can speak Arabic,' said Ophelia.

'It'll be a rest for me; for several days I've been speaking only English with Elias,' said Cyrus in Arabic.

'I'll get your tea,' said Elias as he left the table for the café bar.

'How's life with all the challenges Syria is facing?' asked Ophelia.

'It's sad, beyond sad. I've lived in Damascus all my life. When I was a boy Damascus had sun and culture and life, but now, now we see the purest of evil. A land of sand and death; it's just a matter of time until Assad is gone.'

'We too see evil in Cairo, bombings, terrorist shootings every month, why can't we have love?'

The light in the café recess was dim, but Ophelia took in Cyrus's soft lined face.

'Man has such destructive capabilities. I don't know what brings this, maybe power, greed, ego or should we call it mental sickness. I'm sorry, I shouldn't talk of dark things,' said Cyrus.

Elias returned and placed the *koshary* tea on the table.

'Thank you,' said Ophelia.

'We have a problem,' said Elias. 'I don't like to ask, do you have the credit card?'

'Yes,' replied Ophelia.

'Could you charge twenty-five thousand US dollars?'

'What's this about?'

'Cyrus is Einstein's son,' Elias said.

Ophelia gazed at Cyrus, looked at Elias then returned her gaze to Cyrus.

'What, Einstein's son? The gun, the bike chase?'

'People are after Cyrus.'

'Go to the Israeli Embassy,'

'We have to leave Egypt immediately; I can explain later,' said Elias

'Why the money?'

'For a medivac jet. I'll pay you back. I have money, but my card is blocked.'

'Who's sick?' asked Ophelia.

'No one, we'll use the medivac to get us all out of Egypt.'

'All?'

'With you helping us, it's best if you have some time away from Egypt.'

'Why not fly normal?'

'Not possible, we have to go private.'

'When?'

'I want to book the medivac now, for tomorrow.'

'From Alexandria?' asked Ophelia.

'Yes, book now, then organise the paperwork with Gamal.'

'It's a lot of money,' said Ophelia.

'Yes, and a lot of trust.'

'Einstein's son,' said Ophelia.

'Yes,' said Cyrus.

'You said we leave Egypt? My passport?'

'You may be in danger for helping.'

'The man with the gun?'

'And other men too. We need to get to safety and sort all this out,' said Elias.

Ophelia knew the Tora taught you to help those who came to your door in need. But twenty-five thousand dollars. She had worked and saved all her life. She took a sip of the *koshary* tea then lifted her hands to her mouth.

'Let me show you,' said Elias. Ophelia watched Elias's mobile screen as he typed his ID and password at Bank Hapoalim. Then he selected accounts. Ophelia looked at the balances, over six million shekels.

'My accounts have been blocked; I can't access them.'

'I trust you,' said Ophelia, but now she trusted him more.

'Einstein's son,' she said. 'A friend of Noya's.' Ophelia opened her wallet and placed her card on the table. Elias took Ophelia's hand, and squeezed for several seconds.

'Thank you, thank you.' Online, Elias booked the flight with the German medivac company, departing from Alexandria at nine the following morning. Moments later, Ophelia received an instant payment notification. Elias knew it was also a time location stamp advertising when and where they'd be.

'Where will we fly to?' asked Cyrus.

'I've booked for Frankfurt. Now I need to speak to Gamal.' Elias spoke with Gamal then addressed Ophelia.

'We need to book into a hotel.'

'But—' Her face crinkled.

'A hotel booking in Cairo should keep them looking for us in Cairo.' Elias drummed his fingers on the table.

They left Cyrus then, and an hour later Elias and Ophelia returned. Two nights at the Kempinski Nile Hotel and a hotel car and driver booked to go to Port Said the following morning; a double decoy. Ophelia used her passport as ID and paid with Elias's US dollars. She entered the hotel room, messed up the bathroom and the bed to make it look like she'd slept in it, then left.

○

They ate dinner in the Naguib Mahfouz Café and when Gamal arrived with the ambulance it was quite dark. A driver drove the ambulance for Gamal. During the drive to Alexandria, Ophelia wore a paramedic uniform and sat in the cab. In the back, Elias worked with Gamal and submitted medivac documentation. They passed through two checkpoints on the two-hundred kilometre drive to Alexandria. At both, the police waved the ambulance through. In Gamal's Alexandria villa, it was 10.00 p.m. Eleven hours until evacuation. Elias stood in the villa's office as the printer churned out the documents needed to clear Alexandria immigration. He heard a door open and close; it was Ophelia returning from the supermarket.

Cyrus got up from his chair and took a grocery bag from her. He recoiled when his eyes met Ophelia's.

'Tell me what's going on, please.' Ophelia handed Cyrus a copy of the Cairo newspaper, *Al-Ahram*. Cyrus smoothed a fold from the page which carried photographs of him and Elias. Ophelia stood with her arms crossed.

'What is it?' asked Elias.

The front page had a photo of Cyrus who was described as Syria's leading biowarfare scientist, and of Elias an ex-Israeli spy. Both were wanted in connection with the killing of a Syrian government official in Sharm El-Sheikh. They were thought to be in Cairo and an Interpol arrest warrant had been issued. Elias bent over Cyrus's shoulder.

'A lie,' said Cyrus.

'Biowarfare, a spy and they say you killed a Syrian army man,' said Ophelia.

'It's untrue,' said Elias.

'Why your photographs?'

'The Syrian killed was an army major, he travelled to Egypt with Cyrus, to keep watch on him. When we left Sharm El-Sheikh, the Syrian was alive. Does it say when the Syrian was killed?'

Ophelia scanned the article. 'Shot at 12.15 p.m.'

Elias opened a text message on his mobile from Chris.

'Read this.'

Ophelia read the text. 'It says your passport was scanned in El Tor at 12.03 p.m., Cyrus's at 12.04 p.m.'

'El Tor is over an hour's drive from Sharm El-Sheikh,' said Elias.

'It couldn't be you, why do they say it?'

'Dangerous people are doing things we don't understand.'

'We'll go to the Israeli Embassy.'

'Someone in Israel means Cyrus harm, someone powerful, maybe in Israeli security, until we know, we trust no one.'

'Why harm Einstein's son?'

'I think they're scared, Cyrus could cause political change.'

'It's all wrong,' said Ophelia. 'I'm sorry to have questioned you.'

Cyrus touched Elias on the shoulder and softly said, 'I think we should tell Ophelia.'

'What?' asked Ophelia. She heard Cyrus whisper her name.

'Please sit down,' Elias said. 'There's something we need to tell you.'

Ophelia sat in a yellow chair.

'Cyrus has found proof for the existence of a deity.'

'How?' she whispered.

'He has proven the formation of life required intelligent design, a scientific and mathematical proof.'

Ophelia searched the two faces, in both, she found an unmoving conviction, the certainty of truth. Ophelia's lips trembled, her eyes blinked and filled with moisture. She felt light-headed, thought a thousand thoughts. How could anyone prove God's existence. Man had sought this truth through the ages, but here with her now was a man of powerful intellect. Einstein's own son, fulfilling the prophecies. God vowed to send us a chosen one, a chosen one to save us, to establish a Kingdom on Earth. She gasped for air, her hands and arms quivered as her body heaved. Then tears flowed, flowed freely down her cheeks as she uttered the single word '*Massya.*' Ophelia lowered herself to the floor and kissed Cyrus's feet.

'Please,' said Cyrus. 'People's contributions, my ideas, are based on those who came before, I'm no Messiah.'

Ophelia lifted her head. 'I can't believe this, I can't believe, but I do believe. I knew you'd come, but to be with you, I can't believe it, in my heart I knew but to prove the existence of God. I believe you; I feel your truth. God is in you; you are from above. Cyrus, I'll follow you, serve in any way.'

'I'm feeling the weight of what this means. What to do next? Only we three can know,' Cyrus said.

'I can only do what's in my heart,' said Ophelia. 'I'm sorry, but I also feel frightened. I kissed your feet and called you the Messiah because the Old Testament prophesises God vowed to send us a chosen one—a chosen one to save us. As a Jew, I believe my Messiah to have a political role to establish a Kingdom on Earth. My mind is spinning. The significance, and you're here with me, with us now, the human impact, we need to protect you, people will be jealous of your power, how wonderful, how amazing—astounding you have come to us.'

'There's a danger in claiming to be anointed,' said Cyrus. 'You become a threat, and history has shown people take it upon themselves to prove you are not so anointed —that's what the newspaper is about.'

'But only we three know,' said Ophelia.

'Yes, only we three know this,' said Elias. 'But others know Cyrus may be trying to discover this proof, and that is why they are trying to kill him.'

'We can protect each other,' Elias said.

Then he talked about how the three of them were smart, resourceful, they'd keep each other safe. His audience was Cyrus and he saw Cyrus relax. Elias reflected on Ophelia's powerful response. If most people responded like Ophelia, civilisation would change, the forces mounted against them to stop such change would be colossal. Elias had been mentally preparing for a fight—he needed to prepare for war.

CHAPTER TWENTY-TWO
CAIRO, EGYPT, 30 JULY 2018

THE CAIRO POLICE surveillance team had lost the Jewish woman—and Eidelman—it had to be Eidelman the ex-Israeli special services guy. It was 10.30 p.m. and Nizsm wore his pressed light-brown uniform, with its three rows of coloured ribbons above the right pocket. The top button was undone and exposed a few greying hairs. Nizsm dragged on his Marlboro. He was head of the Egyptian police unit responsible for catching Elias and Cyrus. Nizsm watched his exhaled smoke with his dark eyes and their yellowing whites, and thought of his missed promotion opportunity. They'd let Eidelman and the Syrian bioweapons' expert get away at the Nile. And then Eidelman had disappeared with the Jewish woman after the motorbike chase farce. But the Jewish woman had checked into the Kempinski and planned to go to Port Said in the morning. Nizsm guessed Eidelman and the Syrian would travel to Port Said with the Jewish woman. Nothing else made sense. But then Nizsm knew this was an Israeli special services guy. He would be trained to make sure no one had any sense of what he was doing.

Earlier in the day, Nizsm had sent a search team to the Jewish woman's apartment but found nothing of apparent interest other than a list of syna-gogue parishioners and their contact details and another list of non-parish-ioners with contact numbers. He needed to chum the water, look for a fish to bite, a fish to gaff. Nizsm called the first name on the non-parishioner list, then the second name, then the third. The fourth name he called was Gamal Kouri.

'Hello, Gamal?' asked Nizsm.

'Yes, who am I speaking with please?' asked Gamal.

'A parishioner at the synagogue with Ophelia.' The cop paused, listen-ing, waiting for Gamal to speak, waiting for Gamal to expose information.

'How can I help you?' asked Gamal.

'I apologise it's late, I need to speak with Ophelia.'

'How did you get this number?'

'Have you seen Ophelia?'

'No, I have not. Do you need Ophelia's number?'

'I have it here. I'm a parishioner at the synagogue.'

'I'm sorry I cannot help you.'

'Do you live here in Cairo too?'

'I'm sorry, I don't know who you are. I cannot help you, goodbye.'

The cop stared at his mobile phone, stared in silence, he'd found his fish.

Gamal called Ophelia, who in turn relayed the strange call to Elias.

Elias checked his watch. Ten hours until the medivac jet landed. It was almost eleven. Elias knew the Mossad to be a relentless machine—day or night. But to his advantage, the Mossad focused on meticulous planning. For Elias, operating in a real-time setting levelled the field, in fact, tilted the field in his favour. Elias had the advantage, they were chasing him, by definition he was at least a step ahead. Elias called Gamal, they needed to meet with the ambulance now. Elias grabbed his backpack. That was Elias. Assessment and reaction. He told Cyrus and Ophelia to follow in a couple of minutes. Those chasing them would be looking for two males and a female, anything to sully the scent. The security man at the villa complex entrance did not lift his head as Elias passed through. A minute later, Cyrus and Ophelia followed. The three stole a few hundred metres along the street then waited in the shadows for Gamal's call.

Thirty minutes later, Gamal arrived driving the ambulance. He wore a white coat, his neck was full and soft and his square face fell in a sad smile. He was clean shaven with bushy dark hair and thick dark eyebrows. Elias analysed the settings on Gamal's mobile phone, and found there was a tracking mode. Gamal kept his SIM and dumped the mobile. No GPS on the ambulance; Elias checked. They drove a few blocks then parked in an unlit street. The four climbed into the rear.

At 3.00 a.m. Gamal's house in Alexandria was raided. The police found it empty.

Six hours until evacuation. Ophelia welcomed the time to be close to Cyrus. She lay on her side on one ambulance bed facing Cyrus on the other, while Elias and Gamal sat on the floor. Gamal had his body facing Ophelia but was talking to Elias. In low voices they planned and discussed actions for different scenarios. They talked all night and knew they could sleep on the medivac should their plan work.

○

At six o'clock in the morning, Gamal started the ambulance and drove to Alexandria Airport. He looked like he hadn't slept all night. Beside him, Ophelia again wore the white paramedic uniform.

'They're not terrorists,' Ophelia said to Gamal.

'I know.'

'It's best if you don't—'

'It's okay, I'm not asking questions. I'm in no need of answers.' Gamal's eyes left the road; he smiled at Ophelia then refocused on the traffic. A moment later, his eyes flicked back to Ophelia. He absorbed her presence in an instant and felt a visceral pain at the thought he could be seeing her for the last time. They rehearsed details of the getaway. How they would wait outside the restricted area until the medivac jet landed and create a sense of urgency with the airport security. Gamal would meet in the rear of the ambulance with the medivac doctor. Elias would liaise with the customs' official.

At Alexandria Airport, Gamal parked the ambulance in a lay-by that provided a clear view of incoming flights. Elias squashed into the ambulance cab beside Gamal and Ophelia. They planned and re-planned. Elias knew it was impossible to cover all the scenarios, but he wanted Gamal and Ophelia to be in the right mindset. An hour later, an airport police car cruised past, reduced speed, made a U-turn, then stopped in front of the ambulance. It was 8.00 a.m. An hour before the scheduled evacuation.

◯

A policeman who had spent the night on the surveillance team at the Kempinski called his boss, Nizsm. The surveillance cop had not seen the Israeli woman since she had checked in. On a pretext, he had reception call her room, but no one answered.

He accompanied hotel staff to her room—empty. It looked like she'd slept in the room, but she was gone. *If the Israeli woman is not at the hotel, then my great plan of having an undercover policeman drive her from the hotel to Port Said is not such a great plan,* Nizsm thought. Nizsm cursed; he should have involved the Mossad earlier. He called a colleague in Egypt's GID, who liaised with Israeli Intelligence and asked what information could be found on Ophelia Moschel who lived in Cairo.

◯

Gamal gripped the steering wheel of the ambulance and stared at the police car that pulled to a stop in front.

'What do we do?' asked Gamal.

'Leave it to me,' said Elias. He slipped a blue medical mask over his mouth and nose, then strode to the passenger side of the police car where he asked the policeman in the passenger side if they were the police escort. Of course, the middle-aged uniformed policeman had no idea what Elias was talking about and said no. Elias used a combination of smooth words and cash. The policemen, more interested in the cash than the smooth words, agreed to Elias's proposal.

Elias returned from the police car and with the yellow ambulance's blue lights flashing, Gamal followed the police car to the private jet airport entrance with its security barrier. The policeman talked to the security official at the barrier. The policeman's arm pointed back to their yellow ambulance. The barrier raised and Gamal followed the police car to a private jet loading area on the tarmac. Elias paid the police officer the agreed Egyptian pounds and the police car departed. A door opened at a nearby building and a man wearing a military green uniform slouched towards them. Elias noted with relief he was not wearing a side-arm.

'Follow my lead,' said Elias. He opened the door of the ambulance.

'Are you here for the air ambulance from Germany?' asked the green-uni-formed official.

'Did you speak to our police escort?' asked Elias.

'No, why?' The uniformed official scratched his neck. He looked about twenty years old.

'Are we at the correct gate?'

'This is the private jet gate.'

'Our police escort was correct then.'

'What time is the evacuation?'

'As soon as the jet arrives, maybe in an hour,' said Elias.

'We need to make sure our patient is stable,' said Gamal. Gamal pulled opened the rear ambulance door and climbed inside and pulled the door closed.

'You need to give me the passports of those travelling,' said the official. Elias paused, strode to the rear of the ambulance. He called over his shoulder to the official.

'Of course, but we need to attend to our patient first, if he dies no one will be going anywhere.' Elias scanned the sky. Nothing. He turned from the official and stepped into the back of the ambulance. He checked his watch, eight-twenty, the jet was due in ten minutes. The official banged on the closed ambulance door. Elias stepped out and scanned the sky, still nothing.

'Your passports,' said the official.

'Of course,' said Elias.

'Have you been to Germany?'

'I've never left Egypt.'

Elias shielded his eyes and scanned the sky. A black dot.

'Sorry, I realise there is—' said Elias. He stopped talking, turned away from the official and climbed back into the rear of the ambulance, pulling the door shut.

'Our jet is here,' said Elias. 'Going over this again, you talk to the people in the air ambulance, press for urgency, sign any documents they need, the important thing is to get Cyrus on board as fast as possible. We need to—' There was a banging on the ambulance door.

'Your jet is landing,' called the official. Elias opened the rear door and joined the official on the tarmac.

'We're ahead of schedule; our patient has a high temperature. It may be a bird flu-like virus; for your own safety please keep your distance.' Elias adjusted his face mask.

'Do you have the permit documentation?' asked the official.

'I understand soft copies were emailed to you yesterday from Germany, correct?'

'Yes.'

'Here's a duplicate copy of the documents you need.' Elias handed the official a folder containing the aircraft information, including airworthiness and registration certificates, worldwide insurance, complete crew information, and the flight schedule. He then handed him a second folder with the detailed patient information along with hospital information from Alexandria and Frankfurt.

'May I see the patient?'

'Do you want bird flu?'

'No.'

'Our patient became sick, really sick during the night; we have a serious medical emergency, need to get him into surgery at Frankfurt as soon as possible. When was the last medivac you supervised?'

'This is my first.'

Elias swallowed a smile. 'Then you're lucky.' Elias raised his voice to be heard above the taxiing jet. 'We're dealing with the top air ambulance company in Germany who insist on the highest level of documentation.'

When the jet stopped, Gamal reversed the ambulance and stopped ten paces from the side of the aircraft. Elias hurried to the passenger boarding bridge and greeted the male flight paramedic and female nurse who were leaving the aircraft. He gazed above the blue nose of the aircraft to the cockpit at two men. A total crew of four, as per the documentation provided to Gamal the previous evening.

'How's our patient?' asked the paramedic who looked to be in his thirties. He wore a green paramedic uniform that bore an Air Ambulance Worldwide emblem on the left upper chest.

'Anxious, we need to get him on board,' said Elias.

'I must examine him first,' said the paramedic. After taking Cyrus's pulse, the paramedic exposed Cyrus's bare chest and listened with his stethoscope.

'This man's heart isn't ischemic,' he said.

'The ECG is conclusive showing cardiac ischemia, he needs an immediate balloon angioplasty,' said Gamal as he pointed at Cyrus's chest.

'Not this man,' said the paramedic. 'We're not obliged to transport a patient if his medical condition doesn't match with the medical report.'

'Mr Mahmoud must be transported to the cardiovascular centre in Frankfurt; his life is in imminent danger.'

'I'll speak with our captain,' said the paramedic as he stepped down from the ambulance onto the tarmac.

The immigration official returned to Elias's side.

'I need to see the patient's passport.'

'Do you have a passport?' Elias asked him.

'No. I haven't travelled outside Egypt.'

'This is the same for Mr Mahmoud. There's a copy of his Egyptian ID in the patient file.'

'But he'll need a passport to enter Germany.'

'He'll be granted a visa waiver on entry because of the medical emergency. We need to get our patient on board, excuse me.' Elias rushed to the back of the ambulance where Gamal lifted a finger.

'A problem?' asked Elias.

'The paramedic examined Cyrus. He knows there's no heart issue and is discussing with the captain.'

○

At the same time, Mossad agent, Eliana Sternberg, in Israel's Cairo Embassy, received an urgent request from the Egyptian GID. What information could she find on Ophelia Moschel? Moschel is thought to be travelling with Eidelman and Zaydan. Sternberg directed her field analyst to access the Mossad computer system and search their Egyptian database for Ophelia Moschel. The analyst reviewed age, occupation, address and accessed banking and credit card databases and looked for any detail of interest.

'Anything?' asked Sternberg. The eyebrow over Sternberg's left eye was permanently raised. She questioned everything she read, questioned everything she heard and questioned everything she saw. Sternberg was twice the age of her male analyst.

'Moschel paid twenty-five thousand American dollars yesterday to Worldwide; a German air ambulance company.'

'Get me a phone contact for Worldwide,' said Sternberg. A few seconds later, the analyst called a German number.

'Hello, Air Ambulance Worldwide,' said the operator.

'Hello, who can I speak with to get details of an air ambulance flight from Egypt?' asked Sternberg.

'Our office is not open until nine o'clock, you'll need to call back.'

'I'm calling from the American Embassy in Cairo; we have a critical security issue and need details of a recent air ambulance flight.'

'If you need to book an air ambulance, I can transfer you or you can make a direct booking on our website.'

Sternberg shook her head. 'Transfer me!' She waited and listened to piped music. After several minutes the music stopped.

'Hello?'

'Hello, madam. Do you need to make a booking?' asked a German accented female.

'No, I need to know the details of an air ambulance flight paid for yesterday.'

'Our office for that information is not open until nine. Please call back.'

'This is an emergency.'

'Give me the reference number please?'

'I'm sorry I don't have it. I need to confirm the flight details.'

'Who are you?'

'I'm calling on behalf of Doctor Gamal Kouri, it's his patient. The flight from Egypt was paid by Ophelia Moschel.' Sternberg recited Ophelia's credit card number.

'And the security pin?'

'I apologise, but Ophelia is with our patient.'

'Can you give me the flight details?'

'I need you to confirm the flight details, my assistant made the booking for me, she was involved in an accident last night and is in surgery.'

'Is the air ambulance for her?'

'No, please confirm the details of the booking, the time and airfield the flight will leave from.'

'What's the name of the patient?'

'His name is, is … a mental block sorry, our assistant made the booking, I don't have these details at hand.'

'We're unable to provide any information on the flights without security verification. We need to protect our client's privacy.'

'I'm your client. This is a matter of life and death. I need to call the hospital and organise an ambulance to take our patient to the airfield.'

'This is most unusual. Are you a doctor?'

'Yes.'

'You, of all people should be aware of the need to protect patient confidentiality.'

'I agree with you. It's most unusual our assistant had a serious car accident. If our patient dies, we'll sue you personally.'

'Can you confirm the credit card number again and also the name of the card holder?'

Sternberg repeated the information.

'And you said it was a flight from Alexandria to Frankfurt?'

'Yes.' *Getting somewhere*, thought Sternberg. 'And the departure date?'

'Today, twenty-nine July.'

'The departure time?'

'Ten in the morning.'

Sternberg stared at her watch, nine o'clock. They had an hour, not long but long enough.'

'Oh, no wait,' said the girl. 'Ten is German time, the flight leaves at nine o'clock Egyptian time.'

Sternberg ended the call and spoke to her analyst.

'Get me air traffic control at Alexandria Airport.'

A few moments later, Sternberg told them she was from the police. They needed to stop the departure of the medivac jet and surround the plane with ground security.

○

Meanwhile, as he stood on the tarmac, Elias checked his watch, nine o'clock.

He boarded the jet. The paramedic was discussing Cyrus's status with the captain.

'I need to talk with you,' Elias said to the captain.

'I'm listening.'

'In private, please,' said Elias. The captain stepped into the cockpit and asked his co-pilot to leave. Elias joined the captain and closed the cockpit door.

'Are you familiar with the Canadian Caper?' asked Elias.

'The USA embassy staff escape from Iran?'

'Exactly, I'm an Israeli citizen, my female colleague is Egyptian, our patient Cyrus is Syrian, here are our passports. Albert Einstein and an Arab woman had a child about sixty-five years ago; the patient we are evacuating is Einstein's son. The Egyptians are trying to kill him because his father was a famous German Jew, we must take off now.'

'What? You've brought us to Egypt under a false pretense?' said the captain.

'We're in a desperate position. Can we discuss this further when we're airborne? Einstein's son's life is now in your hands.'

'I have only your word who he is.'

'This is one of those times you need to trust your instincts. Go and have a look at the patient and ask yourself who he looks like.' The captain frowned then ducked out of the cockpit and accompanied Elias and the paramedic to the rear of the ambulance. The captain disappeared inside and climbed out a few seconds later.

'Get the patient on board,' said the captain.

Relieved at hearing his words, Cyrus thought, *if it was Allah's wish, then it would be done.*

The paramedic pulled the collapsed gurney from the rear of the ambulance, stabilised it, then wheeled Cyrus to the medivac jet with Ophelia walking alongside holding an oxygen bottle. The immigration official marched across the tarmac and stood with his feet a hip-width apart and his body facing the gurney. He blocked their path to the jet.

'What are you doing?' asked the official.

'Saving this man's life,' said Ophelia. 'There's a problem with the oxygen in the ambulance. We need to get him to the emergency oxygen supply in the jet. Hold this bottle while we set up the oxygen in the plane.'

The official looked blank but held the bottle while Ophelia boarded the jet. Cyrus was then transferred to a medivac stretcher and taken on board. The official set a foot on the first boarding step.

'We need another blanket from the ambulance,' said Ophelia. The official ambled to the ambulance. A door in the nearby immigration building opened. Two security men carrying carbine machine guns strode towards them. Elias strolled from the tarmac to confront them.

'Please, I need a washroom,' said Elias.

One of the men stabbed a finger in the direction of the building.

'Can you show me?'

'You on the jet?'

'Yeah, but we're not going anywhere. Some engine problem.'

The security man grumbled, and stabbed his finger again. Elias took a slow step closer the kicked the security guy the groin. He grunted and dropped to his knees. Elias flew at the other and smashed his elbow against the top of his head. He folded like a tissue doll. Elias kneed the other guy under the chin who crouched with screaming nuts. His carbine fell and banged on the tarmac. Elias grabbed both carbines, and headed back to the jet.

The immigration official backed up as Elias approached. One of the jet engines sparked up. Another minute to go. Elias fired a shot in the air then aimed the weapon at the immigration man. The second engine sparked.

'*Yarkud!*' Elias shouted. The immigration official needed only one warning to run. Elias darted up the boarding steps.

'Buckle up; we're leaving,' the captain's voice called out over the intercom. Cyrus felt the jet lurch forward and he heard a beeping from the flight deck. The boarding door was still open. Elias tossed the carbines from the moving jet, then several seconds later he tossed the two magazines. Elias stepped back into the cabin, the stairs retracted and the jet taxied towards the runway. The co-pilot closed and locked the boarding door. The beeping stopped. Cyrus stared out of the porthole beside his seat; airport security vehicles raced toward the runway with flashing lights. The captain and co-pilot twisted their heads and scanned the sky for approaching aircraft.

They could not see any. It was now a race to the runway. There was no time to taxi and turn into the wind for take-off; take off would be down wind.

'Need to taxi faster, security vehicles closing,' said the co-pilot. The captain eased the thrust lever forward. Elias sat opposite Cyrus. Ophelia sat behind Cyrus biting on her fists.

'Thirty seconds,' said Elias.

'We'll beat them?' asked Cyrus. The jet seemed to skid sideways as they turned onto the runway then the engines roared.

'We've beaten them,' said Elias. The jet accelerated down the runway, lifted off, and headed on a bearing for Frankfurt.

Ten minutes into the flight, Elias left his seat for the open cockpit.

'There's been a change, we need to go to Zurich.'

'We've lodged a flight plan for Frankfurt,' said the captain.

'We need to go to Zurich. An ambulance will be waiting at Zurich Airport for us.' Elias pulled a wad of one-hundred-dollar American bills from his pocket. 'For your critical assistance and the inconvenience, we've caused you.'

'There is no need for *baksheesh*. I've taken you at your word and have a moral obligation to help.' The captain reprogrammed his flight management computer and submitted his revised flight plan to Zurich Airport. The jet dropped its right wing and veered north towards an air corridor over Italy. A few minutes later, Elias bent forward when he felt a pain in his stomach. He staggered to the toilet at the back of the plane and five minutes later returned to his seat.

'Are you feeling okay?' asked the medivac paramedic.

'I'm fine. I guess it's the Egyptian food.' Elias patted his stomach. Twenty minutes later, Elias was back in the toilet. He coughed, dry retched and smiled wryly at the decision he faced. Should he sit or stand? A few minutes later, he returned to his seat.

'Sure you're okay? asked the paramedic. 'You look pale.'

'I may have a bug.' There were beads of sweat on Elias's brow.

'Were you sick?'

'Almost, I'm going at the other end.'

'What's it like?' asked the paramedic.

Elias gave a questioning look.

'With Giardia for example the stool is clay coloured.'

Elias thought for a moment. 'The colour looked normal.'

'I'll take your temperature.'

'It's okay; I'll be fine.' But he was not fine. He vomited several times over the following hour and had persistent diarrhoea. Elias kept his fluid intake up and his head down.

○

Sternberg received the message from the Alexandria control tower. They were too late. The jet had departed for Frankfurt, but then veered towards Italy. Sternberg's left eyebrow raised further. The flight time to Frankfurt was five hours, veering towards Italy, they could be going anywhere. They needed a new plan.

○

Reznik drained a Red Bull Zero then crushed the alloy can in his fist. A trusted intel source had just informed him Mossad were going to close him down and he knew what being closed down by Mossad meant. He had paid half a million American of his budget to the two Israeli back-up assassins; he instructed them to go to Frankfurt. Reznik didn't want these two assassins anywhere near him, they would betray him in an instant.

Reznik knew Eidelman and Zaydan had crossed the east Sahara Desert in buggies to El Minya then taken a Nile boat to Cairo, where Eidelman was almost captured, followed by a medivac jet out of Alexandria. Two days. Two days to cross the East Sahara, get to Cairo and escape Egypt on the medivac. A fast two days. Reznik thought if they wanted to hide, why not go up the Nile from El Minya, up the Nile into southern Egypt and central Africa. Few police. Even fewer security agents and no security cameras. They could hide in central Africa for an age. It wasn't the Interpol red notice that forced them to run out of Egypt. Their intended plan was to run. He knew they were not going to Frankfurt. The question was, where were they running to and why were they running there? Reznik thought, then thought some more, then bounced lightly on the balls of his feet—with his false passport, he booked a flight to Rome.

CHAPTER TWENTY-THREE

COMO, ITALY, 31 JULY 2018

ELIAS STUMBLED INTO the cockpit holding his stomach and a map.
'We need to land here.' He sharpened his eyes and his finger
pointed to a private airfield near Italy's Lake Como.

The captain, who wore aviator glasses and had short blond hair, looked
at where Elias's finger was pointing. The captain and his co-pilot were about
the same age as Elias.

'It's not that simple; what happened to Zurich?' asked the captain.

For Elias, no regular airport was an option or ever had been. A regular
airport meant checking passports and security and with the Interpol red
notice—no. The private airfield Elias wanted to land at had a two kilometre
sealed runway. It would take the medivac jet without an issue. The private
strip was at Caproni's summer house; the Caproni family made corporate
jets. It was illegal for private jets to enter another country without clearing
customs. Illegal, but there were always exceptions. That was the thing about
laws—written words on a page to cover most situations but with opt-out
clauses for exceptions. Explaining the flight manifest to the IAA would be

easy, Cyrus, Ophelia and Elias didn't board the medivac plane. They were not on the manifest. There was no record of them in Alexandria. The captain of the medivac jet pressed his mic and called Zurich air traffic control. He said they'd experienced clear air turbulence and dropped over three thousand feet; he needed to make an emergency landing at a private airstrip in Como. The Zurich air controller instructed the captain to contact Milan Lineate Airport. The captain switched off his radio.

○

At Caproni's summer residence, an elderly groundsman in blue overalls looked up and raised his hand to shield his eyes as a blue and red branded G505 Gulfstream made a slow fly-by over the airstrip, banked, set up an approach and landed. The groundsman trotted to the main house and called out to Umberto.

'*Signor! Signor!*'

Umberto appeared at a side entrance beside the kitchen.

'*Signor*, an air ambulance Gulfstream has landed.'

'Who do I know with a Gulfstream?'

'The words Air Ambulance Worldwide on the fuselage.'

Umberto Caproni, son of Count Giovanni Caproni who designed and built Italy's first aircraft, drove his Fiat Bambina convertible, from his summer residence through the grounds on a white-pebbled path to the strip. Four German Shepherds padded behind the Bambina. At the end of his runway, a woman and two men descended from the jet; one man moved unsteadily. Umberto drove close and stopped. The German Shepherds stopped too. They froze with their eyes fixed on the strangers.

'*Ciao.*' Umberto waved his tanned arm. His dark hair was swept back; he had a fine frame and his face was a smile. An industrial magnate, billionaire and playboy, Umberto kept his youthful looks playing tennis, hunting with falcons, eating fine food and indulging an endless supply of aspiring Milanese models. A new lover taught you something about yourself and Umberto knew himself better than anyone.

'Hello,' said Cyrus. He and Umberto shared a private smile—recognising each other's youthful looks.

'I'm Umberto.' He jumped from the Bambina and with a smile shook their hands. Elias gave Umberto a rapid explanation of how they came to be in Italy. He omitted the deity constant information.

'We need to get somewhere safe, in a hurry,' Elias added.

'This is wonderful.' Umberto beamed. 'I've led a wasted play-boy life. How could I expect to achieve anything compared to my father? And now, now I get to help Einstein's son, *fantastico*!'

The four squashed into the Bambina. Umberto drove on the white pebbled path past an archery range, a tennis court, a swimming pool, and a private chapel to a three-storey, hundred room 1920s villa.

Cyrus gazed at two cages containing about fifty large birds with dark plumage and sharp beaks. 'Falcons?' Cyrus asked.

'I've just returned from falcon hunting in Scotland. You're lucky to find me here. I'll get car keys. Is there anything you need?'

'I'm unwell; I need a restroom,' said Elias. He had beads of sweat on his forehead and his hair was damp. After Elias's restroom stop, they walked from the villa to a large garage. Umberto swung open the garage door. Inside sat a black Maserati, a white Fiat saloon, and two 18th-century carriages. Ophelia looked inside the small carriage. It was for two people and was lined with deep Persian blue velvet. They took the Fiat.

'We'll take the back roads to Milan,' said Umberto. 'The *polizia* get excited when anything unusual happens, we don't want them getting lucky.'

○

An hour and a half later, in the Milanese suburb of Porta Garibaldi, Umberto braked the Fiat to a stop in the courtyard of a city villa. The villa belonged to a friend of Umberto's who was in Australia for a few months.

Inside, Umberto uncorked a bottle of red wine. 'What are we going to do with you now?' he asked.

'Our situation is more complex,' said Elias.

Umberto's brown eyes shone.

'How so?'

'Elias asked me if I could prove the existence of God.' All eyes were on Cyrus. 'I've proven that life needed divine intervention.'

'Proven?' asked Umberto.

'Mathematically, scientifically proved that it's theoretically impossible for life to have occurred by chance. Life needed a deity.'

'You're telling me God is real?' His face beamed.

'Yes.'

The energy in the room changed. Umberto was silent as he paced in a slow circle, then he sat down and eye-balled them. Each one met his eyes with resolute confidence.

'I don't know what to say … it's like a dream. You've all had time to think about this; my mind is out of control. What does all this mean? What's going to happen?'

'We need Cyrus to get asylum in the Vatican,' said Ophelia.

'Once he's in the Vatican, Cyrus can tell the world.'

'I feel insignificant,' said Umberto. 'This is the most amazing thing I've ever heard. This is incredible.'

'We've been blessed to meet you,' said Cyrus. 'God's will,' he added with a glint.

'We need a plan to get asylum,' said Ophelia.

'I know everyone in Italy,' said Umberto. 'Not because of me, because of my father, he built the first plane in Italy, in the chapel at the Como house we have the wreckage of Mussolini's son's plane. He was shot down in Egypt flying a plane my father built. My father built over three thousand planes for our air force in World War Two. Just telling you so you know. We've seen amazing things before, but proof of God, this is extraordinary. It's going to change our future.'

'We have the Italian A team,' said Elias.

'Not me, but I know the A team,' said Umberto.

'First thoughts?' asked Elias.

'Rothschilds,' said Umberto.

'Why Rothschilds?'

'They have leverage over the Vatican Bank,' replied Umberto.

Elias stood up. As he headed to get a glass of water he stumbled and leant against a chair arm. Ophelia leapt up and steadied him.

'Feeling hot, a bit dizzy. I need water,' he said.

'Lie down and I'll get the water,' said Ophelia.

'Make me a list of the food you need,' said Umberto. His mobile buzzed

'Si.' Umberto listened. The guard from Umberto's gatehouse told him the counterterrorism unit of the *carabinieri* corps were there.

'Give the police Carlo's number,' said Umberto, referring to one of his lawyers. Umberto ended the call, then called Carlo and gave him a brief. Carlo asked Umberto to meet him as soon as possible and they'd go to the police. The counterterrorism unit of the army could shoot and there would be no questions asked. This was not a game. *Not a game. Is this what people think of me … what they think I'm cut out for in life? My life's been a game— huh! That's why they call it playboy. What would my father do?*

After opening cupboards and checking the fridge-freezer, Ophelia wrote a list for Umberto.

'I'm sorry we have no Euro,' she said.

'You can pay me back tomorrow,' replied Umberto.

'Funny man,' murmured Elias who was lying on a couch. The others laughed.

'Do you have identification showing you are Einstein's son?' asked Umberto. 'For Vatican asylum.'

'Photometric data but DNA analysis will prove it,' said Cyrus. 'We need a lab to test a mouth swab.'

'Let me know what you need,' said Umberto. 'I'll be back; I have the list.' He held up the shopping list and gave it a shake.

'Can we get a doctor to look at Elias?' asked Cyrus.

'I'll call one. Her name is Chiara Bertolaso in case she comes before I get back.' Umberto left for the supermarket. The three sat in silence then without warning Elias sat up in a hurry.

'We need to leave now!' he said.

'What?' asked Ophelia.

'Now! They'll have our location from Umberto's mobile.' *I must be sick,* thought Elias, *should have made sure there were no mobiles when we left Como.*

A few moments later, they hurried along the villa driveway where tall automatic wrought-iron gates formed a barrier from the street.

Elias hurried to a pillar beside the gates. 'Look for an exit button,' he said. There was no button on the pillar he examined.

'Nothing here,' said Ophelia.

'Beside … in the garden?'

'No,' said Ophelia.

Cyrus looked closely at a tree. Next to the trunk was a post and a green button. He pressed it. The wrought iron gates opened slowly. They hurried out.

'How can we contact Umberto?' asked Cyrus.

'It was Doctor Bertolaso,' said Ophelia.

'Who?' asked Elias.

'The doctor Umberto was organising, Bertolaso,' said Ophelia.

'Umberto's mobile number?' asked Cyrus.

'Yes,' said Ophelia. 'The doctor must have his number.'

'Good thinking,' said Cyrus.

'You two this side … I'll cross,' said Elias.

'Which way?' asked Cyrus.

After looking one way then the next, Elias pointed in the direction with the tallest buildings. He swayed as he crossed the road. At a rock wall, he stopped and rested his hand the wall, then carried on. He looked across at Cyrus and Ophelia. She was walking and talking on her burner mobile.

'Elias said you're being tracked through your mobile, you need to dump it.

'Ahh … right … okay,' said Umberto.

'Meet us at the doctor's surgery.'

'The doctor?'

'Don't say the name, but the doctor you're organising for our sick friend,' said Ophelia.

'Yes, okay.'

The sky was thick and black. A lightning bolt flashed. Elias blinked and looked up at where the flash had been; the flash lived in his eyes until the thunder rolled. Elias staggered and steadied himself. Another bright fork was followed by an immediate bang that seemed to shake the ground. Elias felt a raindrop. He swayed again and wanted to stop. But they were still too close to the villa. Then came a roaring noise. Elias looked back. It sounded like a truck. Behind him it was dark; there were more big raindrops and then a waterfall. Within two more paces, Elias felt his shirt stick to his back. It was wet and cold and it felt good.

'Elias! Elias!' Was someone calling him? 'Elias!' His name again, a female voice. Then a hand on his shoulder. 'We've got a taxi,' said Ophelia.

'US dollars?'

'Yes, we asked him.' She wrapped her arm around Elias's waist and supported him across the road. Elias almost slipped on white road paint, but Ophelia held him tightly.

'Front seat,' said Elias. He slumped in the seat and Ophelia clipped his seat belt.

'*Ventidue Via Mozart per favore,*' said Ophelia.

Behind them, two black SUVs pulled up at the villa.

Elias bent forward. He sat on the ground, his back against the wall outside Doctor Bertolaso's office.

'He's here,' said Ophelia.

Umberto stopped the white Fiat at the kerb. Cyrus gave Elias a hand up.

'Need the front seat … could be sick,' said Elias. Cyrus helped him in. 'Can they, they, link this car, link it to you?' Elias asked. He had clear thought but spoke through a haze.

'Not easily, one of many in the company.'

'They have evidence we were at the villa with you,' said Elias.

'What?'

'My prints are on record in Israel.'

'Ah.'

'The Interpol arrest warrant, you're an accessory,' said Elias. The wipers swished. Elias looked past the wipers, but still felt his eyes follow the swishing blades. Lots of blurred lights. Unfocussed. His stomach tightened. 'Stop! Stop!'

Umberto pulled over and Elias opened his door, leant out against the safety belt, and retched. Umberto leant across, popped the glovebox and handed Elias a packet of tissues. Elias blew his nose and wiped his mouth, then dropped the tissues in the gutter.

'Okay?' asked Umberto.

'Uh huh.' Elias pulled the door closed. 'Security camera!'

'What?' asked Umberto.

'Does the villa have a security camera.'

'Assume so, didn't see.'

'We need another car. Fast.'

○

At the villa a counter-terrorism agent rolled the security footage back an hour then fast forward. A white Fiat, registration BR227EV and four people.

○

Umberto paused … he was thinking … mid-week late afternoon … who would be home, not away on vacation.

'Stop. Get out … we'll walk … flag a taxi,' said Elias. Umberto stopped the Fiat. Cyrus and Umberto walked fifty metres ahead of Elias and Ophelia. Umberto flagged a taxi with its hire light on. They got in. A *polizia* car, with red and blue lights flashing and the siren blaring, raced past going the other way.

The taxi stopped in the Magenta District at a fine old building of marble and pillars Umberto spoke on the intercom, disappeared inside, and reappeared a few minutes later from an underground parking garage driving a basil-green Peugeot sedan. Ophelia got into the rear seat with Cyrus. There were three large folded towels.

'You'll find towels to dry,' said Umberto.

Ophelia dried her hair, arms and legs and dabbed her dress.

'Where will we go?' she asked.

'Renzano, two hours away,' replied Umberto.

'Why Renzano?' asked Cyrus, who sat behind Umberto.

'A childhood friend with a long driveway, we'll be safe.'

'Should have thought … thought of mobiles … sorry,' said Elias.

'How can mobiles track?' asked Ophelia.

'SIGNIT.' Elias pressed the palms of his hands to either side of his head.

'Huh?'

'Signals intelligence,' said Elias. 'Sweep up signals … and … and create new ones.'

'Create new?' asked Umberto.

'Yeah,' said Elias, 'like stingray … it hijacks a mobile-phone tower … contacts nearby mobiles … even if they're switched off … mobiles respond … giving real-time geolocation … and lots of other data.'

Ophelia thought they should let Elias rest. She touched Cyrus's arm to get his attention. Then she closed her eyes and nodded her head towards Elias. Umberto drove on the A35 to Brescia then turned off to Renzano.

At just after seven in the evening, Umberto nosed the Peugeot into a long narrow drive. The drive wound up a valley. On one side of the drive was a low stone wall and on the other was a wire fence with posts cut from hardwood trees.

'Well done, everybody,' said Ophelia. 'Hard to believe we were in Alexandria this morning.'

Elias stirred. The driveway stopped at a double-level stone farmhouse. A man with a grey moustache came out, squinted at the car then walked to the driver's door.

'*Ciao,* Umberto. He kissed both of Umberto's cheeks then hugged him.

'What a surprise … a fantastic surprise to see you … it's been …'

'It's been my fault. I've been chasing myself around,' said Umberto.

'Chasing yourself?' murmured Giorgio.

Umberto laughed loudly with his mouth open. 'This is Giorgio,' he said. 'Meet my friends, Ophelia, Cyrus, and Elias.' When Cyrus shook hands with Giorgio, he could tell he was a working farmer; wiry, tanned forearms and strong hands.

'Come in, come in, have you eaten?' asked Giorgio.

'No,' said Umberto.

'Fabulous, I'll cook, what're you doing around here, where're you staying?'

'We need to stay with you.' Giorgio's smile got wider.

'I'll take the floor,' said Umberto, 'like when we were kids.'

Giorgio laughed. 'You'll need to.'

'I was going to cook dinner in Milan tonight; it's a long story you'll hear … anyway I'll get the food from the car.'

'Our guests will have two chefs,' said Giorgio.

They entered Giorgio's house and saw an open-plan living area. A cane basket stacked with wood sat beside a wood-burner. Away from the burner on a pink-plastered wall was a stuffed fellow deer head.

'Please, make yourselves at home, it's your home now,' said Giorgio.

'Red wine?'

'No, *grazie,*' said Elias, recalling his promise to himself in Alexandria,

If we get safe I'll stop, although he considered asking if Giorgio had whiskey; he knew he needed something.

'*Si, grazie*,' said Ophelia. Cyrus, being Druze, declined and drank mineral water.

Umberto uncorked a bottle of *Barolo* and poured a small amount into a glass for Giorgio to taste. Giorgio swirled the wine like he'd done a thousand times and looked at the colour and thought about the grapes' journey from the vine. The wine was superb.

'No vegetarians?' asked Umberto.

'No,' said Ophelia.

'Well, you never know, have to ask, so many these days. When I was a boy there were none, people were happy just to have food to eat.'

Giorgio placed a large white plate on the bench for the *antipasto*. 'You've brought everything,' he said.

'Elias is sick and needs a doctor, a discreet doctor,' said Umberto.

Giorgio nodded, left the room, made a call and returned. 'An hour,' he said.

'Thanks. Would you believe Interpol are chasing us,' said Umberto. 'I planned to cook this in Milan, but here we are.' Umberto gave Giorgio details as he rubbed stale *ciabatta* and made breadcrumbs. Then Umberto beat two eggs, dipped veal cutlets in the beaten egg then covered the egg-coated cutlets with the breadcrumbs.

Elias sat and drank mineral water as the two men cooked. They chatted and chuckled like a couple of teenagers.

Ophelia had a shower and after the shower put the same clothes back on. It was two days now. Elias and Cyrus seemed content wearing the same clothes. *It was different for men,* but she didn't want to say anything. She already felt like a burden, yet she had helped with the medivac jet, and was trying to take care of Elias and then there was her help with Umberto's number. She shouldn't feel like a burden, but she did and there it was. And then she realised why she felt like a burden. It was the way the men responded to the questions she asked, questions she wanted answers to, so she could help more, but when she asked questions, there was a change in the air, they were all polite, too polite, unnatural. It made her feel clumsy.

I'm just a simple Cairo girl with these super men. After returning to the living area, Ophelia sat away from the super men.

They ate the *antipasto,* which included artichokes, olives, sundried tomatoes, pepperoni, salami, provolone and Parmigiano Reggiano—it had everything. As they ate, Umberto did most of the talking.

'To the chefs.' Cyrus raised his glass. He sat on a chair with its legs wired together, the wooden stretchers no longer held by glue.

'Time to cook,' said Giorgio. At the gas cook-top he heated three frying pans. The melted butter sizzled when the crumbed veal cutlets were added. It was the water in the cutlets forming droplets under the oil and exploding that made the sizzle. The rangehood hummed. Giorgio eyed the cutlets as they fried. When they were brown at the edges, he dug a fork into each browned cutlet and turned them over. If he were by himself, he'd have flipped the cutlet like a pancake, but he didn't want to be seen putting on a show. They ate the crumbed cutlets with fresh rocket and sliced tomatoes.

'This is fantastic,' said Ophelia.

'Traditional cooking, don't burn or undercook it and it's fine,' said Giorgio.

There were exchanges of, '*Cin cin!*'

'The Vatican is a great idea,' said Umberto.

'It might be,' said Cyrus. 'But I have no idea how to make it work.'

Just then, the doorbell rang. Giorgio left the table and returned with a light-haired middle-aged woman who wore beige and carried a black leather bag and another bag. The other bag was made of heavy brown paper and bore the brand name *Ferretti.*

Cyrus stood up. Elias pushed up from his chair but sat back down. On his second try Elias was able to stand.

'This is my friend, Daniella, she's making an evening house call,' said Giorgio.

'We need our soldier well,' said Cyrus. He moistened his lips, swallowed and tasted a cutlet.

'You must be Ophelia,' said Daniella.

'Yes, hello Daniella.'

'I hope these fit.' Daniella held out the brown paper bag. 'Giorgio said you got soaked in Milan.'

'Thank you. Thank you so much.' Ophelia kissed her cheek, then thanked Giorgio, then turned and thanked Umberto. She blinked her smiling eyes. 'I'll go and change now.' She felt very small, yet she felt very big and she felt very happy.

'In time for dessert,' said Giorgio. He put a plate of biscotti on the table and a bottle of *vin santo*, then he found a glass for Daniella.

'A sweet wine to dip the *cantucci*?' Giorgio held the bottle over Elias's glass

'Thank you.' Elias dipped a *cantucci* into the wine … sucked the wine from the biscuit and dipped again.

After dessert, Elias sat with Daniella in Giorgio's study.

'You've been travelling,' said Daniella.

'Egypt.'

'How long have you been unwell?'

'One day.'

'Symptoms?'

'I feel hot, vomiting, diarrhoea.'

She inserted a thermometer probe into Elias's ear and pressed the scan button.

'You have a fever.'

'What is it?'

'Forty.' She tested Elias's blood pressure. It was slightly elevated, but that was to be expected. 'Any mosquitos in Egypt?'

Elias flashed back to hiding in the Nile under the walkway and the swarm of mosquitos in the waste-water drain.

'Yes, why?'

'Take off your shirt, please.' The doctor touched her fingers to a patch of raised rash on Elias's chest.

'Turn around.'

Elias's turned and Daniela saw his back was covered in the raised rash.

'Does your back itch?'

'A bit.'

'Maybe dengue, looks like dengue. I don't think it's malaria. I'll need some blood.'

'No.' Elias knew malaria and dengue would be notifiable. Nothing to attract attention.

'You have your reasons, but dengue is a serious viral disease.' Daniella recommended paracetamol, hydration, rest and was pleased when Elias told her he had not had dengue before as recurrent infection is more dangerous. Elias was told to expect his fever to go up and down for a few days. He felt better now he had a diagnosis. They rejoined the others.

'In Milan, you suggested Rothschilds,' Elias said when there was a break in the chatter. He drank more sparkling mineral water and raised the back of his hand to his hot forehead.

'I'll call now.' Umberto made two calls, one to get the number, because he was using a clean untraceable mobile, and then to his Rothschilds contact in France.

'Marco will come tomorrow evening,' said Umberto.

'A blood sample, Cyrus?' asked Daniella.

'Yes, thank you.' In Giorgio's study Cyrus gave Daniella a piece of paper with the DNA sequences of thirteen sets of PCR primers, each primer 18-20 base pairs long. Cyrus explained to Daniella the PCR primer sequences were used to generate his father's DNA profile. Chris had hacked into a USA database containing DNA sequences from Einstein's brain and sent Cyrus the PCR primer sequences. These sequences allow amplification and identification of specific regions of DNA. The same DNA regions needed to be amplified from Cyrus's chromosomes to allow a comparison with Einstein.

'How long will it take?' Ophelia asked when they returned.

'Depends if the lab uses the same primers,' said Cyrus.

'If they do?' asked Ophelia.

'In theory, hours, less than a day.'

'If they don't?' asked Ophelia.

'New primers will need to be sequenced. A week, maybe more.'

Umberto impressed urgency to Daniella; an overnight analysis, if possible, whatever it cost.

CHAPTER TWENTY-FOUR

RENZANO, ITALY, 01 AUGUST 2018

H IS FIRST TIME—CYRUS swayed from side to side in a white rope hammock strung between two chestnut trees. The knots pressed on his back. Above him a song thrush in the chestnut sang its flute-like song ... a happy-sounding song. *I suppose other birds think it's a happy sound too.* It was summer, so the singing bird must have a mate from the spring. He didn't hear birds singing in Damascus. Maybe years ago, they sang, he couldn't remember. He swayed slowly from side to side and reflected on the deity constant. A truth released to the wind of time, and time would decide if the wind was a light breeze or a hurricane. Not for personal fame but for satisfaction he hoped to witness his *constant* accepted and not neglected for one hundred years, as was the art of Klimt, before Klimt's art had an impact. He wanted to witness the moral value of his search for truth, and witness the value at finding that truth. Cyrus saw a world that had become divided, a dangerous and oppressed world without hope. The free world strangled by those re-inventing the meaning of truth and democracy, and strangled by the loss of free speech and strangled by the loss of freedom itself. Cyrus saw the deity constant as a new light throwing light on a darkening humanity. Freeing the free world.

As Cyrus listened to the song thrush, he heard the wind above in the chestnut trees and further away he could hear the sound of men's laughter from within the stone farmhouse. Then he heard the sound of a car, the sound grew louder; he thought it must be the Rothschilds man. It was the Rothschilds man. Cyrus rocked from the hammock and strode to greet him. At the car they shook hands and Cyrus found Marco's grey eyes held on his when they spoke. Marco was from Toulon in the south of France, but spoke English with an English accent. His dark hair was cut no fuss short back and sides. He was in his late forties and was an inch or two shorter than Cyrus. Marco seemed happy. Cyrus wondered if he had a mate like the singing thrush, but he didn't ask.

'Greetings, I'm Marco.' He extended his hand.

'A deep pleasure to meet you. I'm Cyrus.' Marco took in a man with lightly tanned skin who was younger than he expected. *Not like an American, and no American accent.*

'Tell me,' said Marco. 'Where are you from?'

'Damascus.'

'Damascus in Virginia?' asked Marco.

'Syria,' replied Cyrus.

They walked and talked as they entered Giorgio's house. As they talked Cyrus mulled his own private thoughts. Syria; a distant memory. After three days of living, he'd found life. Or had life found him. How free he felt.

'*Ciao,* Marco,' said Umberto. 'I see you've met Einstein's son.'

'*Ciao,* Umberto,' Marco and Umberto cheek kissed then Marco was introduced to Ophelia, Giorgio and Elias.

Elias felt his temperature was up, but not as high, the paracetamol were working.

Umberto showed Marco the DNA genealogy data that proved Cyrus was Einstein's son. The Italian lab had the required primers and produced the analysis overnight.

'Why asylum in the Vatican?' Marco asked.

'Safety,' said Cyrus. 'And the Vatican is high-profile to tell the world I have theoretical proof of a deity.'

'A proof of God?' asked Marco.

'Yes,' said Umberto.

Marco sat on the sofa without speaking and one by one looked through his wire-framed glasses at the others. Umberto knew what Marco must be thinking. Thoughts about everything at once with thoughts that collided, and thoughts that hit and crashed and struck and bumped and rebounded, rebounded into space where they could not be caught. It was like being told that proof of God had been found.

'Proof?' Marco asked.

'A scientific and mathematical formula showing life could not have started by chance,' said Cyrus. Marco turned to Umberto.

'You believe this?'

'Yes,' Umberto said.

'Divine intervention?' Marco asked.

'Life could not have evolved by chance,' said Cyrus.

'How can you put yourself back a billion years to say that?' asked Marco.

'Do you know what's required for life, for cell replication?' asked Cyrus.

'I'm sure it's complex,' said Marco. 'But it's a time verses God argument.'

'A very large number of very specific complex molecules are required to be in a specific place at the same specific perfect time to make the first replicating life form.'

'I agree, but you're talking general,' said Marco.

'Today we know what those specific complex molecules had to be and we can calculate the probability of these complex molecules forming by random chance.'

'What's the chance?' asked Marco.

'The chance of randomly making one protein correctly is one chance in a very large number,' said Cyrus.

'What's the number?' asked Marco.

'The random chance of forming one protein with the required structure and function is the same chance as rolling, thirty die with a million-sides and getting a six on every die.'

'Crazy,' said Marco. 'How amazing.'

'Any mathematician will tell you the probability equates to zero, meaning it's impossible to occur by chance,' said Cyrus.

There was a brief silence then Marco spoke again.

'That's the biggest number I've ever thought of, or rather the smallest, you know what I mean.'

'Except, this is for just one complex molecule ... many, many complex molecules are needed. When you take these other necessary molecules into account, the random chance gets really small,' said Cyrus.

'As if the chance was not small enough, a mathematical certainty,' said Marco.

'Yes.'

'I'm sorry, you've all been quiet, patient with me. Assuming the fundamentals are correct, this is stunning, beyond stunning, stunning to the exponential, was it fifteen trillions?' Marco laughed.

'I've called the proof, the scientific and mathematical derivation, the deity constant,' said Cyrus. He wrote the equation for Marco:

$$\Xi = YM(2^{0-PX})4^{-L}$$

○

'I'm no mathematician, but it looks impressive,' said Marco.

'Have you heard of deism?' asked Umberto.

'Tell me.'

'A philosophy based on the belief a deity was responsible for creating life; a large number of leading European scientists, artists, writers and political leaders were deists. Do the names Voltaire and Napoleon Bonaparte mean anything to you?' Umberto asked.

'Bonaparte's philosophy?'

'Yes.'

'The French will—'

'Love it!' interjected Umberto.

'We need security,' said Marco.

'Discreet, there's the Interpol warrant,' said Umberto.

'I'll call the baron,' said Marco, conscious that Rothschilds would not want to compromise their relationship with the Vatican, but he also thought Professor Zaydan could become the most important client in Rothschilds history.

'Somewhere quiet?' asked Marco.

Giorgio stood up and led Marco to his study. 'Say hello from me,' called Umberto.

'You know the baron?' asked Ophelia.

'We have a banking relationship with Rothschilds,' replied Umberto.

In the study, Marco faced the window; his back was to the door as he dialled the London number he'd only called once before.

'Hello, Marco,' answered a soft cultured male voice.

'Good evening Baron, I'm in Italy with Umberto Caproni, who passes on his regards, and with a Professor Zaydan who's Albert Einstein's son. He's a child Einstein fathered out of wedlock. Zaydan has developed scientific proof that a deity was required to begin life, a proof of God's existence.'

'Fascinating,' said the baron.

'Zaydan's seeking asylum in the Vatican, Umberto thought we could help.'

'Asylum?' asked the Baron.

'There's an Interpol warrant on Zaydan, political, and the Vatican is a mountain from which Zaydan can speak.'

'Thank you for calling. Send me a file note, I'll make contact through Umberto.'

'It's best if we work this through me, Umberto's been caught up in this Interpol business.'

'Through you then.' The baron hung up. Marco re-ran the conversation in his head then returned to the living area where the others were talking.

'I've spoken with the baron, I'll send him a file note.'

'Fantastic. Thank you,' said Umberto.

Elias leant forward with his head in his hands. Ophelia asked when he last took paracetamol. Elias said two hours and he felt okay.

'Okay? asked Ophelia.

'No, I need to be in bed.'

○

The following morning, Umberto dropped a copy of the day's *Libero* newspaper on the dining table. The lead story was about two suspected terrorists with Interpol arrest warrants, who had landed at Caproni's private airfield in Como. Umberto Caproni, chairman of the Caproni Group and son of Count

Gianni Caproni, Italy's aircraft pioneer, was missing, presumed kidnapped by the fugitives.

Giorgio turned on his television, it was tuned to the *TV Mediaset* channel; the TV news headlined with the same kidnap story. While the TV channel ran and re-ran the day's news, Giorgio made pancakes and Umberto made coffee.

Umberto and Giorgio dropped a spoon of the resumada into their coffee and also dipped a biscotti into the sweet cream.

'What's the dip?' asked Cyrus.

'We call it *resumada*,' said Giorgio. 'Egg yolk, sugar and sweet wine … shakes the body alive.'

Cyrus dipped a biscotti into the sweet cream too.

Umberto's mobile buzzed—it had to be Marco, no one else knew the number.

'*Ciao*, Marco.'

'*Ciao*, Umberto, have you seen this morning's media?'

'On television … *Mediaset*, yes.'

'*Libero* is carrying the story too, photos of Cyrus and Elias … fears for your safety because you haven't been seen.'

'I've read *Libero* … interesting narrative.' Umberto laughed, but he knew the narrative was a bad twist. He'd seen such stories unfold before. A lie pushed and then a covert police operation no one would ever hear about.

'The Baron insists Cyrus travels to Corsica … and all of you … Rothschilds has a villa … it's safer.'

'Hold on,' said Umberto as he looked at the others. 'Rothschilds are inviting us to Corsica; safer for us.' Cyrus, Elias and Ophelia exchanged glances and nodded.

Marco and Umberto coordinated the logistics of flying to Corsica on a Rothschilds' helicopter.

The men were talking about going to Corsica and a helicopter and Rothschilds. Ophelia bit her finger. 'Going to France, to Corsica, what about our plan to go to the Vatican?' she asked.

'Corsica is as close to Rome as Milan,' replied Umberto.

'I don't know about such things. My life has been centred in Cairo.'

'We need to run faster than those chasing us,' said Umberto. He knew that in business as in life, speed buys time and time creates opportunity. 'Thank you for reminding me about the Vatican though, I need to make a call.' Umberto strolled outside and in the mid-morning sun called his good friend, Archbishop Scola, the Cardinal of Milan.

'Umberto, in the name of our Blessed Mother. I've been praying; the news today,' said Scola.

'I'm fine, dear friend; it's warming to have been in your prayers. Are you in Milan?'

Scola said yes and Umberto arranged to collect Scola from his *Palazzo Arcivescovile* residence at midday and then fly him to France for an urgent meeting.

〇

It was close to midday when Giorgio braked his SUV to a stop at the edge of a small flat meadow surrounded by tree-clad hills. Giorgio painted a large orange cross on the short grass. The goats in the field pricked up their ears, started to walk and then they ran. They had heard the hum of the turbojet and felt the overlaid rotor pulse. The grass around the orange cross was beaten in every direction as the helicopter landed. A couple of minutes later, the helicopter was airborne on a compass heading for the south of Corsica.

CHAPTER TWENTY-FIVE

PARIS, FRANCE, 01 AUGUST 2018

THE GRAVEL RELEASED a soft crunch as Minister Gigi De Zorzi's black Santoni shoes trod the Tuileries Garden gravel path in the heart of Paris. Earlier, Gigi received a call from her contact at Rothschilds who requested she make herself available for a meeting. Such requests were rare, but as Rothschilds bankrolled her election, she was obliged to comply. A louder crunching sounded as a man joined her.

'Good morning, Gigi.'

With her demure form and copper hair, Gigi had been easy for Henri to spot.

'Hello, Henri.' He was fifty-five with greying hair and his sweet tooth won over his self-discipline and awarded Henri a double chin.

'We have a task for you.'

'I didn't think we were here for a social chat,' said Gigi.

'Olivier Dassault will meet with the editor of *Le Monde* in two days; he'll disclose to the editor that Einstein's son has been granted sanctuary at the Vatican.'

Gigi, of course, knew Olivier. He had been in the French National Assembly and headed his family's industrial conglomerate.

'What's his nationality?' asked Gigi as she wondered why he sought refuge in the Vatican.

'Syrian.'

'Syrian?' She blinked slowly.

'The issue is not his nationality but what he's achieved.'

'Which is?'

'In simple terms, he has proved the existence of God.'

'You can't be serious.'

'I couldn't be more so. He'll require friends by his side, powerful friends; you're going to be one of those friends. You're to join the meeting with Dassault. *Le Monde* Thursday morning at eleven.'

'Why's Dassault involved?'

'We work with Dassault on a number of projects.'

'How can you prove God's existence?'

'That's the same question I asked, as will millions and billions of others.

'I can't help but be sceptical.'

'Assuming it's true, what would be the consequence?'

'Ummm …' Gigi paused. *Man will start to behave, or rather stop behaving badly.* Everyone knew the rules, what was black, what was white, what could be argued as grey, the world would operate in white. She thought of the impact on decision-making, a new factor to take into account, the white factor to take into account, a white factor that would trump all other factors.

'Civilisation will change,' she said.

'Which is why Einstein's son needs you and the French government.'

'This is real?'

'Exciting times for you; exciting times for us all.'

'*Ammazza!*' said Gigi, reverting to Italian; she was born in Milan. 'At *Le Monde's* office?'

'Yes, now there's something else. A philanthropic foundation will be established in France for Einstein's son and it requires trustees.'

'What's the foundation's mandate?' She dodged the obvious question.

'Providing social benefit and political leverage.'

Gigi smiled. The two inseparables. 'Within France?'

'Globally, we anticipate the foundation to have a massive funding base.'

'Are you establishing a new religion?'

'The Deity Foundation is expected to stand alongside the major religions of the world.'

'The other trustees?'

'You'll be the only politician, the composition of the foundation trust board is being finalised, we'll have four trustees to start, and will expand later.'

'When you say proved?' asked Gigi, letting herself return to the quintessence.

'Science and mathematics have provided truth since Pythagoras and Archimedes. I don't know the finer details, but experts have confirmed the Einstein proof,' said Henri.

'I see,' she said. Not seeing at all. Henri spoke of a foundation to stand alongside the world's major religions, could this Einstein prodigy seriously rival Christianity or Islam? Or maybe they foresaw religions being brought closer together. Gigi shuddered as she realised why Rothschilds and Dassault were involved. Her first instinct of a shift in civilisation felt like an understatement. 'I'm sure you know,' said Gigi, 'But to be a trustee, and a minister, is there—'

'No conflict,' interrupted Henri. 'Those who need to approve, have approved.'

'The prime minister?'

'And the president.'

'What briefing before *Le Monde?*'

'You'll meet with Einstein's son this evening.'

'He's in Paris?'

'No, you're going to Corsica.'

'They're putting on a play at kindergarten and I promised to be there.' Gigi wanted to remind Henri she had a family life, even though she knew she would miss the play.

'Get your husband to go.'

'He's, he's …' She didn't want to say.

'I'll text your flight details, departure 5 p.m. from memory, come back in the morning, stay the night at the Rothschilds' villa in Corsica.'

Henri headed away along the gravel path and Gigi gazed up at the sky and the puffy white clouds that drifted.

'Hello God,' she said out loud. She'd never said hello to God before.

CHAPTER TWENTY-SIX

CORSICA, ITALY, 02 AUGUST 2018

CYRUS SAT BESIDE the pilot and adjusted his headset; they all wore headsets. As the helicopter descended to Corsica's southern Figari Airport, Cyrus looked down upon pink-red clay, sun-baked pink-red clay in the hills and sun-baked pink-red clay at the edge of the sea. He thought the dark weed beds in the calm sea looked like continents; the scene looked like a photo from space. Further out to sea were white caps.

The helicopter landed and all but Umberto inclined their heads as they passed under the rotating blades to a nearby SUV. A security man sat next to the driver.

Elias opened the front passenger door 'I need to sit in the front,' he whispered.

The security man ignored Elias. Ophelia spoke in French from the rear seat and the security man opened his front door, got out, and held the door for Elias. Elias sat in the front seat and the security man climbed into the back beside Ophelia.

After half an hour they stopped at a gate flanked by a five-metre-high wall with CCTV security. The gate opened. Elias spied four men in the gatehouse and counted six Dobermans. They drove on pink concrete through a natural landscape of bushy trees and pink-red clay. The concrete expanded into a large pink concrete circle in front of the villa. Beside the circle was a flat grass area with a red and white banded windsock. Elias wondered why the helicopter hadn't landed at the villa helipad, he guessed there was a risk of the ADS-B transponder being tracked. He pushed open his door and grabbed the side of the SUV.

'Need help?' asked Ophelia. She touched his shoulder.

'I'll be okay, thank you.'

'Welcome to Corsica.' Marco lifted a hand.

'Thank you for taking care of us,' said Cyrus.

'Come,' said Marco. 'I'll show you your rooms.'

Marco stepped to Umberto's side. 'Cardinal Scola is here.'

'We need to meet with him in thirty or forty minutes,' Umberto said.

'Freshen up first, change your clothes if you like, then come downstairs to the meeting room,' said Marco.

'We'll have a light lunch with the bishop,' said Umberto to Marco. 'Is this correct?'

'Yes, in the main meeting room, on the second level.'

He led his guests to the third level. It was the top level of the villa that was set snugly into the hill. Eight suites were adjacent to a long veranda.

'The stairs in the living area of your suites go down to the second level,' said Marco.

'You'll find clean clothes in your rooms. I hope the sizes and styles are okay.'

Elias lagged behind and slowly placed each foot in front of the other. Inside his suite, beside the king-size bed was a jug of iced water and a glass. He filled the glass, drank it, and collapsed onto the bed. Thirty or forty minutes of rest. Elias wanted to meet with Scola.

Ophelia opened her wardrobe, there were a dozen summer dresses from different designers, blouses, trousers and a number of soft shoes and sandals. The drawers had underclothes, more than she had in Cairo. Ophelia felt tears on her cheeks.

A short time later, Ophelia pushed open the door and entered the meeting room. She glanced at the sideboard selection of canapes, and beverages.

'Self-service,' said Marco.

'Thank you, and thank you for…' Ophelia moved her hands over her blue patterned summer dress.

'Pleasure.'

Ophelia beamed a smile.

With prawns and an orange juice, she sat between Cyrus and Umberto at a large French walnut table; two slabs glued together from the same tree. Around the French walnut table were eight white leather boardroom chairs, and above were two low lights with large copper lightshades. Dominating one wall, was a large oil painting of a mirrored sea moon.

Marco made the introductions and then Cardinal Scola asked Cyrus why he wanted asylum in the Vatican. Scola was short, dumpy, and bald. Cyrus answered the palest man he had ever met and wondered if the cardinal's skin ever saw the sun. Cyrus explained he was Einstein's son and needed somewhere safe, because he was a Syrian refugee who could be killed if he returned to Syria. Scola excused himself from the table. He liked the look of Ophelia's prawns. He'd snacked on Umberto's private jet to Corsica, but there hadn't been any prawns. Scola placed several prawns on his plate and as he held a bottle of red wine, Scola suggested that if Cyrus could be killed if he returned to Syria, then he should stay out of Syria.

'Wine?' asked Scola. Umberto said yes and Ophelia said yes so Scola poured three glasses of red.

'Cyrus is also under threat from people in Israel; Einstein's son not being a Jew is a political paradox,' said Umberto. Elias thought Cyrus was a Jew but saw no reason to undercut Umberto's argument.

Scola broke a translucent prawn skeleton with his thumbnail. He peeled off the skeleton and was most satisfied as the tail came free in one piece.

'It's rare for the Vatican to grant asylum to Catholic refugees. I see a high hurdle for the Vatican granting asylum to a Muslim,' Scola said.

'As we thought,' said Umberto. 'Which is why we need you to lower the hurdle, and Cyrus is a Druze, not a Muslim.'

'If groups in Israel see the professor as a political threat, the Holy See will not willingly become involved,' said Scola.

'Fortunately, your business is miracles,' said Umberto. Scola laughed then Umberto continued. 'Now tell us what we can do to facilitate this miracle.' Umberto stood up, walked behind Cyrus and placed his hands softly on Cyrus's shoulders; the message to Scola was clear. Cyrus thought what a change from when the foul-smelling major gripped his shoulders.

Scola asked when Cyrus wished to apply for asylum and Umberto said tomorrow would be good. The cardinal explained that an asylum application would take weeks to socialise; the Vatican moves slowly; the world watches when there is any change in the Vatican's status quo. The cardinal espoused he'd need to speak with some of his brothers. Umberto heard him say this but knew it was not true for the Vatican had an absolute monarch—the Pope could make any decision at any time. Umberto suggested first a simple agreement on sanctuary. The cardinal said he trusted Umberto, they had been friends for years and he knew to take Umberto's word on issues like this, but his brothers would need proof Cyrus was Einstein's son. *Take my word on issues like this,* thought Umberto, *so on what types of issues wouldn't you take my word?*

The cardinal was on his second glass of wine and Umberto knew he would not have resisted the fine wines on offer during the flight from Milan.

'I'll print you a copy of the DNA evidence,' said Umberto. 'Do you need anything else?'

'After I've spoken with the Vatican there may be,' replied Scola.

'We have a helicopter to fly you to the Vatican,' added Umberto.

'Now?'

'Yes, from Figari. I'll come with you to the airport,' said Umberto.

'It's been a pleasure to meet you, Bishop,' said Ophelia, it was the only words she spoke.

○

The bishop and Umberto sat in the back seat of a Rothschilds chauffeured SUV. Privacy glass separated the front and back seat.

'I'm sorry I gave you little warning, my friend, everything is moving swiftly,' said Umberto.

'The jet commute made it easy, thank you, and what fabulous wine.'

'You could have the jet to fly to Rome. But I thought it would be faster and easier for you to take a helicopter and land on the Vatican helipad.'

'I appreciate your good thoughts, thank you.'

'I trust your influence. The press reports, Interpol, murder, bioterrorism, all character assassination. Cyrus was over a hundred kilometres away from where the Syrian was killed and the Egyptians and Israelis know it.'

'He's a captain in the Syrian army, head of Syria's biowarfare.'

'What biowarfare has Syria engaged in?'

'None—to my knowledge.'

'Right, at high risk to himself, Cyrus has made Syria's biowarfare programme inert.

The French government have more intelligence than we do and a French government minister will meet with Cyrus this evening. The French are protecting Cyrus, not arresting him.' Umberto knew the importance of Scola seeing this first-hand if he was going to influence the Pope.

'Before you arrived, Marco was telling me Baron Rothschild has taken a personal interest in Cyrus,' said Scola.

'The baron wishes the Vatican to provide a safe house,' replied Umberto. 'Einstein was one of last century's most influential people. It's an opportunity for the Vatican.'

'Opportunity … in what way?'

'Moral leadership and peace.'

'On morality the church has fallen short.'

'A good news story.'

The cardinal sat with his head back, the red wine having an effect.

'The high level of media coverage for aberrant clergy has concerned me,' said Umberto.

'Yes?'

'The reputation of all churches has been damaged.'

'True.'

'Who benefits from this damage?'

After some thought the cardinal said 'Governments.'

'Power and persuasion. Aberrations in church morality are nothing compared to the aberrations of morality in governments.'

'You think wisely my friend. Why does Cyrus feel in danger from Israel?'

'No politician likes competition.'

'Mixing of blood lines and religions can invoke hostile responses.'

'We're fortunate Rothschilds are supporting Einstein's son.'

'How did Rothschilds become involved?' asked Scola.

'I'll encourage Rothschilds to show their appreciation to the Milan diocese.'

'We're always looking to increase our practices of charity.'

CHAPTER TWENTY-SEVEN

CORSICA, ITALY, 02 AUGUST 2018

'A BUSY DAY,' SAID Marco as he chopped his hand in the air as though he chopped time. 'A meeting with the cardinal as soon as you arrive, now you need to listen to me. I promise to be concise, and we've another meeting this evening.' He moved his hands a lot when he talked, and it was difficult not to look at them.

Marco spoke of a new foundation, Rothschilds recommendation to form a *Fondations reconnues d'utilité publique*, there was a legal right for for-eigners to form this public utility French foundation. A straightforward process with an initial endowment of one million Euros and approval from *Conseil d'État.*

Cyrus thought about the big words Marco spoke and the two biggest words he thought about were *one million.* 'Where can we find one million,' he asked.

Marco waved his hands like a magician. 'Dassault have agreed to make this initial donation.' Marco said Dassault would pay one million the same way someone says it's raining outside.

'What do Dassault want?' murmured Elias. He had his head on his arms, his eyes closed, and was not watching Marco's magical hands.

'Olivier Dassault's a friend of Baron Rothschild's and Umberto's. Dassault make aircraft in France.'

This sounded like a superficial answer to Elias, but he had no energy to dig deeper. Elias knew Dassault made fighter jets; the Dassault Mirage was the backbone of the French Airforce. Marco said the Foundation would need trustees.

'Trustees?' asked Cyrus.

'An oversight role,' replied Marco. 'We suggest starting with four trustees, Cyrus, Elias, myself and Gigi de Zorzi.'

'Who's she?' asked Elias, thinking her name sounded like a mouthful.

'The French minister of Cultural Affairs—you'll meet her this evening,' said Marco. 'This gives the foundation *de facto* protection by the French government.'

Someone else to deal with, thought Elias—Cultural Affairs, he could imagine. This was going to be more complex than Rothschilds simply providing financial advice.

'I don't understand the urgency,' said Cyrus.

Marco waved his hands in the air. 'When your deity theory breaks, and is made public, we predict tens of millions will donate, we need to establish a religious charity to accept donations.' Marco handed each the foundation application form and the standard foundation charter.

'Requirements for registration?' asked Cyrus.

'Now we have the Dassault money, final approval from *Conseil d'État,* signatures from The Ministry of the Interior and the prime minister.'

'Sounds like a long process,' said Elias.

'Two signatures,' said Marco. 'Twenty-four hours.'

The meeting finished with a few hours to relax and reflect before meeting the cultural minister trustee.

Elias's body called for sleep; the world spun.

◯

With his laptop, Cyrus sat on a lounger by the pool. There was a rolled white towel on the lounger, a high umbrella and a view across the pool, past the pink-red clay and bushes and low trees to the clear sea. As he lay back on the lounger, Cyrus searched *Google* for Einstein—where to start, the information seemed endless, a link to Einstein quotes caught his attention. *Learn from yesterday, live for today, hope for tomorrow. The important thing is not to stop questioning.* Three weeks ago, after 601, Cyrus had no hope of tomorrow and felt his life was a source of regret with no pride, no dignity or self-regard, the failed promise—to Talal to be a King of Kings, and then the longest yet fastest four days of his life, a four-day game of hunter. Talal would laugh. Four days of chase and hide and hide and chase and hide. Talal would nearly always win hunter, a pace faster than him, but Talal celebrated more when Cyrus won as he encouraged the best from his dearest friend; the joy of shared childhood friendship; two clean little minds free from the dark filth time inflicted.

And now on the other side of four long fast days, Cyrus had a message from the present, a message from a vicegerent on Earth, perfect in knowledge and wisdom.

He knew Rothschilds were global players but did not know of their global strategy with its global end game. For the last two hundred and fifty years, Rothschilds had waited and dreamed for someone like Cyrus to appear. And now he was here, they planned to implement the most audacious scheme in history.

CHAPTER TWENTY-EIGHT

THE VATICAN, ITALY, 02 AUGUST 2018

SCOLA DIDN'T KNOW if Rothschilds or Umberto paid. The chartered helicopter from Figari banked high over the Vatican helipad, and the pilot selected his line of approach. A black SUV sat near the helipad; it would take Scola the few hundred metres to his meeting with the archbishop of Vatican Diplomatic Relations.

'Greetings, Dionigi,' said the archbishop of Vatican Diplomatic Relations. Scola could smell wine.

'Greetings, Paul,' said Scola. They held the same rank and both liked wine and that was where the similarity ended. Paul was tall and thin and had a full head of white hair.

'A helicopter?'

'A matter of urgency and others paid,' said Scola.

'I was having a wine. Will you?'

'Yes. A young wine,' said Scola as he held the glass on an angle above his white napkin, and looked at the clean wine edge. A Rioja red.

'From a young wine skin,' replied Paul as he made reference to

Matthew 9:17, the Mathew metaphor of not pouring new wine into old wineskins, for if this is done then the wineskins will burst. The metaphor—the new wine being Jesus's arrival on Earth; the old wineskin the old ways of Judaism.

Scola and Paul sat drinking the young wine and Paul listened to the story of Einstein's son in Corsica, and Rothschilds and Umberto Caproni. They all knew of Umberto Caproni, rectory talk of his playboy lifestyle, talk of sexual deviancy because Umberto partied with not one girl or two or even three; tabloid pictures feeding tittle tattle, satisfying readers' psyches, psyches Freud had written books about. At the mention of Caproni's name, Paul had flashing images of cocaine and champagne and lithe naked women. Paul called the pontiff's private secretary. Thirty minutes and two glasses of wine later the private secretary called back. The pontiff had fifteen minutes available. Paul accompanied Scola to meet with the Pope.

○

Scola glanced at the Pope's private secretary, who was dressed in a dark suit and tie and stood like a shadow at a door covered in cream wallpaper. Above the door frame were the gold letters JOHANNES XXIII PONT MAX—surviving decor from the early sixties—a respect for history.

The Pope, dressed in white except for the gold tassels hanging from his white cloth belt, sat behind a polished wooden desk with his chair turned out. On the polished desk stood a solid gold clock and beside the gold clock a delicate lamp and a large brown leather folder. A metre away, sat Scola, his feet on a red woven rug that covered the marble floor. The archbishop of Vatican Diplomatic Relations sat next to Scola.

'I was in the garden and saw the helicopter. I understand it was you, Cardinal Dionigi.' The pontiff's eyes twinkled.

'Umberto Caproni or Baron Rothschild organised it; I'm unsure, I was in Corsica meeting with Einstein's son who wishes to seek asylum in the Vatican.'

'Fabián mentioned Einstein's son to me,' said the pontiff with a nod to his private secretary who still stood by the door. 'He's Israeli?'

'Syrian Druze.'

'Why not asylum in Israel?'

'He feels under threat from Israel.'

'In what way?'

'The recent press reports about Umberto Caproni being kidnapped, bio-terrorism, murder in Egypt, all appear to be fake news.' Scola borrowed the Trumpism. 'Einstein's son is the Syrian army captain Interpol are looking for.'

The Pope's forehead creased. 'So, we know there's no kidnapping. The press doesn't say Zaydan is Einstein's son, is there proof?'

'DNA evidence, I have a copy.'

'Cardinal Dionigi told me Einstein's son was over a hundred kilometres away when the Syrian was killed and the Egyptians and Israelis know this,' said the archbishop of Vatican Diplomatic Relations.

The Pope turned his eyes to Scola, who nodded.

'I place great weight on the fact that Rothschilds is giving support, we cannot look away because a situation appears difficult.'

'Would sanctuary be an option while asylum is being considered?' asked Scola.

'The concern is,' said the Pope as he brought his fingertips together, 'that we accept Einstein's child but then have disagreement with Israel or Egypt.'

'I understand, Your Holiness,' said Scola. 'But Netanyahu and el-Sisi know the human fraternity you promote both within and beyond our church.'

'We can recognise there may be politics with someone like Einstein's son; there always will be,' said the archbishop of Vatican Diplomatic Relations

'Please give Fabián a briefing paper,' said the pontiff. 'From what I've heard I'm inclined to offer sanctuary.'

CHAPTER TWENTY-NINE

CORSICA, FRANCE, 02 AUGUST 2018

ELIAS'S PALMS AND the soles of his feet were swollen and his torso still carried the red rash. A positive sign the doctor in Renzano had said; cutaneous symptoms indicated a better disease outcome, also a positive sign that it was a first-time infection. Two positive signs—Elias took them both. Determined to go to the trustee meeting, Elias almost fell as he tried to get dressed. He then sat on the bed and pulled on a loose-fitting black track-suit provided by Rothschilds. The tracksuit had EA7 written in white. He held onto the wall as he headed to the bathroom, doused a flannel with cold water and moments later lay on his bed with the flannel on his forehead.

○

Sometime later, Elias stepped down the stairs to the second-floor meeting room, holding the stainless stair rail as he descended. At the bottom of the stairs, he stopped, and made an effort to stand tall. The meeting room door was closed; was he early, or maybe late? He opened the door; his focus fixed on his feet.

There were other people in the room, he didn't try to count, but maybe three, maybe four, maybe five; it was then that he knew he shouldn't be there. He eased himself into an empty chair. Someone was offering drinks, he heard yes to mint tea and someone mentioned *vin rouge* and a different voice said, *grazie.* Another voice was speaking. It was Ophelia, did she just say, *I'm lovely to meet you?* Ophelia was talking again, this time about fever and it not being contagious. Don't they know how sick I am, are they stupid or am I up for an Oscar? Another woman was talking, the one who said *grazie.* Elias heard music, the music of an Italian accent, her voice singing and singing, each syllable finding its place on a multi-octave scale, dancing a trance and infusing a resonating allure. He didn't know the words of this song, but it felt like a hit, it felt good, this hit song felt so good. He looked in the direction of the singing voice, and for an instant had clear vision, a fine-featured angel with beautiful hair, the evening light passed through the window and reflected a thousand shades of copper, then a dark veil descended and his vision became a haze. In his clear vision, she was petite, the Italian woman with the copper hair, and then someone said she was the government minister, and her name was Gigi. He knew female commanders in the Israeli Defence Force and never felt ruffled by their presence, why did he feel ruffled? He thought of Esther, and was pleased she was not in the room watching, she would know, would know he couldn't get enough of *grazie.* He forced himself to focus on the words she was saying. He could hear the words, he couldn't understand the words, she sounded very formal, her voice resonated in his soul. Was he getting better? Elias looked in the direction of Gigi's voice.

'Rothschilds invited me to be a trustee, help expedite registration, give a government presence. The position of trustee is largely ceremonial, day-to-day decisions will be made by the investment committee. I agree with Rothschilds' proposal to have four trustees, Cyrus, Elias, Marco as a Rothschilds rep, and me.' When Gigi said *me,* she cupped both palms under her chin and smiled. Cyrus beamed at Gigi's informal gesture. Elias saw nothing, his head was down.

'I'm sorry, I should introduce Elias,' said Cyrus.

Elias lifted his head and his hand. 'Hello, everyone.' He heard Gigi say hello.

'Rothschilds has given good advice.' Elias heard Cyrus's voice. 'But with respect, it would be great if you could give us some background on yourself.'

Elias opened his mouth to speak, but then Gigi started talking again. It was not background on him Cyrus wanted.

'My father ran Rothschilds Paris office. I've been the Minister of Cultural Affairs for two years and have been in the National Assembly for six. Like my mother, I studied arts at the Sorbonne. I was born in Milano.'

'Elias?' asked Marco. Was it his turn now, did they want him to speak after all?

'The last few weeks I've been helping Cyrus leave Syria and come here to Milan.' But *grazie* called it Milano. 'Umm Milano … ah … Corsica … like *grazie* … Gigi … I have a background too.' *What am I doing talking about her,* thought Elias. *I must be sick … or I must be something … talk about me.* 'My … background is engineering. I started and sold a software company. Tel Aviv is my home.' He wanted to say he liked to drink and liked to smoke hash and didn't like killing and he knew he had done too much of all three and was trying to cut back. He turned away from the woman with the copper hair. He'd called her Gigi, was it Gigi? Someone said Gigi, and didn't Marco say Gigi this afternoon? To think I thought her name a mouthful. Insight—maybe mouthful is the right word. Elias spoke to the person beside him. He thought it was Cyrus.

'I'm sorry, I need to go, I need to rest, can you help me get out of here?' Cyrus stood up and helped Elias; then Ophelia touched Elias's back, and with her arm under his shoulder helped Elias to his room.

Ophelia knew little of men, but Elias seemed captivated by Gigi, and she wondered if the others saw it.

The following morning, Elias woke at dawn in a wet sheet cocoon. His fever had broken and his head was pain free. The peripheral swelling was down. He showered. In the mirror, a hint of rash. He wore a white bathrobe over his black briefs as he sprung softly downstairs to the second level main kitchen. Gigi sat at a table with a coffee and *pain au chocolat*. She looked up as Elias entered, and her eyes softened.

'Good morning … how are you feeling?'

'Oh … Gigi … I'm sorry … didn't know.' Elias closed his white bathrobe and knotted the belt. 'Thank you … feeling better… came down to get moving … for a coffee.'

'Sit down … I'll make you one … you're looking better,' she said. Gigi got up. 'How do you have it?'

'Ah … espresso … thank you … you're up early.' Elias's heart pounded … his words sounded weak … he wanted to find the right words.

'Early flight,' said Gigi.

'Let me … drive you to the air … port,' said Elias. He looked at her freckles. He loved her freckles.

'You've not been well for days I hear … I couldn't … thank you.' The music again … a forever Gigi song.

'If I had my Ducati,' said Elias.

'Oooh … an Italian bike.'

'I love everything Italian.' *Did I say that?*

The coffee machine hissed.

'Here's your coffee … I need to go.' Gigi picked up the *pain au chocolat* that was missing a bite. '*Ciao ciao* … get well, Elias.'

'Thank you … bye.' Gigi glided out of the room. Elias felt eternal.

With her back to him he could not see the gleam in her eyes or the look on her face.

CHAPTER THIRTY

ROME, ITALY, 02 AUGUST 2018

REZNIK KICKED AT a pigeon as he climbed the steps to the entrance of the Archbasilica of St John Lateran. On the top step he clasped his hands behind his back. It would have helped if the non-descript man had given him the motive for the assassin's bullet. That he didn't was telling. Now, Reznik had a meeting with Monsignor Scutari, the Archbishop of the Basilica. A priest in a black robe came from within the church and walked towards him.

'Signor Reznik...?' The priest waited for Reznik to give his full name. He would have to wait forever.

'Si.'

'Let me give you a little history before you meet with Monsignor Scutari,' said the priest. He stared at Reznik with his shaved head and *rosso* birthmark.

Inside the basilica, he pointed out to the shaved *rosso* man the marble statues in six recesses. 'Pope John XVI commissioned the carving of the apostle statues. The carvers were asked to carve from sketches provided by the Pope's favourite artist … all but a French carver agreed.'

'The French haven't changed,' said Reznik. Around them, the hum of tourists' voices bounced and re-bounced off the stone interior. A woman sat fanning her face in this, the oldest Catholic Church in Rome. Although situated four kilometres from the Vatican, it was part of the Holy See and housed the Pope's throne. The priest led Reznik away from the public area, through a door between apostles Simon and Thaddeus. There were corridors and doors and passageways weaving deep into the Lateran Palace. As they wove, Reznik thought Zaydan chose Italy for a reason—the Vatican set Italy apart from other European countries. But what was Einstein's son's interest in the Vatican? The priest knocked on a door and it was opened by Monsignor Scutari. He wore his Monsignor's cassock with its crimson piping and sash. Unlike most of the other Vatican cardinals, the Monsignor had a full head of dark hair and at forty-eight was comparatively young. Some years earlier, in a Tel Aviv sting operation, Israeli police arrested the Monsignor's niece at a drugs and sex party, an arrest that provided leverage to develop the Monsignor as an informant; a *quid pro quo*, for not charging her.

When he was alone with Reznik the Monsignor spoke. 'What do you want?'

'There's a Syrian criminal, Professor Zaydan hiding in Italy. We believe he's trying to contact the Vatican.'

'I saw the press report, a Syrian and Israeli being hunted, but why the Vatican?'

'That's what I'm asking you to find out.'

'I'll make some enquiries.'

Reznik folded his arms and stared at Scutari.

'Something else?'

'Make your enquiries.'

'Now?'

'I'm not a tourist in Rome.' Scutari took a second look at this feeble-looking man with a shaved head and noted his cold pit-bull eyes. He looked like a killer. Scutari called Cardinal Erdo, Vatican Head of Section for relations with states.

'Greetings, Monsignor.'

'Hello, Your Most Reverend Eminence, are you free to speak?'

'Yes, how can I help?'

'A colleague, in the *Corpo della Gendarmeria*,' said the Monsignor, referring to the Vatican police and security force, 'he has asked me about the Syrian, Professor Zaydan.'

'The Syrian is a sensitive issue, Monsignor.'

'I thought this to be the case, hence my call to you.'

'His Holiness has deemed we provide this Syrian with sanctuary.'

'When is this Syrian to be within our walls?'

'In confidence … this week on … ah … Thursday morning.' The Monsignor picked up a pen and wrote *Vatican sanctuary Thursday this week*. He pushed the paper across his desk for Reznik to read. Reznik had already read the message upside down.

Who is Zaydan's advocate? Reznik scribbled.

'I fear we are seeing yet another example of poor judgement,' said Scutari.

'I share your sentiments, Monsignor.'

'Who's advocating we protect this Syrian?'

'Scola.' Erdo had little time for Scola; it was Scola who lobbied the College of Cardinals to support the current Pope rather than himself.

'I thank you for clarifying, Your Most Reverend Eminence. I look forward to enjoying your company when your schedule allows.'

The call finished with Cardinal Erdo wondering what the Monsignor was up to.

'Scola … the Archbishop of Milan has been advocating for the Syrian.'

'Where's Scola?' asked Reznik.

'He could be anywhere.'

'I need to know where he is. Now.' Reznik stood facing the Monsignor, his hands in clenched fists on the Monsignor's desk.

The Monsignor called Scola on the pretext of gaining his input into a policy white paper. Scola's secretary said he had a full day, was in Milan and would return the call.

GIGI'S DRIVER OPENED the rear door of her ministerial car, and after arriving at Charles de Gaulle Airport from Corsica, she headed to *Le Monde's* office in Paris's thirteenth arrondissement. Her car pulled to a stop at *Le Monde's* iconic glass building. On her way inside, Gigi glanced at advertising on the side of a bus shelter; Ralph Lauren men's underwear, the model wore black briefs with a blue and white striped jersey slung over his shoulders. Gigi smiled at the thought of Elias and the flash of black under his white bathrobe. What did he say? *I love everything Italian,* how sweet.

After passing through the *Le Monde* security, Gigi thought of the two hours on the plane and climbed the circular stairs in the centre of the glass building that wound to the editor's fifth-floor office. Yoga kept Gigi's abdominals tight as she climbed and she thought about the kindergarten play she'd missed.

Jerome Fenoglio had been editor of *Le Monde* for eleven years. Jerome fought time; with his hair dyed brown-black, shaped eyebrows and cosmetic surgery that had pulled his face tight. He glanced at Gigi's sheer stockinged thigh. Fenoglio had met Gigi a few times before and never seen her in the company of a man; she didn't wear a ring and he wondered if she swung the other way. He guessed she was in her early thirties and during previous encounters, he'd tried playing the eye-game and touched her arm during conversation, but she appeared oblivious. Gigi, not oblivious to Fenoglio's attention, knew she was in a man's world, but a man's world where soft and sweet found control. Even so, she sat in the seat furthest from where Fenoglio sat and was happy when the door swung open and Olivier Dassault came in. Gigi revered Dassault, a gentleman, a politician—no a statesman, and France's leading industrial magnate. Dassault had full cheeks, ruddy from years of wine.

'*Bonjour,* minister.' Gigi stood up and shook Dassault's hand. Both used a relaxed grip. His face showed he knew Gigi.

'Do you hunt?' Dassault asked Fenoglio.

Fenoglio followed Dassault's gaze to the photo on the wall of him with Somerset hounds. 'Oh … the hounds. Yes … friends… a place in Normandy.' Fenoglio spoke in abbreviated short sentences.

'My cousin hunts hares with Italian bloodhounds. I've been once, but never again,' said Gigi. She grimaced at the memory.

'It's vital and brutal,' said Dassault.

Fenoglio cleared his throat. 'So … what's this get together all about?' He took off his glasses and rubbed the lenses with a small white cloth.

◯

Gigi arched her back and stood up. Fenoglio noted her small breasts. The meeting was over. An hour had passed, Gigi and Dassault had given the editor genetic proof of Cyrus's heritage, and scientific background on the deity constant.

After they left, Fenoglio reread the summary document that outlined the science behind the deity constant. Dassault suggested to Fenoglio he get an independent assessment from the president's science advisor. Dassault left Professor Kamniski's contact details. Fenoglio picked up his mobile phone and called Alexander Kamniski. A few minutes later, he emailed the deity constant document to Kamniski and left for lunch via the circular stairs. Fenoglio strolled for thirty minutes and thought of the implications of the deity constant. He stopped at a café. Seated at a corner table, he ordered a salad Niçoise, Perrier and espresso. Between mouthfuls of niçoise his mobile rang.

'Hello, Alexander.'

'Where did you get this deity constant document?'

'Confidential, unable to say,' said Fenoglio.

'It's unbelievable,' said Kamniski.

'A fraud?'

'The very opposite … the most phenomenal piece of theoretical scientific work I've seen. The science is irrefutable and I can only imagine the implications. I don't know where to begin.'

Fenoglio's adrenaline surged; this was why he was a newspaper man, the once in a lifetime scoop that recorded an event in history.

'I appreciate your comments. I've been told the deity constant equates to a proof of God.'

'The proof is more exacting. It proves intelligent design behind the creation of life.'

'That's what I understand, a god being responsible for intelligent design.'

'Correct, a super intelligence, a god, or deity, it's semantics,' said Kamniski.

Back in his office Fenoglio called an editorial meeting. *Le monde* would go to print with Cyrus and the deity constant in forty-eight hours. He called Gigi with the news of Kamniski's independent confirmation of the scientific and mathematical rigor behind the deity constant. Gigi had already received a call from Kamniski, but she didn't let on. She knew Kamniski had received the Legion of Honour and was head of the Scientific Advisory Council to the prime minister. What Gigi and Fenoglio didn't know was that Kamniski had reviewed a deity constant dossier supplied by Rothschilds two days earlier.

CHAPTER THIRTY-TWO

MILAN, ITALY, 03 AUGUST 2018

REZNIK SWALLOWED THE last drop of Red Bull Zero, dropped the crushed can into a recycling bin, then headed for the taxi stand at Milan Airport. The taxi dropped Reznik near the Palazzo Arcivescovile, the residence of the archbishop of Milan. Reznik joined a late afternoon tour of the archbishop's residence.

As he looked at the other tourists, Reznik could see most were American, the younger ones wore sneakers, university logo garments, baseball caps, free ad-rich T-shirts from marketing events, while the older Americans with fanny packs simply stood in the middle of everything and looked around.

'Does the archbishop live alone in his apartment?' Reznik asked the tour guide.

'Why do you ask?' The guide had her dyed blonde hair in a ponytail.

'Curious if the archbishop has staff, like a chef?' Reznik chewed gum.

'There's an eating hall for the clergy but most prefer to prepare their own food.'

'Are all the apartments the same size or does the archbishop have a larger apartment?'

'The archbishop is a humble servant of God, but he has the largest apartment overlooking Piazza Fontana as he sometimes has guests for dinner.'

Reznik nodded and shuffled to the back of the group. The guide led the tour the length of a broad corridor while she described the history of paintings and etchings of the nearby Milan Cathedral constructed in the sixth century. At the end of the corridor, the tour passed a burgundy cord that hung between two gold stands at the base of the staircase. A sign hung from the cord with the words, *Privato, Divieto di Ingresso*. Above, was a black dome on the roof. Reznik glanced up at the dome, then looked at the tour group in front, backs of heads, no faces. He stepped over the burgundy cord and bounded up the wooden stairs—stairs built in the 16th century, stairs that ended at a locked door. Without knowing what to expect on the other side, Reznik unzipped his jacket and revealed a clergy rabat shirt front and collar. The Milan Archdiocese had over a thousand priests, a large enough number to provide Reznik anonymity should he meet someone. He removed a pick set from his pocket and seconds later, opened the locked door. On the other side he scanned an empty hallway lined with carved wooden relief panels and paintings. The door at the end of the corridor had Scola's name engraved on a brass plate. Reznik picked this lock too.

The bishop's apartment was empty. He'd wait in the study, it had a pink marble door frame, and inside there were gilt chairs at a low table and a heavy black leather chair facing a desk. Reznik sat in one of the gilt chairs. A large tapestry dominated one wall; it depicted a man who played a harp and a man who played a mandolin and another man who sat half-naked on the floor with a flowing burgundy cloth covering. *Half-naked men in a cardinal's private study; made sense,* thought Reznik.

After a two-hour wait, Reznik heard a key in the lock. He stood up and dragged a ski mask over his face The cardinal's study was the second room from the entrance. The entrance door opened and closed and Reznik heard a man humming. He didn't recognise the tune. Maybe a Catholic hymn; he wouldn't know. The man stepped through the foyer that expanded into a small gallery; his footsteps were loud on the wood. Then there was quiet as he walked on a rug in his bedroom suite. He still hummed. Inside his bedroom, the cardinal removed his purple clergy shirt and left it flat on his bed, knowing his secretary would arrive later to cook and attend to him. The bishop opened the middle drawer of his dresser and selected a cashmere cardigan; the air conditioning kept the temperature cool against the summer heat. The cardinal pushed one hand through the cardigan sleeve then turned when he heard a noise. At that moment, a gloved hand covered his face and gloved fingers pulled his bald head back. The cardinal felt the hand clamp his mouth shut. The assailant's other arm held him tightly. The cardinal tried to yell, but the gloved hand muffled his voice. He gasped for breath and felt his chest thump.

'Nod if you're alone,' said Reznik. The cardinal's bald head moved up and down.

Reznik took his gloved hand from the cardinal's mouth and warned him not to yell. The cardinal's head moved up and down again. The black glove glistened with saliva and Reznik wiped the glove on the back of the cashmere cardigan.

'What do you know about Zaydan?' Reznik held the short cardinal firmly against him.

'He … he's Einstein's son, and—'

'Bullshit!' interrupted Reznik. 'It's all a fraud. Have you met Zaydan?' Scola heard his assailant speak with an Israeli accent.

'Yes.'

'Where?'

'Corsica.'

Corsica! 'When?'

'Yesterday.'

'Why Corsica?'

'Rothschilds' villa.' *Why were Rothschilds involved? This was bad information.*

'Where in Corsica?'

'Near Figari.'

Reznik asked who was with Zaydan. The bishop said there was a younger man and a woman.

'Criminals wanted by Interpol for murder and biowarfare,' said Reznik. He demanded Scola prevent Zaydan's entry to the Vatican. When the cardinal said it was not his decision, Reznik pulled a stiletto from his hip and pressed the tip into the back of the cardinal's neck, the skin dimpled, then a red drop formed.

'This is life and death. People have been killed. You'll be next unless you stop Zaydan. Clear?'

Scola's head nodded. Reznik pushed Scola forward; pushed him hard against a bureau.

'Put your hands flat on top.' Scola obeyed. 'Head down, count backwards from a hundred.' Scola stopped counting when he heard the door to his apartment close. Reznik retraced his steps, descended the stairs, stepped over the burgundy cord and left the building.

Scola poured a whiskey. His hand shook. The threat was clear; stop Zaydan entering the Vatican or he'd be killed. Was he Mossad? It was now about his personal survival.

O

Reznik closed his eyes, took a deep breath, then called a colleague in the *Agenzia Informazioni e Sicurezza Interna* (AISI), Italy's domestic intelligence agency. Reznik relayed that Cardinal Scola had met in Corsica with the Syrian and the Israeli wanted for murder and bioweapons' terrorism. The French Police should be informed the wanted killers were at Rothschilds' villa near Figari.

CHAPTER THIRTY-THREE

LONDON, ENGLAND, 04 AUGUST 2018

THE BARON CROUCHED and eyeballed the meniscus, the concave curve where the distilled water clung to the calibrated glass cylinder wall. Then he tipped the measuring cylinder and poured distilled water around the root system of his Venus fly trap. He'd heard overnight that Einstein's son was no longer welcome in the Vatican and as he poured, he wondered what caused the Vatican to rescind the sanctuary agreement.

Chester Morgan, the baron's manservant, knocked and entered. Chester had straight brown hair, a long thin face with a prominent nose. His close friends called him Ascot. With a doctorate in economics, and having been an English fencing champion, Chester was an able manservant who provided the baron with rapier advice. Chester carried an Italian newspaper.

'Excuse me, Baron, an article in *L'Osservatore Romano.*'

The baron stared at the last drop of distilled water to fall from the calibrated cylinder onto the root of the Venus fly trap, then looked up.

'Thank you, Chester.' The baron glided into his well-worn brown leather chair. He was a realist. He had no intention of trying to stop the world spinning or trying to stop the world's orbit around the sun or trying to stop the tides, but there were other things he could and would do. He was fluent in French and his Italian was okay. He pressed the Italian newspaper flat and read the article entitled: *War Criminal Seeks Vatican Sanctuary. Syrian Army Captain Cyrus Zaydan, head of Syria's biological weapons' programme, is seeking to escape international justice by obtaining sanctuary within the Vatican. Zaydan is also wanted by Egyptian Police for questioning relating to the recent shooting of a Syrian army major in the Red Sea Resort of Sharm El-Sheikh. Separately, the Italian police have issued an arrest warrant for Zaydan in relation to immigration fraud. Zaydan, pictured below, is travelling with Israeli, Elias Eidelman. They are believed to be in either Milan or Rome and are considered armed and dangerous. Anyone knowing their whereabouts should notify the police without delay.*

'What do you make of this?'

'Written to influence the Vatican,' said Chester.

'Who's pushing it?'

'The biological warfare reference suggests Israel, disclosure of the sanctuary offer suggests a Vatican leak.'

'Cyrus is secure at the villa?'

'Yes,' said Chester.

○

After Reznik contacted Italy's AISI the previous evening, France's internal security service received notification that Professor Zaydan and his Israeli colleague were at Rothschilds' Corsica villa. Rothschilds' involvement raised a warning. No one in the French hierarchy wanted to sign-off the Interpol red notice, which is at any country's discretion. The issue landed on the defence minister's desk. The defence minister ordered gendarmes to secure the perimeter of the Rothschilds' villa. Not to execute an arrest but to provide Cyrus with added security.

Even so, this situation that Cyrus had with the Vatican was easy to resolve, and the baron looked at a portrait of an ancestor that hung on the wall and thanked him for making it easy.

'Could you place a call to the Pope?' asked the baron. Two hours later the call with the pontiff was connected.

'Your Holiness. Thank you for making the time to talk,' the baron said.

'Baron Rothschild, you must visit the Vatican when you are again in Rome.'

'I'll be overjoyed to accept your invitation. I had the honour of visiting with Saint John Paul in 2003—an exceptional opportunity.' The polite exchange continued for some time until the baron focused on the purpose of his call.

'We have an obligation to protect Professor Zaydan,' said the baron.

'The Holy See views the dark cloud hanging over the professor as an issue.'

'The disinformation in *L'Osservatore Romano* reflects the persecution Professor Zaydan faces.'

'The Italian police are looking for Professor Zaydan. The Holy See must avoid any confrontation.'

'The Italian government has notified Interpol that Professor Zaydan had no part in the assassination of the Syrian,' said the baron.

'I've not heard, but there are the immigration charges.'

'Not unusual in asylum cases.'

'We respect the police action.'

'I understand the Holy See's position, Your Holiness; however, we're steadfast about protecting the life of Albert Einstein's son.' He used his Eton accent and pronounced it '*Ulbert.*'

'We require time,' said the Pope.

'Einstein's son doesn't have the luxury of time; his life is under imminent threat.'

'The Holy See has made its decision.'

The baron knew all decisions sat with the Pope. 'I'd hoped we could keep the good faith of the sanctuary agreement without revisiting history.'

'Can you clarify?' asked the Pope. He knew history was revealing, but never the final word.

'The Rothschilds' family extended a loan to the Holy See in 1832. We negotiated directly with Pope Gregory the sixteenth.'

'I'm aware of our long-standing relationship with the Rothschilds' family.'

'I'm awfully sorry to address this, Your Holiness, but are you aware the Holy See breached this loan agreement?'

'This is news, but the agreement was two hundred years ago.'

'One hundred and eighty-six years ago, Your Holiness. The Holy See should note the penalty interest clause. Rothschilds is now owed a perpetuity debt exceeding the total assets of the Vatican Bank.' There was silence and more silence.

'I doubt you make such claims without good reason. We will review the documentation and make our own assessment.'

'Your Holiness, Professor Zaydan is expected at the Vatican at ten tomorrow morning. We will contact the Vatican office early tomorrow to finalise logistics. I'm appreciative of your support.'

'An informative conversation. When you visit the Vatican, I'll enjoy discussing our historical relationship. Let God be with you.'

'Thank you, Your Holiness. Goodbye.'

CHAPTER THIRTY-FOUR
ROME, ITALY, 04 AUGUST 2018

THE VIP GREETER stopped at the entrance to the immigration fast-track lane and moved a pointed a finger as she did a quick head count to confirm all of her six clients were present. The greeter had short dark hair, a perpetual smile and wore a chic grey skirt and blazer with a red scarf. The official at immigration recognised Williams as the famous Fox cable news host and called over a plain-clothed AISI security officer. The greeter showed the security officer the groups' La Posta Vecchia Hotel booking—a boutique hotel on the coast, thirty minutes from Rome.

The security officer knew with no sign of Einstein's son or the Israeli in Italy, the Italian security apparatus had a credibility issue. Questions were being asked and there were few answers. Recent intel suggested Einstein's son was being guarded by gendarmes in Corsica and would seek asylum in the Vatican; this raised more questions. The security officer knew when it came to politics love and war there were no coincidences. He wondered what Williams knew that he didn't. He looked at Williams' square head with its greying hair and high part. A thin scar above Williams' left eyebrow was the result of a cut sustained in his karate black-belt grading.

'Why are you in Rome, *signor?*' The question was directed at Williams but answered by his producer.

'Scouting footage for a new Christian film.'

'Welcome to Italy,' said the security officer. There was no reason to refuse Williams' entry, in fact, every reason to grant it. He would have Williams fol-lowed, see what showed up. Outside the arrivals terminal, an airport porter and Williams' team loaded their gear into two hotel courtesy vans and departed. The officer called in and requested a watch on the La Posta Vecchia Hotel.

Williams and his crew checked into their hotel, then lugged film equipment to the hotel helipad where a Leonardo VIP helicopter waited.

○

At Rothschilds' villa in the meeting room Elias sat opposite Gigi. Six sat around the table and there was broken conversation. Elias talked to Cyrus, to Marco, to Ophelia and Umberto, but no matter who he spoke to he was always aware of Gigi. Her eyes drifted in his direction and she found his eyes waiting, then her eyes moved on.

How long did she look; what did her eyes say; she's touching her neck now; is that for me? Elias's thoughts were on fire. He'd never been in love with a married woman before. In fact, he knew, until now, he'd never been in love. He took a mint from a table bowl, ripped off the wrapper and popped the mint into his mouth.

They all heard the *whap whap whap* of the approaching helicopter and the engine shut down after it landed on the grass helipad with its red and white banded windsock. Marco left to meet Williams and his crew, and moments later they entered the meeting room and the lives of Williams and his crew changed. Elias watched Williams' life change as he'd seen Ophelia's, Umberto's and Marco's lives change. Williams understood when you roll a dice the chance of getting a specific number is one in six. But that was all Williams understood. Elias listened as Cyrus broke the science into baby steps. Marco pushed the pram and Umberto tied a bonnet on William's square head, a square head with college-jock good looks and the ability to read a teleprompter. Although Williams at one time surprised everyone, and maybe even surprised himself when he said. 'Deism derives from *Deus*—the Latin word for God.' With this comment from Williams, Marco added that deists believe God created the universe, but God does not participate in day-to-day function with the natural laws of science responsible for daily events. It's cause and effect. Marco quoted from his crash course on deism and told Williams that Abraham Lincoln, Benjamin Franklin, Thomas Jefferson, James Madison and George Washington were deists—celebrity influencers. When Williams had no more questions, his film crew set up lights and two cameras for the interview with Cyrus. The others stayed in the room as a supporting audience. The interview would air the following day to coincide with Cyrus's landing on the Vatican helipad at 10.00 a.m.

Ophelia wore a teal floral dress, a new dress for the meeting with Williams. Elias wondered how many dresses Rothschilds had gifted her. She was smiling more than she had been in Egypt. Gigi wore a red couture midi and Elias loved how it hugged her small breasts. He took another mint, then twisted and shaped the wrapper into a ballerina as his mother had taught him when he was a child. Elias placed the mini ballerina in her plastic dress on the oak table. Gigi glanced at the ballerina and smiled. Although she smiled to herself, she knew Elias was watching.

When the interview finished Cyrus got up from his chair and bent close to Elias. 'Can I talk to you?'

Elias couldn't take his eyes off Gigi's red dress as she left the room. It hugged her tight.

'Elias?' Cyrus asked again.

'Oh … sorry my mind was distant.'

Cyrus pulled open a sliding glass door to the garden area outside the meeting room. They sat down in the late afternoon shade of an umbrella with a view to the blue sea.

'I'm troubled about the Vatican,' said Cyrus.

Elias hadn't seen this coming. He looked to the distant sea then back to Cyrus. 'What's your concern?'

'With Gigi, France could give me asylum. The gendarmes; I'm safe here.'

'In a few days, two weeks, I think France will.'

'We're deceiving the Vatican.'

'Yes.'

'People will assume we have papal endorsement.'

'Yes.'

'It doesn't feel right.'

'I understand, we both understand the complexities, the navigation of conscience.'

Cyrus leant back in his chair. He knew his moral compass, but he also knew pure saints are crushed in the colosseum. Cyrus listened to Elias.

'The Vatican provides undeniable gravitas—a pulpit, your deity constant is so important, the Vatican can cope with a little bruised dignity.'

Cyrus was thinking of his own dignity and Elias knew it. Cyrus thought how the lie about he and Elias killing the Syrian major had sailed so easily. The hidden forces out there were prepared to do whatever they could; honesty didn't matter, if it was repeated that two plus two equals five loud and often, people accepted two plus two equalled five.

What would Talal say? Would Talal say it was alright to deceive the Vatican? Cyrus knew what Talal would say. Talal would say fight them all— go fight them my best friend, fight them and win.

'Could you bring a yoga mat?' asked Cyrus.

'A yoga mat?'

'When you first visit me in the Vatican.'

'I'll visit tomorrow afternoon; visit every day.' Elias stood up and clasped Cyrus's hands. 'I'm so proud of you.'

Cyrus stood up and wrapped his arms around Elias. 'Words are inadequate, but thank you for everything.' Elias squeezed Cyrus and patted him on the back.

Cyrus thought once he was inside the Vatican, the cardinals would confront him, confront him and demand he defend, in their view, his indefensible position. But unlike a lifetime ago with deliberate reticence when he spoke to the *al-Ajawid* at Samir's house, this time he'd face the cardinals with discarded reticence and speak with head and heart.

Side by side they left the garden area. Elias stepped through the open sliding door, through the meeting room and into the villa lounge. There was no red dress.

'Where is everybody?' he asked.

'Williams and his crew are loading the helicopter,' said Marco. Gigi had left too—a two-hour commute back to Paris.

◯

The Vatican secretary of state felt his head get heavier and lower as he reviewed the 1832 contract with Rothschilds. He then informed the Pope the baron had the law and history on his side—the penalty interest clause was binding. The pontiff instructed his state secretary to keep his finding *sub rosa* and obtain a formal legal opinion and discuss it with the IOR Board—*le Opere di Religione,* better known as the Vatican Bank. The Vatican would receive Cyrus the following morning.

◯

The Mossad kept a distant watch on the Corsica villa. Agents had seen the gendarmes establish a security perimeter and a helicopter arrive from La Posta Vecchia Hotel. They knew it was Williams. It looked as if Williams was set to announce to the world that Einstein's new son had been found.

CHAPTER THIRTY-FIVE

ROME ITALY, 05 AUGUST

AT 10.00 A.M. a helicopter flew above. Williams turned his head and the helicopter dropped behind tall trees where he assumed the Vatican helipad to be. Williams heard through his ear piece, *You're live*. He straightened to face the camera.

'This is Sean Williams reporting live from St Peter's Square in Rome, Italy, outside the Vatican. We have the most significant breaking news of our lifetime; the most significant news of the last two thousand years. Behind me, in the Vatican, a lost son of Albert Einstein, a Syrian Druze, has been granted sanctuary. Einstein's lost child is Professor Cyrus Zaydan. But this is not the big story. The big story is, Professor Zaydan has discovered scientific proof showing a deity or God was behind the creation of life on Earth. Yes, fellow Christians and those of other beliefs, our long-held faith has now been proven. We have a theophany. A deity has made an appearance before man.'

Williams' opening monologue cut to a split-screen satellite feed and he introduced Nobel Laureate scientist Professor Jim Watson, and Professor Markham, professor of Religious Studies from Harvard University.

'First, Professor Watson, you have reviewed Professor Zaydan's discovery, your thoughts?'

'In my mind this is the greatest discovery for mankind; an unparalleled achievement.'

'People will look to experts like you to give a testimonial credibility rating,' said Williams.

'I give this an eleven out of ten,' said Watson. 'Truly remarkable.'

'Professor Markham, as the professor of Religious Studies at Harvard, your thoughts please?'

'Thank you, and deepest congratulations to Professor Cyrus Zaydan, we now know for a fact, man is not the most intelligent life form in the universe, mankind has no option but to show deference to this deity by realigning the foundations of our civilisation.'

'You said realigning foundations.'

'We're dealing with a new religious reality, I don't think people will remain passive, the majority in all societies are dormant, the people are silent, when the majority stop being silent society changes to the tune of the majority.'

'There are people running and cheering here, coming into St Peter's Square … can you pan the camera onto them?' Williams said. The camera swung to show hundreds of people cheering and running towards the papal basilica. 'There's a crowd coming out of the streets as if all of Rome is arriving.' The camera panned again and showed a never-ending mass of people cheering with their hands held high.

'We need to move now,' said Williams. 'In minutes, it looks as if literally hundreds of thousands of people will be congregated.' With their broadcast running, the Fox crew crabbed to the edge of the square against the pressing tide.

'There's elation in being among the crowd, an incredible din, the crowd is so full of contagious energy and excitement it vibrates to your bones. There's so much to discuss with this extraordinary drama, you couldn't invent it as fiction. What are we witnessing?' asked Williams.

'It's very difficult to determine what we are seeing; we're seeing something that looks like a real prophecy,' replied Markham.

'How do you foresee reaction in America?' asked Williams.

'Well, we know over half of Americans are evangelical Christians, and about one third of American Catholics and Protestants expect a second coming of Christ before twenty-fifty. Is Cyrus this second coming?'

'How do other religions view a second coming of Christ?' asked Williams.

'Islamic texts prophesize there will be a second coming and Jesus will descend at the point of a white arcade, east of Damascus. Cyrus was born in east Damascus. Bahai religion claims Christ will return with a new name, if Cyrus brings peace on Earth Judaism will have their Messiah.'

'How could Cyrus bring peace?' asked Williams.

'I think religion as we know it is over, something new will begin. Religion has always been a kind of glue in the cracks of political systems. It's clear this will influence how people see themselves—it's too early to predict the changes in society or human civilisation, but there will be changes.'

'One last word from you, Professor Watson.'

'People accept gravity as a scientific reality. In the coming days everyone will accept Cyrus's findings as reality, people will accept the deity constant as real and then move on to ask the questions raised by Professor Markham, such as how is this going to impact my future, the future of mankind?'

'History has shown monumental changes can occur fast and take us by surprise,' said Williams. 'We're going to know more about this tomorrow morning when we see the response from around the world. Sean Williams reporting live from the Vatican in Rome.' The live feed cut back to Fox Central.

◯

In his Tel Aviv office, Agmon received a call from a colleague informing him of mega breaking news on Foxtel. Agmon picked up the remote on his desk and selected the Foxtel channel. Two minutes into the report, as he stood in front of the TV screen with his hand at his mouth, Agmon hit pause and made a call.

'On Fox News a report says the Syrian Professor Zaydan is a Syrian Druze. I need immediate confirmation of Zaydan's religious denomination,' he barked.

'Okay,' came the reply.

Agmon ended the call, then his mobile rang. He snatched it. The caller ID said it was Cohen.

'Shalom, Nadav,' said Cohen. 'Are you watching Fox News?'

'I've seen some.'

'They're reporting Zaydan is Druze.'

'I know.'

'Is he Druze or Muslim?'

'I'm double-checking.'

'You should have triple-checked,' said Cohen.

'I apologise. It's a detail we should've got right, but a detail you could've checked with your resources.'

'Don't try pushing this onto us, you should've handled this differently. I'll see you at the security meeting.' Agmon put his mobile phone on his desk. He looked ill.

Agmon's assistant knocked on his door then entered.

'Sir, the prime minister's office is on the line.'

Agmon patched his landline and connected with the PMs' office. An emergency security meeting relating to Zaydan was scheduled in an hour.

◯

The Pope sent messages on his *@Pontifex* Twitter account and other social media along with Vatican Radio announcing an unscheduled address from the large balcony at the centre of St Peter's Cathedral. The balcony that was usually reserved for periodic *Urbi et Orbi* and the, *For the city and for the world* blessings.

At noon, the doors to the St Peter's Cathedral balcony opened and the thousands below saw the Pope dressed in white walk out and sit down on the balcony. He was flanked by two priests and a cardinal cloaked in crimson with a crimson *biretta* on his head. One of the priests moved the microphone on its flexi-stand close to the Pope. Pink and white roses with green leaves sat on top of a burgundy cloth on the balcony façade.

Everyone listened to the Pope's words especially near the end of his address.

'We have welcomed Professor Zaydan from Syria under our roof—' The crowd cheered and the Pope had to wait some time for the cheering to stop before he started to speak again. 'A newly found son of Albert Einstein.' The crowd cheered again, this time louder and the Pope had to wait longer.

'We have another child from one of mankind's great intellects. The church applauds Professor Zaydan's commitment to understanding God's role in making man. As we are taught in Genesis, God made man in His own likeness. In the likeness of God, He made him. He made both male and female.'

'Cyrus! Cyrus! Cyrus!' the crowd chanted non-stop. A demand Cyrus speak to them. The Pope waved to the crowd and finished his address in a faltering voice. 'I wish everyone a serene and blessed day.'

○

At the Rothschilds' Corsica villa, Umberto and the others watched the Pope's address. Umberto waved his arm. 'I've never seen the Pope rocked; he looks rocked off his feet. I know he was sitting down, but he looks shocked by this. He's lost his equilibrium.'

'He sounds shaken, said Elias. 'He's trying to cover this up.'

'The Pope is trying to dismiss Cyrus with his words, but you can see he doesn't believe what he's saying, he's wounded inside,' said Umberto. 'Never confuse what comes out of people's mouths with what they believe or do—three different things.'

'Why this reaction?' asked Ophelia.

'Before now the Pope *thought* there was a God, now the Pope *knows* there is a God. He's shaken because it was Cyrus who delivered this message to him, to the world,' said Umberto.

Elias gulped a mouthful of Perrier. 'After all, from an individual perspective, every person's religious thought is right … there will need to be a reconfiguration of everyone's religious agency to accept what Cyrus says as true. The extent to which this individual reconfiguration or acceptance occurs will dictate the future of the Deity Foundation, we're talking about personal inner transformations.'

'The Vatican is downplaying it,' said Marco. 'They feel damaged.'

'The church needs to be careful not to create a credibility issue,' said Umberto.

'When I met with Cyrus this afternoon, he said Vatican clergy have challenged him that it's no coincidence his work on the deity constant is publicised at the same time as he's granted sanctuary,' said Elias.

'We know they have a point,' added Ophelia.

'Do we have an update on donations the foundation has received?' asked Umberto.

'We'll receive over fifty million dollars in the first twenty-four hours,' replied Marco.

'Phenomenal. Rothschilds did well fast tracking the foundation,' said Umberto.

'Do you think the support will continue?' asked Ophelia.

'In a thousand years' time, I think Cyrus's teachings will continue to impact civilisation,' said Marco.

○

Mainstream and social media, turbo-charged by Rothschilds' financed mega influences, carried headlines: *Einstein's Second Coming; Einstein Proves Deity Delivers Life; And Then There Was Life* with a link to the Deity Foundation donations' page. Around the world, unprecedented crowds amassed outside major cathedrals, temples, mosques and synagogues as people sought out their spiritual leaders for their views on the deity constant.

The foundation's donations were predicted to exceed one billion dollars within three days. Rothschilds' co-ordinated *convince and convert* media strategy had exceeded all expectations.

CHAPTER THIRTY-SIX

ROME, ITALY, 06 AUGUST 2018

IT WAS TWENTY-THREE hours after Cyrus had entered the Vatican and because it was the holiday season in Italy, people from Rome jammed Leonardo de Vinci International Airport.

Reznik prowled through Rome's airport heading for his flight to Paris. He heard excited talk around him, excited talk of Cyrus and the deity constant. No one seemed to be talking about their planned vacations. Reznik stepped onto an escalator.

The lady on the escalator step above Reznik turned to him and asked, 'What do you think?'

'It's a nice day for a white wedding,' said Reznik. His hollow eyes looked up at the stranger. The woman felt the feeble man look right through her; she turned and pushed through people on the steps above. Reznik had been up before light and it was after nine. The top escalator step disappeared and Reznik strode to the nearby food court. For breakfast, he bought a Red Bull Zero. Like super model Kate Moss he was addicted to being thin.

The crushed can hit the recycle bin. Reznik was sure it was Agmon's idea to kill Zaydan. Agmon, the director of the Shin Bet would have balanced, calculated, and assessed the risk, before giving the kill order—the kill order a prophylactic decision to kill Zaydan. A prophylactic decision made by Agmon in case Zaydan discovered proof of God. Now Zaydan had the proof of God, Zaydan was a greater danger than ever. Reznik talked to himself and resolved there were more reasons now for Zaydan to be killed than ever before.

After landing in Paris, Reznik slid into a cab at Charles de Gaulle Airport and an hour later slid out at Hotel Modern, a two-star hotel half a mile from Notre-Dame. Reznik cold called Omid Aleinjad who agreed to meet the next day. Aleinjad was an acclaimed Parisian reporter who wrote on Islamic extremist groups, his theme a justification for the Islamic cause. Reznik had a particular interest in Omid's writings on *Quwat al-Ridha*, a Hezbollah trained militia.

Reznik wondered how Omid may respond, as he left the urine smell of the underground Pigalle metro station. He covered the short distance from the Pigalle station to Boulevard de Clichy and stood outside Brasserie La Marmite near the Arab Quarter. The man Reznik searched for sat at an outside table. Aleinjad looked like the facial sketch accompanying his press articles; a round face with round wire-framed glasses, an open-neck white shirt and dark suit.

'*Bonjour* … Omid?' asked Reznik.

'*Oui.*'

Reznik extended his hand and sat down in the warm shade of a faded red umbrella. A waiter arrived. He was a thick-set man with a twisted black bow tie.

'*Bonjour,*' said the waiter.

'*Bonjour,*' said Reznik. '*Un Red Bull Zero s'il vous plaît.*' Omid had close to a full cup of milky coffee.

'Thank you for meeting. As I said when I called, my name is Reznik.'

'Reznik … Jewish?' Omid's eye drifted to the red stain on Reznik's neck. He gave a fleeting smile. Allah blessed this man by making him look different from everybody else.

'Tel Aviv,' replied Reznik.

'Why seek me?'

Reznik looked at the man—scruffy dark hair, thoughtful eyes and when he smiled unblemished teeth.

'I've read your interesting perspective on *Quwat al-Ridha*,' said Reznik.

'Thank you, but I don't believe you wanted to meet to compliment my writing.'

The thick-set waiter returned. He had the Red Bull on a brown tray

'*Votre Red Bull, monsieur.*'

'*Merci.*' Reznik glanced at the crooked bow tie then he leant forward to Aleinjad and spoke quietly. 'I'd like to meet with a member of *Quwat al Ridha.*'

'The reason?'

'A proposition.' He took a slug of Red Bull and licked his lips.

'I know nothing of you.'

Reznik knew he'd be asked to identify himself. He could lie to Aleinjad, but gambled there were advantages to disclose that he was an Israeli agent. Reznik opened his wallet and showed his Shin Bet identification. Aleinjad's eyes widened.

'This is my job, but I'm meeting you as a private citizen.'

'I prefer to judge a man on his honesty as opposed to how well he hides his deceit.' Aleinjad smiled his white teeth. 'But … oh … we both know security agents are never off duty. I can't help.'

'Listen, I'll meet a member of *Quwat al Ridha* under circumstances that keep identities secret.' He finished his Red Bull in one drag.

'There's no one in the *Quwat al Ridha* group I know in Paris,' said Omid. He did not want to be a pawn in any sting operation.

'I understand your caution,' said Reznik. He leant back and ordered another Red Bull from the thick-set waiter. 'What can I do to give you assurance?'

Aleinjad sat for a moment without speaking and eyed Reznik. 'Give me more information, what type of proposition?'

'I need two or three combat-hardened men and I can pay well.' Using a napkin, Reznik wrote the mobile number for his burner phone, and passed it across the table.

◯

Twelve hours later, Reznik received a call from a man who called himself Dawud. A meeting was set for the afternoon and Reznik was told to wear a red cap and to sit on the steps in front of Montmartre's Sacré Cœur. Reznik again rode the metro to Pigalle and after a short climb from the metro stop, sat on the steps over-looking the rooftops of Paris. Maybe a hundred people sat on the steps. Most were tourists. Arab youths mingled with the tourists and tried to sell hash. Reznik scanned the others on the steps; no red caps. A man roamed then hovered at Reznik's side.

'What do you want?' the man asked. Reznik looked at the middle-aged man. He had a sparse black beard and blistered lips.

'Dawud?' The man nodded. 'The false prophet hiding like a rat in the Vatican.'

'I know this.'

'My people see him as an imposter insulting all religions.'

'Your plan?'

'*Quwat al Ridha* be gifted the chance to cleanse the world.'

'If Israel wants this Syrian killed, do it yourself.'

'I represent private interests.'

'This is not the place for such discussion.' The man with the blistered lips stepped away and weaved through the tourists. Reznik followed him down a set of steps running east away from the Sacré Cœur. A small Renault was parked with a driver waiting. Reznik and Dawud got into the car and were driven to a garage in the nearby Arab quarter

'Do you have a mobile?' asked Dawud once they'd got out of the car.

'I have two.' Reznik leaned his back on the Renault.

'Why two?'

'One mobile I used only to communicate with you.'

'Give them to me.' Reznik was strip-searched, and a black hood placed over his head, then he was handled into the back of a van. They drove for over an hour. When the vehicle stopped, hands dragged Reznik from the van and he was strip-searched again before being frog-marched into a room and shoved onto a wooden chair. The hood stayed on. Reznik held his arms limp at his sides and heard several voices. They spoke Farsi, which Reznik understood.

'Who are you?' asked a voice.

'As I told Omid Aleinjad, my name is Reznik and I work for Shin Bet.

'You're either stupid or you've got iron balls,' said the voice.

Reznik heard a number of sharp words before they moved out of earshot; they would have been told he worked for Shin Bet. It was an ad-hoc interrogation. A few minutes later his interrogators returned.

'Why does Israel want this arch liar killed?'

'It's a private operation.'

'Why kill him?'

Reznik offered a rehearsed answer. 'Iran is the world's largest theocracy. The Syrian's deity theory could be used as an excuse to establish new theocratic regimes in the West. We believe this puts us on a path to World War Three.' There was truth to what Reznik was saying, but he was also driven by revenge— the poison apple of ego.

'Why approach *Quwat al-Ridha*?' asked another voice.

'I need Zaydan dead. He's betrayed the Syrian government.'

'We're not Syrian backed.'

'But you know how to kill.'

'Your timeline?' asked another voice.

'Less than three weeks.'

'I don't like it,' said a voice speaking Farsi. 'I don't like any of it.'

'Three weeks, impossible,' said another.

'I give you the target, I can give you the time and location, the means of attack. You scout the location, organise your escape route and consider your post-attack media strategy.'

'You ever done this before?'

'It's my business,' said Reznik.

'Your suggested way of attack?' asked a voice.

'RPGs, then a point-blank kill shot.'

'Against a motor vehicle?'

'A helicopter.'

'What's the location?'

'The Syrian is in the Vatican. Soon he'll leave; this is when he's vulnerable.'

'You have RPGs in Rome?'

'I assume you'll organise weapons through your networks.'

'An assumption carrying significant risks and costs.'

'Which is why we're talking to a professional group like *Quwat al-Ridha*.'

'Financing?'

'Whatever is needed,' said Reznik. He had ideas to get financing but nothing yet concrete.

'You pay for the RPGs and supply an additional two million dollars' worth of weapons.'

'Small arms?' asked Reznik thinking two million was pocket change.

'Money always leaves a trail. We need the arms delivered to Raftan Tactical.'

Reznik knew of Raftan Tactical, a group that provided military support to oppressed Shia Muslims beyond Iran. A Chinese Muslim of the Hui sect from the Zhongyuan Province ran the organisation. He used the *nom de guerre,* Ma Hongbin after the famous Hui general who defeated the Japanese during the Sino-Japanese War. Ma claimed to have served in Beijing's special forces Arrow Unit.

'I cannot give an answer now,' said Reznik.

'You came to negotiate. Are you not serious?'

'I've approval for less, I don't want to agree if I'm unable to deliver.'

'You seek urgency from us, but you move like a snail.'

'Give me my mobile,' said Reznik, estimating the current time to be 6.00 p.m. making it midday in New York.

'It's at the Paris garage.'

'Get me another, I need to make a call.'

'Who to?'

'I thought you wanted two million in arms.' Reznik knew two million in cash would be a problem, but there was little problem obtaining two million worth of light military equipment. The pentagon invested US$500 million in a Jordanian programme to train anti-ISIS fighters, but only eighty had been trained. The bulk of the money disappeared sideways to support arms ship-ments. Reznik assisted those arms ship-ments with Academi, the American pri-vate military company originally known as Blackwater. They owed him. Owed him big.

'Get him a clean mobile,' said one of the Iranians. Someone dragged the black hood from his head. Reznik thought he was in a farm barn. He stood up.

'I need the Academi contact number from my mobile in Paris.'

Several minutes later Reznik paced on the dusty wooden floor; he paced in a slow circle as he spoke to his contact at Academi in New York. Reznik's New York contact detailed Academi already had a relationship with Raftan Tactical. Academi proposed Raftan Tactical be given a two million discount on their upcoming arms purchase. Reznik conveyed the proposal to the *Quwat al-Ridha* cell, which they reluctantly accepted. In reality, the discount was a bonus. Iran, as their paymasters, ensured *Quwat al-Ridha* were well-funded. To maintain

Iranian financial support, *Quwat al-Ridha* needed to deliver military success. The Syrian was a high-priority target, of the highest possible priority, and his death would find endless favour in Teheran and ensure an endless flow of rials.

'You'll stay with us until the attack,' said Dawud.

This was a dangerous situation, but Reznik knew what he had walked into. No back-up and a pact with an enemy who would think nothing of giving their lives for eternal martyrdom and those waiting virgins.

'I need to coordinate with my contacts in Rome, find out when the Syrian will leave the Vatican,' said Reznik.

'Co-ordinate from here. The Syrian either leaves the Vatican by helicopter, or by car; we'll plan for both.'

'Your man in Paris needs to dispose of my mobiles and erase his connection to the Paris garage.'

'Why?'

'My mobile's location can be traced.'

'GPS?'

'The international mobile subscriber identity allows the location history, calls, texts, everything can be tracked.'

'Location history?'

'Real-time location data is uploaded to the cloud whether the mobile is turned on or not. This is only an issue now I'm off-grid. My people will be relentless in their hunt for me.'

'This is a trap!' One of the men brandished a pistol and pressed the barrel to Reznik's head.

Reznik shrugged. 'If it's a trap, why am I warning you?'

Another man motioned with his arm and indicated for the other to lower his weapon. Their collaborator in Paris was called, instructed to dispose of Reznik's mobile and warned to eliminate all record of his association with the Paris garage.

○

Two days later, Reznik was shaken from his sleep and bundled into the back of a van. Sixteen hours later the van arrived in Rome.

CHAPTER THIRTY-SEVEN

ROME, ITALY, 18 AUGUST 2018

THE VATICAN STATE secretary knelt at the altar of the private chapel in his Vatican apartment. He wore a black cassock, his *zucchetto* crimson skull cap and a silver cross dangled on a fine silver chain. The state secretary finished his prayer and touched his forehead with his fingertips then touched mid-chest and then left to right shoulder. He stood up on aged joints. With his shoulders sloped, he ambled into his spare bedroom. He stopped and looked up at the heavily decorated, gold embossed three-dimensional ceiling. The ceiling he'd stood under ten thousand times before. The ceiling, original in its art and structure from the sixteenth century when Pope Julius II had slept there, the ceiling decorated with Julius's coat of arms, a coat of arms with the crossed keys to the kingdom of heaven and the triple tiara, and a tree. He recalled Pope Julius II was named the Warrior Pope. The Fearsome Pope. The state secretary knew Julius II selected his papal name of Julius in emulation of Julius Caesar, not in honour of Pope Julius I. He wondered what action the Caesar-warrior Pope would take to strengthen his church against a threat like Zaydan. What action Pope Julius II would take to combat this Deity Foundation attacking his church. The Warrior Pope had worn a camouflage of compassion as he restored the glory and respect of the papacy, restoration of papacy, a respect achieved by way of war not spiritual leadership. The state secretary received his sign, Pope Julius II would attack and attack hard and if necessary, fight dirty. His private chapel prayer had been answered.

◯

With millions globally supporting the apotheosis of Cyrus, the state secretary called a crisis meeting of the Pope's cardinal advisors. At the meeting, held in the state secretary's chambers, he extended both palms in front of his chest and encouraged his fellow cardinals to share their true thoughts.

'A rushed decision granted Einstein's son sanctuary; I advised against it and am now even more opposed,' said Cardinal Kesel who headed the Vatican section for general affairs.

'We moved too quickly and didn't consider our ways, and today there's a price,' said Cardinal Erdo. They all knew it had been the pontiff's ultimate decision.

'This Einstein imagines he has wisdom and foresight, his hubris is a mental illness, he's crazy, unwell, and there's nothing more dangerous. For two thousand years the church defended the faith that God created life, and it's not in the Holy See's interest to continue sheltering this Syrian,' said Cardinal Tucci who was head of diplomatic staff.

'The church's compassion has been exploited and raised Zaydan's political profile; we've been duped. It's written in the scripture, the coming of the Antichrist will be preceded by a general apostasy, a Christian loss of faith. This Syrian is apostatising exactly this, a loss of faith,' replied Kesel.

'Zaydan is a personality cult figure who manipulates the mass media with a lie, a propaganda campaign that preys on sentiment,' said Tucci.

'Judaism doesn't recognise Christ as the Messiah. Zaydan is the son of a Jew and Zaydan's key advisors are Jews. He's an enemy of God, undermining faith in Christ. The supreme religious deception of the Antichrist, a pseudo-messiah by which man glorifies himself in place of God,' said Erdo.

'Rather than glorifying himself in place of God, I see Professor Zaydan providing reaffirmation of God. We need to be clear-eyed, ask ourselves why people around the world have embraced his divine pronouncement,' said the state secretary. He was the only cardinal in the room who knew the real reason why Cyrus was granted sanctuary.

'The Syrian offers a false peace on Earth,' said Erdo.

'The Syrian must leave,' said Tucci.

'Professor Zaydan's foundation intends to provide help to those in need, much the way we do. However, I've heard your views and will advise our Holy Father that we should ask the professor to leave,' said the State secretary.

The Cardinals stood up. The state secretary eyed Erdo, then looked down.

Cardinal Erdo hung back, and let the other two cardinals leave. Erdo sat down with the state secretary.

'This is what happens when you have a populism in the papal form. Papal decisions deviating from foundations the church has observed for centuries,' Erdo said.

'I've conducted myself based on Christian values doing God's work but—' the state secretary paused.

'But?' asked Erdo.

'But I must put the future good of the church before myself,' said the state secretary.

'You seemed conciliatory,' said Erdo. The state secretary gave Erdo an insincere smile.

'What do you have in mind?' The two put their heads together.

'Zaydan, the Deity Foundation, have done the church a favour.'

'How so?' asked Erdo

'We've seen an increase in our global church donations over the last week.

'Do you think this can be sustained?'

'Sustained, even increased.'

'Yes?'

'If the Deity Foundation ceases to exist.'

'And how could that occur?'

'The Catholic Church cannot be seen to engage in vengeance; but the FBI...'

○

Later the same day, Cardinal Scola contacted the state secretary. The French government were offering Cyrus permanent asylum. The Pope's office, gratified to learn Cyrus would be granted asylum in France, contacted Rothschild's and they agreed Cyrus would depart the Vatican the following morning.

○

Cyrus looked up when he heard a knock on the half open door to his Vatican apartment. It was late in the afternoon. No one had knocked on his door. Elias, Umberto or Ophelia called out when they visited with their Swiss guard escorts. Cyrus pulled the door full open. A smiling bishop stood facing him. Cyrus had not met him before.

'We hear you are leaving us, professor. An invitation to meet with the Vatican secretary of State and his executive. An informal talk if you have time.'

'Sure … now?'

'If it suits.'

Cyrus welcomed the opportunity to talk with the cardinals and escorted by the smiling bishop left his apartment. After a long walk past art and statues and rare artifacts, such as huge maps of the New World, the bishop stopped at a door, knocked, then swung the door wide for Cyrus to enter. Cyrus passed through a pillared entranceway and stepped from the marble floor onto a Persian carpet. Four cardinals wearing crosses around their necks, over dark robes adorned with crimson, sat at a boardroom table. At one end of the room a book stand supported an open Bible and above the Bible Cyrus saw a towering painting depicting Christ's crucifixion at Calvary. The state secretary stood up, his arms extended in invitation.

'Please, professor, come and sit with us.'

After formal introductions, the state secretary led the discussion.

'I've lived within these walls for many years, we're a family, it's been a privilege to have you with us and I hear you leave tomorrow.'

'I'm very grateful to have been welcomed into your house.'

'We all talk to God and at his will God talks to us. Have you always heard God's word?' asked Cardinal Kesel.

'For as long as I can remember, at times I don't know where my words come from. Not so much the individual words but the message.'

'Do you see yourself as a philosopher?' asked Tucci.

'Like several of you, I have a doctorate of philosophy, we have our doctorates in distinctive disciplines but share an understanding of the philosophical process.'

'How would you describe the philosophical process?' continued Tucci.

'It begins by knowing your subject matter.'

'How did you develop your understanding of spirituality?' asked Erdo. He thought Cyrus looked young and would lack wisdom.

'By reading a lot and knowing myself.'

'Human spirituality is the church's guardian and has been for over two thousand years. Would you describe yourself as a child of God?' asked Erdo.

'A child of humanity.'

'We are all children of humanity, and like you, we are descendants of Abraham. Where do you understand your deity resides?' asked Kesel.

'A deity's intelligence is metaphysical; it doesn't rely on raw biological machine power; by definition the deity existed before man's biological intelligence.'

'Where do you derive your knowledge to make such statements?' asked Tucci.

'Studying science and mathematics.'

'Timothy teaches not to wander from the faith and to turn away from godless chatter and the opposing ideas of what is falsely called knowledge. Is your science and mathematics such godless chatter and false knowledge?' asked Erdo. Erdo thought *It seems Zaydan has no presence, yet also Zaydan has a huge presence. It was odd.*

The cardinal is too strict, too saintly, thought Cyrus. *He talks like the New Testament. He bears no feelings, no appetite for anyone but Christ.* 'The deity constant is based on recognised and proven scientific facts,' said Cyrus. To their faces, Cyrus told them the truth and, in this truth, they had no interest.

'You appear to also possess a wide ability to decipher spirituality, and with this you are truly blessed,' said the state secretary.

'I thank you for the compassion you have shown.'

'It warms our hearts to hear France will help you. We're pleased the Vatican was able to provide a stepping stone to find somewhere more permanent. We thank you for discussing your views with us, but must now ask you to leave as we have pressing business,' said the state secretary. He squared his shoulders and let a simper of superiority replace his cordiality.

The cardinals' eyes bored into Cyrus as he stood up and left the room.

Cyrus thought how closed the Vatican people were, discrete and chary with their true thoughts locked. He knew the cardinals saw him as seeking to flesh Christ's words, infuse Christ's metaphors with human reason, metaphors they thought were not meant to be infused. Christ's metaphors alone were a polished sword to invade man's flesh.

CHAPTER THIRTY-EIGHT

VATICAN CITY, ITALY, 19 AUGUST 2018.

IT WAS A humid day and a big city haze threw a cataract over Rome. A Swiss guard buzzed Ophelia into the Vatican, and after being scanned by a metal detector she passed through the security area and was escorted to Cyrus's apartment. She called out at his open door and Cyrus appeared.

'It's lovely to see you,' said Ophelia. She dragged her eyes from his.

'We have time for a walk in the gardens before Elias is due,' said Cyrus. 'There's a seat in the trees where the birds are social.'

They drifted through the Vatican gardens and passed the replica of the Lourdes Grotto, the original, etched its place in history at Lourdes after a young French peasant girl told of seeing an apparition wearing a white veil with a blue girdle and a yellow rose on each foot. Past the Lourdes Grotto replica, they climbed the incline of Vatican Hill where Cyrus pointed to an olive tree donated by Israel, through leafy arches, passed clipped lawns, and sculptured plants; a vision of man's control over nature. In stark relief, dominating the skyline, the Basilica Dome of St Peter loomed close. They sat at the seat in the trees where the birds were social.

'I had dinner last night with refugees and homeless people,' said Cyrus.

'Yes?'

'Nun's look after a number living here. I ate with them.'

'A gift experience.'

'Traumatic stories,' said Cyrus as he gazed into the distance. 'It's splendid news France will grant me asylum.'

'There's more great news,' said Ophelia. 'The French National Assembly voted to give the Deity Foundation a lease on Chambord Château, so we can go immediately.'

'Chambord Château?'

'One of the largest châteaux in France, around two hundred kilometres south of Paris.'

'How many rooms can we have?'

'The lease is for the complete château complex. You'll have one of the largest châteaux in France as your new home.'

'Gigi organised this?'

'With Dassault and Rothschilds.'

'We're lucky to have great people looking out for us.' Cyrus raised his hand and pointed to a pair of green parakeets on the bark of the pine. One gave a show of iridescent blue when it spread its wings. Then Cyrus pointed to a little bird on the grass. It puffed out its yellow chest, then pecked its feathers with its tiny beak before it chirped. The yellow feathers on the bird's neck pushed out.

'I can think of nothing more special,' said Ophelia. 'We're in the beauty of the Vatican's Eden, but it could be an Eden anywhere.' Ophelia kept a thought to herself—*this nature is God's beauty, why do we talk to God in the artificial grace of a synagogue or church?*

'It feels as if I've been here an eternity; I'll be happy to leave,' said Cyrus.

'The helicopter arrives at ten-thirty, do you have everything organised?'

'I only have a few clothes,' said Cyrus, 'and my yoga mat.'

'I want to come to France with you.'

'But you are coming with us.'

'I only want to come to France to be with you.' Cyrus felt uneasy. He liked Ophelia because she was forthright and kind and didn't know malice, but he never thought about her in any way that was not proper.

'It'll be rewarding to start funding major projects,' said Cyrus steering the conversation in another direction.

Ophelia raised her hand to her mouth, then looked into the trees away from Cyrus.

'There's been a call to the foundation from an Iranian woman,' said Ophelia. 'Her name is Darijani. She knew you in Syria and wants to meet.'

Cyrus smiled and recalled an instant vision of when he and Darijani were last together. A vision that had replayed countless times. A vision of he and Darijani dining near the campus and walking together to her dormitory, facing each other in the dark. She had kissed his cheek. She carried the fragrance of a Persian tulip. After she'd stepped away, she'd turned back to look at him. Her eyes alive had cut through the dark when she'd said goodnight.

'Darijani was in my class at university; she visited our house for dinner a few times and then suddenly left Damascus. I never knew why.'

'Was she more than a colleague?'

'She was the first and only girl I took home to meet my parents.'

'Do you want to see her again?'

'I'd like to know of the life she's lived and why she disappeared from Damascus all those years ago.'

'What do you mean disappeared?'

'We dined in Damascus one evening, then I never saw or heard from her again.'

'It seems strange.'

'It mystified me; I'd like to understand what happened.'

Ophelia looked at her watch. 'Elias said he'd come at ten, we should go.'

They walked down the hill to Cyrus's Vatican apartment. Elias was waiting.

'There's to be a ceremonial welcome when we arrive in Chambord. Umberto will be there too,' said Elias. 'Gigi will travel with us and can tell us about the welcome.'

Two black SUVs arrived outside the apartment; Cardinal Scola and the state secretary stepped from the lead vehicle.

'Ready to go?' asked Scola. Elias caught the aroma of wine. He thought again of the silent promise he'd made to God on the tarmac at Alexandria.

If you let us get away, I will stop drinking. And since Alexandria he kept his promise.

Elias stepped close to Scola. 'Thank you for the help you've given Cyrus.'

'I'm sorry the professor is leaving us,' said Scola with a polite nod towards Cyrus.

'We'd welcome a visit from you at Chambord,' said Cyrus. 'It'll be our pleasure to return your hospitality.'

'Chambord?' asked the state secretary.

'France is providing Chambord as Cyrus's residence,' said Elias.

'The … the complete château?' asked the state secretary.

'Yes,' said Elias. 'For Cyrus and the Deity Foundation.'

The state secretary tensed his lips. Chambord had been built by a French king as a competing structure to the Vatican's St. Peters. 'It'll be a privilege to visit after you're settled. His Holiness asked I extend his best wishes. Unfortunately, our Holy Father is unavailable to bid you farewell.'

'Please pass on my deepest thanks for the safe haven,' said Cyrus.

Elias placed Cyrus's small travel bag and rolled yoga mat into the rear of the SUV, then he climbed inside and joined Cyrus and Ophelia for the short drive to the Vatican helipad. The helicopter was waiting. Its main rotor and tail rotor were already turning. The SUVs pulled to a stop at the helipad where a number of people stood. Elias's heart thumped when he saw Gigi. She wore yellow. The passengers from the helicopter greeted Cyrus and shook his hand and Cardinal Scola and the state sec-retary bid Cyrus a final farewell.

○

The previous day, Reznik received a text message from Monsignor Scutari to say that the target would leave the Vatican by helicopter at 10.30 a.m. on August 17. Reznik and the *Quwat al-Ridha* cell had been in Rome for eleven days. On their fourth, they took delivery of two RPG-7 grenade launches from an arms dealer in Croatia. The attack plan was simple. Enter the apart-ment building opposite the Vatican helipad, kill the ground floor concierge then take control of a third-floor apartment that overlooked the helipad. If anybody was in the apartment Reznik was to gag and tie them while the other two took up positions to take down Zadan's helicopter.

At 9.00 a.m. the day of the attack, Reznik pulled open the side door of a blue van with the words *Roma Servizi Idrici* stencilled on the panel. Two *Quwat al-Ridha* operatives loaded kit bags with the grenade launchers. Reznik pulled the side door closed and huddled in the rear of the van with three terrorists. All wore green overalls. They drove from their safe house to the perimeter of the Vatican and Reznik checked the three faces. They appeared calm. He was trained to read faces and trained how to identify a micro-expression that could expose a lie. He caught Karabiji's eye—the cell commander. Karabiji delivered his best imitation of a smile before Karabiji's eyes drifted away. Reznik thought about Karabiji's false smile. Karabiji had a young but battle-hardened face from fighting with the Houthi in Yemen, but a face too young to have mastered the art of hiding micro-expressions. Reznik hadn't considered killing the terrorists but now it was a front of mind option. His hand rested on the pistol at his waist. A symbol of trust from Karabiji.

Reznik rocked forward in the rear of the van when the driver braked to a stop on Viale Vaticano. Reznik tugged open the side door; one man shouldered the kit bags, and the other pressed the street buzzer to the apartment building. After an exchange over the intercom, the door to the apartment building opened. The concierge stepped from his office. He was led to believe the four men in green overalls were from the water department. He was a thin man of sixty and dragged on a hand-rolled cigarette. It would be his last. One of the men withdrew a silenced pistol, placed the barrel against the concierge's head and squeezed the trigger. The shooter then stayed on the ground floor as lookout. On the third floor Reznik knocked on a door. It was answered by a woman in her early thirties. They expected her to be alone.

'Sorry to disturb you, madam, there's a problem with the water. May we come in?' asked Reznik. He spoke Italian.

'What sort of—' The woman's question was cut. From behind Reznik came a muted plop. The woman's knees buckled. Reznik grabbed the pistol at his waist and spun around. He glared at the dark hole of a silencer inches from his face and knew he was dead. His head snapped back and he fell on top of the woman. Blood seeped from both their heads and stained the blue patterned rug. The two *Quwat al-Ridha* men dragged their kit bags inside and shut the door. The man who shot Reznik put another shot into Reznik's skull then placed a neatly folded paper in Reznik's green overall pocket.

The men hauled the two kit bags from the living area into the bedroom overlooking Viale Vaticano, the two-lane road separating the apartment from the Vatican wall. Each terrorist removed a Russian made RPG-7 rocket-propelled grenade launcher, and a rocket grenade. They both slid a rocket grenade into the barrel of their launchers and unscrewed the plastic safety cap at the grenade's tip. The safety cap was similar to the cap on a plastic 7UP bottle. Each man opened a bedroom window, crouched and rested his grenade launcher on the window sill. The open windows gave a direct line of fire to the Vatican helipad one hundred and thirty-seven metres away. The RPG-7 rocket launcher had an optimal killing range of two hundred metres.

◯

A short time later, the tell-tale thwap … thwap … thwap signalled the approach of the helicopter. The men raised their weapons and followed the slow track of the French Aerospatiale cougar. The helicopter landed and settled on the double nose wheels and the two wheel sets under the fuselage. The reduced whine of the turbo jet and the noise of the chopping blades carried to the men at the window. They observed through their padded tele-sights—two black SUV's approach and stop at the helipad—a group of people left the black SUVs and met another group who landed in the helicopter—a woman's summer dress, a splash of yellow against the suited men from the helicopter. A different woman stepped forward from the helicopter group and ushered two men and a woman from the SUVs; they bent their heads as they walked to the helicopter. The passengers then disappeared one by one into the helicopter belly. The helicopter belly door slid sideways and closed. A few moments later, the sound of the engine increased, the main and tail blade turning faster with a finer pitch. Then the helicopter lifted off, lifted up and lifted back a little, the nose dipped and the pilot banked the cougar and headed away from the Vatican grounds and over Viale Vaticano towards Leonardo Di Vinci Airport.

The first shooter looked through his tele-sight at the middle of the helicopter and squeezed the trigger. A huge boom. The rocket propelled grenade raced with a bang in a line towards the helicopter. The shooter followed the vapour trajectory then a second later an explosion as the grenade hit. The helicopter lurched. The second shooter fired—the RPG exploded the tail rotor. The helicopter cartwheeled.

○

Ophelia leant in close to Cyrus. 'I've missed spending quality time with you.'

Cyrus gave Ophelia's arm a friendly squeeze and moved his mouth close to her ear. 'When we arrive in—' but his words stopped when his body felt a sudden jolt. An explosion rocked the helicopter and sent a flash of light and a pressure wave through the cabin. Pieces of hot jagged metal flew through the air. Elias felt the pilot lift the nose and turn the wounded machine back towards the helipad. Passengers screamed—women and men. Elias yelled *brace* and crouched forward over his knees. Another explosion and a searing hot flash. Cyrus jammed his mouth shut tight in reflex to the hot air.

Elias lifted his head and his eyes whizzed. Outside an apartment building spun by, then the Vatican wall spun by, and a road below came up fast. Elias bent forward and again yelled *brace.* The helicopter hit the road hard and snapped the nose wheels. Elias's head jerked and a driving force pulsed up his spine and catapulted him against his safety harness. His ears zinged. Elias opened his eyes. He could still see. Everything looked smoky and sounded quiet. Moments later, those conscious in the helicopter started to make noise. Someone shouted 'help me.' Another moaned. Elias straightened from his brace position. His brain said Cyrus, then Gigi. He twisted and through the smoke he could see Cyrus. Cyrus sat still. Ophelia lay slumped beside him. Elias knew she was dead. Part of her head was gone. Elias unbuckled his seat belt, unclipped Ophelia's seat belt and pulled her to the floor so he could reach Cyrus. A deep red bruise rose on the side of Cyrus's head and blood pulsed from his leg. Elias dragged the belt from his own trousers and fashioned a tourniquet above the red pulse before he pulled Cyrus from his seat. Elias used a fireman's lift, heaved Cyrus onto his shoulder and carried him several steps to the cabin door. He lowered Cyrus to the floor; shoved the exit slide-door but it didn't move.

○

Above in the Viale Vaticano apartment, the backblast from the rocket grenade launchers flamed the wall and a broil of smoke swirled. Karabiji and his terrorist colleague dropped their launchers; ran from the smoke-filled room and charged down the stairs to the ground floor courtyard. Karabiji pressed the rocker switch to the communal entrance, the door clicked and he burst onto the street. The two other green overalled terrorists followed a few paces behind. To the left Karabiji saw strewn metal and the downed helicopter, to the right their getaway van. Karabiji could hear a slashing metal sound; someone was alive trying to get out. He cursed, whipped his pistol from his belt and raced towards the wrecked helicopter. The two others followed, a few paces behind.

◯

Elias bent his knees and thrust against the door handle. It didn't move. Beside the door was a fire axe with a red handle. He grabbed the axe and swung at the sliding door lock. The axe punched through the alloy fuselage like a giant can opener. Elias swung the axe until the door was cut away around the lock. He pushed again and this time the door slid half-open—half-open was enough. He dropped the axe with a thud and stared out the half open door along Viale Vaticano. Elias threw himself to the cabin floor as shots zinged past. Lying flat, Elias reached to his shoulder holster, grabbed his pistol and squeezed two rapid shots; he heard the thump as both hit. The green overalled man buckled. Two others, behind the buckled man, had weapons raised and were now also shooting. Elias spun through the half-open door and hit the road. He lay prone. Bullets pinged and road chips flew close to Elias's face. He sighted on the closest man's chest and squeezed two quick shots. Both hit with a thump and the man fell. Further back, the other man spun around and ran towards a blue van. Elias fired two more shots. A hit and a miss. The man stumbled, hit the ground, got up and continued towards the van more slowly. Elias squeezed another shot and the man fell. Umberto had done well having the weapon placed in the helicopter for him. Elias hauled himself back into the helicopter. The smoke scorched his nose, Elias coughed and his head spun. He pulled Cyrus close to the half-open door, jumped to the road, and looked down Viale Vaticano. All three men dressed in green overalls lay still. He lifted Cyrus out of the helicopter onto his shoulder and staggered as he carried him from the wreckage to a doorway at the side of the street. He lay Cyrus down, then straightened up. Elias grabbed the doorway to steady himself. Images of

Gigi in her yellow dress flashed. His head said to stay with Cyrus until help arrived but his heart screamed, he needed to help Gigi. With his hand on the building, he sucked in deep breaths, then stumbled back to the helicopter. He threw himself into the cabin and collapsed onto the floor. His body wanted to stay there, rest on the floor, but he forced himself to where Gigi sat. He put his cheek close to her mouth and nose and felt her breath against his skin. His hands found the buckle of her seat belt and he fumbled as he undid the buckle and tried to pull her free. She didn't move. He tried again. His ears pounded and his vision was filled with purple and his legs felt like lead. It was impossible to breathe. The cabin was filled with toxic smoke. He dropped to the floor where the air was clearer and gasped a breath. Then he saw Gigi in her yellow dress. She stood in a meadow surrounded by red flowers and called to him. He could hear her voice but could not understand what she said. He tried to walk closer to Gigi, but the red flowers wrapped around his legs and held him tight. Then he dragged one leg free, but the red flowers wrapped around his legs again. With each step he inched closer to the yellow dress. 'I know you can do it, get us both out now,' in his head he heard Gigi say.

○

A *Polizia Roma Capitale* car was the first emergency vehicle to arrive at the crash scene. A cloud of smoke and the odorous smell of burning flesh ballooned from the cockpit. A police officer grabbed a fire extinguisher from the boot of his car, and doused the cockpit fire with foam. An ambulance carrying three paramedics arrived. A paramedic with a fire extinguisher, and a medical kit, ran to where the police were at the front of the helicopter. The paramedic stared through the broken glass of the cockpit to the charred pilots belted in their seats. Their skin dripped and the blackened muscle tissue made it difficult to recognise their faces as human. One of the pilots uttered a low guttural sound.

'He's alive!' shouted the paramedic.

'Give me your fire extinguisher,' said a policeman. The policeman rushed to the half-open sliding door of the main cabin. More police cars and another ambulance arrived.

As a policeman climbed into the main cabin, orange and yellow flames licked behind him. He held his breath and blasted the fire extinguisher. The flames died. Then he returned to the half-open door and gasped a breath. A paramedic climbed inside.

'Help get them out! This could explode.' It was what they yelled in movies, but the policeman was right. On the floor of the smoke-filled cabin lay a female passenger with a severe head wound. He moved on and examined another passenger; a male with minor facial lacerations and blood seeping from an abdominal wound. He wasn't breathing.

'Pass a stretcher!' called the paramedic. They bundled the man onto the stretcher and pulled it out of the cabin door. Then more paramedics pushed their way into the main cabin. One of the fire crew cut at a contorted seat to extract a male passenger, while at the front of the helicopter, fire crew cut through the frame of the glass cockpit for access to the pilot who grunted. A male passenger lay on a gurney and was being wheeled to an ambulance. Another female passenger in the cabin was not breathing. A male passenger seated in the rear section bore the brunt of the second explosion. There was no need to check his pulse. Shrapnel had passed through him and shredded his torso before it ripped into the male sitting beside him. A second group of paramedics helped three passengers found some distance from the wreckage. A man lay in a doorway with a make-shift belt tourniquet on one leg; his cream trousers blood red. He was lifted onto a gurney with a saline drip in his arm. A middle-aged man lay on the road beside an unconscious copper-haired woman wearing a yellow dress. She was in the recovery position.

Of the twelve people on board, eight died at the crash site—one of the pilots, six males and one female passenger. The grunting pilot who survived the crash died on the way to the hospital. A man dressed in green overalls and holding a silenced pistol lay dead twenty paces from the helicopter. He'd been shot twice in the chest. Two other men in green overalls had been shot. Both were alive. Smoke wafted from two open third-floor windows in an apartment up the street.

The Rome anti-terrorist squad swept to the smoking third-floor apartment that overlooked the Vatican helipad. They found the dead concierge, a dead woman and a dead man in the third-floor apartment. The bedroom that overlooked the helipad had scorch marks on the wall from the RPG's rear breech.

The digitised fingerprints of the dead were compared against a number of databases. Within an hour, the Rome police identified the man found shot dead in the apartment. He was Reznik Abravanel, an Israeli Shin Bet agent. The Israeli government and the Shin Bet were asked for an explanation.

In Tel Aviv, the front page of *Haaretz* carried a photograph of the helicopter wreckage with background commentary on Cyrus, Elias and Ophelia and their links to Israel. At the bottom of the front page was the news line: *Director of Shin Bet Dead from Gunshot Wound. No one else sought—see page two.*

CHAPTER THIRTY-NINE

ROME, ITALY, 20 AUGUST 2018

ELIAS DRAGGED SHALLOW breaths in the cocoon-like hyperbaric oxygen chamber at Rome's Gemelli Hospital.

When his two-hour oxygen therapy ended, the nurse unlocked the chamber door seal, swung the door open and pulled the patient table from the chamber. An orderly wheeled Elias away from the chamber— the lights on the sterile white ceiling made Elias feel dizzy. He closed his eyes. The young male orderly who wheeled Elias's bed said something about him being a hero, but Elias was thinking of Ophelia and wished he'd thanked her more for the help she'd given. Some have subtle ways, and others not so subtle, of eliciting thanks, but Ophelia gave no time to seek recognition. For her, it was not what she had done but what she had yet to do. Actions and words define us all. It was good Tzvi was going to her funeral in Cairo.

The orderly opened the door to his room and Esther with her ombre braids looked up from reading *Catch 22*. Beside her on a low table was a copy of Rome's daily *Il Tempo* with a photograph of the downed helicopter and inset photographs of those who had been killed. Esther stood up and wrapped her arm around Elias's chest and helped him to his bed. She thought Elias felt stiff. His weight was not relaxed against her and his eyes … his eyes were his eyes but not the eyes she knew. She asked if he could breathe better and he said yes.

Elias saw himself back at the helicopter. Gigi was in her yellow dress and beside her was another with ombre braids. He only had time to save one … he blinked hard and picked up a glass of water from beside his bed. Don't go there. But it was too late, he had gone there and he knew who he would save. Elias wanted to ask about Gigi. He knew she was at Gemelli Hospital too and was doing okay, but he wanted an update. With a croaky voice he asked about Cyrus, then Tzvi and then the French minister. Esther said she had a room at the other end of the ward; this was news. She'd met the French minister's husband and little daughter at the ward station and spoken with them in French. Elias was about to ask what the minister's husband was like, but the door opened and Elias's father walked in. His father's eyes swarmed with tears, and his face smiled.

◯

A few kilometres away at Rome's Celio Military Hospital, an aseptic band of blue linoleum covered the floor under Cyrus's bed then rolled up the wall to the ceiling. Cyrus grasped the pull-up assist on the bed crane, contracted his abdominals, and pulled up. He propped himself up with two pillows at the head of the bed. A good-looking nurse, in her mid-twenties with dark hair, then sponged Cyrus's face and chest, and when she was finished, asked if he wanted the patio doors opened. He said yes. She was about to leave his room when she turned and spoke.

'Your leg's healing well, you'll be leaving us soon. Time heals everything.' She smiled and shut the door. Cyrus looked out the open patio doors to Cyprus trees fringing the private garden, while closer were three soldiers of the *Gruppo Operativo Incursori*, part of the elite special forces combat battalion guarding him at the military hospital. Cyrus raised his palm and a soldier raised his thumb.

Ophelia had died, eight others had died and he was alive. Nine innocent lives taken in an attempt to kill him and kill the deity constant. No eleven. The two Italian civilians in the apartment building. For several decades in Damascus, he had lived in fear or lived with fear. Evil people did things to make you scared. And the punishments could be scary, very scary. He'd seen the veneer during his visit to 601 and on the flight from Damascus to Sharm El-Sheikh, the major had bent his foul-smelling mouth close to his ear and warned of the consequences if he didn't obey. He'd be a guest in the 601-dance studio watching prisoners have ropes slipped around their necks and tightened then tugged and pulled until they danced a final dance. And when he'd watched the last dance studio prisoner, complete his or her dance, it would be his turn. Cyrus thought about what the nurse had said; *time heals everything*. She was right. Time healed life and healed everything back from there. For the first time in his adult life Cyrus felt fearless.

There was a light knock at the door and Umberto walked in. Umberto glanced at the white bandage wrapped around Cyrus's head, then he leant forward and kissed Cyrus on both cheeks.

'How are you, my friend. Your head?'

'My head's okay, thanks,' said Cyrus. His head had been tilted close to Ophelia's when the first RPG hit. Ophelia's head smashed into his.

Umberto sat beside Cyrus's bed and said Ophelia's body had been flown to Cairo. She was to be buried at Basatin, Cairo's Jewish cemetery, the second oldest Jewish cemetery in the world. Tzvi, Elias's cousin, would go to her funeral and Netanyahu said he'd attend.

'Ophelia was a rare gem,' said Cyrus.

'She made me smile inside, in the best way possible. She wanted to know exactly what was going on, so she could see where she could help,' said Umberto.

'Ophelia paid for our medivac jet.'

'I didn't know, I assumed Elias had.'

'Elias's funds had been frozen.'

'A saint,' said Umberto. He'd never called anyone a saint before.

'How are Elias and Gigi?' asked Cyrus.

'They're going to be fine—healing fast.'

'I've heard nothing of the foundation.'

'A beehive of three hundred are in a wing at Chambord. They hit the ground at a sprint, and are humming to process the tsunami of donations.

We've got security at Chambord that exceeds that for most heads of state. An army is guarding you here.'

'I've seen them outside.' Cyrus nodded to the double patio doors.

Umberto stood up and stepped to the patio doors. Outside he saw three military men, one was talking into a mouthpiece.

'I passed about a hundred military to get to your room, and you're the only patient in this ward.'

'It'll be good to get to Chambord, a new home.'

'You could go to Chambord today. We've installed a medical facility.'

'The doctor said I shouldn't fly for a week with my concussion.'

'Ask your doctor if a helicopter is okay.'

The following day, Cyrus flew on a helicopter from Rome, with a refuel stop in Monaco, to Chambord Château.

CHAPTER FORTY

CHAMBORD, FRANCE, 28 AUGUST 2018

AFTER RESPONDING TO calls from around the world to speak, Cyrus agreed to an interview with *Talk Asia* Anchor Christine Chan at Chambord Château. A doctor advised Cyrus to delay, but his own opinion differed. Cyrus believed people needed to see him, understand him, see how he viewed the world, see his authenticity. The mega donations reflected the faith shown in him and he needed to say thank you and let people know he was working for them.

'It's not as if I'm a politician and need to speak with a guarded voice,' Cyrus said. A week after the helicopter tragedy a small white bandage covered his head injury and Cyrus's leg was healing, but that was not the case for his heart. Cyrus now viewed his life as being sandwiched between the brutal and senseless killing of Talal and the killing of Ophelia and the others. But he did not have the time to think on this. The live interview would start in fifteen minutes.

Cyrus extended his hand to Chan and thought it must be her blue day. She had a streak of blue hair, a blue dress and pale-blue lipstick.

'We need to give you make-up,' said the production woman.

'I'm fine like this,' said Cyrus who wore a white shirt with the top button undone.

'It's for the lights,' she added. 'To stop your skin shining.'

'Oh … okay.'

The make-up artist powdered Cyrus's face, then placed the powder puff back in her make-up box and picked up a lipstick.

'I'll pass on that,' said Cyrus.

'Just to—'

'Thank you, I'll be fine,' he said.

'We want you looking your best.'

'You're about fifty years too late.' Those who heard laughed.

'Do you know you've got blond eyebrows. It's rare with dark hair.'

'Maybe they are grey.'

'People must compliment you on how great you look,' said Chan.

'It's diet, healthy living.'

'Can we talk about that?'

'No.'

'Which seat would you like, professor?' asked the producer. The seats were on an angle.

'Either, thank you.'

'Most people prefer their right side to the audience.'

'I didn't know that,' said Cyrus, after he gave the comment a quick thought.

'We're live in five,' said the producer.

Two others sat down where Cyrus and Chan would sit while lighting from three lights was optimised. There were three cameras. Cyrus sat with his left side to the audience and opposite Chan. Between them was a low table, glasses of water and a green plant. Chan opened the interview.

'We've been invited here to Chambord Castle to speak with Professor Cyrus Zaydan, he's asked me to call him Cyrus, to discuss his deity constant and the Deity Foundation, which as you know have dominated world news over the last month. Let me start by thanking you, Cyrus for talking to us and my sincerest condolences, our sympathies to the family and friends of those who died in the Vatican attack. I would like to ask for your thoughts on the motivation behind this attack?'

'It's a pleasure to be with you, thank you. My deepest condolences also to the family and friends of those killed and injured.' Cyrus touched his palm flat against his heart. 'Please let me read their names and we'll share a moment's silence.' After the silence, Cyrus continued. 'Some people are, seem to be, threatened more than others by new ideas, by change. Violence is the most exercised weapon to protect self-interest.'

'We now know the Israeli government has apologised, but with the apparent suicide of the head of Israel's internal security, and one of their agents directly involved, what is your view?'

'I accept the Israeli government's position that rogue people were involved. The foundation has an outstanding relationship with Israel, with the Israeli government.'

'Could you comment on your relationship with the Vatican?'

'The Vatican provided a safe house for me, provided sanctuary and I owe my friends and protectors at the Vatican huge thanks.' Cyrus ignored the cameras as he spoke Chan.

'Let me move on to your discovery. We see you have wide support from leading scientists, but how is what you have proposed with the deity constant different from the European movement of Enlightenment in the 17th and 18th centuries?'

'The philosophers of Enlightenment looked at the relationship between God, nature, reason and humanity ... so as a result of the dramatic advances man has made in understanding science since the 18th century, we can today apply advanced science to deduce the origin of life. It's this ... this advanced science that is captured in a mathematical formula proving that life could not have arisen by random chance.'

'You've called this formula the deity constant.'

'Yes.'

'There has been comment from some church leaders that supporters of the Deity Foundation are suffering from false consciousness, a blind acceptance ... even a seduction by what is non-sophisticated science and non-sophisticated mathematics.'

Cyrus leant forward, took a mouthful of water, paused, then spoke. 'I haven't engaged in religious criticism, or engaged in criticising people's free will to follow a religious doctrine or philosophy. This is a fundamental right of man.'

'A comment on non-sophistication?'

'Non-sophistication?'

'Some have said your deity constant is not sophisticated science and mathematics.'

'A comment I agree with. I'm all in with the view that solid science is elegant in its simplicity.'

'Thank you,' said Chan. 'I was interested to learn your family in Syria was Druze. I've read that ultimate reasoning and Neoplatonism are central to the Druze dogma.'

'You're right, so you know such thought is embraced by Druze, but logic is the base of all reasoned argument. All discoveries must begin somewhere, with someone. One needs to be fearless to see it through; to see it through to find the truth.'

'I appreciate the way you express a refreshing lens in an era of media sensationalism and lack of rational thinking,' said Chan. 'I would like to ask … we have learnt some are calling you the Messiah. How do you react?'

'We are too quick in this world to fix labels to people; it's not constructive.'

'I understand that labels are not always constructive, but what words have you for those who see you as the Messiah?'

Cyrus reached for his water and took a drink. 'I'm not claiming to be the Son of God.'

'Would you say you're a religious prophet?'

'A prophet gives further insights into what has come before them and lays new groundwork for those to follow … religious prophets teach a religious philosophy. I've not proposed a religious philosophy; I've simply constructed a scientific proof on the origin of life.'

'I want to stop you there because you are saying so many important things. How does your deity constant differ from religious philosophy?'

'It's not possible to summarise religious philosophy in a few words, but I see religious philosophy expressed in metaphors … expressed as scholarly prose or verse … as a canvas for the psyche and spirituality of man … and this canvas is palpable, powerful and engaging to create a spiritual relationship with God. By comparison the deity constant is a factual basis of mathematics and science.'

'Deism is a religious philosophy,' said Chan.

'Yes, my scientific proof aligns with the fundamental principles of deism.'

'I've read in preparation a number of the Western world's political, scientific and literary leaders have been deists, yet deism has received until now very little public profile; why is this?'

'Let me say first, Émilie du Châtelet, Benjamin Franklin, Abraham Lincoln, Napoleon Bonaparte, George Washington, and Thomas Jefferson were deists. Also, literary leaders Voltaire, Victor Hugo, Jules Verne and Mark Twain were acknowledged deists, and the scientists … the scientists who have subscribed to deist philosophy are many including Michael Alberto, Earnest Rutherford, Carl Gauss, Max Born and Dmitri Mendeleev. And now to your question on public profile. Unlike other religious philosophies, deism has not engaged in political or commercial activity to increase its member base, in fact, it has not had an organisational structure to do so.'

'Until now?'

'We've not sought any funds, but we've been obliged to establish the Deity Foundation to manage donations offered and then use this money to help, to advance people's quality of life.'

'We've heard there's been unprecedented global financial support.'

'The Deity Foundation has been very fortunate to receive significant financial donations.'

'Are you able to give an indication as to the scale.'

'Donations run to many billions of dollars; we're putting in place the governance to administer this money with infrastructure projects planned in needy regions of the world.'

'This makes you one of the richest and most powerful men on Earth.'

'It's not my money; it's controlled by the foundation.'

'Even so, you must now be a very wealthy man, have you always aspired to be rich?'

'When I was growing up, I never dreamt about wealth or how to get it. It may sound like a cliché, but as a child, all the wealth I needed was within the four walls of our home.'

'I would like to discuss the concept of *faith*. It's widely acknowledged religious *faith* is a pillar, if not the most important pillar of all religions. In a broad sense I understand *faith* is a belief held in the absence of evidence or reason.'

'I'm sorry, I'm not sure what you are asking.' Cyrus sat straight.

'Let me say it this way … if *faith* is a belief based on the absence of evidence, hasn't this now changed with you giving us the evidence? As I understand it, you have a scientific proof life needed God's hand?'

'Life needed an intelligent intervention.'

'So, *faith* has been superseded.'

'Science has provided clarity of understanding in many areas.'

'I'm sorry if I seem like I'm repeating myself, but with an excepted certainty around the existence of a deity, it seems we no longer need *faith*. How will religions respond to this colossal shift.'

'I'm not placed to judge how different religions may respond. But if we look at history, we see early religious writings and scriptures reflected an understanding of the time. In two thousand years mankind will have a different understanding from today.'

'I'm pleased we are reflecting on history. The single most fundamental question challenging mankind through thousands of years of history is whether God is real.' Chan raised both her hands and drew quotation marks in the air before continuing. 'And I say, *God* in inverted commas, as different religions have their own interpretation of God. I've profound respect for you having provided an answer to this question. What do you say to the media commentary around the world claiming this will cause a seismic shift in civilisation.'

'Ah yes, a great question: a great question with many answers. Mankind has an opportunity, in fact, an obligation to address and solve humanitarian challenges, if this can be the primary focus of our civilisation going forward then it's a seismic shift I welcome.'

'We've heard this call before. The call to solve humanitarian challenges, heal the scars man has inflicted on society; heard the call from many political and religious leaders. Why do you think such a previous call has failed?'

'There needs to be unified effort and commitment, when we have this unity, solving humanitarian challenges will not fail.'

'Are you suggesting with the certainty of God's existence there will be this unified effort?'

'Political will of our leaders is necessary for unified effort. I believe people will demand unity from their leaders, and demand humanitarian needs are met, and demand peace and demand a right to dignity and—'

'So, what … sorry to interrupt you … there is just so much to discuss in this extraordinary situation. What are the inner sanctums of governments thinking … the power centres?'

'Ah, a difficult philosophical question. Philosophy is outside my … I'm a scientist, but one way to look at what power centres may be thinking, is to ask how proof of a deity effects our view of death. Birth is less complicated. It's merely the start of life. It's not linked to moral judgement. Not linked to sin. Not linked to punishment or to reward.'

'But death is,' said Chan.

'We see death linked to judgement in all religions. Some religions more than others and some less so now than a few centuries ago, but whether by intention, or not, I'm not giving a verdict here, but the linkage of death to moral judgement gives those in power control, gives a lever to control people, to control their behaviour, to control their submission, to control their compliance, to control their faith. This control comes from a church, temple, synagogue or a mosque's perceived monopoly position on God, on God's word, or control from theocratic governments and even control from governments in the West functioning within Christian societies. So, I think these power centres will be asking in what way proof of a deity could be a threat, a threat to their power.'

'Is that why the Israelis tried to kill you; you were a threat to their power?'

'It's possible.'

'You mention Christian societies. Nietzsche proposed with science understanding, Christianity fades,' said Chan.

'It's interesting that Nietzsche thought this because the science of his time was thin. When was Nietzsche, 1840s to 1900? And not being a scientist, Nietzsche gave too much credit to thin ideas, as non-philosophers also do.'

'Following on then … you remarked about power centres, how could your deity proof be a threat to these power centres?'

Cyrus sat for a moment. 'Individual enlightenment, free thought, history has shown the greatness of individuals lies in their ability, their ability to unite, unite against their own insignificance.'

'The world's media is full of talk about a seismic shift in civilisation. It's important to talk about this because people are asking, *what now?*'

'What now? As Carl Jung and others have written,' said Cyrus. 'There's social benefit to us all when individuals increase their spiritual awareness. Time will decide the impact and dictate the *what now.*'

'I agree we're seeing an increased spiritual awareness. The scale of donations your Deity Foundation is receiving is a reflection. Now, before we finish, I want to ask you, do you believe God speaks to people? There are many accounts from people claiming to have heard the voice of God. Did you hear God's voice when you developed your proof?'

'I conceived an inner inspiration of thought. I suppose such inspiration is a combination of my life's contract with nature, with man and with God.'

'An inner inspiration that could have been directed by God?'

'It's possible.'

'It may be God chose to reveal Himself through you. Which takes us back to my first comment … some … well, in fact, many are calling you the Messiah. God chose you to reveal His true existence.'

'It's important to draw a line here. I'm a scientist.'

'People believe you were chosen by God, and you now sit above all other men on this Earth. I can't begin to fathom how you must feel.'

'I feel insignificant and free.'

'It's been said humility is one of the greatest blessings God can bestow on a human being. To finish. Returning to the money you've raised. What specifically does your foundation plan to do with the funds you have and will be raising?'

'This week we've approved our first two infrastructure projects. We'll build a world-leading hospital in Sudan and a university in the West Bank of Palestine.'

'Why have you chosen these two projects?'

'To help the Sudanese and Palestinian people.'

'What of the political implications.'

'Israel has agreed to provide logistical support for a West Bank University; France will assist in Sudan.'

'Are we seeing a peace initiative?'

'We are seeing peoples with a shared pride, a shared vision facilitating these ventures. The more Israel and Palestine work together the stronger the path to a lasting peace.'

'I thank you for your time today, professor and congratulate you. And once again extend our condolences to you and the family and friends of those killed in the helicopter attack at the Vatican.'

The camera panned out and showed Cyrus and Chan sitting opposite each other across a low table.

○

Donations spiked following the helicopter attack and spiked again after Cyrus's globally televised interview on *Talk Asia*. Branding, content and social media; the foundation's message was being sold everywhere, twenty-four hours a day, and at the buyer's donation price.

CHAPTER FORTY-ONE

WASHINGTON DC, USA, 30 AUGUST 2018

CARDINAL ERDO FLEW from Rome to Washington, DC. Erdo had a suite for his Washington stayover in the Apostolic Nunciature of the Holy See to the United States; a three-storey brick building set behind mature elms and oak located on Massachusetts Avenue. Erdo's silver Maserati SUV swung past the mature trees then stopped at the main entrance. Cardinal Rusconi stood on the bottom step under the yellow and white Vatican flag and welcomed the Vatican secretary of State. The two cardinals kissed cheeks in a traditional Italian welcome.

'Would you like to rest?' asked Rusconi in Italian. Rusconi was the archbishop of Washington. He smiled showing buck teeth that pushed forward from his face as did his prominent nose. Rusconi's smile lines ran to his ears.

'I rested well on the flight.' The bridge of Erdo's nose was sharp and his top lip was thin. He had silver grey hair and his silver-grey eyebrows were two narrow lines. Erdo had a double chin, and the vapid eyes of a judge.

'I'll show you your rooms, then if you like, we have a sauna,' said Rusconi. They climbed the steps together and stepped inside the Embassy.

'How long have you had a sauna?' asked Erdo.

'Before my time.'

○

Erdo pulled the sauna door open. Cardinal Rusconi was lying flat on a wooden bench. Erdo lay down on a wooden bench opposite. The air was hot and heavy and Erdo inhaled fast shallow breaths. Rusconi picked up a ladle and threw cold water from a wooden bucket on the hot rocks. The rocks hissed and the water formed a humid mist.

'It's been years since I had a sauna,' said Erdo.

'I keep a room here just for the sauna and stay over once or twice a week.'

'Thank you for the meeting tomorrow.'

'You said it was urgent.'

'The Deity Foundation,' said Erdo.

'Why was Zaydan allowed in the Vatican?'

'The Vatican was ambushed, blackmailed.' Erdo breathed more slowly. He lay on his stomach; his folded arms supported his head. He looked down through the gaps in the wooden slats.

'Blackmailed?'

'Rothschilds is behind the Deity Foundation and Rothschilds has leverage over the Vatican; fine print in a his-torical loan agreement.'

'When was the loan?'

'Over a hundred and fifty years ago. The *Opere di Religione's* lawyers have provided an opinion; the Vatican bank's assets can't meet the debt accrued to Rothschilds.'

'Rothschild's own the Vatican bank?' Rusconi threw more water on the hot rocks.

'If Rothschilds call in what's owed the bank will collapse.' Erdo was covered in sweat.

'What's the peace plan with Rothschilds? Debt restructure; partial or full write-off?'

'We've got to eliminate the Deity Foundation problem first.'

'Eliminate?'

'We can be passive, or— '

'Or?'

'I'm cooked. I'll tell you over dinner.' Erdo stood up, wrapped a white towel around his waist, pushed the sauna door open, then took a cold shower.

At dinner, Cardinal Erdo said grace then made the sign of the cross. Cardinal Rusconi made the sign of the cross too. The two cardinals dined alone. Rusconi tilted a bottle of California cabernet and half-filled Erdo's glass.

'Why meet with Goss?' asked Rusconi referring to the meeting he'd organised with the director of the FBI.

'Pressure the FBI to destroy the Deity Foundation.'

'Pressure?'

'Goss is a paedophile.'

'You're going to threaten him to his face?'

'Do you have a better idea?' Erdo cut a chunk off his prime rib.

'If that's what you think is best.'

'That's what I think.'

'Has his Holiness approved?'

'You have to maintain a relationship with Goss, let me deliver the threat.'

'Another?' Rusconi held the cabernet.

'Grazie.'

It was early afternoon the following day when Goss's FBI motorcade pulled to a stop on Rhode Island Avenue, Washington DC. Goss was six feet eight, his dark hair was cut short and he had a pixie nose that some said looked too small for his face. Goss got out of his armour-plated SUV, glanced up at the bland red brick exterior of St Matthew's Cathedral then climbed the cathedral steps. Behind him were two FBI bodyguards. When Goss was halfway up the steps Cardinal Rusconi's assistant stepped from the cathedral. Goss looked past Rusconi's assistant and expected to see the cardinal.

'Welcome, director.' The assistant wore a dark suit and black tie. He had a close stubbly beard. Goss thought he looked more mafia than Catholic Church.

'The cardinal is…?'

'Waiting to meet with you.'

They stepped inside to an inner opulence that rivalled any cathedral in the world; an opulence perhaps designed to mimic the inner rich soul of man. The assistant and Goss walked together on burgundy carpet and as he walked Goss brushed his hand on the American oak pews. Sunlight fell from the octagonal dome above the sanctuary onto the hand-carved marble altar. Around the altar were colourful mosaics and murals. Goss followed the mafia man past the altar. The Cardinal's assistant opened a wooden door, took a few steps, then knocked on another and showed Goss into Cardinal Rusconi's chambers. Goss's bodyguards stood outside the closed door. Rusconi and Erdo stood up and shook Goss's hand. They wore formal cardinal robes that conferred a cloak of authority.

'Greetings, director,' said Rusconi. 'Thank you for making time.'

Both Cardinals smiled, and continued to smile. Goss wondered what their smile-masks hid and was sure time would be thin before he found out. He'd never seen Rusconi smile like this before. It made Goss feel he had to smile too.

'Hello, cardinal.' Goss smiled. Goss had not been informed that another cardinal would be present; an obvious slight. Goss couldn't place this other cardinal but thought he was part of the Vatican government.

'This is Cardinal Erdo, he's visiting from the Vatican,' said Rusconi.

'His Holiness asked me to extend his appreciation to you, director, for your security advice in the recent papal visit to Cuba,' said Erdo.

Erdo, the Vatican Secretary of State, thought Goss. 'When the American president speaks of Cuba, he acknowledges the Pope's diplomatic efforts.' Goss's eyes flipped between the two cardinals.

'I'll include your comment in my report to His Holiness,' said Erdo.

'Thank you.' Goss took a deep breath. 'How long will we be honoured to have the Vatican secretary of state as a guest in our country?'

'Unfortunately, I return to Rome tomorrow. It's important you are also of our faith, director, we can be open,' said Erdo.

'If not, we do an injustice to our time,' said Goss, waiting for the injustice.

'We have a shared problem,' said Erdo.

'We do?'

'This Deity Foundation.'

'Why is it a problem?'

'Do you know the global value of religious donations?' asked Erdo.

'No.'

'Last year over six hundred billion dollars; this year we predict the number will be over eight hundred billion, with up to a third going to the Deity Foundation.'

'Where's the problem for America?' asked Goss.

'The Deity Foundation is an existential political threat to America. We both know it's a common political strategy for strong governments to create problems in strategic locations around the world, then step in and provide solutions. Governments do this to control resources and support their internal arms industry,' said Erdo.

Goss thought that was a fair summary. He kept his smile.

'And the basis of this existential threat?' asked Goss.

'The Deity Foundation is funding Sudan to construct a state-of-the-art hospital, the French may help, and the foundation will fund the PLO to build a university in the West Bank. Israel is in tacit support. This is a first tangible step towards a Palestine-Israeli peace accord—shredding America's faux-peace broker influence. Foreign policy is won and lost in the court of public opinion, and this is one fight the Deity Foundation will win. The foundation has established a template for success and has the funding to replicate this template around the world time and time again,' said Erdo.

Goss was aware of the foundation's Palestinian initiatives but refrained from direct comment. The cardinal's comment did cause him to think maybe the FBI had dropped the ball because they were too focused on trying to take out Trump.

'I didn't think I was invited to be given a treatise on geopolitics and economics,' said Goss. His smile turned superior and smug.

'On the contrary, and with respect, director, this is the very reason why I asked to meet,' said Rusconi, thinking those who are smug wear their inferior intelligence for all to see.

'What's the church's concern with this foundation?' asked Goss.

'His Holiness extended the Syrian mercy and granted him sanctuary. The Syrian used the platform of the Vatican to announce a proof of God's influence on Earth. He deceived His Holiness and used the Vatican as a pulpit to proselytise to the world and undermine the Catholic Church,' said Erdo.

'Has the foundation affected the Catholic Church's revenues?' asked Goss.

'We have higher revenues. Our true concern is the religious and social damage. We hear talk of the French granting the Deity Foundation state status, a mirror Vatican,' said Erdo.

'The French have always been opportunists,' said Goss.

'The Deity Foundation was formed less than four weeks ago, but we estimate it has received ten billion dollars, three times the annual budget of the United Nations. It's a front for financial terrorists,' said Erdo.

'As you know, money flows in murky waters,' said Goss.

Erdo ignored the director's jibe; both knew the Vatican had laundered Mafia money for years.

'Does America support France's use of the Deity Foundation as a conduit for foreign policy?' asked Erdo.

'We've not given it deep consideration.' Goss thought they had given it no consideration.

'A minister in the French government is a trustee of the Deity Foundation,' said Erdo.

'You offer some interesting points for reflection,' said Goss.

'Do you know where the Deity Foundation is based?'

'An old castle in France,' said Goss.

'Chambord, it's one of France's premier châteaux. There are more than three hundred staff based at the château. Rothschilds looks after the foundation's financial management. Dassault are involved; it's a global enterprise.'

'You're well informed,' said Goss. He reached for his glass of water.

'More than anyone, director, you understand the value of intelligence,' said Erdo.

'This discussion will stimulate me to review our files.' Goss wondered where the conversation was headed.

'We encourage you to eradicate the Deity Foundation as soon as possible,' said Erdo.

'I grasp the church's views, but due process will occur.'

'The church is sitting on a time bomb capable of destroying the American political establishment,' said Erdo.

Goss raised his hand to his mouth and cleared his throat. 'Meaning?'

'We have thousands of young American men and women, sometimes very young, confessing indiscretions to our priests every day. We encourage these vulnerable young people to fully disclose the nature of their sin and who they have sinned with or sinned against. Of course, we keep these confessions secret. Confessions are kept on a centralised server in the Vatican for the future protection of these young people. Confessions about judges who have sinned and politicians who have sinned and business leaders who have sinned and even confessions of high-level intelligence officials who have sinned.'

'Are you trying to intimidate me?' asked Goss. He'd stopped smiling.

'I see young teen girls in my congregation looking like twenty-year olds. I think we both understand your situation, director, without getting into sordid details,' said Erdo.

Colour faded from Goss's face as he realised, he was a wounded bull in the cardinal's bull ring. Erdo with his crimson *muleta* in one hand and cross in the other. Goss was sweating in front of the smiling cardinals. The three sat in silence. Rusconi looked at the director's white face.

'God has work for everyone in His kingdom,' said Rusconi.

'The church gives me daily support,' said Goss breathing quickly, trying to think fast but thinking slowly.

'The FBI should have an urgent interest in the billions of dollars leaving America for the Deity Foundation's French bank accounts—then to wherever. We'll be watching for action,' said Erdo.

'We investigate any people … any group reaching a certain money … umm … fiscal threshold, if I … we decide to indict the Deity Foundation it will be because they've broken … violated United States law.' Goss spoke in a toxic mist.

'This has been a most welcome pleasure, director. If you and your wife are free after taking the Holy Sacrament this Sunday, it would be a joy to have lunch with you,' said Rusconi.

'I'll look at our weekend plans. I confess I defer to my lovely wife to organise my time away from work,' said Goss.

The cardinals and Goss bid each other farewell having committed to make a Sunday lunch when the time suited, although Rusconi knew, that time would be some way off.

Goss stopped before he opened the door, turned and came back.

'Listen,' said Goss. 'I do what I can to protect the church. We have active investigations into those at the highest level. I'm talking cardinals, being an accessory to abuse,' he stared at Rusconi. 'Covering up abuse complaints is a criminal offence. I hope we understand, cardinal, I need to know from you there will be no indiscretion.'

'Indiscretion?' Rusconi looked through Goss. He had not foreseen this. Goss was a blackmailer, a damn coward as well as a paedophile.

'With the confessions,' said Goss. He knew the smell of fear, but the cardinals were odourless. Goss sweated under his arms, his stomach had a hollow feeling, his mouth was dry—a jellyfish before the cardinals.

Cardinal Erdo stepped inches from Goss's face. The cardinal spoke quietly. 'The decisions with regard to your future will be made in Rome. Rome will watch for results, then act or not act.'

'I'm sorry, I didn't mean to press,' said Goss. He didn't look Erdo in the eye.

What could Erdo say? He'd been professional, indirect and broken it off neatly, given Goss an off-ramp, and now the bastard was apologizing after slighting them. Both cardinals looked at Goss's dilated pupils and enlarged whites and they saw beads of sweat above his top lip.

'Do you read the Bible?' asked Rusconi.

'Not a lot.' Goss meant not ever.

'Read the Bible,' said Rusconi. Both cardinals stared at Goss, their smiles gone.

Without speaking, Goss made a slow spin on his heel, and opened the door.

As he climbed into the back of his armoured vehicle he thought about those crimson pricks, and that little bitch he'd paid—she got paid twice—McCarthy paid her too.

Goss called McCarthy and organised to meet for a drink, he needed to meet that little bitch one last time and find out how she knew his name; he'd kept her blindfolded when the lights were on; it didn't make sense.

In his office later that day, Goss reviewed an analyst's file on the Deity Foundation.

A few moments later, the analyst was in a secure lift to the director's office on the seventh floor. The analyst was shown to a meeting room and sat at a polished cherrywood table. In a corner, were the American and FBI flags—security agencies like their flags. Goss strode in.

'When did you open the deity file?' he asked.

'When Cyrus entered the Vatican,' replied the analyst who wore a brown gilet with FBI in white letters on the back. She had a prominent but not unattractive nose, fine manicured eyebrows, brown eyes and brown hair.

'Give me a one-line summary.' Goss stood with his hands in his pockets. He looked at her manicured eyebrows and wondered where else she was manicured.

'A phenomenon. I predict they'll have revenues greater than two-fifty billion this year.'

'Revenues?' asked Goss—the same ballpark number given to him by the crimson pricks.

'Donations.'

'Two-fifty billion is the asset base of the World Bank,' said Goss. 'How many in your team?'

'One.'

'A team of agents will join you today. You're doing a good job, a damn good job.'

The analyst left and Goss called his deputy, Weldon Potts, for a meeting. Potts was ten years older than Goss, near retirement, his pinched cheeks had grey stubble.

'What do you know of the Deity Foundation?' asked Goss.

'A religious charity organisation. In my opinion, Cyrus has made the greatest contribution mankind's seen. He's proven the existence of God,' said Potts.

'Do you know how much money they've raised?'

'A lot, billions I would guess; I've donated and so have many of my family and friends.'

'What do you know of their Middle East projects?'

'The prime minister of Israel issued a joint announcement with the Palestinian prime minister, a university in the west bank, and they'll build a hospital in Sudan.

'Are American donations being used?'

'Indirectly.'

'Indirectly?'

'It's normal practice for donations to go into a pooled fund; the projects funded from this pool.'

'I want to know how many American dollars are going into the pool. We're opening an investigative file; we need to be prepared for any DOJ or congressional oversight of the Deity Foundation's US operations.'

'Are you going after them?' Potts asked.

'Find out what they're doing, then we can assess,' said Goss.

Potts raised his eyebrows but didn't speak. On first thought, Potts could see no scenario where the FBI would not be damaged if it tried to take down the Deity Foundation.

The following day, the lead analyst provided Goss with an updated file. An estimated seven billion dollars had been donated to the Deity Foundation from America. This seven billion provided an opaque basis to construct a case that focused on donation solicitation, interstate electronic banking trans-actions and targeted support for the PLO and Sudanese government. Goss then met with the deputy assistant attorney general for counterterrorism and counterespionage, James Anderson, to discuss a case construction strategy. Anderson's face was expressionless, as if he had a neurological condition, but the only condition he had was an addiction to money.

Goss used bureaucratic speak. 'When I took office, I swore an oath to protect the interests of the United States, if a foreign company or country threatens American interests, I'm duty bound to protect America using the legal instruments available.' Goss grimaced, thinking this should keep the Vatican quiet. Goss had yet to learn that truth sharpened your vision.

Anderson had never liked Goss. Goss told lies. Sometimes they were small lies, small lies where Goss would claim as facts apocryphal events in which he was the white knight and other times Goss credited himself with achievements others had made, or events others had seen. Anderson thought Goss didn't have the strength to carry his own ego. He'd kissed and conned his way to be FBI director and never seemed to believe he was fit for the job. But here Goss presented him with an opportunity, an opportunity to take down the Deity Foundation.

Two days earlier, Anderson had met with a director of America's largest defence company, Lockheed Martin. Geopolitics was Lockheed's business, peace and the Deity Foundation's talk of God were red ink to the company.

Anderson was asked by the Lockheed director if the Deity Foundation could be neutered. Greed had come to be fed and laid its head on Anderson's desk. He could smell its breath, and here was Goss two days later, gifting him a razor-sharp knife to dice greed's food, an opportunity to enrich himself from appreciative military corporates, an opportunity not to be missed.

Anderson straightened his back. 'Could you explain how the Deity Foundation threatens our interests?'

'They're on track to be the wealthiest corporation in the world, and with this financial resource, a political mandate not aligned to America, and a widespread public devotion, they're in a position to destabilise the globe,' replied Goss.

'In what way destabilise?' asked Anderson.

'Change the status quo, change countries' policies, facilitate events not in America's interest.'

'Such as?'

'Funding construction of a university in the West Bank and a hospital in Sudan; the Sudan project is far more than a hospital, it will include a solar power facility, a desalination plant, wastewater and sewage processing. A major infrastructure investment and America played no role in the decision-making.

'Israel supports the West Bank university project,' said Anderson.

'The PLO and their affiliates are designated as a terrorist organisation. Sudan is on our state sponsored terrorist list. It's a federal crime to provide material support or resources to designated foreign terrorist organizations.'

'How do you want to get control of this?'

'I want a grand jury empanelled; get indictments on money laundering, wire fraud and supporting a known terrorist organisation, and anything else you can think of.'

'A state preference for the grand jury?' asked Anderson.

'Stay clear of the Bible Belt, New York Jews and Washington politics.

'Virginia?' asked Anderson. Goss nodded.

'I want indictments immediately, we need to shorten the Syrian's tongue,' said Goss, stealing a line Putin had made regarding Gorbachev.

'We should get AG sign off,' said Anderson.

'Get it.'

Meanwhile, nearly five thousand miles from Washington DC, on the island of Malta, Oliver Dassault walked down the boarding steps from his private jet, got into a vehicle and transferred to The Grand Harbour in Malta's capital—Valetta. A security gate to the private wharf opened, the driver drove through and stopped beside the first boat. With his overnight bag, Dassault removed his dockside shoes, and with bare feet boarded the baron's seventy-metre super yacht. The baron waited on the teak deck at the top of the gangway. The baron's thin face smiled at his dearest friend. Dassault's tanned face smiled too, and he passed his carry bag to a deck hand the baron called Chester. The baron hugged Dassault and kissed both his ruddy cheeks.

'My bag please, I'm sorry,' said Dassault. Chester passed Dassault his bag. Dassault removed a bottle of wine, rezipped the bag and gave it back to Chester.

The baron glanced at the bottle; it had a cork.

'Bring a corkscrew,' he said to Chester then climbed a glass staircase to the upper deck main salon. In the salon, Dassault's bare feet padded across the polished New Zealand kauri then onto white carpet where he sat in a cream leather chair. Chester pulled the cork; it came out clean.

'Nice wine,' said the baron.

'Australian. Barossa Shiraz.'

Dassault felt a slight vibration as the vessel nosed from its berth into the Grand Harbour. The yacht pivoted on its bow; the stern moved in a slow arc.

'I met with Macron yesterday, he said Europe needs to take more responsibility for its security, and make the EU more sovereign,' said Dassault.

'We wouldn't have a security issue if NATO had let Russia in; Yeltsin and Putin wanted to join,' said the baron. 'Putin tried with Clinton and Bush two.'

'If Russia had joined NATO, the American military complex would have no real enemy to fight,' said Dassault. He stood up and stepped to the starboard deck rail holding his glass. It was more than half full—a measure of his optimism. Dassault stared forward and looked at the stone fort guarding the Grand Harbour entrance, then looked down at the passing water, mirror calm and ink blue. He looked again at the stone fort. It was getting bigger. Dassault turned slowly and faced the baron.

'The military complex will not give up; arms sales are the major strand in the warp of world politics. I know these guys, if they feel boxed in, they'll start shooting in the boardrooms, shooting in the lobbies, shooting in the streets. These are not people who are going to pack up their bags of money and move out of their power position. They're going to fight, and when they start losing badly, which they will, they'll put whoever they need to in their sights and really start fighting.'

'We need to push our power lever. The Chinese are ready,' said the baron.

'Is Cyrus primed?'

'Not yet.'

'When?'

'The Vatican attack spooked him,' said the baron.

'Understandable.'

'We'll get him to Taiwan one way or another. That I promise.'

'The Chinese think they're coup proof,' said Dassault.

'An emperor, or dictator, doesn't matter which country he rules, he's a coup target when the lie he rules by is exposed,' said the baron. And this is where they knew Cyrus could unite the Chinese population by exposing the lie pushed by Beijing, the lie that the Chinese are soulless, a lie the Chinese population lives by in silence, a lie that denies the individual the divine spark felt within, a divine spark felt within by everyone.

○

Later, as he ate dinner, Dassault used his fingers to pick a rabbit bone from the stew on his white porcelain plate. He bit off the tender meat, cleaned his fingers on his napkin then repeated to the baron a warning he received from a French NATO general, who asked why he, Dassault, was supporting the Deity Foundation. Why did he threaten the decades of progress made by the establishment, decades of progress where the church's influence on society had been diluted. On a white napkin, the baron wrote the words *NATO, governments, Russia, USA, China, kinetic partner, Deity Foundation. Taiwan and Elon.* Then he drew boxes and arrows, and when the baron had finished drawing and talking, Dassault nodded and said 'I agree.'

○

Few realised the force multiplier effect that the Deity Foundation could exert, and those who did know were either the foundation's best supporters or the foundation's mortal enemies—mortal enemies driven by the usual suspects—ego and power and greed; the three wolves that crafted an unwarranted influence on civilisation.

We're in a control position, the baron told himself, the billions in donations are validation of Cyrus's truth. Our foundation is bursting onto the geopolitical stage, bursting uninvited, redefining the rules, threatening political and military incumbents, incumbents who would be committed to destroy the foundation at any cost—people killed each other over bar fights, the baron and Dasault knew this was about leadership of the world.

CHAPTER FORTY-TWO

CHAMBORD FRANCE, 10 SEPTEMBER 2018

THE FLOWER DELIVERY van passed through the foundation's perimeter security at the twenty-mile-long wall that surrounded Chambord Château. Cyrus watched the van from the château steps. At first, it was a small dark-coloured speck moving slowly along the grey shingle road with trees on either side. Then came puffs of dust from the tyres before he heard the low engine hum of the van. It was mid-morning and the air was still and the van had yet to reach the waterway surrounding Chambord on two sides. The waterway was a protective moat. The van was painted dark green. It swung in close to the château and stopped by the front steps. Cyrus, with an assistant at his side, paced down the marble steps and onto the gravel beside the van.

The delivery man got out then opened the van's dark-green sliding door.

'One bunch of red tulips and five bunches of red roses,' he said.

'I thought I ordered five bunches of red tulips,' said Cyrus.

'I'm sorry, we only had one of red tulips there's a free bunch of red roses for you.'

'Better than no tulips,' Cyrus said quietly.

'Pardon?'

'Thank you,' said Cyrus. A foundation assistant took the flower box.

'In madam's room?' asked the assistant.

'The tulips on the bedside table, please,' said Cyrus.

'Do you live here?' asked the flower delivery man.

'Yes,' said Cyrus.

'What do you do?'

'I work with everyone.'

'With the new Messiah?'

'With everyone. Thank you for bringing the flowers, I need to go.'

○

It was mid-afternoon and Cyrus traipsed from the helipad to the moat and back to the helipad. A short walk to snack time before the helicopter arrived. He looked down. The toes of his shoes were dusty. He glanced at his watch, and this time traipsed the other way to the tree-line. Back at the helipad, he glanced at his watch and this time traipsed down a path bordered by low shrubs and wild herbs and French oak seedlings, each tethered by soft rubber to a tripod of wooden stakes.

Cyrus had sent a foundation helicopter to transport Darijani to Chambord from Paris's Charles de Gaulle Airport. He checked his watch yet again, then he heard the noise he'd been waiting for. Cyrus stood behind the helipad safety line and looked up at the helicopter's approach over Chambord's huge woodland. It made a banking circuit around the châ-teau and then eased down onto the helipad's yellow H. A few moments later, the boarding door opened, and it seemed an eternity before Darijani stepped into view. Then Cyrus saw her and raised his hand as she grinned and stepped slowly down the stairs then quickly across the helipad. *In only a few seconds Darijani will be by my side.*

'Hello, wonderful to see you,' he said and their eyes locked for an instant and then Cyrus looked away. He hesitated, put out his hand briefly before he retracted it and stood still.

'And you. Look at you. Cutting a youthful healthy figure and everything you've achieved.' Darijani spoke with the passion Cyrus remembered. She stepped forward and kissed him on the cheek. He felt his heart bounce, and as he looked into her face, he saw two familiar alive eyes and a warm soul.

'Come inside, let me find out what you've been doing for the last, um … we'll not count the years,' Cyrus said.

Darijani stopped and extended her hand towards the helicopter.

'I have a bag, or rather three bags.' She giggled.

'We'll make sure they find you. Do you have the baggage tags?'

'Wait.' Darijani opened a zip in her handbag, but as soon as she saw Cyrus's grin, she stepped forward and cuffed him on the shoulder. They laughed and moved closer, their shoulders touched as they strolled to the Chateau.

'I'm so sorry about the attack. I watched the interview where you spoke about losing Ophelia.'

'Ophelia was critical in getting us out of Egypt and she stood by my side in Rome. We only knew each other for four weeks, but I'll feel her presence forever.'

Darijani stepped close to Cyrus and wrapped her arms around him. She held him tightly. She saw in him the vulnerable young man who she fell in love with in Damascus.

'Trust me, my heart goes out to you,' she whispered.

Cyrus felt as if they had never been apart, and in essence, they hadn't. It was as though Darijani had stepped out of a room and returned a minute later, even though she had returned a few decades later. What would Einstein have said about love and relativity and time? The Druze doctrine— keep silent and wait.

'Do you have any children?' asked Cyrus.

'A daughter.'

'Tell me about her.'

'She has a son, a devoted husband and much to my chagrin is seduced by Italian and French fashion.'

'And your daughter's father?'

'He passed away four years ago. Tell me about you.'

'I've lived the life of a clergy,' said Cyrus, his asceticism rooted by life's cruel fate.

Darijani giggled but let her smile fade when she saw Cyrus looked serious. 'Why did you just disappear?' he asked.

'A man came to me in the university grounds; he gave me a one-way air ticket to Teheran and demanded I leave Damascus that day. He threatened me and said if I told anyone their life and mine would be in danger.'

'I'm so sorry.'

'Look at this beautiful château.'

'King Francis built it as a hunting lodge.'

'I guess if you're king of France you can build a huge hunting lodge. How many rooms?'

'Almost four hundred and fifty bedrooms.'

'A spare one for me?'

'A suite for you.'

'Did what is happening with you start back in Damascus?'

'Several months before I was even born,' said Cyrus. 'I've learnt there were people in Syria who knew I was Einstein's child. I fear the people who tried to control my life in Syria, were the ones who threatened you.'

'What was going on? What were you part of?'

An hour passed as Cyrus gave Darijani a summary of the events as he knew them to be.

'When will I meet Elias?' she asked.

'We'll dine together this evening. Would you like time to rest?'

'A hot bath would be divine.'

'Give me a call when you're ready to eat and an intern will bring you to our restaurant, or we could walk in the grounds before we eat.'

'A walk first, please.'

Cyrus called an intern who showed Darijani to her suite.

Darijani strolled into the suite's living room then gazed out of a tall window at the moat and beyond to the forest. Beside her bed, she looked lovingly at the red tulips—her favourite flowers. Did she tell Cyrus? She tried to recall. And other flowers too, red roses. In the bath, she scrunched a bunch of bubbles between her painted red toenails then cleared the bubbles from the line of her thigh and examined the skin tone as she had inspected the tapestry and framed paintings in her suite. Her skin was not the spring leaf of her prime, but it was not yet a leaf in autumn. And with Cyrus seemingly yet to experience the heaven a woman can offer, she would not feel judged by where she lay in life's calendar. She didn't want an affair—she wanted the loving romance stolen by time.

◯

That evening, Cyrus, Darijani and Elias dined together in a private room adjacent to the executive dining lounge. To begin with, sourdough bread, cold pressed olive oil and balsamic were served. They all ordered fish.

'Cyrus told me of your adventures, although I'm not sure if *adventure* is the correct word.'

'We had challenges. Cyrus got us through by putting one foot in front of the other.'

'Your *parikrama,*' said Cyrus.

'*Parikrama?*'

'Strength and resilience, a Sanskrit term,' said Cyrus.

Elias recalled Druze beliefs were influenced by Hinduism; he inflected a smile at the compliment.

Darijani squeezed Cyrus's hand and kissed him on the cheek. 'This wonderful man filled my room with flowers.'

'I remember you telling me you like red tulips,' said Cyrus.

Elias saw an aging woman who was still a girl in her heart, alive from being in love.

'What's been the response to the deity constant in Iran?' Elias asked.

'The ayatollahs and mullahs decry it as a blasphemy against Islam but give no sound argument for their opinion.'

'What of the people?'

'They engage in intelligent discussion, and I believe there's extensive acceptance. This is the likely reason the ayatollahs condemn it. Anything with the potential to unite our people, the regime sees as a threat.'

'Divide and distract and divide and conquer, a recurring political theme,' said Cyrus.

'Do you have a partner?' Darijani smiled at Elias.

'I live with my girlfriend in Tel Aviv; it's been three years.'

'Will she come here?'

Elias paused, he had no idea of the answer, and Esther was back in Israel staying with her parents after a short visit to Chambord.

'I'm not sure yet, Esther is taking time with her family in Israel.'

Darijani nodded and Elias directed his attention to cutting the fish on his plate.

After sorbets, they finished their dinner and bid each other goodnight.

When he was alone, Elias thought of Gigi.

○

The following morning, Cyrus woke after the best sleep he could remember. He sang his own lyrics in the shower before he met Darijani for breakfast in the management restaurant.

Darijani knew she loved Cyrus; she loved his devotion to what he saw as the truth. He was a glittering light who didn't lie to himself, a free life, who accepted consequence, shouldered his weight and did it correctly. After taking more time in front of the mirror than usual, Darijani walked downstairs to the restaurant for breakfast. Cyrus stood waiting by the door.

At the breakfast bar, Darijani asked the chef for an omelette with capsicum and when the chef asked if she wanted cheese she pointed to the Leerdammer and gruyère.

Cyrus placed his fork on his plate and looked at Darijani. 'Tomorrow we're meeting with people from the Israeli Ministries of Education and National Infrastructure. The Foundation's first major project is the construction of a university in the West Bank. I can speak with Elias about you working on this project with us if it interests you.' Darijani smiled an effortless smile.

'I'm not suggesting you're going to stay here forever, of course, you can, but while you're here it may be more rewarding for you to be involved.'

'I would love the opportunity to contribute.'

'It's more complex than I ever imagined. There are different Israeli ministry considerations, the Palestine Authority, and we have yet to award the engineering, procurement and construction contract, consents, independent auditing, provision of utilities, the lists go on. And then there's the Sudan hospital project.'

'Are you subcontracting all services.'

'Yes. We have an external project contractor, hub and spoke, jargon I'm learning.'

'The support infrastructure for the hospital in Sudan?'

'We'll build a desalination plant, water treatment plant and solar power plant to safeguard utility supply. These infrastructure projects will also provide services for a lot of the general population.'

'You're rebuilding Sudan.'

'After breakfast, I'll speak to Elias about you working with me … ah … with us.'

Once they'd eaten, they left the dining room and made their way along a passageway with its barrel-vaulted ceiling embossed with salamander emblems. As was the custom of the 14th century when Chambord was constructed by the French King, as a secular rival to St Peter's Basilica in Rome, aristocrats chose an emblem for self-representation. King Francis selected the salamander as it embodied one who believed in God and always had peace in his soul. Darijani left Cyrus's side to look at a wall of medieval battle paintings while Cyrus spoke with Elias.

'Is it okay if Darijani attends our project meetings. She's a lawyer.'

'Of course, you're the president of the foundation. It's up to you to have whatever expert advice you wish.'

'I wanted to clear it with you first.'

'Thanks. You know I'm always watching your back. If you're getting advice from Darijani then she should get paid. I'll get our lawyers to organise a draft engagement contract for her.'

Elias was elated with the change Darijani brought. For the last two days Cyrus had worn a constant smile.

There was a light tap on Elias's office door and Enrico, a mid-thirties in-house Rothschilds manager, entered.

'Do you have a minute?' he asked.

'Sure.'

'Marco wants an urgent trustee meeting.'

'Why?'

'Something critical in the States.'

Elias co-ordinated with Cyrus and a meeting was set up for later that day.

It was mid-afternoon when a helicopter landed with Marco, two lawyers and Gigi.

Marco and the two lawyers came into the boardroom and Elias said hello. The lawyers, two conservative middle-aged men. *Where's Gigi,* he wondered. Then he thought maybe she was in the restroom. His chest tightened. *Don't get excited. Don't get nervous.* Gigi came in.

Introductions between those gathered were interrupted by a foundation intern taking coffee and tea orders. A few minutes later, they were all seated around the two-hundred-year-old French oak table in the foundation's boardroom.

Gigi looked cool and fresh and gorgeous in the hot room. She always looked that way to Elias, maybe it was how she dressed; she loved colour and Elias loved the ache in his heart.

'Thank you all for meeting so promptly.' Marco placed his black briefcase on the table. 'The FBI has indicted the foundation, and issued extradition requests for the foundation's directors.' Marco extended his arms as he spoke then brought his hands together on the word extradition.

'Extradition!' shouted Elias.

'It's a political move from the USA. France can and will refuse extradition when it's inspired by political motives.'

'Does that mean the extradition will go away?' asked Gigi who had a heads up on this before the meeting.

'It will be a protracted legal process, but with the support we enjoy from the French government I can say with confidence, yes, in time it will go away,' replied Marco.

'The indictment is on what basis?' asked Elias.

'There are two counts,' said Marco. 'Count one: conspiracy to commit money laundering and fraud by wire and count two: aiding and abetting fraud by wire.' Marco dug into his briefcase then handed out copies of the summary charge sheets.

Elias scanned the charge sheets.

Count One 18 U.S.C. 1956(h) Conspiracy to Commit Money Laundering. Members of the Enterprise committed money laundering, attempted to commit money laundering and conspired to commit money laundering to facilitate the Enterprise's criminal operations which affected interstate and foreign commerce, and

Count Two 18 U.S.C. 2 and 1343. Fraud by Wire and Aiding and Abetting Fraud by Wire.

Members of the Enterprise and their associates derived a scheme to defraud, commit wire fraud, aided and abetted wire fraud and attempted to commit wire fraud which affected interstate and foreign commerce.

'The FBI have named Cyrus, Elias, Gigi, and me as defendants. They have also filed a separate lawsuit against all of the Deity Foundation's assets.'

'What does this mean?' asked Cyrus.

'The lawsuit against the Deity Foundation is technically entirely separate from the indictments against the individuals. It is USA versus all assets of the Deity Foundation. This is a deceptive strategy to steal all the assets.'

'Where does this leave us?' asked Cyrus.

'This is an asset forfeiture case; the US government is technically filing the lawsuit against the money, arguing the money itself is guilty. The foundation has limited ability to block the US government from taking it all. The FBI are unreasonably using the argument that as Cyrus and Elias were being pursued in Egypt by Israeli, Egyptian and USA intelligence operatives, they are, in fact, fugitives. As fugitives, the FBI argues that they are disentitled, which means they are unable to stop the forfeiture of the money being sought, and in America it's a *fait accompli* for the FBI to find a judge to agree.'

'But we've never been to the United States; how can they say we are fugitives?' said Cyrus.

'The foundation receives donations in the United States,' replied Marco.

'Cyrus and I were in Egypt before the foundation was even formed,' said Elias.

'The position of the FBI is that the intellectual property, in other words the actual deity constant, confers the value on the Deity Foundation. This intellectual property was developed by Cyrus while he was a fugitive. The FBI argue the Deity Foundation is monetising the fugitive intellectual property.'

'This is insane! How can a court give the FBI the legal right to steal billions of dollars from the Deity Foundation?' asked Elias.

'The FBI has global reach; if they believe a financial crime's been committed on American soil or against American citizens, they can file to have all assets of the offending party frozen. We'll file an appeal arguing how ridiculous this entire case is,' said Marco.

'What'll you argue?' asked Cyrus.

'The FBI is being disingenuous classifying the Deity Foundation

executives as fugitives and is being disingenuous using the fugitive classifi-
cation as an excuse to seize the foundation's assets. Fugitive disentitlement
has previously only been applied to criminals who have escaped custody
while appealing a conviction.'

'This is sophism, how can the FBI abuse the legal process arguing the
foundation executives are fugitives?' asked Gigi.

'I agree, we believe it's unconstitutional, by using the fugitive disentitlement standard the FBI is stopping the foundation's executives from even
challenging the seizure,' replied Marco.

'What's the redress?' asked Gigi.

'We'll apply to a circuit court in the US to challenge the seizure and
have it thrown out as unconstitutional,' said Marco.

'When can they theoretically seize the Deity Foundation's assets?' asked
Elias.

'The assets are under a seizure order as of today. All financial institu-
tions and banks must comply. If a bank doesn't cooperate, the American
government can revoke their banking licence.'

'How long will a resolution take?' Gigi asked.

'If the FBI slow plays us and appeals every decision that doesn't go their
way right up to the supreme court, then years not months.'

'Years!' said Cyrus.

'We now have a legal war on our hands,' said Marco.

'Who's behind this?' asked Elias.

Marco's thought was a Catholic Church-FBI conspiracy, but he kept
this thought to himself. 'We can guess, top of the list are the organisations
in America which may suffer as a result of the foundation's initiatives. For
example, companies not wanting to see the foundation's projects in the
Sudan and West Bank go ahead.'

'Companies opposed to peace,' said Cyrus.

'Many American companies are in the arms' business, their business is
war, the Deity Foundation's business is peace; we're threatening their financial security,' said Marco.

'What funds can we access for day-to-day operational activity?' asked Elias.

'In the short-term Rothschilds will provide funds from our holdings.'

'And the long-term?' asked Elias.

'There may not be a long-term.' Marco was grim faced.

'What about future donations?' asked Cyrus.

'They are criminalising any access to future donations. The filed *cease and desist order* maintains the foundation is a criminal enterprise. We'll file to oppose this accusation too … I know there's a lot to digest.'

'Next steps?' asked Elias.

'Rothschilds legal will give a more detailed assessment tomorrow. I'll give you an update following.'

Cyrus looked at Gigi and Elias. Both nodded.

'One more thing,' said Marco, 'we expect news of the FBI indictments to be leaked to the press, part of the strategy to destroy the foundation's reputation.' Marco knew the indictments would not be resolved in court but in the corridors of political power.

The two lawyers picked up their papers, filed them into their satchels and with Marco they left. Elias, Gigi, and Cyrus stared at each other.

'I have a trust in God,' said Cyrus. 'In His time, I'm sure we'll be delivered a solution.'

Cyrus looked at Elias who was looking at Gigi.

'I need to catch up with Darijani,' said Cyrus. He opened the door and it tapped shut behind him.

'You understand the indictment?' Gigi asked Elias.

'More or less, complicated by the lingo.'

'Law has its own language.'

'We can sometimes make things too complicated.' Elias held Gigi's brown eyes and she didn't look away. He felt a smile and his heart danced.

'How did I get out of the helicopter?' asked Gigi.

'I don't know.'

'A doctor at the hospital said I was found by paramedics with you lying close by.'

'Think I blacked out.'

'It's my life, Elias; I have a right to know.' Gigi knew those not killed by injury died of smoke inhalation.

'Maybe you saved me,' said Elias.

'*Dai!*' Gigi used the Italian word for *come on* or *stop it.*

Elias took a breath. 'After I got Cyrus out, I returned for you. My last memory is fighting to lift you out of your seat. A fire had started and it was difficult to breathe and hard to see. My mind was black and then you came to me in a vision. I swear, you came to me and you said, *I know you can do it, get us both out now.*' Elias looked into Gigi's brown eyes; she was two paces away, but her brown eyes seemed ever so close. He stepped forward, one step, two steps then reached out and rested his palm on the pale blue cotton of her sleeve. He felt an electric shock. Gigi's arm was warm and slender and soft, so soft.

'I was looking forward to seeing you today,' he heard himself say, his voice sounded anxious and shrill. Gigi would hear how nervous and high-pitched it was and know it was for her and that was fine, more than fine. She giggled coquettishly. He dropped his eyes to her lips. They were relaxed. Then he lifted his eyes to hers—they met his. Elias had reached somewhere new in her eyes and read what he wanted to read, but Gigi broke his touch on her sleeve and lifted her arm away. She pressed her hand against his shoulder and Elias felt himself pushed back. Gigi's eyes looked up; brown eyes, universe deep with blue mascara, brown eyes with flecks of gold and a future promise, brown eyes choosing to forget about the photos at home. Her soft lips the perfect shade of pink; the perfect shade with their freckles. Her lips two perfect pink sentries guarding her heart.

Elias took a chance and brushed Gigi's lips with the softest kiss. Her lips were warm and soft and they quivered. His arm wrapped her in reassurance. He felt her gasp, then relax, and relax again as they kissed once more. Their kiss a light breeze on a warm spring day, a breeze carrying an orchid fragrance. Gigi's pink petals were receptive, soft and smooth and smooth and soft, and with passing seconds the breeze strengthened—honesty and trust were unleashed. Elias held Gigi tight until their lips parted, and when their lips parted Elias sighed.

'Thank God you feel like I do.'

Two hours later in his apartment, Elias lay back. Gigi's head rested on a soft white pillowcase. He tugged free a few strands of her fine copper hair and looked at Gigi's full pink lips with their freckles, the arc of her cheekbones, at her universe eyes and tousled copper hair and at the fine pale skin on her neck. Gigi pressed her limp body close. Her toes kissed his leg like a kitten's nose kisses your skin. Elias loved the intimate feel of Gigi's kitten-toe kiss. He let go of the fine strands of Gigi's hair and encircled her slim wrist with its freckles and creamy soft skin. Her fine fingers had nails that were ice clean. He lifted her hand to his mouth and kissed the soft skin on her palm. Then he turned Gigi's hand over and kissed the back. He felt warm and confident and safe, knowing Gigi felt that way too. He had taken and the taking was giving and taking in silent agreement. Taking with a touching reassurance of more taking and taking; with a gentleness and soft kisses and hard kisses with a soft caress and chances and trust and laughing at shared delight.

'A thousand kisses should do,' Elias said.

'A thousand?' She looked at him through her copper hair.

'To kiss you every millimetre.'

'This is going to be hard,' she said and turned on her side. Her eyes were wet when she looked at Elias. Their lips touched and he tasted salt. A warm wind through the half-open window brought in vanilla from the French oaks.

'I'm so happy,' he said.

'Me too. Tell me more.'

'Your mind dances and your words trap, every time we speak my love for you gets more complex and more alive. The moment I first saw you, the moment I first heard your voice, my heart thumped, and the thumping hasn't stopped; its non-stop, every time I see you, I fall in love, my world has changed colour, changed colour forever.'

'Wow! … what have I done?' Gigi wanted her life to go smoothly, but now it was tossed in the air, but inside her she wanted it tossed there.

'I love my family. I'm married.'

'It's easy to un-marry.'

'I have a little girl.'

'What a treasure she must be.'

'*Si*,' she said. 'Thinking of her now and thinking of us troubles me.'

'Children's hearts are protected by love,' said Elias.

'And adult hearts.'

'You have seven sweet little freckles on your top lip.'

'I know.'

'What month were you born?'

'July.'

'One for each month.'

'A lip calendar?' Gigi asked with smiling eyes.

Elias smiled too. 'Say it to me in Italian.'

'*Un calendario labbra?*'

'Give me a calendar kiss,' said Elias. They kissed softly, then their teeth touched and they kissed hard. Their lips parted and Elias stroked his fingertips on Gigi's face. 'Stay with me; I'll get us a place in Paris.'

'I need time,' said Gigi. 'We don't know each other; I may do things that drive you insane.'

'You already have.'

'Incorrigible, that's what you are,' Gigi said, thinking that if he'd just grabbed her arm, she could wriggle free, but he'd stolen her heart; she'd need to do a lot more than wriggle.

'I don't want you to feel troubled,' said Elias.

'I want you to know how I feel, so we can work everything out together,' said Gigi.

Elias lay on his bed and watched Gigi dress.

'Yes?' she said and smiled a shy smile.

'Yes, yes,' Elias said. He dressed quickly.

Elias carried Gigi's computer bag.

'*Ti amo.*' Elias repeated *Ti amo*, about twenty times, as he and Gigi glided to the helipad; Gigi giggled with misty eyes.

Elias flew to Paris with Gigi but spent the night alone. In the morning, Elias heard a strong Paris wind blowing and the early sun dashed in and out behind the clouds. He was awake in that soft dreamtime before you are wide awake thinking about Gigi and then he heard the wind and saw the sun flashes. He had gate-crashed Gigi's life. He wondered if she felt the type of love he did, or was it as if both were looking at the same painting and walking away with a stunning appreciation, but a different stunning appreciation. Meeting Gigi had lifted the shroud concealing his soul, and when he'd seen his soul revealed it was fused with another energy—Gigi's soul was in his. *Is this how we find our souls,* he wondered. Elias thought that if the *energy of hearts in love lasts a lifetime, the energy of souls in love will last an eternity.*

CHAPTER FORTY-THREE
PARIS, FRANCE, 12 SEPTEMBER 2018

'WHAT DO YOU think Chester, institutional corruption—FBI games, US attorney general and US presidential sign-off?'

'Time to drag heads to the executioner's block, swing the axe, shove their play book down their throats.'

'I tend to agree, Chester.'

The baron knew Macron had called the American president and had been rebuffed. A polite call to the FBI director would have no effect, an impolite call the same. The counts against the Deity Foundation amounted to the corrupt use of the law to destroy the law.

The baron called Florence Parly, the French Minister of Defence. Parly considered her options; a cabal of American and French intelligence was running interference against the Deity Foundation, the FBI indictments, rumours of another assassination attempt. Until these hostiles were identified and neutralised it was safer to outsource.

Parly's limousine exited through the security gates of the Russian Embassy onto Boulevard Lannes. She wore natural lipstick, a shade that made you look twice, her light brown shaggy bob pushed behind her left ear showed a silver streak and her eyes drilled to your core. Four motorcycle police accelerated ahead, sirens blared, red and blue lights flashed, and hands waved traffic to pull over. Parly's SUV nestled in the middle of her ten-vehicle motorcade. She and the Russian ambassador had met several times over the previous five weeks with the same subject matter; the deity constant and the new future of the world. Parly's motorcade swung left onto Avenue Victor Hugo, a direct track to the Arc de Triumph. Today's meeting had a new discussion item; Parly asked the Russian Ambassador to investigate what leverage the Vatican had over the FBI. Governments the world over had contingency plans for expected and unexpected events. No government had a contingency plan for someone like Cyrus bursting onto the world stage and proving the existence of God. No government had such a contingency plan, but that did not mean such a plan didn't exist at a sub-government or supra-government level. They'd be dammed if the FBI or Vatican thought they could get onto the field and influence the play.

◯

Gigi, who always wore soft lipstick, looked up at the sound of a knock on her open office door; her private secretary entered. Gigi's private secretary was in her early sixties and guarded Gigi's life as she would her daughter.

'Minister, we have a call from the president's diplomatic unit, asking to meet.'

'Any details?'

'No.'

'Do we have a time?'

'You can do 5.00 p.m. today.'

'Confirm with them, thank you.' Gigi's gut feeling told her the meeting was related to the FBI indictments and extradition requests. An FBI attack on France, as much as an attack on the Deity Foundation.

The meeting at the diplomatic unit did not last long. The Russian Embassy had contacted the French president's office to say they had information helpful to France regarding the FBI indictments. Gigi was invited to meet with the Russian ambassador to discuss details.

Lunch between Gigi and the Russian ambassador was scheduled for the following day; the urgency to meet reflective of two motivated parties. In the grounds of the Russian Embassy, a female attendant dressed in blue met Gigi at her black Citroën, then escorted her, up the marble steps and into the embassy entrance. Gigi glanced above the entrance to the Russian coat of arms with its double-headed eagle; the duality of mortal man, having traits both good and bad.

Inside the reception area, Gigi circled two large white clay pots of chamomile with their small white petals and yellow capitula. A door swung open and the Russian ambassador appeared.

'Hello, ambassador.'

'Let's drop the formalities, its Aleksey.' Aleksey's soft round face had vodka cheeks and soft eyes that could turn to steel. His greying hair was rough parted in the middle, and he had a neat ginger-grey moustache. 'It's good we can talk one on one without the usual entourage trying to interpret and reinterpret every word.'

Gigi knew; however, that every word between them would be recorded.

'Thank you, I'm Gigi.' Her Italian accent was obvious.

'An Italian French minister, how charming.'

Gigi smiled. 'I spent my early years in Milan.'

'And then France won and Italy lost.'

'A draw at best.'

Aleksey laughed. 'Come, let's eat. Have you visited Russia? Do you know Russian food?'

'I've eaten *pelmeni,*' said Gigi, referring to the Russian national dish of meat dumplings.

'I made *pelmeni* when I was a young boy, the family said we know the *pelmeni* Aleksey's made, they're the ones falling apart, everyone but me laughed.'

'A warm family story. I must admit I had similar trials when I first made ravioli.'

'Families the world over have more in common than not,' said Aleksey.

'I didn't know chamomile was Russia's national flower. I saw it in reception.'

'Chamomile grows everywhere; it's the peoples' flower. The yellow head is used as dye and the flower can be eaten, or made into tea, would you like a chamomile tea?'

'Yes, thank you.' He picked up a small silver hand bell and flicked his wrist. A young woman entered and Aleksey spoke to her in Russian.

Aleksey congratulated Gigi on the success with the Deity Foundation and extended an invitation for Cyrus to visit Russia.

'Our president is a devout orthodox Christian,' he added. The world had seen the cross the Russian president wore in his promotional shirtless macho photographs, but few in the world knew the cross to be a gift from Putin's mother. The President's cross was blessed in Jerusalem, and he never takes it off.' As Aleksey talked, he moved the salt and pepper like king and queen chess pieces. Then he held the pepper shaker and looked at it.

'I understand the FBI is being problematic.' He placed the pepper shaker on the table with a thud.

'Playing their games,' said Gigi who was unaware the French defence minister and Aleksey had devised a plan to kill the FBI's attack on the Deity Foundation.

'The FBI are polishing the Vatican's shoes,' said Aleksey.

Gigi took a sip of chamomile tea. 'Why does the FBI bend to the Vatican?'

'Kompromat,' said Aleksey. It was always kompromat, an intangible commodity, easy to find and easy to trade. Even behind apparent acts of goodwill one finds self-interest or compromising leveraged action; the common ease by which people fall to corruption is frightening.

Gigi sat in silence, waiting for more detail.

'The Vatican's computer security is a honeycomb for our IT gurus.' Aleksey reached into his pocket and placed a silver cross-shaped USB flash drive beside the pepper shaker. 'You'll find a solution in the cross to make the FBI indictments go away.'

'Thank you; it's great to have very good friends. If I may ask, I'm intrigued to understand your interest.'

'What is Russia's interest? Let's keep it simple and say our president has embraced Cyrus. In Russia, we have a saying, for *a big ship a big voyage.* Know we'll always be supportive to help the Deity Foundation's voyage and please tell your famous Professor Zaydan the president extends an open invitation to visit.'

'Thank you, it may be some time; Professor Zaydan wishes to stay in France for the foreseeable future.'

'The professor is a ship anchored in port,' said Aleksey. 'We all see the benefit of the Pope's and Deli Lama's travels.'

'It's but three weeks since the Vatican attack. We'll see what time brings.'

'Only three weeks; it feels an age. I'm sorry, of course you were on the helicopter too.'

'It feels like yesterday, and yet feels like an age as you say.'

'Your resilience is to be admired.'

'I don't feel resilient. I think of those who died and ...' Gigi's voice trailed as she thought of those who died.

'I can see why you're trusted.'

'Trusted?'

'Global politics is like a Russian doll; the final beautiful little doll is a group of people who share the deepest trust.'

'My daughter would love her mum being called a little Russian doll.'

Aleksey picked up the silver cross and handed it to Gigi. '*Fiat justitia ruat caelum.*' Gigi translated Aleksey's Latin in her head. Let justice be done though the heavens fall.

Gigi weighed the silver cross in her hand; it was heavy like silver. She wondered why she felt like a messenger and then realised she was a messenger. Parly had sent her to Aleksey to pick up the USB. Why did Parly want her in their Russian doll club. What value could she bring. She was close to Cyrus and closer to Elias but did Parly know about Elias?

Gigi discussed the Aleksey meeting with Parly but kept the talk of Russian dolls to herself. She and Parly were close friends, two of the twelve women in the twenty-eight-person French Cabinet. Parly told Gigi to make a copy of the USB flash drive and give Bernard Émié the silver original. As director of France's external security service, Émié would know what to do. He was already expecting the USB and after Émié reviewed the information the USB contained, he made a secure call to the private number of his American friend, the director of National Intelligence known by the acronym DNI.

Two days later, Goss was asked to attend a private briefing at the office of the DNI. The DNI oversaw FBI intelligence. Goss, as requested, arrived alone, an unusual request but not without precedent. Two people from National Intelligence were in the meeting, the deputy director and someone else. The deputy director was the most powerful intelligence bureaucrat in America and Connor was his alpha attack dog. Goss and the deputy director shook hands, then Goss turned to Connor, hand extended. Connor was a former marine with a Harvard doctorate in psychology. An artist could sketch Connor's face using a handful of geometric lines. His short scissor-cut brown hair was about the same length as his dark stubble. When Connor's eyes locked onto you, you felt trouble—he knew the worst about you.

Connor ignored Goss's hand. 'What's your view of Zaydan's claim?' Connor asked.

'You didn't say your name or your role with intelligence,' said Goss.

'Correct,' said Connor. 'Your view of Zaydan?'

Goss paused. *Who was this arrogant prick?* He reached for his smartphone.

'You gonna take my photo?' asked Connor. 'Do that and I'm gonna break your wrist.'

Goss withdrew his hand.

Connor laughed. 'Just joking.' He strode behind Goss and patted him hard on the back. 'Man, you shoulda seen the look on your face.'

Goss forced a laugh and looked at the deputy director, who looked at Connor. *A rat in a trap,* thought Goss. *No, not a rat,* but he couldn't retract his thought.

'I've given little consideration to Zaydan's claim. I've … we've given more energy to investigating the legality of his foundation's money launder-ing—hence the indictments.'

'The Rams do a better job than you,' said Connor.

Goss's mouth twisted. He hadn't felt boxed like this since meeting the two cardinals. The LA Rams just beat the Arizona Cardinals 34:0. Is this what this prick means—sending a duplicitous message?

'Where can this go?'

'Where can this go?' repeated Connor. 'It can go where people demand. A new path for their lives and herein lies the political threat, people are asking questions that cannot be taken off the table, people are asking what if we don't follow traditional religion? This alternative is more real and more available, an enlightenment. There's a huge urgency for us to eradi-cate. Rothschilds is canny, they've co-opted Dassault to support the Deity

Foundation, co-opted the French government—got top cover, info-warriors on social media, a serious enterprise.'

'I tell you, religious governance is opaque, a blend of corporate board and mafia,' said Goss.

'Zaydan's been *de facto* elevated to the level of the Pope, even higher because the Pope has no aura of a prophet. Rothschilds knows what they've got hold of and what they helped create.'

'You think Zaydan's the most powerful religious leader in the world.'

'Without doubt,' said Connor.

'I agree there's wide euphoria.'

'Taking out Zaydan's helicopter was the right idea, but poor execution. We tried to influence it,' lied Connor. Connor found there were a thousand and one sides to every story. The truth and a thousand sides of perceived truths and lies, and people were happier to believe lies than the truth. The truth required commitment, a self-response, self-reflection and self-adjustment—all too invasive and energy sapping, lies were a short-cut.

'You knew?' asked Goss.

'RPGs don't get moved around Europe without us knowing,' lied Connor again.

'We'll take them down with the FBI indictments,' said Goss.

'But we were talking about the cardinals,' said Connor. 'Tell us the deal.'

Goss swallowed. He thought for an instant he'd shaken free.

'The deal?'

'The deal you made with the Vatican,' said Connor.

CHAPTER FORTY-FOUR

PARIS, FRANCE, 18 SEPTEMBER 2018

A S WELL AS being a US National Intelligence attack dog, Connor was also the baron's secret intelligence liaison in America. The TGV departed from the *Gare de l'Est* for Strasbourg, the track-side graffiti art exhibition became a blur. Connor arrived in Strasbourg one hour and forty-six minutes after departing from *Gare de l'Est*, then headed to the rendezvous on the canal motor launch. Working in the field these days was rare, but deceit necessitated a *tete-a-tete*.

Connor glanced at a pair of inflatable fenders that squeaked as the launch lifted against the Rhône jetty, then he stared up river at a church, a large, stained rosette window and beside the rosette window two spires and two gold clocks. The time on both gold clocks was 3.20 p.m. Connor convinced himself he could see the minute hand move. The meeting with Frederic Panel, head of the J2 intel unit in the French Directorate of Military Intelligence, was set for 3.00 p.m., the French called it *ça s'appelle le retard de convenance,* fashionably late; the Americans called it rude.

'Hello, Connor.' Everyone called him Connor, most didn't know if it was his first or last name or even his real name. Frederic found as long as he kept speaking, he could win any argument, but this approach had never worked with Connor. Frederic's tortoiseshell-framed glasses sat on his oval face. At the corners of his eyes, he had pale white wrinkles that grooved carelessly when he smiled. He smiled at Connor now. Frederic stepped down onto the launch.

'Come aboard colonel.' They shook hands.

Frederic's wondered why Connor used his military rank and then realised he broken old school etiquette by stepping aboard the launch without being invited. 'Is he your man?' asked Frederic; he nodded towards the motor launch driver.

'Yeah. Cast the stern rope, will you?'

Frederic stepped to the back of the boat and grabbed the rope. Connor pulled a bottle of single malt and two crystal glasses from his backpack.

'Duty free and it's 16 August today; a whisky to celebrate,' said Connor

'What's 16 August?'

'Today.' He splashed whiskey into one glass, then poured a solid slug in the other. Frederic released the rope from the jetty cleat; it made him feel like a seasoned boatie. He liked that.

'To friendship and co-operation,' said Connor. They chinked crystal.

'You didn't say what brought you to France,' said Frederic, wondering what antic Connor would play. With Connor there were always antics.

'To meet with you. Now tell me, what's going on with the Deity Foundation?'

'It's being run out of the president's office.'

'You're passive?'

'Total.' Frederic looked at Connor's short hair. It made Connor look aggressive, confident, unwavering.

'You agreed with Zaydan entering the Vatican?'

'Didn't know.'

'No heads up?'

'Knew when the rest of the world knew.'

'Your arts minister knew.'

'Cultural affairs,' corrected Frederic. Connor knew it was cultural affairs.

'She's a Rothschilds puppet,' said Connor. 'Thought your job was to provide political and strategic intelligence, are you letting Rothschilds and Dassault replace you?'

'Can't have the defence minister as a trustee, the foundation is a philanthropic, not an arms company.'

'More dangerous than an arms company.' The crease between Connor's eyebrows deepened.

'You think?' Frederic swirled a mouth of whiskey.

'Where's the line between geopolitics and philanthropy, you know the gambit, there's talk of a French Vatican; a self-sufficient embryonic state in waiting.'

'The Vatican is a foil for Italy, the Deity Foundation is now a foil for France, a French asset, an asset for the world.'

'Do you believe the bullshit you're saying? You need to exert control, decrease Rothschilds influence.' With his bright blue eyes, Connor stared at Frederic.

Frederic held his gaze. 'Your interest?'

'Protecting our country's interest. This year the foundation will receive donations a hundred times greater than your military intelligence budget. Our influence, your influence, internal and global is under threat.'

'You're proposing?'

'We've two choices, either use the foundation to our advantage or eliminate.'

'Too big to eliminate.'

'Too big? We eliminate governments and control countries.'

'I can't go along with this.'

'You're ah, *already in* as they say, we both know your past, life's simpler if there's no scrutiny, people hate the entitled thinking one rule for them, one rule for others.'

'I paid.'

'Loyalty keeps paying.' Frederic stood silent thinking blackmail not loyalty keeps paying. Connor pulled the cork and poured Frederic a multi-shot and another big one for himself. 'Lighten up.'

Frederic was lightening up.

'You're proposing?'

'For survival, the Deity Foundation needs to sever the FBI stranglehold,' said Connor.

'You want to tighten the FBI noose?'

'Cut the noose. Win the Foundations trust.'

'Russia intel will kill the indictments. Bit convenient you're only now talking to us,' said Frederic.

Connor knew Russia provided France with the hacked intelligence. It was his and Parly's idea to involve the Russians.

'Russia, you sure?'

'Positive.'

'The White House have picked up the FBI mantle; blocked the indictment withdrawal while publicly saying it was an FBI decision. We need to change the White House position. I need the best dirt you have on our president.'

'Why me?'

'The French *reynard* sits atop of the hill.'

'I dig dirt on the French, not the Americans.'

'Which is why, I'm is talking to you. Frederic my dear friend, you have leverage on every important French bureaucrat. I want the best your intel can deliver. Call Bernard.'

'I can't just—'

'You can just.' Connor saw Frederic's face tighten then relax. The whiskey helped him relax.

A half hour later, Connor had a video clip on his mobile. A video clip from when the US president was a senator. A hidden camera filming inside a French hotel room. A lithe Asian on her knees taking the senator in her mouth. The senator lying back on the hotel room bed, the lithe Asian entering the bathroom, then coming out dressed in black lace. Connor stopped the video and enlarged the image. Connor's smile grew.

'A productive river cruise,' said Connor. He pulled the cork.

'No thanks,' said Frederic.

'For the road, but we're on a river, what should we say?'

'Ok, I'll have one more with you.'

Conner filled their glasses half full. 'Now, he said, 'there's one last thing.'

Frederic thought with Connor there was always one last thing.

'Zaydan is travelling to Taiwan in nine days. We'll kill Zaydan in Taiwan, but we need help from the Chinese. We've got to finish this, kill Zaydan; get it done.

'Why are you telling me this?'

'Because you, dear friend Frederic, are going to arrange for one of your Chinese colleagues to have a VX nerve agent delivery for our pick up in Taiwan. An early Chinese New Year gift. Zaydan is eliminated, and the Taiwanese get the blame.'

○

Conner had different ways of occupying himself when he flew. On the eight-and-a-half-hour flight from Paris to Washington DC he watched The Disaster Artist cult movie, penned a thousand words of his American political satire, dozed, and planned how to garrotte the FBI.

Connor called the US president's chief of staff.

'I need to see the president tomorrow, late afternoon.'

'Not possible.'

'I need five minutes, make it possible.'

'Topic?'

'I can't tell you.'

'Don't get all silver-back with me.'

'Five minutes.'

'It's not happening.'

'A foreign government will contact the president if I don't.'

The chief of staff didn't want anything hung on him and said 'Alright, five minutes.'

Connor sat in the back of his black SUV; his driver passed through the two security checkpoints at the White House. After ID checks the white bollards descended in front of the SUV. Inside the White House, the chief of staff barged into the room where Conner stood. The chief of staff had a pudgy jawline and a round chin.

The chief of staff peppered Connor with questions such as, what are you doing here? What do you want? Why don't I know? Conner let him ask the questions; it passed time before the President arrived. After his questions the chief of staff still knew nothing. 'I have a message for the president from a foreign government' was what Connor said. He told the chief of staff if you want to know more, ask the president.

'It doesn't work like this,' said the chief of staff. His face reddened.

Connor looked at his watch. 'I'm trying to make a masonic meeting. How long will the president be?'

Several minutes later, the president came in.

'Hello, sir,' said Connor and flicked his eyes towards the rose garden. 'How are the roses, sir?'

'Sure,' said the president. Behind Connor the chief of staff followed and stepped towards the rose garden door.

Connor turned his head and glared. No confusion in the message. *You stay the fuck here.*

'I've got five minutes.' The president stood beside Connor and stood beside the roses.

'I'll take two,' said Connor. 'The French want you to drop the extradition and FBI charges against the Deity Foundation.'

'I've already spoken with Macron, it's not happening.'

'The French told me there was a covert operation you helped them with when you were a senator—code named ladyboy.' In the evening light Connor saw the president turn ashen. Connor's words greased the impaling stake.

'Who did you speak with?' asked the president. Connor heard the falter in the president's voice.

'A random DSGE agent. A woman. Don't know her name.' The president knew this was a lie and Connor knew the president knew it was a lie.

'One other matter,' said Connor, the first matter was sealed. 'Goss needs to go. He's being blackmailed. Has a young teen girl problem—too young. We'll make his death look natural, avoid any scandal.'

'Do it. You've made me late for a dinner.' The president scowled, spun on his heel and a satisfied Connor eyed the hunched president plod back into the White House. Connor stood by a white column. The door behind him opened.

'What does this concern?' asked the chief of staff.

'It's been good to see you. I'm late for my lodge meeting, got to go.'

The double set of bollards dropped, and Connor left the White House complex. He'd make his lodge meeting.

◯

Three days later, Goss felt his private mobile buzz. It was McCarthy.

'I've got that girl,' McCarthy said.

'What'd she say?'

'I thought you wanted to talk to her.'

'The situation has changed.'

'Do I let her go?'

'Where is she?'

'In a suite at the Dupont Circle.'

Goss swallowed. When he first met her, he'd given her a hit of ecstasy and taken one himself. A night of tight hard pleasure. Ecstasy with Stacy. An adventurous hot little tight slut. Breasts a mouthful and sweet nectar tang. And she was there now. He could have it all again. And more. He'd spent a lot of time thinking of the more. If there was a next time, he would—.

'Book me a room. Same arrangement as last time.' Goss ended the call. His mouth was dry.

◯

Four hours later, Goss opened the door to his Dupont Circle Hotel room. On the desk inside the room lay a key card to the Stacy suite. He swallowed an ecstasy pill and swallowed a Viagra, and then put an ecstasy pill in his pocket for the pet. Goss left his room, slinked to the lift, swiped his master floor security card and pressed 15 for the top floor. At the Stacy suite Goss pressed the room card against the reader; a green light flashed and he heard the lock click. Goss stepped inside. AC/DC played loud.

'Stacy! Stacy!' called Goss. Three men burst from a bedroom. They knocked Goss to the ground. Two other men barged in from a second bedroom and pinned Goss prone. Strong hands dragged Goss alongside a three-seater couch. Goss's wrists were bound using two soft Velcro straps. No bruising. The Velcro straps were knotted to the legs of the three-seater couch. Goss stared at the men. No effort to conceal their faces.

'I can help you. I can help you all!' said Goss.

One man bent over Goss and ripped open Goss's shirt. Another knelt beside Goss then placed the paddles of a defibrillator onto the exposed white skin.

'No!' Goss bucked with his hips and thrashed around.

The paddles pressed down hard.

'Stand back!'

Goss bounced with the two thousand volts. A plastic bag was placed over Goss's head. Goss continued to thrash.

'Stand back!' Another two thousand volts. Twenty minutes after Goss stopped thrashing and stopped vomiting and stopped breathing, an ambulance was called.

Heart attack. Vomit inhalation. Death. Open and shut. More discrete than the grassy knoll. No autopsy, a speedy funeral followed by cremation and a large payout to Goss's family.

CHAPTER FORTY-FIVE

PARIS, FRANCE, 20 SEPTEMBER 2018

'M IN PARIS; can we meet?' It was a week since their calendar kiss. Elias ached to see Gigi.

'You're here, a surprise.' Elias heard a different music; a different tone. One of the billion things he loved about Gigi was her honest spontaneity.

'Where are you?'

'I'm picking up Maria from *école maternelle.*'

'At her school now?'

'I'm driving; on the way.' Gigi glanced in her rear-view mirror.

'You're not in your Ministerial car?'

'No.'

'Where is Maria's school?'

'Quai d'Orsay.'

'I'm close, at Musée d'Orsay, I'll meet you there.'

'Don't know if it's a good idea for Maria to meet you.'

'I'm a work colleague.'

'She'll pick up our energy; children are more attuned than adults.'

'What number.'

'Okay,' said Gigi. '*Soixante-cinq,* the Montessori school, you can keep an eye on my car while I get Maria. We'll take her to the park, then we can talk.' Gigi glanced again in her rear-view mirror.

'Four short,' said Elias.

'What? Four what?' Gigi sounded flat.

'You okay?'

'Don't have much time; a family dinner.'

'What's your car?'

'White Peugeot.'

Elias trod down the exit steps of Musée d'Orsay, and took the riverside *Rive Gauche* path. The Seine flowed slowly on his right. What did Gigi say, *we can talk. What did that mean? We need to talk?* The pain in his gut had come back, but this time the pain demanded an answer to a different question. As he passed the *Assemblée Nationale,* the lower legislative chamber of the French Parliament, Elias's thoughts touched on Olivier Dassault, and Umberto's genius to have Olivier as the Deity Foundations' financial sponsor. His mind returned to Gigi. Five minutes later, Elias stood outside the Montessori school, a building that looked as though it had been plucked from Oxford University's campus with its conflated Gothic Baroque style. Gigi's white Peugeot came down the one-way street. Elias raised an arm and Gigi doubled-parked. He opened her door. She wore a pink skirt and white blouse.

'Hello.' He held her hand as she got out of the car then air kissed Gigi on both cheeks. He resisted an amorous kiss; he knew other children's mothers would have a sharp eye for a hint of spice.

'Watching eyes,' said Gigi as she let her fingers slip from his. He wanted to hold her hand forever.

'I need to tell you. I'm staying with my husband—'

'But Gigi—' Elias interrupted.

'Let me talk.' She stood with her hand on the white car roof. 'If I didn't have a little girl, it would be different. As a mum I see the world through her eyes. Her world is herself and her mum and her dad, I'm sorry Elias, so so sorry.' Elias felt he'd been shot in the gut with a heavy-calibre, soft-nose exploding bullet. After their calendar kiss he knew Gigi would leave her husband—in his heart he knew—in his soul he knew.

'Was it a reward for saving you?' The words were out before he could stop. Gigi's face drained to white; her bottom lip quivered. 'I'm sorry, I didn't mean …' Elias said.

Gigi turned and hurried away into the école maternelle.

Elias knew the rule of consequence; a man took ownership of his actions, his dreams. He cried.

◯

At Chambord, Cyrus and Darijani promenaded before dinner beside the edge of the moat. Darijani knew Cyrus had his thoughts elsewhere; his eyes were fogged. She asked if he was feeling alright. Today would have been Talal's birthday.

'I need to tell you something,' said Cyrus. He apologised for not being open and true and then described their trip to Bosra, and how he'd pressured his father to bring Talal. Children played on the side of the road, the bump, the sickening bump he could still hear and feel, the sickening bump, the bump of bone on steel, then strange men's hands on him, being dragged away and his father calling *stop*. He'd told no one before that his father had said, *Take the other one*. Cyrus said he was sorry to Darijani and would understand if she wanted to leave.

She stepped close to him and placed a palm on each of his cheeks—she looked into his eyes and spoke softly. 'Marry me, you lovely, lovely man.'

'Yes, yes,' said Cyrus. When he was young, he'd dreamt of being king, and then he became one, and now he had his queen.

CHAPTER FORTY-SIX

PARIS, FRANCE, 24 SEPTEMBER 2018

AT THE DEFENCE Minister's residence there was another black car parked. A man in a suit stood on the steps of the 18th-century mansion on Rue Saint-Dominique in Paris's 7th arron-dissement; his eyes followed the arrival of Gigi's black ministerial Citroën.

The security barrier lifted and Gigi's driver brought the car to a stop beside the other black car.

After a moment, the security barrier lifted and Gigi's driver brought the car to a stop near the mansion steps. Gigi spoke to the man in the suit, who ushered her inside and together they climbed the curving marble staircase to Parly's first-floor office; their feet soft on the tapestry green carpet runner, with its brass stair rods.

'Let's go down and walk and talk in the garden,' said Parly.

At the back of the mansion, Gigi looked at the secluded grass lawn and wondered how her heels would hold up. She rocked forward on the balls of her feet.

'Do you like to garden?' Parly asked.

'When I was young, I had my own little vegetable patch,' said Gigi. She saw flowers but no vegetables.

'These are my weakness,' said Parly pointing to orchids with a mauve-pink pouch and magenta petals.

Gigi crouched and looked at the capricious beauty of their labellum. 'I wonder what bees think when they see this?'

'The orchid makes the same sex pheromones that female insects use. With the smell and velvet leaves the orchid is like a female virgin.'

'Lucky bees; did you grow these?'

'Three years ago. I bring them inside when it's cold.' The orchids grew in pots.

'I need to resign from the Deity board.'

'Why?'

'Personal reasons.'

'Who is he?' Parly asked. She knew it was Elias. One of Parly's people who spied on Gigi had reported her interaction with Elias outside the Montessori school four days earlier. Parly's immediate thought was, *Fabulous, Gigi's got more influence than ever.*

Gigi gazed silent at the orchid then spoke. 'Elias, the Israeli guy on the board.'

'I've seen his photo. He looks a wolf.' They both laughed, Parly more than Gigi.

'Elias was a mistake.'

'Lucky orchid,' said Parly, only *she* laughed this time. 'We need Cyrus to give a talk in Taiwan.'

'Taiwan?'

'At the National Stadium.'

'I don't know; after the attack in Rome.'

'I have a meeting with the Taiwanese defence minister. We'll use Macron's presidential plane.'

'When?'

'Two days.'

Gigi shook her head. 'Have you asked Cyrus?'

'We need you to make it happen.'

'Why the short notice?'

'Security, logistics, an opportunity window.' Cyrus's talk had to be in two days because China's Politburo meeting was in three. All the key details had been finalised. A Chinese agent would have the VX nerve agent in Taiwan. The aircraft carrier Shandong had been positioned close to Taiwan. The Chinese president must have approved the mission.

Gigi called Elias. 'Florence has a meeting with the defence minister in Taiwan. She said Cyrus could travel with her on the presidential plane, give a talk at Taiwan's National Stadium.'

'What's her angle?'

'Two days' time—full diplomatic security.'

'Two days!'

'We can come today, meet with Cyrus, finalise logistics.'

'Florence?'

'You can ask what her angle is.'

'Marco should come too,' said Elias.

'He's in Taiwan.'

In Taiwan, Elias wondered why pieces were being moved around them and moved around so hastily. He didn't like the sound of this but accepted time would tell.

'I didn't mean it, Gigi. In my heart I swear I didn't mean it,' said Elias

'I know.'

◯

Later that day, Florence Parly and Gigi met with Cyrus and Elias at Chambord. In preparation for the meeting Cyrus had read a number of articles on Taiwan's response to the deity constant. He dressed in a clean white shirt and rolled up the sleeves, ruffled his hand through his hair and headed to the meeting with Gigi and the French defence minister.

'Elon donated a billion dollars yesterday. The world is uniting behind the foundation,' Gigi said at the start of the meeting.

'We should invite Elon here. Thank him personally,' said Cyrus.

'I'll contact him,' replied Parly. 'I know Gigi's spoken about this, but let me give you more background on the Taiwan talk.'

Cyrus shifted in his chair; his eyes had stayed on Parly since she began to speak.

'The first Emperor of China, Qin Shi Huang, was buried with his Terracotta Army, all facing his tomb because Qin saw the greatest threat to his rule coming from within. The same is true today—China crushes the Uyghurs, not for any terrorist threat, but because they're Muslim. China also persecutes Christians; the Chinese government has released a rewrite of the Bible. We estimate there are at least one hundred million Christians in China; this is a serious number of people. The Chinese Communist Party is atheist and prohibits its one hundred million party members from hold-ing religious beliefs. In essence, the Chinese government wages a war against the Chinese people, wages a war where nihilism is propagated. This is a war the Chinese regime will not win; it's a war against the strongest power of all; a war against people's souls. Read this,' said Parly. 'It's our intelligence summary of the Chinese government's reaction to the deity constant.' Parly handed Cyrus and Elias a single sheet of paper. There was silence while they read.

○

The Chinese government has allowed internal media reports of the previously unknown Einstein child seeking sanctuary in the Vatican. However, all report-ing on the deity constant and intelligent design has been banned. The Chinese social media site WeChat is abuzz with news a major spiritual discovery has occurred. The government-controlled tech giant Tencent, which controls WeChat, implemented a word censor algorithm to stifle social discussion. But just as people discuss the president of China in cryptic terms using words such as Winnie and Poo, because of the president's similarity to A A Milne's character, they have largely circumvented the government censorship effort on Cyrus's spiritual discovery.

Larger than normal congregations have flocked to the three Christian churches in Beijing. People are seeking the advice of church elders and ministers on the implications of the Deity Constant Theorem. Following the first three days of these large congregations, temporary security barriers were erected around churches, with Chinese State Security only allowing entry to people holding foreign passports. Within the last week, Professor Liu, head of Religious Science at the Beijing's pres-tigious Tsinghua University has been detained for telling students Cyrus Zaydan's teachings will transform civilisation. Tens of thousands of students gathered outside the Great Hall of the People in Tiananmen Square and called for Liu's release. The Beijing City government has warned protesters; they risk severe punishment. Tens of thousands of Chinese students in China's five largest cities have staged the biggest demonstrations of their kind since the Tiananmen Square massacre in 1989.

'My Taiwan talk is aimed at China?' asked Cyrus.

'Everything we do in Taiwan is aimed at China,' said Parly. 'Cyrus can unite Chinese spirits, light the fuse of the Chinese populous, catalyse their realisation that we are all a deity's child, win their hearts, win their souls, and with this belief lit, at warp speed there will be spirits freed all across China.'

'Why the urgency—two days?' asked Elias.

'Beijing issued a blanket warning last month against any country that allowed the Dalai Lama to visit. Beijing will haemorrhage when they hear Cyrus plans to talk in Taiwan; there's a security advantage; minimal lead time.'

'Haemorrhage? The people or the government,' asked Cyrus.

Parly squared her shoulders. 'In their own way, both.'

'What logistics and security can be organised in two days?' asked Elias.

'Maximum French and Taiwanese diplomatic protection. The French president has made his plane available for Cyrus. We have five hundred legionnaires on an exercise in Taiwan; we'll use them too. French military helicopter from Taiwan's airport to the National Stadium, bullet-proof glass protection in the stadium. After Cyrus speaks, Taiwan will host a state dinner, then fly out.'

Elias thought no. It didn't add up.

Cyrus sat silent for a moment. There was no inner conflict about what to do or not do. He'd made his decision weeks earlier when in the Rome hospital. Cyrus said yes.

○

When she was alone, Parly called the baron. 'Cyrus is going to Taiwan.'

CHAPTER FORTY-SEVEN

TAIPEI, TAIWAN, 27 SEPTEMBER 2018

THE SECURITY MAN raised a finger to his earpiece then knocked on the door to the aircraft's presidential meeting room. Elias stood up from his chair at the meeting table, which doubled as a dining table, with its white linen table cloth to the floor. Elias opened the door. The security man looked at Elias.

'Sir, we're ready.'

○

With Darijani at his side, Cyrus followed Gigi, Parly and Elias down the boarding steps. Drops of rain fell. Cyrus glanced at the grey sky, then an umbrella opened. Across the tarmac was Taiwan's Taoyuan International Terminal. It looked about a mile long, and closer there were a number of vehicles, all black, and a hundred or so people who stood on the tarmac. Half were Taiwanese government officials who all clapped. The others were French security. At the bottom of the boarding stairs, Marco stood beside Tsai Ing-wen, the Taiwanese president. Thin-framed glasses sat on Tsai's small nose and the oval frames rested on her chubby cheeks. As a legal scholar, Tsai weighed evidence and truth and stood in awe of the truth before her. In awe of what Cyrus had found and with a feeling of reverence at what Cyrus had unlocked within herself. Grey streaked her black hair. Tsai clapped too. Cyrus lifted his hand. Marco raised his. At the bottom of the boarding steps warm words and handshakes were exchanged between Tsai and Cyrus and the rest of the party from France, then they all spent thirty minutes meeting in a VIP airport suite.

Cyrus, Darijani and Elias then boarded a French marine helicopter for the short flight to Taiwan's National Stadium. It was the same model helicopter that crashed at the Vatican.

Cyrus bent his head to Elias. 'I'm nervous.' He buckled his seat belt.

'The helicopter will be fine.'

'Not the helicopter, the fifty thousand people who are expected.' With the Williams and Chan interviews he'd spoken to millions, but that was talking to three or four in a room; the reporter, camera men and lighting.

'You'll do great. Chat to them just like you're chatting to me, and you've got your presentation.' Elias tapped his hand on the computer bag. Cyrus's presentation had been forwarded in advance, but Elias had a back-up copy; he'd seen too many glitches with presentations using IT. Darijani sat on the other side of Cyrus and she squeezed his arm.

The French marine helicopter hovered over the centre of the stadium then descended onto the stadium turf. Cyrus looked out the window and saw the biggest crowd he'd ever seen; he had never been to a football match or live concert. Everyone was seated; a vibrant mass.

Elias looked from the helicopter and thought *No mosh pit.*

When the rotor stopped and the door opened, Cyrus heard and felt the crowd cheer and thunder and clap. It was as though everyone tried to make more noise than the person next to them and they all succeeded. It was crazy. All wore T-shirts printed with the deity constant equation. Some T-shirts were red, some black, some white. A scrum of men formed around Cyrus as he left the helicopter—a rolling maul to the stage with its bullet-proof glass box around the speaking platform. Two hundred armed legionnaires stood on the turf that surrounded the platform. On the stage, Elias spoke to Cyrus. Cyrus cupped a hand to his ear but could not hear. Elias mouthed, *it's okay* before he sat with four security men on black leather seats behind a rostrum with a microphone. The computer bag was at Elias's feet.

○

Before he spoke, Cyrus looked around and looked up. Above, the silver oval rim of the stadium framed the grey sky, and below, the silver oval rim was a large seating section all black, black with T-shirts except for a twenty-row high white Greek upper case letter *Xi* where people had worn white T-shirts; *Xi* the symbol for the deity constant— social media coordination as to what colour T-shirts to wear in which seats.

Cyrus tilted the microphone. It was midday when he said, 'Hello, Taiwan.' Then the crowd unrolled a huge red banner, hands reached up, held onto the banner and unrolled it over their heads. The banner was more than thirty metres wide and ten metres deep and flowed down over heads like a sports teams' flag. Printed in white on the pulsing red banner was the deity constant equation. With the banner unrolled, the crowd roared. Cyrus's face smiled on the big screen, then he spoke for almost an hour and thanked everyone for their generous support before he detailed the projects the foundation would fund. Then he explained the deity constant, much as he had to Elias on the Nile. In the stadium, molecules and numbers flashed on the big screen as Cyrus talked. When Cyrus said thank you, the crowd screamed for more, so he spoke for another ten minute—an encore at a spiritual rock concert.

○

The helicopter lifted off and Cyrus felt lighter. He'd left something of himself in each of the fifty thousand disciples.

'You did great,' said Darijani. She wrapped her arm around his shoulders and squeezed.

'Thank you. I enjoyed it a lot. The crowd gave me energy.'

The helicopter left the stadium and after a few minutes banked over Taoyuan Airport. Elias looked down. Four Dassault Rafale fighter jets and a French air-tanker were on the tarmac and he wondered what they were doing in Taiwan. The helicopter landed on the tarmac close to the presidential jet with its tri-colour tail and the words *République Française* emblazoned on the fuselage.

On the tarmac, a security man told the group to board their jet. The Taiwanese prime minister had taken ill; the state banquet was cancelled. Ten minutes later they took off. Elias thought they turned east and kept flying east. He checked the GPS on his smartphone. They were eighty-nine miles east of Taiwan. Elias found a member of their security detail. 'Why are we flying east?'

'We have intelligence there are disturbances in Beijing. A security decision has been made to fly east back to Paris, a precaution to keep clear of Chinese airspace.'

'As a precaution you fly directly away from China to the other side of the world?'

'That's what we do in security—we take precautions.'

'And the French fighter jets?'

'The Rafale's will escort us; part of a long-range training exercise.'

'Do we stop in the States?'

'Refuel in New York.'

Elias thought; 'A rushed departure from Taiwan and cancelled state banquet, a fighter escort, over eight hours added flying time because of disturbances in Beijing, *disturbances in Beijing, we take precautions*, the actions they were taking were precautions against Chinese military activity, not a few banner wielding protestors in Beijing.

'What was going on?'

◯

It was 1.00 a.m. in London, and 9.00 a.m. in Beijing.

'In twenty minutes,' Chester said to the baron.

◯

Images and short-form videos from Cyrus's deity rally at the Taiwan National Stadium and his meeting with Tsai Ing-wen, were shared on Chinese social media apps; rocket fuel images for protesters riling against Beijing's suppression of spiritual freedom. Tens of thousands teemed into Tiananmen Square protesting the Beijing government's censorship of Cyrus—censorship of themselves.

Politburo member, Hu Qiang, strode up the stone steps leading from the courtyard to Xi Hua Hall with its burgundy and gold pillars and grey artichoke leaf traditional tile roof. Hu Qiang made what would be his last walk past the presidential guard, as he entered Xi Hua Hall in the President's Zhongnanhai residence, adjacent to the Forbidden City in Central Beijing— Zhongnanhai, China's 'White House' equivalent, dated back over eight hundred years to the Jin Dynasty. Hu's stride was a stride of brave caution. Inside Xi Hua Hall, for the regular meeting of China's seven-member Standing Committee Politburo, Hu glanced at the red and gold Chinese government emblem, which dominated a wall. The ruling emblem had five golden stars, golden bundles of rice and wheat and golden Tiananmen, and below the Tiananmen the golden cogwheel of industry. Like each of the Politburo executives, Hu wore a white shirt and red tie with his photo ID pinned to his dark suit. Set on the table in front was a pot of green tea, a porcelain tea cup, a bottle of mineral water, a crystal glass, pen and a white pad. A few minutes later, the president entered the room and the other six Politburo members stood up. The meeting started and Hu glanced at his watch. It was 9.06 a.m. He poured water into his glass, took a nervous gulp, then took a deep breath. He pushed himself up and held his stomach. Hu had dyed black hair like almost every man in China over fifty. Hu's eyes were black, with heavy black bags on either side of his flat nose.

'Excuse me, *Zhuxi*,' Hu said, calling the president by his preferred title of chairman. 'I fear I ate something last night that is not agreeing with me.' Hu looked ill; he was sick with fear. The chairman nodded. Hu navigated around the table so as not to walk behind the president, left Xi Hua Hall and trudged along a corridor to the washrooms; his polished black leather shoes made a slow cadence on the stone. With a light head and fast heart, he continued past the washrooms, and was stopped by one of the hundred or so presidential guards.

'No one is to leave the building before the president.' The guard was dressed in black pants and a fashion-styled black combat jacket.

'Our *Zhuxi* needs a document from my car.' Hu spoke, barely moving his lips, his tone dismissive. The guard hesitated then nodded and marched a step behind Hu.

'I don't need a shadow.' The shadow followed Hu.

Inside his car, shielded by tinted windows, Hu texted; the single Chinese character for 'go'. The war to rule China and then the world began. Hu eyed his watch—9.13 a.m.

The presidential guard banged on the rear window with the butt of his pistol. *Give me a hundred seconds,* thought Hu.

'Tell him I'm finding the document,' Hu said to his driver.

The driver opened the door and got out of the car. '*Ni Hou.* Mr Hu find the document.'

'We return now,' said the guard.

'Get back in the car,' said Hu. His driver poked his head into the car and looked at Hu.

'Get in now and lock the door,' hissed Hu. *It's bulletproof, let him shoot,* thought Hu.

In the Politburo meeting, everyone heard the shot and jumped to their feet. Hu bent forward in the rear seat of the car. He stared at the second hand of his watch—9.15 a.m. Hu braced and smiled, and thought if the panda smiled too, he would become the new ruler of China.

A few seconds later, a missile exploded. A pressure wave slammed into Hu's car. Then a second explosion. Hu's driver yelled. Hu stared wide-eyed and gave a broad smile. Through the smoke and dust, Xi Hua Hall was a pile of burning rubble. Hu watched tens of uniformed men holding automatic rifles run past, then throw themselves flat as two more explosions rocked the ground. Above, came the low rolling rumble of two stealth Q5 ground attack aircraft that arced high then tracked back to Huairen Airbase in the Northern Shanxi province. Around the rubble of Xi Hua Hall, the breeze blew the smoke and dust as soldiers got to their feet and ran madly. Most sprinted in the direction of the hall, some tripped as they ran and fell beside others who lay on the ground and would never get up.

'We need to leave. Go!' yelled Hu.

'Our president! The explosions. We need to help,' said Hu's driver.

'It's an order! Give me your pistol,' shouted Hu. The driver gave Hu his side-arm then Hu felt his car lurch forward then brake hard at the external security gate to Zhongnanhai. A guard rushed to Hu's car.

'The compound is on lockdown,' the guard yelled. Hu screamed at the guard that he was injured in the gas explosion and needed to get to the hospital. The guard shouted back it was missiles and not gas. Hu threatened the guard with being shot, and ordered him to open the gate. The guard froze. His allegiance first and foremost was to the president. When indecision played on the guard's face, Hu aimed the pistol at him. The guard lowered his head, dashed to the booth beside the steel gate and moments later the steel gate rolled open. Hu's ten-vehicle security detail waited on the other side. With red and blue lights flashing, Hu's motorcade raced the few hundred metres to Tiananmen Square. En route, Hu made two calls. Hu's first call to a general in the 82nd army, one of the best-equipped and well-trained armies in China. The general would neutralise hostile officers in the 82nd army; march on Beijing and seize control of key government and military buildings. Hu's second call was to a general in the Central Theatre Command; a China wide strategy implemented to exert control of China's seven million strong army and police security apparatus.

O

'The coup has started,' said Chester.

'Update?' asked the Baron.

'The missile attack destroyed the Politburo meeting; unknown status of the Chinese president.'

'He was a sitting Peking duck. If he's not dead this has all been for nothing. Has there been any statement from Hu?'

'Minutes ago, he was on Chinese State television and announced he's acting president.'

Another line buzzed in the Rothschilds office. The Chinese president had been killed. The following twenty-four hours would be critical. Hu needed to consolidate power. The Baron called the UK foreign minister, a long-time friend and explained that Rothschilds had an eye witness account of missiles that destroyed the Politburo—the president was dead— this was a coup. The baron suggested Hu would be less expansionist and more pro-Western than his predecessor. The implication from the baron being; do what you can Britain to support Hu. In reality, the options were limited for Western crisis management, short of painting red stars containing the Chinese characters for eight and one on cruise missiles, and attacking designated targets for Hu. Any Western support would be minimal; restricted to actions such as US Intelligence breaking secure codes used by Chinese generals opposing Hu's coup, and passing onto Hu the information, much as the US had done years earlier when they helped Boris Yeltsin grab power in Moscow.

It was 6.05 a.m. in New York.

'This is Louis, your captain from the flight deck. Sorry to interrupt if you've been sleeping, but we've been given clearance for take-off. Everyone be seated please. There'll be a few bumps as we climb out of here, but otherwise expect a smooth seven-hour fifteen flight to Paris.'

Cyrus pulled the strap on his seat belt and beside him Darijani did the same.

When they levelled out, Darijani turned on the 26-inch screen in front of their seats. She selected the news channel *France 24*. A breaking news ticker ran on the bottom of the screen and said, *Suspected gas explosion at Beijing's seat of power, Zhongnanhai. A number of the Politburo reported injured.*

'Elias,' said Cyrus. Elias sat across the aisle with headphones on. Cyrus waved his arm.

Elias turned his head and pulled down his headphones.

'There's been an explosion in Beijing. See *France 24*.'

Elias switched to *France 24* and watched the newsfeed which then switched to graphic footage of Chinese soldiers shooting unarmed protesters in Tiananmen Square. Unarmed protestors massed against the suppression of spiritual freedom. Protestors who wanted freedom like the people in Taiwan who had attended Cyrus's rally. A General Hu confronted the armed soldiers after they opened fire. Hu snatched the weapon from one soldier then threatened the other soldiers. They lowered their weapons. Hu was an instant hero. He won the heart and souls of millions across China. When interviewed, General Hu condemned the attack on civilians and said all military personnel responsible for this crime against the people of China would be detained. Hu said he sympathized with the Tiananmen protestors, and he would allow the prophet, Professor Cyrus Zaydan, and other spiritual leaders such as the Dalai Lama to visit China.

◯

Here we are, thought Elias. *A general talking about Cyrus in the same breath as an explosion at the seat of China's power. Our fighter escort and a flight east away from China.*

'You following this?' Cyrus asked Elias.

'Watching, not sure about following.'

The TV action then switched to breaking news; the Chinese president was wounded. Then came a report from officials who worked in the president's office. Bank account records showed the president had billions of Yuan in secret off-shore accounts and many unaccounted property assets including seven properties in Hong Kong worth over one billion Yuan. A formal corruption investigation was ordered by General Hu, the acting president.

'What the hell! The Chinese president must be dead,' said Elias.

'Hu speaks against the regime,' said Cyrus.

'A coup. Now we know the urgency for your speech.'

'Parly knew?' asked Cyrus.

'Any other explanation?' They both saw the jigsaw.

Elias knew enough to know coups required detailed planning, broad planning for a year or two. Longer in a country like China with its huge military apparatus. Billions of dollars, recruiting the right generals and eliminating Chinese whispers. The fine minutiae, false flags, well-positioned dominos over the last month, the last week, the last hours. People waiting for "go signals" and the moment Cyrus boarded the flight for Taiwan a "go signal" would have been sent. Rothschilds, Dassault, the French government, the Taiwanese government, other governments, Gigi, how deep did this go?

Elias unbuckled his seat belt and headed aft from the presidential suite. Parly sat and watched *France 24,* ate *mousse au chocolat* and drank champagne.

'Unusual breakfast,' said Elias.

'A celebration.'

'Cyrus was a pawn,' said Elias.

'What's the issue?' asked Parly.

'The issue—the coup.'

'History has been changed. A new China gifts its people spiritual freedom. Cyrus deserves our congratulations.' She raised her glass. 'Will you join me?'

'How long have you been planning this?'

'Does it matter? We've secured the foundation's future. China and the foundation will be new partners. Muscle out the nonsense coming from the USA.'

Parly drained her glass and refilled it from a bottle of Krug in an ice bucket. She then pushed the Krug back into the ice. 'We have a collective responsibility to do what's best for mankind. Let's have this conversation again in two months when you see the political impacts unfold.'

'And the state banquet?'

'Fluid plans. Security advised not to hang around too close to China.'

'I will have a glass, thank you.'

Parly handed Elias a glass and Elias grasped the neck of the Krug bottle. After a couple of gulps, he remembered his Alexandria promise.

'Russia worked with us to make the FBI indictments go away. We're all on the same side here,' said Parly.

'Thanks for the words.' In two minutes, he'd learnt how global politics worked.

'Take care of your orchid,' said Parly.

Elias gave Parly a sincere fleeting smile. Parly had been watching him when Gigi was about.

○

In the dark of the previous night, flying somewhere over the North Pacific, Gigi had been talking to herself and it came quicker than she thought it would. And she didn't know why it had come so quickly. There was no written checklist, but there had been a mental checklist, nonetheless. Two checklists, in fact. One list headed with the name of her husband and Elias headed the other. Under her husband's name she thought of words such as marriage and daughter and responsibility and commitment, and promise and lifetime and tolerance. When she thought of Elias there was just one word—love.

◯

Elias walked through the plane and found Gigi sitting in her mini-suite with the privacy curtains held back.

'May I sit down?'

'Of course.'

Elias sat on a half-circle seat facing Gigi. 'Did you know?'

'About the coup, no.' News of the coup in China had raced through the plane.

Elias looked down at Gigi's bare feet with their painted pink toenails.

Gigi leant forward. 'You love everything Italian?'

'You're gorgeous, *Ti amo.*'

'You're going to need to broaden your Italian.'

'You want to do this?'

'I want to do this.'

'I'll never stop loving you. You know I love you.' Elias held Gigi's eyes, they danced and he held the dance.

Elias unclipped the two curtain stays and the two drops of grey fabric closed.

In private, Gigi reached up and pulled Elias to her. Two sets of lips pressed together said what words could not. Their lips pressed a truth, a wild truth, a truth beyond truth, an endless, bottomless, timeless calendar kiss of love.

◯

In Beijing, the sun rose on a new China—a new China with a spiritual awakening—a new China with spiritual freedom.

The End.

ABOUT THE AUTHOR

NEIL DOMIGAN

The Deity Constant, a geopolitical thriller, is Neil's debut novel. His inspiration to write this book is to communicate an earth-shattering truth to the world.

Neil has a PhD in Biochemistry from Otago University, and completed an OECD funded Post Doc at *Institut Pasteur* in Paris.

9 781764 149204